XZA

· a novel ·

by

Cassandra Leuthold

XZA: A Novel
Copyright © 2013 Cassandra Leuthold

Published by Green Hill Press
South Bend, IN

ISBN-10: 0991131916
ISBN-13: 978-0-9911319-1-4

to Josh for his constant support and unending humor;

to my friends and family for all the great memories I wove into this book;

and with grateful acknowledgement to Kris Torrey for her thoughts on an early draft

Ten Years Ago

Xan

I didn't notice him until he was third in line. The line was mostly women, ages twelve through fifty-five. A lot of them talked while I wrote brief inscriptions, sharing how much my stories meant to them, how they identified with my characters, and why they hoped I kept writing the same kinds of books. These conversations were sometimes punctuated by much more personal stories about abuse and coping with becoming a woman, which usually made any men in the vicinity squirm to get away. It was a rare man who braved my readers to get an autographed copy for his daughter, wife, niece, or himself.

This was an even rarer man. His attractive face loomed over the shoulders of the two women in front of him. His dark hair fell in half-curls and waves almost to the base of his neck. He had either just rolled out of bed or he knew how to style his hair so the effects looked effortless. His skin was almost as pale as mine, the slightest tan stretching across his clear complexion.

I stopped ogling him to sign copies for the woman in front of me, who wanted them addressed to her daughter. I chatted with her for a minute until she went on her way, watching the man take a step closer. He didn't fidget as the men sometimes did, their eyes swimming everywhere but the line. I spotted a worn copy of *Satan, My Father* in his hand, which told me he was a longtime fan, not one of the new initiates clutching a shining copy of my latest work. He stopped reading the nearby book titles on the shelves and started paying attention to me. I shifted my focus to the teenage girl at the head of the line, signing my name in her crisp copy of my newest book and sending her out into the world again much better prepared for it.

My curiosity buzzed. The closer this man came, the more I noticed how good-looking he was. The ceiling lights gave warmth to his hair, revealing it for chocolate brown instead of the black I thought it was. He stepped up to the table and held out his book. I took it and set it in front of me, not ready to sign yet. I was much more interested in the man.

"How are you?" I asked, my pen dangling uselessly between my fingers.

"All right. How are you?" His voice was delicious, heady like wine and gently raspy.

I couldn't keep from smiling. "I'm fine. What brings you here today?"

"My name is Michael Singer." He gave the slightest pause. "I work for Underrated Media dot com. I write book reviews."

My eyebrows slid upward. "Really?" I had been interested. Now I was rapt. If he wanted his book signed, he hadn't written any bad reviews of my work. I swept my eyes over his face, taking in the unique details of his features. His nose, although straight, had a slight bump below the bridge. I moved on to his lips, the well-defined kind I always said were too nicely shaped for a man's, although I appreciated every pair.

His eyes, the caramel color of worn leather, watched me above his warm but professional smile.

My expected, innocent questions probed for information. "Have you reviewed my books?"

"Of course."

"You liked them, I assume."

He nodded.

"How long have you been reading me?"

Michael pointed at the book in my hands. "Since the day that came out. That's a first edition hard cover."

"I know." My fingers smoothed the dust jacket.

"I think I picked it up the day it came out. I've read it several times."

"That's what I like to hear. I'll have to stop by the site and see what you've been saying about me."

"It's all good," he assured me. "The reviews are still up under the books section. They're some of the easiest I've ever done."

Michael wasn't giving me the answers I really wanted. I couldn't tell from his tone if he was being polite or if he was flirting with me as much as I was flirting with him. "You said it was a site called Underrated?"

"Yes."

"Do you think my work is underrated?"

"Far too much. It's well written and well planned. There's no part of life that you'd ignore, and I admire that. Too many books focus on what everybody already knows, and they never push to move beyond the way things are."

I opened the front cover of the book, but I was stalling. I had one more trick to try. "Would you like an interview? Is that something you do?"

Michael's eyes widened, and he leaned forward. "Yes. I'd be very interested."

"Are you available when the signing is over? We can talk over coffee."

"That'd be great."

"You don't mind waiting for me?"

"No, not at all." Michael checked his watch. "It's only about an hour."

"There's a coffee bar in the back if you want to meet me there."

"I will."

I poised the tip of my pen over a blank space on the title page. "Should I make this out to Michael?"

"Yes. Please."

In the neatest version of my chicken scratch I could manage, I wrote beneath the title, *For Michael, as underrated as I am.* I closed the book and handed it back.

He gave me a grateful smile. "Thank you."

"Thanks for the interview. I'll see you in an hour."

Michael walked away, and I leaned back in my chair to watch him. His jeans were loosely cut but hugged his butt closely enough to show me a drool-worthy shape. Out of the corner of my eye, the next three women in line stared with me. Michael disappeared between the shelves, and I leaned toward the waiting women.

"Do you think we could talk him into becoming a gynecologist?" I said.

The women laughed. A teenager with braces peered out from between them. She stretched her lips in an uncertain version of our shared smile. It might take several years for the joke to make sense to her, but it would make her laugh all the harder.

I met Michael in the small café as agreed, but I didn't want to stay there. With copies of my books on display and my picture on posters throughout the store, I didn't want the interview to be interrupted. Usually, I welcomed opportunities to meet my readers, but Michael counted as a fan and a business contact. He deserved my undivided attention for his credentials if not just his looks. I offered to drive, and Michael climbed into my car.

Michael nodded his head down the road. "I think there were stores down this way."

"It's been a few years since I've been here," I admitted, squeezing my purse between my thigh and the car door.

"I've never been here. I just remember them from the drive in."

We followed Michael's hunch to a local coffee shop. It was mostly empty, and walking in put us first in line. Hand-written chalk-on-blackboard signs offered an impressive mix of old classics and more complicated specialties. Michael ordered first, a flavored, sugary concoction topped with whipped cream and a dusting of cinnamon. I asked for coffee straight and black.

The young man behind the counter glanced at the coffee maker. "I'll get a fresh carafe going. That coffee's probably burnt by now."

I put my hand out. "Don't throw it away. That's what I want."

He shook his head as he rang up my order, but he didn't argue with me. I tucked two extra dollars into the tip jar.

I tasted it as soon as I got it. The coffee wasn't scorched, but it was close.

Michael and I settled in at a table halfway across the room, not drowning in the noise of small drink machines or tucked too intimately into a corner. He pulled a palm-sized digital recorder out of his coat pocket. "I hope you don't mind. It's easier than trying to type everything into my laptop."

"That's fine."

"I don't want to miss anything." Michael set it on the table between us.

"Are you the only one who listens to it?"

"Yes." Michael's eyes twinkled at me. This was more than an interview, and he knew it. He had to. His thumb pressed the round red recording button. "Thank you, first of all, for agreeing to this interview."

"How could I resist?"

"I wasn't expecting it. I came as a fan, not for business reasons."

"I appreciate it either way."

"I wanted to start with a quote you gave several years ago. It was always one of my favorites. You said the phrase, 'A woman only needs four animals: a tiger in her bed, a mink around her shoulders, a Jaguar in the driveway, and a jackass to pay for it all,' should be the phrase by which all women live their lives. How facetious were you?"

I laughed. "Only partly. The other part of me was extremely serious. I think a lot of women – and men – could benefit from cutting loose and getting some of what they want."

"That's the opposite of what most people would say."

"And that's the problem. When you've got a restriction or a constriction of some kind, it creates a fixation." I formed a circle with my hands over the table. "It puts a bull's eye on whatever it is. Sex, drugs, music, clothing, movies. It makes it a target, either something to strive for or something to avoid. The problem is that most people are confused, so they say they're trying for one thing but they really want the other. That's how you end up with hypocrisy."

"Hypocrisy is something you deal with a lot in your books."

"It's one of the few things I really can't stand. Heavy traffic I can deal with. Blow your cigarette smoke in my face. I'll deal with it. But hypocrisy is so dangerous on the individual and the social level. It reminds me of another quote. 'The greatest trick the devil ever played was to make us believe he doesn't exist.' Hypocrisy is the real devil. People think if they pretend they're being honest that they're being honest."

Michael folded his arms on the table and shifted his shoulders. "Walk me through, if you don't mind – I like this theme – your two books and how hypocrisy plays a part in each of them."

"Sure. In *Satan, My Father*, you've got a huge disconnect between how the family wants to be seen and the way they are. It's not just the father. There's a much bigger smokescreen going on. He's pretending he's a good person when he's not. The mother refuses to accept what's going on, as if turning a blind eye will make it cease to exist. The one major character who's not a hypocrite is the narrator. She hates what's happening from word one. She never denies the horror of it. She's simply powerless to change her situation."

Michael nodded, intrigued and patient, his eyebrows relaxed and solemn.

I went on. "As far as *F*CK, F*CK, F*CK*, it's kind of the same thing, except that Chessa's more culpable. She's hurting herself and keeping silent so she can keep doing it. What makes her a hypocrite is that she wouldn't let any of her friends hurt themselves like that, but she's also a victim of other things going on in the book."

"You've also said survival was a common theme."

A smile tugged at my face. "You know a lot about what I've said."

"I spent most of the last hour looking you up on the Internet, refreshing my memory."

"Thank you. You have no idea how many interviews start with where I'm from or what my name is."

"What is your name? Why do you write under your initials?"

For once, I tried not to sound too forward, even though I relished the answer. "My name is for friends and lovers only."

Michael echoed my coyness back to me. "I see."

"I write under my initials because it's fun. It's confusing and eye-catching. It lets me keep some privacy, although most people aren't that interested in who I am. I think they'd like to learn some terrible secret about me, but I don't have any, so they'll always be disappointed."

Michael took a sip of his sweetened beverage, making a brief grunt of remembrance at the top of his throat. "I had asked you about survival."

"I want to draw a line between surviving and thriving. Survival is important, but it's not the same thing as thriving. It's what gets you through to a point where you can start to thrive and open up and enjoy what's going on around you. Both of these characters, the narrator and Chessa, are stuck in the survival stage. It's not until the very end that we start to see some possibility for anything better than that. It's much closer for Chessa. The narrator might never get there."

"Is this a mode you found yourself in at some point? Or am I getting too personal?"

I gave Michael a genuine smile. "Get as personal as you like. I was in survival mode for many years, but writing was always a great way to work through my problems. I always wrote characters who were worse off than I was, so my problems didn't seem so bad."

"There's no bulimia in your past?"

"No, but I get asked that a lot. Every book signing. Almost every interview. It's a lot easier to answer when it's a scared, desperate teenage girl than when it's a hardened, crusty reporter."

"Have you had many crusty reporters?"

"More than I wanted to deal with, if I'm being honest." I drank more of my coffee. "There's a big difference between asking me out of real interest and asking because it's the popular, controversial question. It's not as immediate, which rubs me the wrong way and brings us back to hypocrisy again."

"What would you say set off the worst of your survival years?"

The rest of my smile faded. The interview was getting real now. I appreciated Michael's honest questions, but I had not expected this to turn so bleak. "My uncle died when I was a kid. We were very close."

"I'm sorry."

Michael's lips remained parted, as if about to say he'd move on to another question. I continued before he could speak. "I wasn't even thirteen. It was very unexpected."

Michael repeated his apology.

I stayed on the subject. "He was the one who gave me my name. My mother was too exhausted and drugged from medication after she had me, and my father was off somewhere getting food or getting the car ready for the trip home. The nurse wanted to know what my name was for the paperwork. My uncle was there, and he gave her the name he thought was best for me. Alexandria Zenobia Alexander. Such a Russian thing to do, make my first name so close to my last."

"It's very Gogol."

"Exactly. I waited my whole school career for a teacher to make that joke, and no one did. I was very disappointed."

"Did you take Russian literature?"

"No. I didn't think I had to. I inherited my uncle's books. Most of the authors were Russian. I read *Lolita* for the first time the summer after he died." The pain was still palpable, and I forced myself to stay in the present. "So now you know my name. One of numerous cities named for Alexander the great, and a Syrian queen, also used for a character in Hawthorne's *Blithedale Romance*."

"Not Russian literature."

"No. It's a typical American idea that a group of people who set off to make the perfect society would be so flawed that it would fall apart from the very beginning."

"That's what your books seem to focus on, the destructive aspects of society rather than the collaborative or constructive."

"I don't do it to be pessimistic, but I don't want to write to make people feel good. I write to let them know I see the problems that are going on, and I want the people who are in those situations to know they're not alone. Reaching out is more important to me than putting a smile on someone's face. If I see a smile, it's because somebody knows I understand, not because I can make a clever joke."

"What about people who think you write for shock value?"

"They must have no knowledge of the world or any creativity of their own. What I write isn't about them or their preferences. It's about uncovering things that people shouldn't have to go through in the first place. If it's that shocking to you – and it should be – go volunteer. Go out and prevent and help stop these things from happening. Then I wouldn't feel such a compulsion to write about them."

"Are there things other than teenage girls in bad situations you want to write about?"

I narrowed my eyes playfully. "Are you trying to find out what I'm currently working on?"

"No. Well, maybe. I think any of your readers would want to know what you're working on."

"I'm sticking with that theme for now. Hypocrisy and the teenagers it affects. That's all I'm willing to say."

"I understand."

Michael's smile still had a coyness to it that intrigued me. Was he trying to seduce me, or was I just being hopeful? I glanced at the digital recorder on the table. It was time to really test the waters. "Well, you got what you wanted. You lured my name out of me. Which do you want to be, Michael? A lover or a friend?"

He rubbed his chin, the squared bone structure making it the most rugged of his features. "I wasn't expecting questions directed to me."

"Let's be honest. You've read my interviews. I can spot a single man from fifty feet, and you find me attractive."

Michael hesitated. "I can't deny it."

"So which is it going to be?"

Michael's grin wavered, interested but weighing the consequences. "You're serious?"

"Why not? We're two adults, like everybody else. I'm sure you can write a professional, unbiased article whether we fuck like rabbits or not."

Michael reached out and turned off the recorder. His eyes shone. "I'll do my best. Lovers it is."

We collected our things, and Michael tucked the recorder into his pocket. We discarded our cups in the trash and moved outside to my car. We said very little. We'd decided everything that needed to be known: he thought I was a genius, and I thought he could give me a much-needed good time.

I started to appreciate that stretch of over-commercialized road. Past a dozen restaurants and an outlet mall sat a compact but adequate hotel. The sun was already setting, getting stingier with its light as it moved toward the darker half of the year. We registered at the desk, using his lesser known name and my credit card. We rode the elevator to the fourth floor and unlocked our door.

What the room looked like didn't matter. A clean bed waited in the middle, and that was good enough for me. We pushed the door closed at the same time, his lips finding mine as the door clicked shut. I pulled him closer by his open jacket, the zipper teeth pressing into my palms as his hand warmed against my neck. He kissed me with an urgency I was glad for. I wouldn't have to spend the next few hours alone and bored. I had met the right match in Michael Singer.

Michael tugged at my jacket sleeves. Like him, I'd unfastened the front in the too-warm lobby. I shed it, letting it slip to the floor as we stumbled toward the bed. The breathing in the room was audible, almost desperate. Michael's unhurried conversation had tipped me off to his single status, but his eagerness told me he'd been single for some time. The possibility he might've turned me down seemed ridiculous. He needed relief as much as I did – badly.

Michael stripped away the V-neck and black wide-leg trousers I'd chosen so carefully. I was more intent on getting him naked, ditching the polo shirt and jeans I thought too conservative for his hair if not his impetuous actions. His body deserved better, his light tan stretching across his sturdy chest and flat stomach. Dropping his jeans revealed long, muscular legs.

I edged Michael toward the bed and eased him into a sitting position. He bent his head and nuzzled his face against the exposed inner curves of my breasts. His hands wandered up and down my sides, over my stomach and across my lower back. I unhooked my bra and let the warm flush of Michael's breath heat my chest. His mouth closed around my nipple, and my fingers tightened in his hair to keep him close. He shifted to my other breast, and I exhaled grateful curse words under my breath. When he pulled his face back, I set each knee up on the bed to straddle his legs. Michael fell back, and I leaned my hand against his chest to keep him there. I scooted forward to grind against him as he moved against me.

I hadn't figured out how to solve the underwear problem when Michael turned us onto our sides, rolling me onto my back. He slid his hands down my hips to catch the sides of my underwear. I raised my butt off the bed, and he slipped off my only remaining clothes. I wasted no time, keeping Michael from making his next move. I hooked my fingers under the waistband of his underwear and pried them down. Michael lay down next to me, and I stripped off the last piece of clothing between us. He started to sit up, but I pressed him down again. I straddled his hips, running my fingers over his chest and his stomach. His eyes closed for moments at a time, savoring each sensation. I gripped my hands firmly around his staff, and I got his full attention, a continuous gaze full of intent. His hands met mine, and I lifted my hips to help him guide it inside me.

Relief flooded my muscles, softening my mood and heightening the tension. I laid my hand on his stomach, steadying myself as I followed my body into a rhythm. Michael moved with me in an unerring sense of timing, and even though I wanted the sex to last, I didn't have the patience. I leaned back, deepening every feeling inside me. I obeyed the rhythm until the spasms clenched and rippled through my body. Michael exhaled, his fingers gripping my thighs. He came in a series of moans, and I was surprised to feel my body respond with a second wave of pleasurable twinges. I slowed the rhythm of my hips until we both stopped moving. I felt almost triumphant sitting on top of Michael. Two hours had passed since we met, and I'd gotten everything I'd wanted since the moment we met.

My skin began to cool, and the temperature of the room pricked at my pores. Michael pulled the comforter toward us from the head of the bed, and I gave up my conquering position. Michael drew the comforter back far enough to slide under it, and I hesitated. Cuddling was not something I condoned on the first night or most other nights, but I did like Michael. He wasn't a hopeless romantic with puppy dog eyes. He knew what this was. I climbed under the soft sheet and stiff comforter beside Michael, my body languid with happiness and my mind blank with contentment. I closed my eyes with a sigh, letting random thoughts come and go as they pleased. The book signing had been successful enough for as small as it was. I'd planned to drive straight home afterward, but I wondered whether I should spend the night in town now that my body was closer to sleep than awake.

Michael was silent, and I was thankful for that. I liked talking to him, but I avoided after-sex conversations at all costs. They were often awkward and unnecessary.

Michael cleared his throat softly. "What do you think about love at first sight?"

I pushed a resentful exhale through my nose. At the first hint of the L word, I sat up and swung my legs over the edge of the mattress. I kept my back to him, looking over the hotel room for the first time. The mauve carpet was slightly worn. The wallpaper was a shiny striped mix of cream, turquoise, and pink. A large painting of Victorian ladies carrying parasols through a park hung above the cheap wooden desk. A threadbare armchair sat past it in the far corner by the window.

Michael spoke up again. "Let me clarify that. I'm not saying that's what I feel."

My answer remained the same, irritated and cold. "I believe in lust at first fuck." I crouched over the floor and sorted through the scattered clothes, piling my own at my feet.

"Don't be like that. I just asked you a question."

I stood up to face him. My hand sliced the air for emphasis. "I don't do love. Not in my books, not in my life. Not in interviews, not in post-coitus questioning."

"I'll take that as a no, then."

"It's a no." I lowered myself back onto my haunches long enough to scoop up my clothes. I dropped them on the desk and pulled my underwear on first, a red thong outlined in scalloped lace, apparently wasted on Michael. "It's a no at first sight and all the other sights."

"How did you get so bitter?"

I hooked my bra behind my back with quick, practiced fingers. So I was seeing the real Michael now, as romantic and self-possessed as he was flirtatious.

Michael propped himself up on his elbows. "The usual high school tragedy?" he prompted.

I pulled my pants on and zipped them up. "I've managed to avoid tragedy in that area, thanks to being observant as a child."

"Is that so?"

I put on my socks. "People say I was jaded before I could get my heart trampled on, but I think I was just correctly informed."

Michael laughed, genuinely enjoying my attitude. "Why are you getting dressed? Get back in the bed and let me explain myself."

"You can explain yourself from there. I never get back in the bed after the L word comes out. I'm done with this."

"I feel a connection with you. That's all."

"Connections lead to relationships, which never lead anywhere good." I pulled my shirt on and adjusted the fit of it to hug my body in the best places.

Michael raised his eyebrows high. "Are you saying you've never had a relationship?"

"I've had *relations*, just not relationships."

"That's crazy. You have to be my age. When did they warn you against relationships? In kindergarten?"

My mother's voice popped into my head, as sarcastic as Michael's. "Preschool."

"That must've been some bad relationship you saw."

It wasn't really a relationship that came to mind. It came down to one sentence, really, uttered by Uncle Grigori when it was all over: *I loved her, Xan, and she broke my heart.* His grey eyes had been so dark, focusing farther than they needed to, avoiding my young face.

His hair, usually combed with neat precision, was left disheveled over his forehead and the tips of his ears. I circled his neck with my thin, insignificant arms. *I love you, Uncle Grigori. I'm still here.* It might have comforted him later, if the harsh sting of his rejection wavered, but it barely tilted the corners of his lips away from a frown. I was thinking more of Uncle Grigori's girlfriend than the end of their relationship when I answered Michael. "It was ugly."

"And you swore you'd never get hurt?"

"It wasn't that dramatic." I moved closer to the door, where I'd left my shoes. "Get dressed, and I'll drive you to your car."

"You're really not getting back in?"

"Why should I?"

"It's still early. There's more fun to be had before I drive back to Chicago and you go where you're going."

"I'm going home to my empty house."

"You don't have any pets?"

"Why would I want that responsibility? What would I do with them on book tours? What would I do with them when I'm trying to write and they want to climb all over me?"

"You could get a fish."

I picked my purse up off the floor.

"Dogs make very good companions," Michael added.

"Is that what you have?" I asked with distracted interest.

Michael nodded. He was still in bed and hadn't ticked a muscle toward getting out. "Jack Russell terrier."

"What's his name?" I liked to think I could tell a lot about a person by the names they gave their pets.

"Jack."

The obvious simplicity was almost a let-down. Michael probably liked its overt irony, and on that point, I did, too. But Michael had destroyed the mood by dropping the L word. I wasn't climbing back into bed with him because he was clever. "Are you getting up, or are you walking?"

Michael took his time sliding out of the bed, his once-hard cock no less impressive for having returned to its resting state. "Should I walk down there naked and see who else I can pick up tonight?"

"Do you know what would happen if I gave in to everybody who thought I was smart and sexy? I'd be dating until the end of time."

Michael stepped over his clothes and walked up to me. "You said let's be people, let's be adults. I'm being myself. I like your writing, and I like getting to know the real you even more."

It was a good speech, but my mind was made up. "I'm sorry you ruined things, Michael. I liked talking to you, too."

He watched me, and I hoped he wouldn't try to kiss me. He walked back to his clothes and got dressed, still moving in his unhurried pace. He put his jacket on last and lifted the recorder out of its pocket. "I don't have to post the interview if you don't want me to."

"It's up to you. I trust you to keep the flirting between us."

Michael slipped the recorder into his pocket. "It'll be erased by noon tomorrow."

I felt a little disappointed that the evening had soured, but I reminded myself the L word had been dropped. There was no recovering from a mistake like that. "Are you ready to go?"

"I have all my stuff."

I felt bad for him, but it proved my point. I lowered my voice. "This is why I don't do relationships." I opened the door.

Michael walked ahead of me into the hallway, and we made our way back to the bookstore. I was grateful he pointed out his car without me having to ask which one it was.

"The little grey one. Over there."

I pulled in next to it, missing the curve and squeeze of Michael's ass already. "Good luck editing the interview," I said.

"Good luck on your book."

The tone in Michael's voice reassured me. It was candid and bright. There were no hurt feelings here, but his eyes gave him away. Even in the hazy lamp light of the parking lot, they were serious and preoccupied.

"Have a safe drive to Chicago."

"I want to see you again."

"That's not a good idea."

"Based on what? We both have literary backgrounds. We know we have chemistry."

I tried to make a flimsy excuse sound valid. "Chicago is a few hours from where I live."

"I'd make the drive. I'm as determined as you are to get what I want."

"Nobody's as determined as I am. Thank you for the interview. I do appreciate it."

"I do, too."

"Goodbye, Michael."

He tilted his head amicably and stepped out of the car. I waited until he unlocked his car and opened the driver's door. I backed my car up and sped out of the lot.

In the morning, I was plagued by memories of dropping Michael off at his car. I could see his eyes and the unspoken thoughts behind them. He hadn't suddenly given in to me. He was plotting something. I picked through the day-old mail on the entrance hall table. The seal on the front door lost suction as it opened, and my part-time assistant stepped into the hall. Instead of my usual "Good morning," I grumbled an order. "If anybody named Michael calls, I don't want to talk to him."

Melody's agreement couldn't hide the lilt of confusion in her voice. "Okay."

I looked up from the mail. Melody studied me, surprised by my mood. She closed the door behind her. Her copper hair was secured in a streamlined ponytail, and her glasses gave her the look of an older, more accomplished secretary.

"Which Michael?" she asked. "I don't want to drop the wrong call."

"Michael Singer. He's a book reviewer from Chicago." I lifted the unexpected home décor catalog off the table. It was worth a flip through before I dropped it in the recycle bin. "The rest of the mail can be put in the shredder."

"What happened?"

"I don't want to talk about it. I'll be in my office. Start some coffee for me, will you? I'm running behind."

I left the back half of the hall, turning in front of the kitchen and taking the short jaunt to my office at the rear of the house. I opened the blinds to the backyard and turned on the computer. I ignored my email for the time being and opened the current draft of my novel in progress. I'd left a note on the desk about a paragraph I'd added before leaving for the book signing, and I returned to scrutinizing its intricate wording. It needed just the right tone.

Unnumbered minutes slipped by before Melody knocked on the open door. She held the cordless phone to her chest, and a smile stretched across her lips.

"It's Michael," she said in a pleased, breathy voice.

My eyes narrowed. "Hang it up."

"Xan, he sounds so sophisticated, and his voice is so sexy." Melody carried the phone to me, still pressing the microphone against her white t-shirt. "Why wouldn't you want to talk to him? I don't understand what happened."

I resented stealing time from writing to explain my private life. "He said the L word to me, and we're not speaking."

"He thought you were a lesbian?"

"He said love."

"He wants to talk to you." Melody held out the phone. Her crisp brown eyes lit up with hope and encouragement.

I didn't want to waste any more time arguing with her. I snatched the phone from her hand. "Hello?" I croaked.

Michael's voice, as sexy as it might've been, wasn't as welcome in my ear. "Good morning."

"How did you get this number?" I was vaguely aware of Melody slipping out of my office, her sneakers squeaking across the hallway's wooden floor.

"I called your agent in New York."

So Sheryl had betrayed me, too. "I'll be calling her later. What did you say to her?"

"I told her the truth. We had an interview, and I had more questions for you. She was ecstatic about the interview, by the way."

"I'm sure she was. I'm also sure your questions have nothing to do with my books." I heard Melody rummaging in the kitchen, closing cabinet doors and sliding drawers open. "You charmed my assistant, too. I told her I didn't want to take this call."

"I wanted to call you before you forgot how much you like being with me."

"You're very sure of yourself, aren't you?" I turned my chair away from the computer, unable to concentrate on my book. Outside the window, the sun had come up over the rest of the horizon, lighting up a summer blue sky in the autumn landscape.

Michael persisted. "Am I lying?"

I didn't answer for a long time. I never liked admitting the truth when it didn't serve me. "No."

"How about this? We meet again, and we fuck like rabbits, and I won't use words that annoy you anymore."

I sat through a longer silence. It was an intriguing idea, but I wasn't sure he could do it. "I wouldn't mind seeing you again for a short visit, but I have my doubts."

"About what?"

"You get attached too easily. You seem like you're ready to jump into a relationship with the first person who interests you enough to look twice, and that someone can't be me."

Michael chuckled. "At what point did I give you the impression I couldn't just sleep with someone?"

"The second you dropped the L word."

"That was a slip, I promise. It's not what I meant."

"Just the same, when was your last relationship, and how long did it last?"

"An actual relationship, or one of those three-week things?"

I thought for a moment. Even I was capable of a three-week fling if he was busy and independent. I could forgive those. "A full-on relationship."

"I was with Janelle seven years. That ended four years ago."

"I'm checking for rebounds."

Michael laughed. "You're checking for serial monogamy."

"Yes, that too."

"Believe it or not, I am not the Casanova of Chicago."

"It's a good title, though, for a book or a person." I turned to my desk and picked up a pen and notepad I always kept nearby. I scribbled down a note: *Casanova of Chicago*.

Michael pressed on. "If you want to see me, there's no reason we can't get together. Do I pass your screening?"

"Surprisingly, yes. It has more to do with your performance last night than anything you've said this morning."

Michael didn't answer, and I imagined him grinning like a fool.

"Don't be smug. If you'd called when Melody wasn't here, I wouldn't have talked to you. I know how to screen my calls."

"Why did you take it, then?"

"You are nicely built, Michael."

He laughed harder. "You make me sound like a boat."

"You were a very good ride."

"I'll take that, if that's what it takes to see you again."

I needed to give him another test. I still didn't believe him. "Do you want to see me for pleasure or conversation?" I asked.

Michael paused slightly. "Mostly for pleasure."

"You're learning fast."

"The interview will be up on the site by tonight, so we won't have as much to talk about."

"People shouldn't say more to each other than what gets them in bed. All that other stuff is what gets people in trouble."

"That's a great quote. Do you mind if I write it down?"

"Go ahead." I gave Michael several seconds to get started. "When did you want to get together?"

"It's early yet. How about tonight?"

I wondered if he assumed I'd label this as more evidence of his clingy personality. I found it a relief, the thought of seeing Michael so soon and finishing the tryst I shouldn't have started. "That's fine."

"I could drive down."

"All right." I liked his willingness to please me, but I realized this meant either paying for another hotel room or inviting him into my home. I looked over my office, a room no one but Melody and me had been in for years. Books packed the built-in shelves I'd had custom built after moving in. The plant in the large ceramic pot by the door was yellowing and starting to wither, in need of more attentive watering. Could I see Michael here? Did I want to see Michael here? His silence dragged on, and I thought he might be mulling over the same question of where to continue our ill-imagined coupling.

"I could pay for the hotel this time," he offered.

Hearing it made it sound silly. "No. My bed is better."

"That's a fact?"

"Yes. I know where to spend my money." I lingered over the books, crammed onto the shelves more than they were stacked. The vertical rows served as shelves for thinner layers of horizontal and diagonal volumes. A sentence slipped out of my mouth I was surprised to hear myself say. "You might be interested in the extent of my reading collection."

"I'm sure I would be. I don't usually get invited to writers' houses."

"You don't sleep with that many writers?" I joked.

"Posers, mostly. Everybody says they're working on a novel, but maybe it's only an excuse to get me back to their apartment."

"I can understand that."

I gave Michael my address and told him it was the white one outside the city with the white door and wholly unoriginal white fence. "I keep meaning to replace it."

"I'll find it," he assured me.

We set a time and said goodbye. I laid the cordless on the desk.

Melody poked her head in the door, leaning her body against the frame. "So what happened? What'd he say?"

"You'll be gone before he gets here." I picked up the cordless and held it out to her.

Melody skipped across the office and took it from me. Her bright smile was impossible to ignore. "You're having an affair?"

"Did you think I didn't have them?"

"I don't usually get exposed to them when they're going on." Melody stayed in front of me, clutching the phone to her chest.

I didn't want to linger on the cordless or my recent call. "The plant needs watering."

"I'll do it."

"Where's my coffee?"

"It's coming. I'll bring it."

My voice lowered into an ominous, cranky warning. "Now, please."

Melody smiled as she swept out of the room, taking the accursed phone with her. I returned to the books filling the far wall, wanting them reorganized but knowing I would have to do it myself. Melody would have no way of knowing which were my favorites and which I kept out of obligation for various reasons. Some were old and tattered, smelling too strongly of must and mildew for me to read them. Some were the compact trade paperbacks I loathed for the boxy feel of them in my hands but tolerated for transportability. Soon Michael would be here, scanning the titles, clicking his tongue at them and telling stories about his own reading history. I was ready for that, but I wouldn't let him break the spell of this room. Books and their material were boundless. They belonged to everyone. This office was mine.

I heard Melody's rubber soles on the hardwood floor and called out before I saw her. "I need all my books moved out to the living room, please. This afternoon. Before you go."

Melody turned into the office, a substantial mug streaming steam from her delicate hand. "All of them? To the living room?"

"Exactly. I'll go through them later, but I need you to move them for me."

"All right." Melody eyed the massive shelving unit taking up the entire wall. The shelves were only interrupted by a row of white cabinets at the bottom used for storing printed manuscripts and office supplies. She seemed to be counting the books, not in their number but the number of trips, the number of hours it might take her to move them. The intimidated tilt of her eyebrows belied the cheerful tone of her voice. "I can do that."

"Coffee, please."

Melody set the mug on the desk. "When is Michael coming?"

"Why does it matter? You're not meeting him." I sipped the coffee to make sure it was pure and bitter, knowing it would be too hot to drink by the mouthful for several minutes.

Melody was practically bouncing up and down. "It's exciting. All I'm doing tonight is reading the rest of *The Ya-Ya Sisterhood*, eating ice cream, and going to bed. By myself."

"He's not staying here. He's just coming over."

"You're saying I'll never get to meet him?"

"No, you won't. Not in my house. If you're so interested, go to Underrated Media dot com. His picture's probably there with a cute little bio."

Melody brightened her smile.

"He's more your type than mine. He comes across as desperate." I tasted my coffee again, craving the caffeine but hoping not to burn my tongue.

"You mean affectionate? Loyal?"

"Smothering."

"Don't you like to feel needed, Xan?"

I dipped my face for another sip of coffee, but my lips stopped above the edge of the mug. I raised my eyes to Melody's hopeful expression. "Have you read my books? I prefer to feel sane and grounded. Save the plant and move the books. I have to finish this chapter, or I'm going to waste the whole day."

Melody left the room, and I swiveled the chair back to the computer. I put the coffee down and returned to the handful of word choices I'd jotted down as questionable. Most readers wouldn't notice the difference, but I would, and I took it as a personal responsibility to represent my ideas as clearly as I could.

Later that night, if Michael insisted on bringing up his feelings or future meetings, I was prepared to make myself clear. We had no future. I had no future with anyone, nor did I want one. If he could have sex without strings attached, he'd better be prepared to have it with me. That is all that had ever interested me.

Ten Years Later

Chapter 1: Xan

Annoyance tightened my chest, the same tension that plagued me every time I argued with my mother. Her familiar opinions squawked into my ear from the phone. I knew what all of them were without listening. I stood in the foyer, not sure when I'd wandered there during the long conversation. The phone's unforgiving plastic sent a burning soreness through the ridge of my ear. My elbow ached from its bent position even though I'd switched hands several times. My jaw clenched in defense as I started listening again.

"How can you not think of getting married?" my mother asked. "You're forty-three. What are you waiting for? Your death?"

I jumped right back into defending myself. "That's the one question left, isn't it? You can't ask me about having children anymore. You had a good run with it, though. Over twenty years."

My mother huffed. "Is it such a strange question to ask? Is it such a horrible thing for me to want for you? All of my friends have the cutest little grandbabies to play with. I'm the only one who doesn't except for Sofia, and you know how sad that was." My mother let a few beats pass for Sofia's daughter's miscarriage, which was a heart-rending situation. "I don't understand why you were so opposed to the idea of having children."

I'd been over it a thousand times. "What part of it was supposed to entice me? The lack of sleep, the diapers, the drool?"

"The love, daughter. The pride of seeing your child grow and succeed. The fulfillment that comes from raising a child into independent adulthood."

"Tell me, then. How fulfilling was it?"

My mother remained upbeat despite her firm honesty. "With you, awful, but there were some good years. We had good times together. You remember them, too."

"Yes, those were such good times before I learned to talk."

"It wasn't your talking that got you into trouble, at least not until you were in school. It was walking that gave me the most to worry about. When you started reading, you were easier to keep in one spot. I always knew where you were."

"Don't romanticize my reading habits." My eyes fell on the wide doorway to the living room, and I glanced behind me the length of the foyer to make sure no one was coming through the house. I liked to keep my arguments with my mother as private as possible. "You didn't like what I was reading any more than you like anything that I've written."

"Your books," my mother sighed, defeated. "I don't want to talk about them today. You know how I feel. The things they tell me your books are about. It makes the family look awful. Your father's heart can't take it."

"I'm not surprised you only know about my books from other people. I don't think you've read any of my writing from the day I wrote my first poem." It had been about daisies when I was eight. My writing had changed considerably since then.

"Would it be so difficult to write about something else?" my mother insisted. "Don't you care at all about what you're doing to us? The image you're giving our family?"

"I write for women, not for the family."

I heard the footsteps I'd been dreading, crossing the linoleum of the kitchen at a slow but steady pace. I turned my back to them, turning down the volume on the phone to keep my mother's tirade inside my ear.

My mother scoffed in disbelief. "You write for women? Women don't want to read about such things. We want to read about shopping and dating and food. My friends are reading these funny little mysteries that come with recipes right in the book. Why can't you write something like that instead of this trash?"

Michael set his hand on my shoulder, ducking his head to kiss the free side of my neck. His lips moved close to my ear. "Is that your mother?" he whispered.

I nodded.

"Have you been talking a long time?"

I shifted the phone away from my mouth and answered him. "Interminably."

"Let's put her on speakerphone." Michael dropped a fingertip onto the phone base on the table. Where I was tired and irritated, Michael was fresh and casual. "Hello, Anna, it's Michael. How are you?"

My mother's terse tone barely softened. "Hello, Michael. I'm fine. How are you?"

"Good. What are you two lovely ladies talking about today?"

I set my hand on my hip, leaning closer to Michael while I watched for changes in his expression. "She wants me to think about getting married."

Michael started to laugh but turned it into a smile. "Anna, be honest. Would you really pick me for your son-in-law?"

"No, I would not."

"You know Xan does things in her own time." Michael paused. "Remember how long it took for her to warm up to me? It was years before I moved into the house."

"We've had our talks about that, too."

Michael set his hand on the table. He smoothed his voice over even more, all but crooning into the phone base. "Come on. Don't be angry with me."

My mother relaxed, but I could hear the distance, the resentment. "We don't all have your patience, Michael. I wish I did."

"It's not about patience. It's about respecting what Xan wants."

"Forgive me, but what Xan wants hasn't always made sense to me or most other people. I'm still trying to convince her she should find new subjects for her books."

"I don't think she should." Michael straightened up and wrapped his arm around me. "I love her books the way they are. Her fans would riot if she changed what she wrote about."

My mother turned to pleading. "Are you sure you can't talk her into toning it down? There must be something else that interests her, something else she could write about."

What other subject did I like enough to write about? "Erotica," I muttered.

Michael stifled a chuckle and left a kiss on my cheek. "The literary community, not to mention society, needs more writers like Xan with honesty and persistence. These are stories that need to be told."

My mother's tone lowered to a more serious one. "Don't placate me with your ready reviews. I always considered you the more practical of the two."

"Practical, yes, but my loyalty is to your daughter."

"I hope it serves you well, Michael. I'd hate to see you waste your life. I've spent over forty years trying to reason with Xan and give her what she wants. You might find out as I have, that above most things, Xan doesn't want to be reasoned with."

I eyed the red button on the phone base. It would be easy to press it and end the call right there. My mother wouldn't bother to call back to argue with me twice in a day.

Michael carried on, his voice light and assuring. "It's not wasted, Anna. Don't you worry."

"I hope not," my mother replied. "Just because I wouldn't want you for my son-in-law doesn't mean I don't like you."

Michael was finally stumped, and I met his glance with a shrug. She'd rendered me speechless and confused my whole life.

Michael's response wasn't as easy and prompt as the others, but it came out pleasantly. "Thank you. I appreciate that. Have a good rest of your day."

My mother hesitated, realizing Michael was brushing her off and ending her conversation with me. "You, too. I'll talk to you later, Xan."

I had nothing more to say. I was glad she was taking the graceful way out instead of asking to talk to me again. "Bye."

Michael pressed the button I'd been eyeing, and the phone fell into silence. He shifted half a step away from me. "I was only out back for half an hour. How did she get through the weather and family health to the M word so quickly?"

I couldn't explain it. It made my head spin to follow her deft weaving between subjects. "She's got years of practice. She always says exactly the same thing. She blames me for Dad's heart problems instead of his diet. She doesn't know what my books are about."

"Maybe you should mail her some copies."

"I will if I want to see them covered in dust the next time I'm there."

Michael pulled me into a warm hug, his long hair brushing my cheek. "What makes you think she wouldn't mail them back?"

I rested my temple against Michael's shoulder. "She could never look that ungrateful. But she'd put them in the basement where they couldn't bother Dad and his sensitive heart."

Michael kissed the top of my forehead. "Your readers know none of those things ever happened to you."

"For Mom to know that, she'd have to read my interviews. That's asking too much of the woman who gave birth to me. She got me here. Now she's done with me."

"I can try explaining the difference between fiction and non-fiction again."

I pulled away. "You've told her that every year for the last ten years. It hasn't changed anything."

Michael smoothed over the air with his hand. "Your mother's like a rock. She has to be worn away slowly over time."

"Wake me up in a million years, then, when she's finally accepted modern literature and us living together."

"She's predictable, isn't she?"

"Yes." Knowing my mother's favorite subjects didn't keep them from exhausting me. I was glad Michael had inserted himself into our conversation and come to my rescue. How he could soothe and tame my mother, I'd never know. "You could've been a hostage negotiator."

Michael laughed with amiable appreciation. He stepped in close and kissed me. Ten years hadn't softened the effect he had on me. The silky strands of his hair still caught my attention and kept my hands there. His lips moved with a pressure and familiarity that reassured me and kept me wanting more.

But this wasn't a spare moment in my day I could stretch into more. My mother had interrupted me making lunch between work and more work. I leaned away from Michael as much as I hated to. "I should get back to my book."

"*Bitches and Assholes*? How's it coming?"

"It's all right. It still needs a real title, though. I'll be relieved when it's done."

"How much more, do you think?"

I shrugged, trying to calculate how far I was into the plot. "Thirty, maybe forty thousand words."

"You're closer than you were."

"True."

I started for the kitchen, and Michael walked with me. "I came in for something to drink," he said.

"How's the book you're reading?"

"It's good. There are some pacing issues, but the characters are good. It's another one of those that benefits from crossing over between adult and YA."

"Woe to us who only write for adults or advanced YA readers looking for a nightmare."

A small plastic tub of ham salad sat on the kitchen island. Two pieces of bread waited on a plate, hastily smeared with mustard. I picked up the butter knife while Michael opened the refrigerator.

"You've always had a diverse audience," he said, the packed cavern muffling his voice.

I spread a thick layer of ham salad across a piece of bread. "I have, but they read my books the same way I read my favorites at that age. In secret. It's okay to read about first ladies and Anne of Green Gables and the Amish, but if a book about summer camp has one mention of underwear, nobody's allowed to read it. Did you know my mom objected to Shakespeare because of the violence?"

"She probably wasn't a fan of Ben Jonson, either."

"She doesn't know who that is."

Michael set the pitcher of sun tea Melody had made on the counter and lowered a glass from the cabinet. "There are so many books I'd like to buy her for her birthday."

"Don't bother. The look on her face wouldn't be worth it, no matter how little you spent."

"This is the first time I ever heard you say a book wouldn't be the right present for someone." Michael poured himself a tall glass of tea.

I stacked up my sandwich and snapped the lid into place over the ham salad. "I'd prefer to keep the book and leave my mother out of it. It's a thought for the next time we're supposed to see her."

Michael returned the pitcher to the fridge and stopped by the island to give me a kiss. "Good luck with the bitches and assholes."

"Thank you. Do you mean my characters or my mother?"

"Whichever applies."

Michael swept out of the kitchen, and I heard the door open to the back patio. Out the window, I saw him sit down at the table and open his book. In a few more weeks, after one last belt of warm weather, the table and chairs would be covered with plastic sheeting for the winter. We had more room in the house than we needed, but Michael liked to sit out with the birdsong and the fresh air as long as the weather stayed tolerable.

I put the ham salad in the fridge and dropped the butter knife in the sink. I carried my belated lunch through the back hallway of the house to my office. Even before I sat down at the computer, the unfinished page on the screen glared white at me.

I was used to filling blank pages, but in recent years, most of those were for freelance jobs to pay the bills. I'd put all that on hiatus to finish my book. In two or three months, I needed to add seventy pages and edit them towards presentability. I couldn't spare my full attention too much longer than that. Even my lunchtime was no longer sacred. I took a bite and chewed it automatically, barely tasting the ham and sweet mustard as I returned to the daunting expectations of the page.

Chapter 2: Jessie

Willa never gave me a present before. She leaned toward me from the couch, holding the package out to me. "I got you something. For your birthday."

I hadn't expected this, but Willa never did anything anybody expected. Even the wrapping paper was classic Willa, either left over from last year or bought early for this coming Christmas. It was covered in fat, jolly Santas floating like bearded stars over a forest green background.

"I'm only a couple of weeks late," Willa said. Her dark hair slipped forward to frame her slender face. She couldn't stop smiling as she pushed the present into my hands. "Aren't you gonna open it?"

I turned the rectangle over, trying to guess what it was. "Yeah, I just feel bad I didn't get you one."

"It's not my birthday."

"I know, but I wasn't expecting anything."

Willa huffed. "So get me something in December, and we'll call it even." She got up and tore the wrapping paper off the far end of the gift in my hands. She slid a book out of the jagged sleeve.

Filling the cover, a young woman in red plaid pants screamed silently at the top of her lungs, crossing her arms to cover her bare breasts. The young woman's head was bald except for a narrow purple mohawk. The title stretched across the top in chunky black letters: *F*CK, F*CK, F*CK*. I wasn't surprised Willa had picked out such a bold book, but I wasn't sure why she had given it to me.

"What's it about?" I asked.

Willa wadded the wrapping paper into a ball. "If I told you that, you wouldn't have to read it."

I looked for the author's name. All I found were the letters XZA in the lower right-hand corner. I pointed to them. "What's this 'Egza' down at the bottom?"

"That's the author. She writes under her initials. She's pretty cool. It's not her latest book, but you'd be seriously missing out if you didn't read this. I read her first two books in something like three days. It only took me that long because I had to run out to the store to buy *Satan, My Father*."

I studied the details of the cover. My voice slipped out sheepish. "I haven't heard of that one, either."

"Really? Trust me. Go down to Used Books right now and get it. The second you finish this, you're gonna wanna read it." Willa raised her palm and trailed it across the air as if tracing an invisible banner. "The dedication page says, 'To the devil himself.' It was brilliant. Everybody thought she was this Satanist or something, but it didn't have anything to do with that. If they would've read it for three seconds, they could've figured it out. It was great publicity for her, though. Everybody was talking about it."

I flipped the book over, hoping for some clue as to what it was about. Instead, the glossy back was covered in critics' praise for *Satan, My Father*. *A dark, realistic look into the unspoken horrors often covered up by patriarchy. The X stands for the unearthed and uncharted, and this book covers them from Z to A. Brutal, blunt, and uncommonly necessary.*

I glanced at Willa. "You said she has a newer one out?"

"Yeah. *Hypocrisy*."

"Is it good?"

Willa shrugged and blew out a breath. "I haven't had time to read it. I've been so busy working. Frank's gonna be pissed at me for the five dollars I spent on that."

"You guys are still together?" I opened the book to the dedication. *For little girls everywhere.*

"Yeah," Willa said, and I could hear a smile giving her voice a little lisp. "Things with Frank are pretty good." She paused and spoke up again. "Used Books had the other books when I was there. Both of them."

I nodded and turned to the first chapter.

1: Bulimia

Chessa spent half her life on her knees. Praying in church, dropping onto the hard tiles of bathroom floors, sinking to the rough carpet of strangers' bedrooms at parties in front of teenaged boys she barely knew.

Willa poked her finger against my knee. "What do you think?"

"It's good. I think I'll like it."

"Of course you'll like it. You'll read it, though? The whole thing?"

"Yeah."

"Good. Let me know what you think." Willa patted my arm. "Happy birthday, kiddo."

"Thank you."

My eyes barely left the page. I kept reading even though Willa stood over me, silently demanding my attention.

> Chessa had barely eaten anything. For lunch. For days. She swallowed hard, staring down into the familiar rounded shape of the porcelain bowl. Most of it was white, but parts of it were stained. She stared at the brown chunks and yellow streaks, making herself nauseas already. Chessa stuck her fingers into her mouth as far as she could. She gagged and lurched forward with dry heaves until stringy, partially digested lettuce leaves dropped into the still water.

Willa's voice intruded again. "Hey. Earth to Jessie. Come in, Jessie."

I closed the book to keep from reading any more.

Willa jerked her thumb toward the other side of the room. "I'm gonna take off. I just wanted to give you the book and wish you a happy birthday."

I stood up and left the book on the seat. I gave Willa a hug, her quilted coat making her feel like a giant stuffed animal. The fact that we could hug, that she'd greeted me with one, assured me nothing had changed. No matter how long we'd gone without talking, we were still friends. I hadn't lost her to life changes and the rest of the world.

I stepped back. "Thanks for stopping by. It was really good to see you."

"Yeah. We'll have to get together one of these days when Frank is sleeping and I'm off work."

"That'd be great."

"Are you working?"

I cringed because my answer always made me feel like a slacker. "No, I'm still in school. I don't know what I'm doing with my degree. I'm only taking a couple of classes this semester, so I'm free every night. I get done around either four-thirty or seven. No classes on Fridays."

"Perfect. That should be easy, then." Willa's lips puckered toward the center. "Are you still with that guy?"

"Dick?"

Willa's face tightened around the eyes. "Yeah. Dick."

I didn't want to go into details. We were on and off and back on again. We'd broken up for part of the summer, but since I'd taken him back, I was trying to make the best of it. I sounded perkier about it than I had a few weeks before. "Yeah, we're still together."

"Have fun with the book."

"Okay. Thanks again. It looks really good."

I followed Willa to the door. She bounced out onto the porch with a wave goodbye, and I locked up behind her. I walked back to the recliner and sat down, moving the book to my lap. I had a few hours until my parents got home. They'd have a completely different reaction to it, so I'd have to be careful when and where I read it. I could get through a few chapters now at least.

I skimmed what I'd read and launched myself eagerly into the new material.

> She was trembling when she sank back on her heels. She felt weak, but that didn't bother her. There was nothing in her life she felt she needed to be strong for. She could skate through it, do the bare minimum at school, nod her head to anything said to her at home, and perk up if she felt like it with a wine cooler with her friends.

Chessa liked the feeling of being weak. It made her feel she could get what she wanted most out of her disease, which was to fade away and disappear like a cloud. What would happen, her health teacher had assured the class during a section on eating disorders, was that bulimics got dangerously thin. She would waste away like a cancer patient, her cheeks looking pale and perpetually sucked in. Her stomach acid would eat at her gums until her teeth loosened and fell out. She already had dark patches not only under her eyes but around them. Those eyes, once large and wondrous, were sinking into tired bruises. If she didn't stop, her next class picture was going to look like the meth addict's mug shots she'd seen on the Internet.

Chessa wiped her mouth with toilet paper thinner and rougher than notebook pages and flushed it down the toilet with the remains of her modest lunch. She pushed herself up off the wall of the bathroom stall and dragged her feet out of the claustrophobic space to the long, shared sink. While she was still alone, she rinsed her hand and dotted it across her lips. She drank cold, metallic tap water out of her cupped hand. The second the bathroom door squeaked open, she threw her hand down from her face to fill the shaky palm with liquid soap. The other students roared by in the hallway, the volume shooting up as if on a dial. It died again as the door closed with a subtle thump.

Natalya Black, the most popular girl in school, stopped two feet behind Chessa. She smiled at her in the mirror. "You look good," she said. She pushed open a stall door and disappeared. The rest of her posse waited by the door, their open mouths chomping on wads of gum the size of ping pong balls.

Chessa finished washing her hands. Yes, she was

beautifully thin. It was the only good thing to come out of her terrible habit, the easiest part of her miserable life. She was too busy picking at her food to break a sweat taking the stairs. She was too busy retching into toilets to find out how hard it was to find a well-fitting dress in a size 16. When she set her hands on the narrowest part of her waist, her fingers nearly touched. Chessa hoped to make them touch by the time school let out in the summer, a sickening goal, but the only one she had ever set for herself.

She popped a piece of strong mint gum into her mouth and moved out of the restroom into the hallway. She walked like a zombie, vaguely aware of where she was going and how much time she had to get there. She gave no reaction to the students who bumped shoulders with her in the packed confines of the hallway or the close shouts that made her ears ring. The best way to make it out alive was not to pay too much attention to anything. Feeling like half a ghost, Chessa did not find that hard to do.

Keeping the book open, I hunched sideways, trying to get comfortable. I laid the book on the chair arm, crowding my ribs together on one side while the others stretched apart. It wouldn't last long, but I would shift again when it bothered me.

Chapter 3: Jessie

A warm breeze brushed my legs as I walked across campus. It felt good to be out doing something, getting some exercise and seeing people I knew. My books slapped against my back with every step, a weight I had not missed over the summer. I waved to people I'd met in previous classes but didn't stop to join their conversations. I didn't know them well enough to stop and talk.

I let myself into the student building and headed for the cafeteria. The identical clocks in every hallway showed I had a good twenty minutes before I needed to head to class. Even though it was after eleven, I didn't think the cafeteria would be too crowded. Competing voices echoed down the hallway, but when I turned the last corner, I saw the cafeteria was sparsely occupied. Perfect for reading.

I wove my way across the room to an empty table and lowered my backpack into the chair beside me. I sat down and unzipped it, revealing *F*CK, F*CK, F*CK* in front of my less appealing books for class. Half of them were dry, oversized volumes of literary criticism and classroom discussion questions. The other half was literature, some books I'd heard of and others I hadn't. I pulled out *F*CK, F*CK, F*CK*, carefully obscuring the cover with my hands. Even with the strategically placed asterisks, it could attract the wrong attention. I cracked the book open and held it low against the edge of the table.

5: Cling

Chessa's mother stood at the sink, rubbing the sponge so hard across the plates, she splashed great deluges of water over her stomach and onto the rug under her slippers. Chessa tried to concentrate on her homework at the kitchen table, wishing she had never let Jeremy into her room. The five minutes she'd stolen with him weren't worth losing the convenience of her desk lamp after he broke it. She wished she hadn't been too proud to borrow money from her friends to replace it. She was defenseless here in the kitchen with no head phones to put on and drown out her mother's droning. If the sun was shining instead of skulking behind the clouds, she would have moved herself outside.

Her mother's volume increased with every comment she let loose. "That stupid slut."

The equation Chessa had been trying to memorize flew out of her head as if it had never been there. All that remained was an empty space highlighted by confusion and the torn feeling of loss. She wondered why she tried to keep her grades up at all.

The woman at the sink shook her head at the window in front of her, making her greasy, unwashed curls sway side to side. "She thinks she's so hot with her mini skirts and her push-up bras. She can afford to get manicures now. Six months with your father, and she'll be wishing she'd never laid eyes on him. Eighteen years, and he throws me away. For what? That skinny bitch?"

Chessa stared harder at the math book lying open across the tablecloth, trying to force the equation into her brain. The letters and numbers might as well have been swirling on the page instead of standing still. She couldn't make sense of any of it.

"I gave him everything." The woman's voice finally wavered, and she laid her hands on the ledge of the sink, her knuckles frothy with white soap bubbles. She took in a scraping breath that came back out a rounded sob. "Everything I had."

As her mother began to cry in a noisy outpouring of stopped-up grief, Chessa regarded her hunched back with disdain. Her shoulders shook unevenly as she cried. Chessa had no idea her mother owned such an ugly housecoat, mint green with large white polka dots. Pink quilted slippers covered her feet, the toes pointed in opposite directions. Chessa's upper lip curled away from the bottom one. She knew she should feel sympathy, but she couldn't. This is the woman who's supposed to be raising me, she thought. This is my hero, my guide, my teacher. She was falling apart, and she didn't have enough shame or self-respect to do it in private.

The woman sniffled as she returned to the motions of washing and rinsing and setting aside. Chessa ignored her homework to watch her mother, unable to concentrate on anything else. The chore sickened her with her mother's attention to every detail, the squeaking sounds of her fingerprints rubbing away hardened specks of dinner. The dishwasher her husband had been promising for years would never come.

Chessa wondered if her dad would ever come home. She didn't think he would, but she wondered if he saw the house the same way she did, as something that needed to be escaped, never something nourishing to crawl back into. Only her mother seemed content to stay there. How long would the woman stay there now that the illusion of a happy family was permanently broken? She insisted on finishing the dishes while she cried, not even stopping to wipe her face or catch her breath.

Chessa wished she was anywhere else, anyone else. She wished she could make herself into one of the punk girls she had met in the park, Mandy or even the wilder Toria. They could help her leave this self behind. They could help her shave her head, leaving a strip of hair half an inch wide the whole way down the center. They would help her dye it purple or blue or neon green. They would help her ditch the bra digging into her ribs, a set of three dimensional rods carved from hunger like the hull of an abandoned shipwreck. They would let her scream, let the frustration blast out of the tar black depths of her. She wanted to scream, not to say any exact words, but to release the pressure that had been building inside her for years.

Chessa realized she did want to go outside. She wanted to run and search the park for any signs of them. She needed to make some new friends if she was going to get out of that house. It might be the only way.

I felt a tug on my hair before I realized anyone had come up behind me. Something metal crashed onto the table in front of me and slid scraping to a stop. Dick stepped into view, hovering over me. "Here," he said, gesturing to the table. "I got you something."

Still recovering from the tug and the slap of metal, I closed the book over my fingers as I reached for the gold chain. I lifted it into a bracelet, a simple chain holding an oval-shaped plate engraved with flowers. "It's pretty."

"Put it on."

I hesitated, the book still filling my hands.

"What's up? Oh, you're reading. Whatcha reading?" Dick dove for the book, his brown hair falling down over his forehead. Unruly curls flopped around his ears.

I swung the book out of his reach. "Something a friend gave me." I eyed my bookmark and the backpack just past it where I could stash the book out of view.

Dick lunged across my lap and twisted my arm, turning the cover towards him. "Let me see that. That looks hot. Is she naked?"

Dick grabbed my wrist and snatched the book out of my hand. My fingers slid out, losing my place. He grinned and crowed as he looked it over, but his wide smile fell into a disapproving sneer. He looked it over from front to back. "This is one of those women power things, isn't it?"

I swallowed, trying to find a convincing lie. "I don't know. I just started it." I picked up the worn bookmark I'd been using for years.

"Of course it is," Dick insisted. "If it wasn't, her tits would be bigger." Dick waved his hand over the cover. "What is this? What's this chick's name who wrote it?"

I sat up straighter to point out the initials in the corner. "XZA. She writes under her initials. It's different."

"She's lame." Dick waved his hands in the air. "Ooh, look at all the power she has. She can't even use her real name." Dick dropped the book carelessly into my hands, the cover flapping open and slapping closed. "I'm starving. Let's get out of here."

I skimmed through the pages, looking for the one I was on.

"Starving," Dick repeated. "Let's go."

I gave up, knowing I could find it later, and stuffed the book into my backpack. "I can skip my first class, but I should probably go to the second one." I zipped it closed and followed Dick across the cafeteria. "We could eat here. It is a cafeteria."

"All they serve is shit. I wanna go to the diner."

"All they serve is shit," I echoed. "Everything's so greasy."

Dick stopped short. I was so busy fastening the bracelet around my wrist, I almost slammed into him. I stopped with a high-pitched squeak three inches behind his new fluorescent shoes.

Dick studied me over the shoulder of his hooded blue sweatshirt. His dark eyebrows crouched down over his sleepy eyes. "Are you paying for dinner?"

I didn't have any money, and he knew it. "No."

"When you do, you can pick the cafeteria or the fanciest place on the river. I'm paying, and we're going to the diner."

I nodded, and Dick continued to stare at me. "Okay," I said in a tiny voice.

"Jesus. I'm doing you a favor."

"I know."

We started walking again, Dick barreling down the hallway as I tried to keep up. I realized for the first time the colors around me were brown and yellow. The walls were painted a faded canary, and the floors shone a speckled brown and white. I was going to school in a toilet like the one Chessa threw up in. I stifled a laugh, and Dick jerked his face toward me.

"Are you laughing at me?" he demanded.

"No, I was laughing at something I read."

"In that book?"

"Yeah."

"So it's a funny book?"

"Not really."

"I like funny books. Maybe I should read it."

I tensed at the idea of Dick opening that book. One scene about Chessa despising her mother and giving up on Jeremy, and Dick would tear it apart. He'd drop it into the garbage, saving my parents the chance to throw it out first. "I don't think you'd like it," I said.

"Why not? Don't you think I read?"

"You read. I just don't think you'd like this one."

"I probably wouldn't. I don't read stuff by chicks."

I cringed at his bitterness. "Women write funny books. I read Mary Roach's book about astronauts. It was really funny."

Dick swung his arm around me and pulled me up against him. He pressed his lips hard against my cheek. "Whatever, Jessie. You're so blonde sometimes."

I adjusted the strap of my backpack and shut myself up. Arguing with Dick never got anybody anywhere.

Chapter 4: Xan

Marcy lit her cigarette and blew the first puff of white smoke towards the sky. She always smoked dramatically, like she was a Hollywood starlet sans the holder. She relaxed in the patio chair across the table from me. "You'll be editing before you know it. I don't know why you worry so much."

Stacey laughed, seated between us on my right. She snorted lightly. Her honey blonde hair hung over her shoulders, silken and straight. Her thin bangs covered her forehead, bringing extra attention to her big green eyes. "How can you say that? Do you listen to yourself? Every time you send a poem to a magazine, you hyperventilate for days."

I smiled at Stacey. It was an accurate accusation, but I was too tired to back her up. I'd been writing for too long without a meaningful break. Sitting in the cool autumn breeze listening to my friends tear each other down gave my mind the perfect distraction while it repaired itself. I waited for Marcy's answer while she studied Stacey's smirk.

Marcy brushed her dark bangs off her forehead. Her once-casual tone rolled with baiting sarcasm. "You don't know what it's like, do you, Stacey? You rub down total strangers for a living."

Stacey, a successful masseuse, jerked her chin at Marcy. "I rubbed your boyfriend down for free."

Marcy made a sour face and sucked on her cigarette. "You did not. You're not his type."

"He prefers blondes. I heard him say it. What are you going to do? Get a wig? You'd fry your hair trying to go platinum."

"I'm not talking to you. I'm talking to Xan." Marcy raised her cool blue eyes to my face. "What does Sheryl think about your book?"

I was almost disappointed. A few half-hearted insults, and we were already back to the subject of my book. "Nothing yet. I haven't shown her anything."

"Have you shown Michael?"

"No. He won't see it until at least draft three. Draft two if I'm impatient."

Stacey sat up straighter, peering through the windows of the house. Her fingers smoothed the length of her hair. "Where is Michael?" she asked, the urgency of her words underlying her attempt at indifference. "I thought he was coming right out."

Marcy ignored her and shot another question at me. "Do you have an ending?"

"No."

"It could be worse. You don't have thirty people watching you while you work. When you make a mistake, you can delete it."

I offered a lazy shrug. "Who told you to be a teacher? I don't know why you suggested I do it."

"I just wanted you to work with me so we could raise some hell. It didn't have anything to do with teaching. Well, not everything." Marcy glanced behind her at the house, her solemn expression giving way to a smirk. "You know, Xan, my offer still stands. If you ever want to send Michael my way – if you're getting tired of him or feeling extra generous – I'll still take him."

Stacey adjusted her blouse, a hot pink satin that hugged her small breasts. She'd left it unbuttoned a few inches down her chest but slipped one more button out through its hole. "I'll flip you for him," she chimed in without hesitation.

I gave a half-smile. My friends always fought over Michael's attention, ever since Stacey's "Try me on for size" comment slipped out years ago when she was half drunk and her ex-husband was dating somebody new. Marcy had followed it up by tousling her hair and arguing, "He obviously prefers brunettes." Their attempts to snag him for themselves had never worked, and Michael handled it so well, I'd never bothered to stop it. It amused me and reminded me of wilder times. "Michael and I are fine," I said.

Marcy held her cigarette farther from her lips, her two fingers extended on either side. "Don't look so morose about it. You should be ecstatic. When Michael walks down the street, he leaves all the women, ages twelve through ninety-five, quivering in his wake. He's given more women their first unintentional orgasm than we'll ever know."

I gave a short hum, both thoughtful and smug. "I was never multiorgasmic until I met Michael."

Marcy narrowed her eyes at me. "Now you're just showing off."

The patio door slid open, and Michael walked out onto the deck. He smiled graciously at my friends, as he had when they'd arrived. He didn't sit down in the empty chair as he passed it. He came to stand behind me and started massaging the back of my tortured neck. I appreciated the gesture more than I could put into words. His practiced thumbs found the knots and ropes in my muscles, slowly but firmly encouraging them to let go.

Marcy glowed as she looked over my head at Michael. "What were you doing in there?"

Michael's voice rumbled gently above me. "I had a few more paragraphs I wanted to read. I wasn't doing anything interesting."

"You underestimate how interested I am. I want to know everything about you."

Stacey looked Michael over, muttering, "Everything about his body."

Marcy spared her half a glance. "Not true, but you know, Michael, we were saying, if Xan is too old for you, you can come over to the younger side of the table."

Michael continued rubbing my neck, his reply distracted and subdued. "I'm sorry, Marcy. I prefer older women."

Marcy scoffed, her mouth gaping open. "Xan's only older than you by two weeks."

"So why would I leave her for you?"

"Let's face it, darling. You're aging like the finest of wines, and Xan's already beginning to droop."

"Nice try, Marcy, I've seen Xan naked." Michael bent his head and kissed my cheek. "She pleases me in ways I don't think you could."

Marcy grinned back with a hint of defiance. "You can't hurt my feelings, Michael. I'll always want you. I'll give you five hundred dollars for a moustache ride right now."

Michael deflected the impromptu offer with his usual humor. "Ah, one more reason to stay clean shaven."

Stacey threw Marcy a disapproving glance. "Cheapskate. I'd give him a thousand." She pushed her chest out before she spoke to

Michael. "I thought the goatee looked very good on you."

"Thank you."

"Of course, I'd look good on you, too."

Michael said nothing. He repositioned his fingers on my neck, which were working wonders for my strained muscles.

Stacey pouted at Michael. "How come I never see you in my office? I could give you a great massage." Stacey flexed her fingers as if imagining them on Michael's shoulders.

"Do you have to ask? I'm afraid I'd get mauled in there."

"I'd be very professional."

Marcy coughed into her sleeve and turned to Stacey. "When people do what you're thinking of doing in a professional context, it's called prostitution."

Stacey stuck her upturned nose in the air. "I'm more sophisticated than that. I'm like a call girl."

"With your shirt half open, you're a floozy."

"Eat it, bar fly."

Michael gave my neck a few soothing strokes and kissed the side of it. He settled into the plastic chair on my left.

More languid than I'd been in weeks, I met his laidback gaze. "Thank you."

Michael swatted Marcy's smoke away from his face. "You're welcome."

Marcy jammed her cigarette into the ashtray she'd brought from her apartment, smashing the cherry until the smoke disappeared.

Stacey sighed with resignation and fastened the lowest open button on the front of her blouse.

I looked across at Marcy. "How's your new boyfriend working out?"

She shrugged. "The magic's gone. I give it another month at the most."

Stacey finished arranging her pointed collar. "What happened?"

Marcy moved her fingers toward her mouth before she remembered she'd put out her cigarette. "He makes me want to smoke just thinking about it. Every time he comes over, he brings these tiny bottles of milk. They get kicked under the furniture, and then I have to figure out where they went before they stink up the apartment."

"That's disgusting. Why doesn't he bring a gallon jug and pour himself a glass?"

"Are you ready for this? He says it tastes better." Marcy paused for effect, her eyes sharp under bunched-up eyebrows. "It's the exact same goddamn milk as all the other goddamn milk, the milk that does not fit under the couch or disappear under the dresser. Yes, I said dresser. I've found one there before."

"Why are you with him?"

"Do I have to spell it out? Is nothing obvious to you, Stacey?" Stacey shrank away from her, and Marcy pressed on. "He's five years younger and has the sexual experience of someone five years older. Maybe even fifteen."

Stacey sat up again, recovering her poise and confidence. "So he's a manwhore."

Marcy nodded, tossing her eyebrows up. "I always wanted to get checked for an STD. No time like the present."

Stacey held up two fingers. "Two words for you: double bag."

Marcy raised a finger for each word of her reply. "Planned. Parenthood."

Stacey extended a smooth gesture to Michael. "You can see why we won't give up on you. You're the only decent man we know."

"I see that," he assured her.

"Don't you have any friends you could introduce us to?"

Marcy fished around in her pocket. She set her pack of cigarettes on the table and pushed them away from her. "It's the least you could do."

Michael thought it over, clasping his hands behind his head. "My closest friends still live in Chicago."

"It's not the other side of the world. Why don't they drive down?"

"Do you expect them to speed here with possible STD's waiting for them?"

"Wise-ass." Marcy scooted lower in her chair. "I'll bring you a clean bill of health so you can see for yourself. Give them a call. See if they want to come out for a little meet and greet."

Stacey raised her hand. "I'll bring the bowl we all throw our keys into."

Michael pulled his phone out of his pocket and looked through his contact list. "It might be nice to get the old crew together. What do you think, Xan?"

I was so grateful for the neck massage, I was prepared to say yes to any plans Michael wanted to make. "What old crew?"

"The boys of Underrated Media. We could have Nick and John down for a night."

"That's fine with me."

Stacey leaned forward and set her forearms on the table. "Now we're talking. What do they do?"

"John writes music reviews. Nick does movies."

Stacey's breath of exultation was filtered through a thick screen of indignation. "Why haven't you told us this before? What do they look like?"

"John has a huge, hairy mole on his face." Michael gestured at his cheek with undulating fingers.

Stacey grabbed Marcy's pack of cigarettes and threw it at Michael. He laughed and barely bothered to dodge it. It bounced off his shoulder and clattered to the patio floor. "I'm forty-one and single. I'm not joking around, you liar."

Marcy bent over and picked up her cigarettes, tossing them back on the table. "You're divorced, not single."

"I'm not dating anyone with a milk fetish."

Michael pressed a few buttons on his phone. "I'll send them a text and see when they want to come out."

Marcy raised her eyebrows high. "Don't mention the STD thing. I don't want to ruin my chances."

"I wouldn't do that to you. How much notice do you need to break up with the milkman?"

"About five minutes."

"Really? What happened to fifteen years of extra experience?"

Marcy leaned toward him. "Get single. I'll show you how fast I can do it."

Michael smiled but didn't look up from his phone.

Marcy rested her head on the back of her chair. Her admiring eyes roamed Michael's upper body. "You're so gorgeous. You're like Russell Brand with that hair."

Stacey piped up. "Who's Russell Brand?"

"Let's wait and let Nick explain it to you. That should be fun."

Michael tucked his phone in his pocket. "It'll be too cold to sit outside by the time they drive down, but we still have one good bottle of wine from my parents. We could break that open and have a nice time."

I nodded.

Marcy looked Michael over, more approving than devouring this time. She shook her head. "How did you ever get him, Xan?"

I answered honestly. "I have no idea."

Michael held his hand out to me, and I offered him mine. He kissed the back of my hand. "Because you're a genius writer, and when you asked me if I wanted to sleep with you, I found it impossible to say no."

Marcy let out a small, jealous moan. "I'm a genius writer."

Stacey snorted. "You're a writer in your spare time."

Michael held onto my hand, and I gazed back at him across the length of our arms. How had this grouchy, aging writer hooked such an enduring person as the often-pursued Michael Singer?

Stacey spoke more pleasantly to me than she had to Marcy. "You're so lucky, Xan. I'm happy for you. I'm still pissed you wouldn't let us do anything special for your anniversary."

Marcy adopted a flat, low tone. "She was doing something special, all right." She sent a loaded sidelong glance to Michael.

Stacey snickered.

Michael fielded their drama for me. "Maybe Marcy has a point for once. Who says Xan didn't do anything special for our anniversary?"

Marcy guffawed with her mouth open while Stacey turned her head and tittered, every sound bouncing off the back of the house. They gave up on their inquiries, and I waited to hear what inappropriate subject they would pick up next.

I'd watched our ten year anniversary approaching for months and made sure Michael knew I didn't want to make a big deal out of it. We took a night off from writing and reading to cook together and enjoy a low-key evening at home. We talked about old times and present projects. The date itself was arbitrary, anyway. Michael wasn't sure what date to mark as our anniversary, and since I wasn't willing to set one, he'd settled on the night we met. I knew even as we discussed letting it pass without a group celebration that my friends would whine in protest. But the details were none of their business, and if they wanted to picture wild escapades through the house in silky things and handcuffs, I was going to let them.

Chapter 5: Jessie

Mom called me for dinner, and I called back while I sped-read one more paragraph for class. The information barely stuck in my brain as I got up and wandered out to the dining room table. Bowls of vegetables and side dishes lined the table runner, and embarrassment took over my thoughts of school. My parents shouldn't be cooking full meals for me every night. I wasn't a kid anymore, thinking dinner magically appeared on the table. My parents put in full days at work and came home to another hour in the cramped, hot kitchen. All I'd done was read all day.

Mom carried out a bowl of mashed potatoes and set it on the table. She muttered to herself about finding a spoon for it.

"I can get it," I said, moving past the table.

Mom patted her hand towards me. "Sit down, Jessie. I'll bring it."

She disappeared into the kitchen, and I lingered by my chair. Dad came out with plates and silverware. He looked tired, but he brightened with a smile when he saw me.

"Have a seat," he said. "It's almost done."

"I could've helped," I insisted. I reached for the plates, but Dad didn't give them to me. He set them at our usual seats around the table.

Mom addressed me as she swept back into the room. "You were studying." She slipped spoons into the mashed potatoes and the green beans.

"You could've called me," I grumbled.

Their eyes scanned the table, and they headed back to the kitchen without another word. I slid down into my seat to wait for them, trying not to think about how nonequivalent a full-time job was to a few hours of classes and studying.

Dad returned with filled water glasses, and Mom carried out a plate of baked chicken.

"I could've set the table," I tried again.

"Don't worry about it." Mom nestled the chicken between the other dishes. "Dig in. Help yourself."

I reached for the serving fork.

Dad talked to Mom as they settled in around me. "So once the copier got fixed, everybody who needed copies ended up getting back in line. They were snaked out of the copy room all the way to my office." Dad shrugged. "I just waited until all was clear. I think I was the only one who left on time except for Mack."

I added a pile of green beans to the chicken on my plate. If Dad was already mid-story, I'd missed the initial generalities about their day. It was another reason I hated being excluded from the kitchen. I had no idea what their days were like. "How long was the copier down?" I asked.

"About three hours."

"How was your day, Mom?"

"Exhausting," Mom sighed. "It feels so good to be home with my shoes off. Oh – " She fluttered a hand at Dad. "I ran into..."

I stopped listening and piled my plate higher. I didn't want to hear about some school friend of Dad's or anybody's daughter or new job. As I took my first bites of juicy chicken and over-buttered mashed potatoes, my thoughts drifted to Willa. She was probably at work, maybe even on her break for dinner. I tried to imagine what she would've packed for herself. She had brought all kinds of crazy snacks to class when she was in school. Would she have packed some kind of leftovers? Nothing too fancy, nothing that would cost much to make. Knowing Willa, it was macaroni and cheese in fun shapes meant for kids.

I started on my green beans, thankfully the fresh ones, not canned like every school cafeteria I'd ever known. Willa would've packed a side for dinner, too, something besides macaroni and cheese. What was it? Not an apple – too obvious. Maybe a pink apple sauce cup. And a chocolate pudding cup for dessert.

"Jessie?" Mom asked, breaking into my thoughts. "How was school today?"

I tried not to cringe. It sounded like I was in elementary school. "Classes were fine," I said, choosing my words pointedly.

"Do you know anybody from last semester?"

"A couple of people."

"That's nice."

I stuffed my mouth with food so she wouldn't ask me any more. I wondered what Dick was doing. He was surprisingly more unpredictable than Willa. He could be speeding down back roads with friends, sitting in a darkened movie theater, or stuck at home with his mom and step-dad. What were they having for dinner? It was probably worse than Willa's ensemble. I'd only eaten with his family once, and I tried not to grimace at the memory of what we had. Canned corn, not well-rinsed and barely lukewarm from the microwave. Greasy meat and wilted lettuce stuffed into taco shells from a brightly colored box.

Dick had only had one meal at our house, too. The biggest disaster of my evening with his family was the food. His step-dad's attitude hadn't been so abrasive then. It would be uncomfortable at best for me to try it now. But even I had to admit Dick's evening with my family had been one disaster after another.

It started out all right, I thought. Dick looked nice. He wasn't as late as he'd been other times we were supposed to hang out. He was enthusiastic about what Mom had cooked for dinner, licking his lips and rubbing his belly in a spontaneous dance of gratefulness.

But as soon as Dad appeared, Dick's mouth didn't stop moving. "Hey, Mr. T. Mr. T, what happened to your gold chains, man? Where'd you put 'em? Did you lose 'em? You're looking a little bare tonight. Hey, Mr. T, say something tough for me. Come on." Dick put up fists and started shadowboxing with thin air.

The way Dad gave him a blank stare and then set in to ignoring him was not a good sign. Mom tried to be polite and ask Dick all the normal questions, but he either gave way too much information or none at all. After a while, the questions stopped coming, and Dick rambled on without prompting.

At the end of the night, I walked Dick out to his truck to say goodbye. I lingered on this part of my memories, a tight hug and long kiss. As I walked back into the house, I thought the night had mostly worked out. I'd learned things about Dick I hadn't heard before. The dinner was good. Dad's silence seemed normal. I said, "That went well," and Mom turned to me with disbelieving eyebrows above her open mouth.

"Jessie, that boy is awful," she said. "My head hurts from

listening to him. I don't know how you put up with him."

"What?" I asked.

Dad's head jerked toward me, his eyes sharp. "He's obnoxious. If I heard one more Mr. T joke, I was going to throw him out."

"Like we're going to have to throw this food out?" Mom chimed in, lifting a dish from the table. "I watched him spit all over everything every time he talked. You don't really expect me to eat this, do you, Jessie? That's disgusting."

I looked at the food left on the table, a few meals' worth headed for the garbage can. "I'm sorry. Maybe he was just nervous. He's not usually..." I stopped myself before I could lie.

Mom's eyebrows disappeared under her drooping bangs. "Not usually what? So loud? So arrogant? So mouthy?"

"Forget it," I mumbled.

"We invited him," Mom reminded us without enthusiasm as she cleared the table. "I think it'll be a long time before we invite him again. I certainly hope we won't feel the need to do that."

I dropped the subject, and my parents seemed to forget about Dick as I'd muttered for them to do. They never asked about him. They never asked about our plans. When I offered such information, my parents only nodded with comprehension while condemnation wrinkled stress lines into their foreheads.

I looked up from my plate and listened in on my parents to see how far they'd gotten.

Dad was saying, "...in the army. He was a real hero over there. Saved half a dozen people at least. Confirmed. I just felt pretty proud to be shaking the guy's hand."

I spoke up before Mom could respond. "Do you think they'd take Dick in the army?" I watched for their reactions to see if their attitudes had changed.

Mom stared at me then turned to Dad. "I'd rather hear about a hero any day than some of those other stories you hear coming out of there."

I cleared my throat. "I mean, Dick gets through school all right, but he's not really a college type of guy. Maybe the army would be better for him."

After a long pause, Dad forced out a tense, "Maybe."

"He should join," Mom piped up, nodding like a Bobblehead. "It'd be good for him."

Dad stifled a laugh, and I went back to finishing my mashed potatoes.

"How's Willa?" Mom asked. "Didn't you see her recently?"

"Yeah, she dropped by for a minute. She's good."

"What has she been up to?"

I swallowed, distinctly remembering my parents not liking Willa very much. She was nosy and nontraditional. I couldn't drag them into a conversation about Dick, but they were suddenly interested in Willa. I didn't want to answer, but finally I said, "She works at a laundromat. She lives with Frank."

"Oh, Frank," Mom cooed fondly.

"You never met Frank."

"But you talked about him sometimes. Wasn't he always doing something nice and thoughtful for Willa?"

I hung my face over my plate so Mom wouldn't see my eyebrows scrunching up. Was this a deliberate dig at Dick? "Yes," I mumbled.

"Well, I'm glad that's working out for her. He was such a good catch."

"He's not a fish, Mom," I muttered into a forkful of mashed potatoes.

"I just want you to have good friends who are doing well. That's all."

It was the grown-up version of the advice she'd given me in third grade: make friends in the morning so you'll have someone to sit next to at lunch. Pick someone who doesn't push you down on the playground or steal your lunchbox. I shoveled the last bites of food into my mouth and took my plate to the kitchen. On my way back through the dining room, I thanked my parents for dinner and said I still had reading to do for school. I tried to ignore their understanding replies as I continued to my room and shut myself inside.

Chapter 6: Xan

Michael stepped quietly into the doorway to my office. New ideas had swum in my head while we watched TV, and I was so intent on typing the intricate dialog that I barely acknowledged him.

He kept his voice low, trying not to distract me. "I thought you were coming to bed."

"I am. I just have to..." I backed up and retyped the last few words correctly. "Have to get this down."

Michael drifted away, and I finished the scene the way I wanted it. It was a rough draft to be sure, but it was progress. I turned off the computer and wandered off in search of Michael.

He came out of the kitchen and met me in the hallway. "Did you get everything?" he asked.

I nodded, feeling the full weight of my tiredness now that my ideas were preserved. "Did you get all the lights?"

Michael put his hand on my back and guided me toward the stairs. "Don't worry about it. I'll get them."

I started up the stairs, listening to the gentle clicks as Michael flipped switches behind me. I led him into the bedroom, and Michael continued our nighttime ritual by closing the door.

It was an old habit of mine born of living with my parents and fighting on a regular basis with my mother. The rest of my house sat empty and silent, but I didn't know if I could sleep with the door open. I'd never tried. Closed doors meant isolation to most people, but they'd always meant privacy to me. I'd never asked Michael if closing the door was left over from his past or if he'd picked it up from me. I couldn't remember if his terrier Jack slept in bed with him or not. Jack had never had the opportunity to live here. He'd suffered eye and leg problems for several years, and Michael put him to sleep months before I offered the option of moving in with me. I still had no pets of my own, so there really was no one to wake us up at night if we left the door ajar.

My flighty mind stuck on the fact I'd never questioned the closing of that door. I didn't know who we intended to keep out or if we were keeping each other in. No one but us had been by the house since Friday, as Melody took long weekends off from helping me organize my career to spend time with her growing family. I was happy for her, proud her life had opened up beyond her work for me. She had a kind husband and a joyous three-year-old daughter. Her second child was set to be born in the summer, but Melody was convinced it would come a few weeks early.

The house felt still and sleepy after the sound and action of the television. It had been almost this quiet most of the day except for my typing and reading aloud. Michael had driven up to Chicago to touch base with the other members of Underrated Media. I'd spent the day cooped up alone, trying to hammer out the final few details of my book, but I was unable to answer any of the long-range questions. Who would turn out to be the most self-serving, the most callous? Who, if anyone, would redeem themselves? How could I possibly wrap this up, and what useable title would I eventually suggest to Sheryl?

I peeled off my thick socks and started getting undressed. Michael lingered by the door, unbuttoning the line of black buttons down the front of his shirt. Neither of our stomachs was as flat as it used to be, but we weren't in bad shape. The glinting white-silver hairs on Michael's chest gave away his age more than anything else. He covered the grey in his hair to keep himself looking young, hair that was as long if not longer than when we'd met. I imagined hiding the grey was the only thing that kept my friends from cyberstalking him the way they did Anthony Bourdain. Michael's face was still handsome, his arms and legs strong and well toned. He dropped his clothes into the hamper, and I carried mine over to do the same.

Michael laid his hand on my back and pressed his lips to my temple. "You look exhausted."

"You look tired, too." I knew Michael spent as much time staring at text as I did.

Michael held my gaze. "No, you look exhausted. You're working way too hard on this book."

"You never told me that before, that I was working too hard."

"You used to take more breaks. You used to read more print and rest your eyes more. You weren't this obsessed."

"I'm getting older. I want my book to be finished before I'm ancient."

"You have plenty of time. You're not as old as you think."

"I owe it to Sheryl. I owe it to my fans. I owe it to myself."

"You owe yourself good health."

I started for the other side of the bed, one half of the bed I used to sleep in alone. I decided I wouldn't need to put a nightgown on if I climbed under the covers in the next half a minute. The air was chilly but not as cold as it was going to get by the end of the year.

Michael wasn't putting pajamas on, either, pulling down the comforter from his side of the bed. "Is Sheryl pushing you to finish it?"

My eyes landed on the short stack of books beneath the lamp on Michael's bedside table. Nick Hornby. Chuck Palahniuk. Bret Easton Ellis. This was Michael's personal collection rather than the shifting assortment of authors he read to review. I forced myself back to Michael's question. "Not directly. I know she'd side with you. I should make sure I'm taking care of myself. But she's gone to bat for me a million times. She found me editors when other agents wouldn't even look at my work. She talks highly of me in every interview I'm mentioned in. If I have a chance to make both of us some money, I have to do it. It's been too many years since *Hypocrisy* came out."

"Your fans will be fine. Sheryl will be fine. She has other authors."

I climbed into bed, my skin retracting against the cold cotton sheets. "I want to be done with it. I want to know how it ends, how I'm going to get all of this figured out."

"You will." Michael walked over to the light switch beside the door and turned off the lamp on the dresser. He came back to the bed and climbed in beside me. "I don't know how you do it, but you always do."

"What?"

"Find the perfect endings for your books."

I laid my head on my pillow, shifting position for the right placement and cradle. "If I always found the perfect ending, I wouldn't have so many partial manuscripts downstairs."

"Don't worry about those. They don't count. Nobody has to know about them." Michael propped himself up on his elbow and leaned down for a kiss. He brushed his fingers down my cheek. "Other writers would be lying if they said they didn't have two dozen of those, too."

That was true. We all had our little graveyards of hopes and plots and uncelebrated characters.

Michael patted my hand. "Don't stay up all night thinking about it."

"All right. I'll try not to."

"Good night, Xan. I love you."

I ignored the three little words, also part of our ritual. "Good night, Michael."

He kissed me again, softer, and lay down next to me mere inches away. I closed my eyes in the dark. I wanted to carve out eight hours of restful sleep.

I was glad I'd added some fresh ideas to my novel, though. It gave me hope that one day I could fill in all the remaining blanks. It was yet another story that was coming out anti-marriage, and my mother wouldn't be thrilled with that. But how many years would pass until she heard that secondhand?

I took a deep breath. My mind was stirring itself up instead of cooling down for sleep. As Stacey had once taught me to do from her years of practicing yoga, I focused on my breathing and tried to forget the stories that haunted me. My book and my parents crept into my slowing thoughts from time to time, but gradually, my mind gave in. The persistent questions disappeared, and I slipped into sleep before I could protest anymore.

Chapter 7: Jessie

It wasn't that far into the semester, and my room was already a mess. It had seldom been spotless, but I'd reorganized it before fall classes began. Walking into it from the kitchen with fresh eyes, I could see how bad every pile had gotten. A tornado could have passed through it with less destruction. The closet door gaped open, exposing hanging clothes and clumsily stacked boxes. Papers and school books covered my desk. My stereo, seriously outdated, sat layered in dust, and it would be years before I could afford to replace it.

The cleanest part of the whole room was in a photograph on the wall. It was a black and white picture I'd taken of my room after I'd spent a weekend detailing it two years before. As a joke – or a sign of resignation – my mom matted it and framed it. It hung above the stereo, the mat graced by a slip of paper proclaiming what she'd named it: *The Rise of Jessie's Blue Moon*. Very funny.

There was no use in putting anything in its place now. I could find everything I needed, and the rest could wait until winter break.

I made my way around the bed to the small table beside it. I set my glass of water on a coaster with a kitschy country cat on it and returned to my place on the bed. The black and white photo taunted me from the opposite wall. I used to take pictures all the time, and it reminded me how much I wanted to do that again. I pushed the longing away, stretching my legs out in front of me and picking up *F*CK, F*CK, F*CK*. I peeked ahead to the last page to see how far I was from the end. Only a few pages remained. I settled further down into the pillow stuffed behind me, determined to finish the book before I got up again.

"Fuck it," Toria said. Her bright blue eyes shone in the leaf-filtered sunlight. Even though her teeth were yellowed and oddly shaped, they stood mostly in a straight line, and her smile was contagious. She held out the cigarette again, the harmless white stick.

This time Chessa took it. She set it between her

lips as she'd seen Toria do a thousand times. Toria flicked the lighter into flame and held it out for her. Chessa's hand shook a little as she tried to calm her nerves and keep the bouncing cigarette above the steady fire.

Toria slid her thumb off the lever. "Let me do it." She pulled the cigarette away and curved her lips around it. In seconds, Toria drew fire into the cigarette until it caught a red and yellow glow. She passed it to Chessa. "You have to puff on it first to get it going."

Chessa nodded, getting used to the reassurance of the cigarette between her fingers.

"And stop throwing up," Toria said. She tucked the lighter into her pocket. "That shit is sick."

"I will. I've been meaning to."

Toria watched her, not the intense observation of her parents, but a cool, even waiting. Chessa returned her attention to the cigarette. She hoped not to embarrass herself and inhaled her first mouthful of acrid smoke. She choked on it harder than she wanted to, afraid Toria would laugh at her and call her a baby.

Toria gave an encouraging smile. "You'll get used to it. I puked my first time smoking."

Chessa could hardly believe that. Toria seemed too tough, too resilient for throat irritation or stomach problems. Chessa had imagined Toria being born with a cigarette in her mouth and a metal bar through her navel. The head of her recent snake tattoo slithered up the side of her neck above the collar of her wrinkled, military-style blouse. Chessa wanted to be as brave as Toria, but she was light-years away from gritting through the pain of a needle dragging across her skin.

Toria winked, and Chessa knew she'd be okay. She could learn to be tougher. It would only take time. Her stomach rumbled uncomfortably, begging for food.

Toria pursed her lips. "You need a cheeseburger or a mondo taco salad or something."

"Yeah."

"But you have to keep it down this time and not leave it in a toilet somewhere."

"I will." It was easy to listen to Toria and do what she said. Chessa wished she'd met her years ago. By the time her father left, she might've been too independent and apathetic to hate her mother.

Toria started back the way they came. Chessa took another small inhale from the cigarette, not as offensive to her lungs this time, and followed Toria over the uneven gravel to the truck. The hole rusted through the side of the faded maroon bed looked even bigger than it had the day before. Toria stuck her hand in from the underside and wiggled her fingers through the hole, shaking her head at how ridiculous it was. Chessa said nothing. She didn't mind riding in it. She wasn't embarrassed. She felt like a human version of the truck, rusted through with unfortunate, rough experiences but still running. With a few replacement parts, Chessa could be good as new.

I lingered over the last pages of *F*CK, F*CK, F*CK*, letting the words absorb and echo through my head. Chessa was going to be all right. I could see that. I appreciated the bittersweetness of the ending. I could see Chessa being friends with Toria for a long time despite how much Toria had intimidated her at first. I was glad Willa got the book for me. It was the best present I'd gotten in years. Mom and Dad did all right, but they never would've picked this up for me.

I closed the book, trying to pull my head out of Chessa's fictional world. Except for a few short breaks, I'd been immersed in it for hours. Willa was right. I should've run out and bought XZA's other books before I finished this one. I wanted to know what Willa knew.

I looked at my watch. It was only five-thirty. I still had time to get to the bookstore.

Climbing off the bed, I swung my purse off the back of the door. I stuck my feet in my shoes, the laces already tied. I slipped out of the house before Mom or Dad could get home and ask me where I was going. They wouldn't understand a mission like this. I jogged out to my car at the curb, grateful the most damage it had was a few scratches from shopping carts and car doors. Willa had told me to go to Used Books. Within fifteen dollars and half an hour, I could be back on the bed reading *Satan, My Father*, dedicated to the devil himself.

As I drove, I thought about how hard I'd worked to hide a book with a cover exclaiming *F*CK, F*CK, F*CK*. I'd have to work even harder with *Satan, My Father*. Dad would assume it was a blanket tirade against all fathers or at least against the religion they were trying to raise me in. Mom would instantly sense its feminist roots, roll her eyes, and point to the trash can. There was no telling the kinds of reactions I could get from my classmates, and then there was Dick. He would probably give this book the same reaction he gave *F*CK, F*CK, F*CK*, getting excited about the cover's potential controversy and quickly turning cynical at the reality of the story inside.

I parked hastily in front of Used Books. I found it a small, cramped shop with discolored flooring and books crammed into every possible space. I had no idea how I'd find anything, and I was relieved when a hippy-looking girl with a nose ring called out a greeting from behind the counter. I walked over, slightly nervous to share my reading preferences in front of the overweight man reading a sci-fi novel on a stool behind her. She blinked at me earnestly.

"I'm looking for *Satan, My Father* by XZA."

"Cool," she sighed softly. She came around the counter and led me to the literature section. We couldn't find *Satan, My Father*, but Used Books had retained a battered but tightly bound copy of *Hypocrisy*, which I snatched up immediately.

I left the store and got back in my car. Where to next? I had to find *Satan, My Father*. I couldn't wait for another day, and I was already out of the house. Preoccupied with the idea of putting together an entire set of pre-owned XZA novels, I avoided the chain bookstores, but I worried I'd end up there. I finally found a copy at a dusty, book-packed shop by the college less than two minutes to closing.

By the time I got home, my parents were, too. I didn't get to read a page of the book for days, but it was still worth it.

Tuesday night, I left my bedroom door open to listen for my parents going to bed. I flipped through a textbook until they stopped by to say good night. They waved to me from the doorway, their eyelids drooping after another night of sitcoms and reruns.

"Don't stay up all night," Mom said, wagging a finger at my littered desk.

"I won't," I promised.

"I put the reminder for your dentist appointment on the fridge."

Wishing my mom didn't still pose as my secretary, I smiled so I wouldn't look ungrateful. "Thanks."

"Don't forget to call and reschedule it if you have class at that time."

Mom rubbed smudged mascara off her face and wandered away towards their bedroom. I got up to close the door as if I didn't want to disturb them while I studied. Seconds later, I heard the door latch to their room. I left my homework on the desk and dove to my knees to reach under the bed. I pulled out the copy of *Satan, My Father* I'd driven all over town to find.

I flopped down on the bed and stretched my legs out, leaning back against the pillow. The cover of *Satan, My Father* was much plainer than XZA's later books, dominated by a cherry red background and the title in shocking black letters. As always, XZA's cryptic initials hovered in the lower right-hand corner. I opened it to the infamous dedication. *To the devil himself.* In bubbly letters, in purple pen, someone had written, *Ha ha! Die, bastard!* They had drawn a little smiley face beside it sporting curved horns and angry eyebrows.

Biting my lip, one anxious ear turned to the hallway in case I heard my parents' footsteps, I flipped the page to chapter one.

1

Are you done now, Daddy, are you done?

There is so much that I could never tell anyone or write down on paper. There are things I couldn't have dreamt up in my most terrifying nightmares, things that I wish were not real.

There is a list of family crimes, and my father is going through them one by one – revolting, terrible, retched, disgusting. The horror never ends, and if it did, I would still be too scared and shocked to notice.

I think I figured out when it first started, about a year before I was born. It started at a party fifteen years ago. Mama was stupid like I was. Virgin, you would call it. And in five minutes of pain, maybe less, that was gone and I was there. Mama thinks she wishes that wasn't true. I wish it more.

I went to a party once last year. I didn't think they'd let me go, but Mama didn't argue with me this time. She said it was okay. I didn't get a new dress, but I put a different belt and a nice cardigan over my old one. Mama didn't say anything about how I looked, so I knew I must look all right.

Most of the girls weren't my usual friends, but I knew them from school. We didn't play the games my friends liked to play, card games and board games that talked through battery-powered boxes. We were playing truth or dare. Bethany, who we all loved for her perfect, shiny hair even though we were all jealous of it, sat in the middle of the rec room floor. Her jeans were new, no stains or loose threads, and the cuffs were rolled up to expose the paler underside of the fabric. She grinned as she leaned toward me, her legs folded under her and bent to one side. It was the worst question she could've asked me.

"Have you ever seen..." She could barely get the question out. It was such a private thing to say. "...you know, a boy's..." She laughed, and all the girls giggled, covering their toothy mouths filled with braces with their nervous hands.

Instantly I felt sick, my stomach doing more than churning. I knew what she meant. My stomach jolted, squeezing the acid and ice cream cake together inside it. I stood up from where I sat a few feet in front of her. My hand flew to my mouth, but not because I was laughing.

I didn't want to see it. I didn't want it to come for me! And I didn't want to throw up all over Bethany Zubecki, but I did. I ruined her, all of her. Her hair, her blouse, her jeans, her watch. I coated her in vanilla white vomit like bubbling milk. She screamed and jumped to her feet. Everybody was shouting. At Bethany. At me. At Bethany's mom, who had come down to the basement to offer us a tray of drinks.

Mrs. Zubecki tried to fix everything. She passed the tray to one of the other girls. She sent Bethany to the basement bathroom to shower in the corner rig her dad used when he got back from long days on the road as a truck driver. I was crying, and Mrs. Zubecki tried to calm me down. Her smooth fingers touched my bare arms. I'd taken off the cardigan in the warmth of the house. "It's all right. I'm so sorry. I must've given you too much cake." She led me upstairs and gave me some water. She held a wash cloth under the running faucet and washed my face for me. The water was cool, and it didn't smell funny like our water did at home.

Why couldn't my dad disappear for days at a time? Why couldn't he go away without coming back?

Mrs. Zubecki tried to fix things.

Cassandra Leuthold

But for me, they would always be broken.

Chapter 8: Xan

I had never told Michael I loved him.

It wasn't a phrase in my vocabulary. It wasn't an emotion I let myself feel. It was too brief and too fragile. Michael had asked me when we met why I was so opposed to it. I'd thought instantly of Uncle Grigori and the incredible suffering his girlfriend had caused him. That formed the cornerstone of my beliefs. But I'd found dozens if not hundreds of additional answers in the past ten years, whenever his question popped into my head.

There was my parents' strained marriage to serve as exhibit A. It was hard for me to imagine them young and happy, whether it was the day they met or the day they got married. I'd seen them half-heartedly content at best. They didn't vacation together. They shared no hobbies. They saw everything in life from a different perspective. My mother claimed it was out of love that she stood up for my father against the supposed bad press my books earned for the family. I knew better. It was duty that stuck her to his side. If my mother lived by her heart, they would've divorced years ago. They had some feeling left for each other, dogged respect if nothing else, but I wondered how much of that was purposefully cultivated.

There was Stacey's divorce not long after I met her. I'd made an appointment for a massage to work the kinks out of my back. She made it through most of the session before she started to cry and talk about her marital problems. These were not the spoiled milk, surface problems of a relationship no sooner begun than ended. Stacey had known her husband since high school. She insisted he used to be doting, complimenting, and romantic. I doubted it because the present found him inattentive, unsupportive, and controlling. After knowing her for forty-five minutes and her situation for less than ten, I told her to leave him. Stacey was one of the few people in my life who took my advice, and although she griped about her occasional singlehood, she knew she was better off without him.

There were my books, of course, the stories I told myself and others about the dangers of long-term relationships. None of them lasted in my books without secrets or turmoil. Relationships were portrayed as cesspools where resentment bred and spread malcontent like a fungus. Friendships were much safer and often redeemed those hurt by love.

I watched Michael across the table in the breakfast nook. He broke a muffin in two, one of two dozen treats he had hand-selected for us at a new bakery downtown. He drizzled honey on one half and took a bite out of each.

"It's good either way." Michael wiped honey off his finger onto a napkin. "It's almost too sweet with the honey, but it's pretty good."

How did I not adore this man? How did I keep him with me, and how did his patience never run out?

Michael held out the honey jar. "Did you want to try it?"

I thought of all the things "it" could mean. Monogamy. Commitment. Life together. He was so innocent to the thoughts plaguing my head, blinking casually as he waited for my decision on the honey.

I took the jar. "I'll try it. We have different tastes."

"That's true, but I still think it'll be more sugar than you want."

I lifted the knife out of the jar and spread honey on a bite of my muffin. The moment it reached my tongue, he was right. The orange and cranberry were sweet enough. The added sugar was overkill. How did he know these things about me?

Michael left his chair and opened the refrigerator. "Do you want some orange juice?"

He skipped from knowing the exact sensitivity of my taste buds to offering a common breakfast drink with no transition and no hesitation.

"No, thank you. Just the coffee."

Maybe it was the closing of my nonproductive child-bearing years, but since our tenth year came to an end, I couldn't stop thinking about our relationship.

Michael poured himself half a glass of orange juice. "Worth the trip downtown, don't you think?"

I took a second to realize he meant the muffins. "Definitely."

"I'll make a weekly trek if I have to. I don't know how we lived without them."

"We could get Melody a cookbook and see if she'd make muffins for us."

"She would if you asked her to." Michael returned the juice to the fridge and carried his glass to the table. His cell phone rang somewhere, and he found it on the counter across the room. He looked at the screen. "It's John. I better take it." Michael walked over to kiss my temple before he wandered away down the hall.

He'd always obeyed my rule of no phones in the eating areas, and he'd never laughed at it.

Was this more than I deserved? I might be fooling myself. It could be over in a matter of days, and Michael would be gone. My withholding of the three magic words would be validated. The house would be mine again. I wouldn't earn any more stern looks from my mother by introducing Michael as my lover to friends and family as opposed to a term she would prefer such as boyfriend or live-in partner.

Having Michael live with me hadn't always been so natural. One day several months after he moved in, I recognized the huge difference in my house. I sensed the massive increase in intimacy and treated it as an affront to the life I'd built for myself. Suddenly the occasional became the rule. It wasn't a spare toothbrush in the bathroom. It was Michael's toothbrush. His grey and green razor sat on the sink in direct opposition to my pink and white razor in the shower. His shoes moved from the door mat to the closet floor. Bottles of Starbucks Frappuccino and boxes of strawberries appeared in the refrigerator. Marcy, Stacey, and even my parents had tried out the guest rooms, but no one had ever rivaled my supremacy over the master bedroom.

Michael seemed more comfortable in my house than I was the first few months he lived with me. I second-guessed my decision to let him move in every time he interrupted my writing or took up the bathroom when I wanted a shower. Stacey told me I was lucky he didn't snore like her ex-husband did, keeping her up all night with gurgling and sawing. At least I could sleep, and I knew where he was. Michael gave me space as my moodiness demanded it, which I appreciated. We found a more effortless flow, and I thought things were working out pretty decently. Then he started the unnerving habit of saying he loved me.

I came up with numerous ways of responding. I pretended I didn't hear it. I changed the subject. Sometimes I gave him a warning stare like he should know better than to say that to me. One morning, I was brushing my hair in the bedroom mirror when Michael walked in from the hallway. He stopped and watched me for a second. Out of nowhere, he said it.

"Xan, I love you."

I turned my head away and brushed my hair in long, decisive strokes.

Michael came closer and laid his hand on my arm. "I know you hear me. I love you."

I let him turn me to face him, giving up on my hair as he took my upper arms into his hands. I gazed back at him and tried not to grimace, knowing he didn't deserve that strong of a reaction.

Michael took the brush out of my hand and set it aside. He guided me several steps to the bed and eased me down on my back. His face hovered over mine, his hands pinning my arms down. Softened by a dark cascade of hair, his expression was serious. "Listen to me. I love you, and I'm going to say it even if you can't say it back to me. I can't take this awkwardness. Will you just let me say it? I mean it."

Michael's eyes and voice weren't swimming with hurt feelings. They burned from frustration and genuine affection. He was being level with me, and I decided to be level with him. I was the one who'd asked if he wanted to move in with me. I gave in and nodded. Michael kissed me and pulled me to my feet. It was one of the few displays of raw emotion he'd shown me over the last decade including his candid tears over the loss of his terrier, Jack. I respected him for his honesty then and now. Michael continued to love me, and I started to let him. He never pressed me for more, and I learned to accept the L word I'd always despised.

Michael walked back into the kitchen and left his phone on the counter. He came over to the nook and sat down across from me. "John checked his calendar. He says it'll be a while before he can make it down for an evening of wine and your friends. He's looking forward to it, though. That surprises me."

"You must've put the emphasis on the wine and not my friends."

Michael smiled, which I realized was one of the best sights of my day. His smiles were mischievous and gorgeous, never more arresting than when he aimed them at me. "Do you think they'd drive down if I told them a divorcee and an English teacher were waiting for them?"

"It's all in the words you use. The divorcee becomes an expert in massage, and the English teacher you can sell as an educated listener."

"I'll have to tell Marcy the next time I see her that you're trying to sell her to my friends."

"My friends would sell themselves to you."

Michael laughed and picked up half a muffin. "They've tried so many times."

"Does that bother you?"

"What?"

"Their obsession with you."

"No. I find it flattering."

"One of the biggest differences between men and women."

I knew it was much more than that, but I hoped my glib answer would stand in for the fact I had never understood how Michael kept his cool under their teasing. The way they ogled him the night I introduced him made me look tame in the way I admired his body.

Michael finished the first half of his muffin. "Does it bother you?"

"No."

"I never expected you to have well-behaving friends. It comes with the territory. I can handle it."

We fell in to breakfast and left the subject behind. I tried to imagine how Melody and her husband went through their day. Maybe she poured a bowl of cereal for him and started the coffee maker while he showered and shaved. He'd sit at the kitchen table for no more than ten minutes before flying out the door, leaving Melody to take care of their daughter or drop her off at day care to work for me. I couldn't imagine him not saying he loved her or Melody giving him the cold shoulder in response. I didn't think she was a fool for marrying him. The thought of me echoing their verbalized vulnerability tightened my muscles with fear.

And yet there sat Michael, innocently sucking honey off his finger. He finished his orange juice and carried his empty dishes to the sink. He hardly looked like he was planning to leave me, much less do it in a dramatic, heart-rending scene. Michael came all the way back to the nook to kiss me, his cell phone in his hand.

"I guess I'll get started with work. I'll be upstairs if you need me."

"Okay." I kissed him, trailing my hand down his rough, unshaven cheek.

Michael caught my hand and kissed my fingers. He hummed a note of recognition. "Fruit and honey."

I studied him, not sure what to say.

Michael raised his eyebrows with another, more serious thought. "I forgot to tell you. The site is going ahead with the local underrated idea. I'm going to start looking for local writers, probably from the Chicago area out to Fort Wayne."

I was very excited about the project. It would give unpublished, unheard-of writers a boost in their confidence and their careers. All I said was something Marcy or Stacey would've said. "I'm local talent."

Michael smiled, still holding my hand. "I know you are."

I didn't want him to think the sentiment was mine. "You already interviewed me. Go find those who need it."

"I will." Michael squeezed my hand. "Once one of them finds out what the website is doing, they'll all know about it in a matter of days."

"That's probably true." It had been almost twenty years since college, but I remembered how closely the writing community stuck together. Marcy gave me occasional anecdotes about the creative writers toiling through her grammar- and structure-based English courses. "Maybe you could put up fliers at the college or ask Marcy who the faculty advisor is for the campus writer's group. If you gave a short talk about what you're doing, it could be good for the project and good advertising for the site."

"That's a good idea. She'll have a heart attack when my name shows up on her phone."

"At least you know she won't blow you off."

"It's to her credit she's had my phone number since we coordinated that birthday party for you several years ago and she's never used it to send me dirty texts in the middle of the night."

"She never gets drunk unless she's with Stacey, who would keep her from sexting you out of pure envy. If Marcy ever hit send, you'd get one from Stacey, too."

"I'd change my number before she got the chance." Michael leaned down for one last kiss on my forehead. He walked out of the kitchen. His footsteps creaked up the stairs, where his avid reading, typing, and phone calls wouldn't disturb my writing.

I finished my muffin, devouring it rather than deliberating over every fruity bite. I poured another mug of coffee and walked into my office. Michael had never asked for a workspace of his own. He was content, or he said he was, to carry his laptop and books anywhere in the house. I wished I had his uncanny ability to settle into any space, not just in my house, but the places we visited together. He was at ease in his parents' cramped but homey ranch outside Chicago and more comfortable than I was at my parents' atomic-era box in a child-ridden neighborhood on the other side of town. The corrugated metal window overhangs bothered me for aesthetic and structural reasons. Even though I'd kept my home a clean slate with pale neutral colors, I often imagined redoing their drab, outdated walls in bold, colorful hues.

Unlike Michael, I had no intention of going straight to work. I sat down at my desk and typed *review* into the computer-wide document search. I didn't have to sift through Michael's reviews online. I'd copied and pasted them into my personal documents years ago. They quickly showed up in the search, and I skimmed them for the juiciest parts. *Sheer genius. Makes your skin crawl in a way you'll never forget. Characters so real, you want to spend time with the good ones and prosecute the bad. Sad but perfect. It could end no other way.*

I went back to the search and changed it to *interview*. It turned up the only formal interview Michael had done with me. Considering the intimate nature of our relationship from that night on, I'd worked to keep our relationship separate from my writing career. He continued to champion and review my work, but we never again sat down together in the name of business. Not only had Michael started and ended the interview transcription in the right places, his introduction was more evenhanded than I'd expected. He noted that I'd offered him the interview, side-stepping the flirtation involved to say I was as genuine and forthcoming as he'd hoped. It was so well written and ego boosting, I might've slept with him for the compliments alone.

I stopped perusing the past and opened up the novel in progress that haunted me every moment I was awake. Where was the perfect ending for this one? The common-sense if not pessimistic closure to everything my characters had done to each other? Writing closer to the end made the solution no more apparent.

More than the plight of my characters, my brain lingered on Michael. He didn't always work out of earshot. He used to work downstairs in the living room or sometimes at the dining room table. He had started disappearing upstairs to dispel the tension caused by interrupting me, especially during my final edits of *Hypocrisy*.

I couldn't imagine Michael interrupting me for a petty reason. We'd talked about writing before. He understood what went into a novel to make it worth-while rather than unimaginative. Why had he interrupted me? I had to think a little harder to remember those details, and when I did, they made me feel worse. He'd approached me to offer me food or coffee, or check on me after I'd been working for long hours without a break. I treated his questions as insufferable intrusions, working hard to answer him while holding onto the thought he had broken in half. I'd met his generosity and concern with scowls, ungrateful for offerings of water and adjustments to the window blinds.

Maybe Marcy had a point. Why did Michael stay with me?

Chapter 9: Jessie

I carried *Satan, My Father* in my oversized purse in case I got a chance to read it. It didn't seem right to meet with Willa and not have an XZA novel with me. We'd already been over the finer points of *F*CK, F*CK, F*CK* over the phone, but we hadn't talked much about XZA's first book. I was worried Willa might spill some spoilers, but it didn't really matter. It was probably going to be just as shocking whether I saw it coming or not.

I parked my car in the truck stop parking lot a few miles out of town. Willa was already standing out front, silhouetted against the brown wooden boards of the building we'd chosen in homage to Mr. Zubecki's fictional job. I was happy to see her, dressed in her classic baggy overalls and a striped long-sleeved shirt, but not waiting on her meant putting off more reading until I got home.

Willa greeted me with a hug and ushered me inside. "Have you been here before?"

"No."

Like the college, the walls were yellow. These were more of a goldenrod, probably stained darker than painted by decades of cigarette smoke. It caught in my lungs, sticking there and stinking up my nose.

Willa crashed into a nearby empty booth. "I used to come here to people-watch sometimes."

I slid onto the bench across from her, relieved it was clean and dry. There were no cockroaches in sight. Yet. "I bet you saw all sorts of crazy things."

"Yeah, but not too much crazier than I see every day at the laundromat."

I took my purse off and set it in the corner of the bench against the partition.

Willa raised her head to get a better look at it. "Why is your bag so big?"

"So I can carry books in it."

Willa's eyes lit up. "Yeah? What you got?"

"*Satan, My Father.*"

"No way. Let me see. How far are you?"

In the safe anonymity of the truck stop, I handed the black and red book across the table. Willa opened it automatically to the bookstore receipt I'd been using as a bookmark.

"Chapter ten," we both said.

To my embarrassment more than my excitement, Willa began to read aloud. "Ten. I think a lot about running away. I continually tell myself, if it happens again, I'll run. Mama has always made sure to warn me of the dangers of the outside world, but I don't care about them. How could they possibly be worse? How can she stand it in this house? I can't. He is always here, watching. He can see through walls. I'm sure of it. I'm always afraid to do anything I know they wouldn't like. But I want to run. I dream about it three nights a week, crying when I wake up and realize I'm back in my bed, beating my fist against my pillow."

I reached for the book over the discolored teal tabletop.

Willa grinned and pulled the book closer to her side, out of my reach. "If I can dream it, I can do it. I mostly dream that I run out of town, past the sign for the city limits and past the highway. Sometimes I dream we're having a family picnic in an impossibly gigantic field of grass, and I run away from them there. They call my name, but I never look back." Willa turned the page. "When I'm awake, I dream of running to Mrs. Zubecki, right into her strong, sturdy arms. Tears stream down my face, and she asks me what's wrong. She doesn't hit me. She doesn't demand that I explain myself. She holds me and waits, saying it will be all right. I wish I was a little, tiny girl again so she could really hold me close. I bet Bethany had the best childhood anyone could dream of, but she doesn't seem to care. As much as I hate her now, I wouldn't switch places with her. I wish we could both grow up with Mrs. Zubecki and her often-absent husband. I bet Bethany feels safer than I ever could."

I lurched across the table and succeeded in grabbing the book from Willa. The flimsy receipt slipped out of the pages, falling past the table and gliding off her bench seat to land on the floor by my shoes. I left it there without looking any longer. I didn't want to know what lurked by my feet.

"Dang it," Willa said, peering under the table. "Do you need me to grab it?"

"No. I know what chapter I'm on. I don't need it for anything." I tucked the book in my purse. "So what's new?"

Willa blew out a breath with her lips too close together, making her mouth puff up for a few seconds. "Nothing, I guess. Frank is trying to get off the night shift so we can see each other more. Night shift is all they had open when he applied, so that's what he's been stuck with for the last three months. Can you believe we've been together almost four years? God, that's weird."

I forced a smile and shook my head.

"It's the longest relationship I've ever been in. It's been good, though, for me because Frank taught me I can be in total control of my life. I was hanging on to these friendships with people for no good reason, and I realized I didn't have to do that anymore. I started kicking anybody I didn't need out of my life." Willa hung two fingers in the air like legs and kicked one out. "Bam! Gone. Outta here. That's what Frank did. It was like what characters do in the movies when they have their big moment and walk off with that determined look on their face. I've felt so much better since then."

I nodded, wondering if Willa was hinting that I give Dick the boot. If she was, she didn't push the issue to make sure I understood it.

Willa gestured to my arm. "Nice bracelet. Where'd you get it?"

"Dick gave it to me."

Willa hummed thoughtfully but doubtfully. She pulled my wrist closer for a better inspection. "It's nicer than I would've expected from Dick."

The way she spat his name out made me uncomfortable. "How's work?"

Willa shrugged and let go of my arm. "It's okay at the laundromat, but we get some really weird characters in there. If you want to watch people or feel better about your life, you should stop by some time. It's a freak show every night."

"I think I'll pass. I hope my life isn't so bad I have to people-watch at a laundromat to make myself feel better."

A short, round-bellied waitress stepped up to the table. Her wiry golden-red hair curled on itself in frizzy ringlets, stubborn grey hairs poking out from the curls. Her thick makeup was caked into every ridge and wrinkle on her face. She spoke with a chain smoker's throaty gruffness. "Welcome to the Last Truck Stop. My name is Rhonda. Have you been here before?" Her small, pudgy hands gave us each a menu.

"I have," Willa volunteered.

"Okay," Rhonda continued, as if the question and its answer made no difference. "The chef's special today is bacon. We're all outta bacon. What do you want to drink?"

"Something filtered."

"Bottle of water?"

Willa's head bobbed up and down.

Rhonda turned to me, and I nodded.

"I'll be back to take your orders." She waddled away, betraying a slight limp in her right leg.

Willa opened her menu. "Did you want some bacon? They don't have any. They probably ran out at three o'clock this morning."

I tried not to look too hard at my menu. There seemed to be a thin half-moon of dried pancake batter at the top of the front cover. I opened it, cringing at the sucking sound of the sticky plastic pages separating.

Willa looked over from her menu, crinkling her nose. "That's disgusting. I can read mine to you."

I gratefully set my menu aside for Rhonda to take, although I didn't want her to have to touch it, either. "What do they have?"

"Eggs done any way. Sausage. Ooh, toast. That's a classic."

"Willa, it's six o'clock at night."

"Breakfast was meant for any time. You want dinner?" Willa flipped her menu over to the back. "Here it is. We've got a tuna melt, tuna salad, tuna wrap…"

I put my hands on my head. "You can stop."

"Pick your side, Jess. There's onion rings or chili fries."

"This place is horrible."

"This picture is horrible." Willa turned her menu to show me a picture of the chili fries, a heaping mound of chopped white onion, too-yellow cheese, and grey-brown beef atop thin fries gleaming with grease.

"This is worse than the diner Dick always makes me eat at."

"How is Dick?" Willa asked, emphasizing his name. She went back to perusing the menu.

"He's all right."

"How is he to you? How are you doing with him?"

I shrugged, wishing my menu wasn't so disgusting. I felt like I had nothing to do with my hands. "He's a little rough sometimes, but we're doing okay."

"Does he still treat you like shit?" Willa glanced up at me, her usually soft eyes sharp.

"He pays more attention to me than anyone else ever has."

"I pay attention to you."

I appreciated her friendship, but it wasn't my point. "Guys, I mean."

Willa closed her menu and set it at the edge of the table next to mine. "Guys probably don't know much about you because you don't say too much. Or they're intimidated because you're smart."

I sighed. One thing I couldn't change, and the other would be too hard to try.

"You need to find somebody cool," Willa said, leaning her jaw into her hand. "Somebody smart and funny and nice."

"Like Frank."

"Yeah, the opposite of Dick."

Rhonda hurried across the dining room, and I turned the conversation back to food in case she came to the table. "What are we having?"

Willa took a second to catch on. "To eat?" She looked at the menu. "I think eggs are our best bet. We can tell right away if they're cooked through or not."

Rhonda dropped off a straw at another table and doubled back to the kitchen. I didn't want to argue about Dick, but it bothered me that Willa still hated him. "Why don't you give Dick a chance? I'm sure he's not as bad as you remember."

Willa sprawled out across her bench, her head in the upper right corner and one ankle draped over the left-hand corner of the table, dangling a red shoe above the floor. "I gave Dick a chance. He told me my eyes were the color of doggy doo. I'm not really in the mood for Dick. Ever." She searched the ceiling. "Ever. Ever. Ever."

"Come on. It'd be fun. We could make fun of the food. Make up nicknames for the wait staff."

"Where would we go?"

Without trying, I pictured bright lights in a white room.

Willa eyed me. "Don't tell me the diner. You're thinking of it already."

I was, but I didn't want Willa to be right. "No, I wasn't."

"You know if you tell Dick you want the three of us to get together, he's going to insist on the diner."

I opened my mouth to contradict her.

Willa raised her index finger before I could form words. "Which you said he always does."

"What's wrong with the diner? We decided to meet here at grease central."

Willa leaned her arm on the edge of the table. She thought better of it and pulled it off again. "We met here specifically because of the truck stop, truck driver, *Satan, My Father* connection. Is Dick going to let us talk about XZA? Does he even read?"

"He reads."

"I guess I should've started with the simpler question, *can* he read?"

I took a breath in through my nose and let it out the same way. "He can read."

"Well, if it means I get to spend more time with you, I'll do it. I just wish Dick would shut his pie hole, and I haven't even dealt with him yet."

Rhonda limped up to the table and picked up the menus, seemingly immune to their questionable condition. She dropped two water bottles on the table with matching thumps. "What're you having?"

"Two eggs over hard. Very hard," Willa added. "And the hash browns."

Rhonda looked at me, her mascara clumping her stubby eyelashes together like spider legs around her watery blue eyes. They looked a little red, either from smoking or wearing contacts for too long.

"Two eggs over hard." My eyes landed on the back of the menu in Rhonda's hand, and I spotted the dessert list at the bottom. "And a sundae."

"Vanilla or chocolate?"

"Chocolate, please."

Rhonda shuffled off to the kitchen.

Willa picked up a bottle of water and twisted off the cap. "Good choice. It's pretty hard to screw up a sundae. It's vanilla the narrator pukes up in the book, right?"

"Yeah."

"It makes me want to go back and read it again. I wonder where my copy went."

"Used Books sold theirs before I got there."

"Really?" Willa smiled faintly and took a sip of water. "Another reader joins the fold."

I picked up the other bottle. "So if I tell Dick the three of us should meet somewhere, you'll do it?"

"Sure. What the hell? As long as Frank's working or sleeping, I'll go. I'm not sacrificing Frank time to sit around with Dick even if you're there."

I drank some water, trying to disguise how excited I was.

Willa tapped the side of her bottle. "Did you ever read these labels? Half the time, it's tap water from some other town. What a racket, huh? Getting people to pay a couple of bucks for tap water."

"Yeah."

"But it's gotta be better than any water that comes outta this place."

"Yeah," I agreed quickly. I didn't want to think about the truck stop water, whether it was rinsing my hands or being served in a glass. Anything I needed water for, I was getting out of that bottle. Otherwise, it could wait until I got home.

Chapter 10: Xan

Marcy came through for Michael better than we could've hoped. She sent him contact information for the college writing group and gave the faculty advisor a glowing review of Michael and the site. When Michael called the advisor, she was over the moon at the idea of Michael offering such an opportunity to the students. I was glad Marcy was able to do more for him than ogle him and polish the pedestal she put him on. It would be a great benefit for everyone involved, and it was such a brilliantly simple idea, I was jealous I hadn't thought of it first.

I snuck back to my computer to look at the outline for my novel while Michael changed for his big presentation. I read through my scene list, following the characters through their highs and lows. Everything made so much sense, I wondered why I couldn't see how it would end. It was usually easier than this, and it irked me when I couldn't grasp what should be an obvious conclusion.

Michael came into my office long before I figured it out. "How do I look?"

I took my eyes off the screen to size him up. Michael was wearing a long-sleeved button-down under a chocolate-colored sweater vest. His unkempt hair falling on his uptight outfit made him look adorable. I stood up to meet him. "They're going to eat you alive."

Michael smoothed his hand over the fibers of the vest. "You don't think it's too *School of Rock*? I've never had the guts to wear the vest before. I think my parents gave it to me."

"You look perfect. You need a certain amount of unwavering authority. Anything less would make them swoon harder. You have to remember you're not just eye candy. You're offering them professional reviews of their work."

Michael held up a finger. "If it's underrated."

"How are you planning to get around the ones that aren't?"

"I'll explain it's a limited part of my job to deal with local talent, and I can only read and review so much of it. I hope they'll assume if

I don't review their work, I liked it but didn't have time or space to review it. I can send them emails to that effect at least."

"You can explain whatever you want, but they'll be too busy daydreaming that vest off of you to hear what you're saying."

Michael's lips drew to one side. "The more time you spend around Marcy and Stacey, the more you talk like them."

"I used to talk like this all the time. It's what got us from the book signing to the hotel room."

"How could I forget?" Michael glanced past me at the computer. "Don't work too hard. The end will come to you when you least expect it. You have to give your brain a chance to do that."

"I will. I want to see if logic will kick in faster."

"How about a weekend off? Mom called while I was upstairs. It'd be nice to have them down before the holiday rush at the end of the year."

Michael's parents kept me more honest about my writing breaks than anyone else, Michael included. They were such engaging, vivacious people, it was hard to leave the room if I thought to try. My desires to be a good hostess and enjoy good company were some of the only things that could override my compulsive work ethic. I needed a full weekend off from the book to reboot my brain, and the Singers were my best bet to accomplish that.

"It sounds good. What do you want to do?"

"Mom's always up for wine tasting. I thought we could placate my dad with another round of mini golf."

"Sure. That should fill up two days."

"It's so rare he makes it out to the actual golf course. Mom keeps their spare time so busy."

"She's a smart woman. It can't be easy keeping your dad out of trouble. She's lucky you calmed your life down."

Michael tilted his head as if I should know better. "I've never been trouble for her, just everybody else."

"You've mostly been trouble for me." I leaned up and gave Michael a kiss so he knew I was joking.

"I only cause enough trouble to keep people guessing what I'm going to do next."

Michael turned toward the door, and I followed him to the foyer.

He pulled his coat out of the closet under the stairs.

I folded my arms. "It's too bad you don't like the way I talk after I meet with my friends. Stacey asked me to go lingerie shopping with her on Wednesday. She has the day off, and she wants to look good for when your friends come down."

"They're not going to see her in her underwear." Michael shrugged his coat on and buttoned it. "I don't think Nick and John are as wild as we once were."

"Let Stacey boost her confidence where she can. She'll find a way to get her underwear out there."

"Is that designed to lure them closer or scare them away?"

"Stacey has attracted better-looking men than Nick and John with her bag of tricks. She needs to start going for smarter men, though, which is why I think this is such a good idea."

Michael stepped toward the front door. "I never thought I'd see the day you played matchmaker."

"Matchmaker's a dirty word, Michael."

"I'll file it away, then."

I caught up to Michael on the entry rug and kissed him goodbye. "Good luck, and by that, I mean good luck escaping in one piece."

"That's what the coat is for. I cover up the cuteness, and the riot dies away. Instant crowd control."

"That's what your parents are going to be for us after I go lingerie shopping."

Michael winked at me. "Nothing I can't get off in less than five seconds."

It was more of a joke than a rule, but it made me smile. "I know."

Michael let himself out into the early hours of sunset. I returned to the computer, not to wear myself out over my story, but to search online for vineyards we hadn't visited that weren't too far away. I scratched down a list in a hurried script, most of them in southwestern Michigan. I pulled a white piece of paper out of the idle printer to start a grocery list. We couldn't have wine without cheese or cheese without crackers. We couldn't have any one thing without variety. We needed muffins from the downtown bakery plus an assortment of bagels and cream cheese spreads. It looked like a lot as I wrote it down, but I always enjoyed having Mark and Claire for the weekend.

It was one of the best parts about owning a house that was too big for me. I could fill it with whomever I liked. I never turned down a guest unless I wanted to. My parents had gotten snowed in with us once, and I was grateful they could stay in a guest room instead of sleeping on the living room couch and loveseat.

When Marcy, Stacey, and I were younger, we'd have what Marcy called grown-up sleepovers. We'd drink a bottle or more of wine over the course of an evening, always watching two carefully selected movies. We'd watch a romantic comedy, which they enjoyed, and follow it with an action movie powered by some short-haired heroine to please Marcy and me. That way, each of us had something to cheer about and something to heckle. At the end of the night – or early the next morning, more often than not – all we had to do was stumble up to bed. No one had to drive home drunk. It was the best of all worlds, eventually replaced by relationships and digging deeper into our chosen careers. Surprisingly, it was a man sneaking into my life that probably put the most definitive end to those days.

As a writer, I was fascinated by the scope of Mark and Claire's adventures across America. From small towns nobody'd heard of to national monuments to major cities a thousand miles away, they had done a lot. And they were always eager to share.

I realized I hadn't asked Michael how he planned to conduct his local author interviews. I was too wrapped up in my novel to think of much else. He would probably do them by email or phone or meet them on campus, but I almost pictured them coming to the house. I envied him, getting to meet the new, fresh talent of the region. I pushed myself because I was getting older. They pushed themselves because they were young and enthusiastic or else took long breaks between writing poems and short stories because they didn't yet feel the crunch of time. Marcy had tried to talk me into teaching years ago when *Satan, My Father* came out to its anticipated mixed reviews and I hadn't bought the house yet. I was between day jobs, giving interviews, touring for book signings, and saving up for a down payment. Marcy told me teaching would speed up the process and end my frustrating job search. I hadn't wanted to stall my writing by teaching the basics in English grammar or the more creative side of its usage. I couldn't picture myself as a writer in residence somewhere. They were usually classier, better known, or displayed a charming renegade attitude foreign to me.

Teaching still wasn't my cup of tea, but the thought of new ideas circulating around me was exciting. I didn't want to step on Michael's toes. He was already reaching out to the local writing community, but I could too, if I wanted. I could start a writer's group or oversee one made up of a younger crowd. I could offer a workshop in a local hotel meeting room or host some kind of online contest. Michael was better at networking than I was, as was Melody. Sheryl might have some ideas if I cared to ask her.

Having Mark and Claire down for a weekend would give me a good distraction to focus on and let my story clear out of my head. Until then and again after, I would wrack my brain and my environment for answers. There was no disease without a cure and no story without a good ending. Michael had said so, and the universe was often impatient to prove him right.

Chapter 11: Jessie

Dick flopped down on the couch, managing to land in a sitting position, and pulled his shoes up onto the far cushion. Dirt covered the yellow soles, and my jaw tightened like he'd already muddied the entire couch.

"What's the matter?" Dick said, interrupting a story I'd already heard about spilling hot nacho cheese all over his friend Kyle. "You look like I sat on your cat or something."

"We don't have a cat. It's my parents' couch. Could you please take your shoes off if you're going to put your feet up?" I didn't add what I wanted to, that I didn't want my parents to know he hung out there sometimes while they were gone.

"Jeez, you act like this thing is valuable or something." Dick hesitated but kicked his shoes off. Dirt and grass flaked off into chunks on the beige carpeting.

I'd have to vacuum it after he left. "It is valuable. To my parents."

Dick snorted. "What do they know? They don't have any taste. My uncle had a black leather couch. That thing was sleek. It was classy. That couch was a work of art. He wouldn't let anybody touch it, it was so cool."

I sat in the recliner, not feeling the need for functional art in the living room, just a lack of reasons for my parents to kick me out. I returned to the conversation we were having before Dick's thoughts on nacho cheese. "So why don't you want us to go hang out with Willa sometime? She said she'd be willing to do it."

Dick's eyebrows bunched closer together. "Are you sure I met her before?"

"Yeah. Several times. She was taking classes with us."

"Is she the stupid one?"

"No."

"Is she the creepy, smart one?"

"No."

Dick held his hands a foot out from his chest like he was cupping two large balloons. "This one?"

I curved my back into the recliner, hunching my shoulders to hide my much less noticeable breasts. "That was somebody else."

"There was that skinny chick who read a lot. She was weird. She wore the same clothes all the time."

The bottom of my stomach dropped another inch. "That's Willa."

Dick glanced at the kitchen. "Can you get me a soda?"

I rocked myself to my feet and walked into the kitchen. I got a cold Pepsi out of the fridge, making a mental note to replace it before my parents got home. The extras were sitting in the pantry, and if there weren't enough cold ones, my parents would know why, unless I lied and blamed it on Willa. I didn't want to do that. I walked back to the living room and handed the can to Dick. "Willa's not that weird."

"Does she still read all the time?" Dick flipped the pop tab back, reclining at an angle that made me nervous as he took his first swig of soda.

I sat down, my fingertips digging into the recliner's pillow arms. "She likes to hang out and eat greasy food the same as we do."

"Does she read that what's-her-name stuff you started reading?"

My stomach drooped even farther. Not only did Willa read what's-her-name, she had picked up a used copy of *Hypocrisy* to read alongside me when I got that far. "I don't think so."

"I guess we can meet up with her. I don't see why we have to." Dick took another drink. Dark bubbles dribbled down his chin, popping along his lower lip before his hand wiped them away.

I stared at his chin to make sure no soda hit the couch. I had to be ready to jump up, wet a towel, and wipe it away the second it did. "We don't have to. I like her. She was a good friend of mine for a couple of years. It's been good to catch up with her. I thought it'd be nice to see both of you at the same time."

"What are we gonna do?"

"I thought we'd go to the diner and eat and talk about what's been going on since she left school. That was when we stopped seeing her so much."

Dick belched so loudly and suddenly, I didn't realize he'd opened his mouth until the sound was reverberating through the house. He finished it off with an audible exhale. "That's fine. Whatever. I'm going to a movie with the guys in a little bit." He set the can on the corner of the coffee table. "I don't make you go out with my friends."

I was grateful for that. Willa could say what she wanted about Dick excluding me from his guy plans, but I wanted no part of them. "She's one friend. If you don't like it, you don't have to hang out with us again. I'll see her by myself."

"What's she doing since she left school, anyway?"

"She moved in with Frank, and she works in a laundromat."

"Real exciting." Dick sat up and set his feet on the floor. He drank the rest of the pop and left the can on the coffee table. He stood up and pulled his phone out of his pocket. "I'm gonna see if they're ready to meet at the theater."

"What are you seeing?"

"I don't know. We'll figure it out when we get there." Dick flipped his phone open and pressed a couple of buttons with his thumb. "Why do you have to know everything? Just because you make all your plans way ahead of time doesn't mean we have to."

Dick jumped into his phone conversation, and I sat trying to tune him out. His voice filled the room as his belch had, talking way too loud for the small house even with its open floor plan. I remembered where I'd left off reading *Satan, My Father* before Dick picked me up that morning. The book sat in the top drawer of my desk, mere pages from the end. Dick was laughing, and I wished he'd hurry up. As soon as he left, I could run to my room and finish the book.

Dick continued to wander around the coffee table and pace along the sides of it. He traded jokes and stories before he finally stopped laughing long enough to check what time he was supposed to be at the theater. "Okay, I'll leave now, and we'll get the best seats." He blurted out a cheesy "Peace!" and closed his phone.

"You're leaving?" I felt relieved.

"Yeah."

I stood up to see Dick to the door. "Have fun. Let me know what you see and if it was any good."

"Why? Are you going to see it with Willa?" Dick said her name like she was a dirty diaper.

"No. We only went to the movies once or twice. We like to talk too much for the movies."

"Oh, yeah. I forgot."

I followed Dick to the door, where he turned and slid his arms around me. The silent hug was the best part of our day together. I could feel his muscles against me as he kissed me. I was starting to relax from his constant jabbering when he slapped my butt. I could've recovered from the surprise of it, but he missed the second time and hit bone. He settled for grabbing my butt with both hands, probing his tongue deeper into my mouth at the same time. What had been a good kiss turned my stomach as his tongue swirled as far into my throat as it would go. I stood it for as long as I could before I pulled back. I'd never decided how to tell him to change his technique, only how long I had to wait before I pulled back so he wouldn't try to kiss me again.

Dick squeezed my butt. "I'll call you later. Maybe tomorrow."

"Okay."

Dick let himself out, and I locked up behind him. I didn't bother to stay at the window in the door and watch him walk to his truck. I didn't replace the pop can in the fridge. I crossed the house to my room and pulled the book out of my desk drawer. I flopped down on my stomach on the bed and opened the book to the tortured narrator's latest attempt at a normal experience.

> I want to run as soon as my knuckles hit the Zubeckis' front door. I'm terrified. My heart races faster than I think it ever has. I would run if I didn't think Mrs. Zubecki would arrive at the door in time to see me. I would die if she thought I was pulling a prank on her.
>
> She answers the door wiping flour from her hands onto a kitchen towel, its checkered border and fruit design faded with use and repeated washings. She smiles to see me. I wish I could smile back. "Hi. How's your summer going?"
>
> "Okay," I lie.
>
> "I'm sorry you came all the way over here. Bethany's out with other friends."

"That's okay." The lines I rehearsed about wanting to spend my afternoon with Mrs. Zubecki won't come out of my throat. They stick there sounding fake and memorized from too many movies. "What are you doing?"

"Baking a pie. It's not Bethany's favorite, but my husband's birthday is coming up. I'm baking it for him."

Ask if you can help, my inner voice says. Instead, I ask, "What kind of pie is it?"

"Apple pie."

"Are you putting the lattice on top like they do at the store?"

"I was thinking about it. It looks so pretty that way." Mrs. Zubecki is still wiping flour off her fingers. "I'd hate to send you all the way home already. It's so hot outside. Why don't you come in for a glass of water?"

I nod, too eager to speak. I don't want to ruin everything by saying something wrong. Mrs. Zubecki steps aside, and I step into the cool, quiet house.

"Let me see if there's some lemonade. Bethany says she's too old for it, but when I buy it for her brother, she always has some."

"I like lemonade," I tell her. I feel nervous to be in the house with her, just the two of us rounding the corner into the kitchen.

Mrs. Zubecki lays the towel down and checks the fridge. Her face lights up, and she pulls a plastic container of lemonade off the shelf. There is only an inch or two sloshing at the bottom, enough for one more glass.

"Oh, no," I insist. "I can't take the last glass. I'll take some water." Water is free. When you take it from the tap, nobody misses it.

"Don't be silly. The kids can do without. I'll put it right on the shopping list. We'll have more in no time." Mrs. Zubecki gets a plain blue glass out of the cabinet and fills it with the last of the lemonade. She sets it on the counter and starts rinsing the container in the sink. She tilts her head at the glass. "Go ahead. You must be thirsty. You live on Tenth Street, don't you?"

"Yes."

"That's at least a mile or two." Mrs. Zubecki sets the container in the sink to dry. "Did you want to see the pie?"

I step over to the other side of the sink with Mrs. Zubecki. She points out the pie, still sitting in pieces. A thin layer of dough covers the inside of the pie dish. She shows me a bowl filled with sliced apples, flour, and brown spices. It smells wonderful.

Mrs. Zubecki lays her hand over a ball of dough wrapped in wax paper. "This dough here is supposed to cover the top in one plain sheet, but I think you're right. I'll slice it after I roll it out and make a lattice." She dumps the apple filling into the pie crust and spoons out what sticks to the edges of the bowl. She glances at the glass of lemonade. "It's going to be room temperature if you don't drink it. Why don't you have a seat at the table, and I'll finish up with the pie?"

I want to help her with the pie, but I don't want to waste the lemonade she poured for me. I take the glass to the table just outside the kitchen, where I can still see Mrs. Zubecki over the serving counter between the two rooms. She drops the ball of dough onto its surface and presses it down with a rolling pin. I watch her strong, careful movements as she thins the ball into a broad, even layer.

I sip the lemonade. Even though there is a whole glass full of it, I want to make it last. It is the best lemonade I can remember, not watered down like the concoction Mama sometimes makes.

Mrs. Zubecki almost starts to sing as she slices the sheet of dough into strips. She smiles at me and says, "Sorry," in a gentle voice before falling silent.

I don't want her to stop singing. I don't want to ever not be sitting in her house, calmly drinking the best lemonade in the world. I can't stop myself from crying. I hang my head to my chest and wipe the tears away as quickly as they well up in my eyes. Even though I don't make a sound, Mrs. Zubecki is kneeling by my chair before I can dry them up.

Mrs. Zubecki's big brown eyes are even bigger with concern. "Are you okay? Did the heat get to you?"

"No."

"Is the lemonade all right?"

"Yes."

"Can I get you a tissue?"

"Please." Mrs. Zubecki is back in a flash, handing the Kleenex to me so close to my face, I think for a moment she might wipe my eyes for me. She sits down in the chair beside me. Now it is she who watches me, bending towards me at the waist, her forearms propped above her knees. I wipe the Kleenex across my eyes and cheeks, glad for the first time that I'm not allowed to wear makeup. It would've smeared and streaked all over my face.

When Mrs. Zubecki speaks again, her voice is low and serious. "You know, I don't want to ask you this, but I worry about you. Since the night of Bethany's party, I've wondered. Is there something going on at home? Something you might not want to tell me. Something bad."

I can't look at her. Deep inside me, or maybe not so buried, is a voice screaming for me to tell her.

End this. Tell her! The things you hear and see and feel will never make you throw up again. I sneak a peek at Mrs. Zubecki, waiting patiently at my side. How can I tell her? What words can I use? *My daddy*... No.

I'm too scared. I thought knocking on the door was shockingly brave. My stomach twists in knots at the thought of opening my mouth.

Mrs. Zubecki's patient expression tenses, and she reaches out to lay her hand on my arm. "Tell me."

I push the screaming voice further inside when I want to let her up and out. "There's nothing wrong."

Mrs. Zubecki's eyes get shiny, too. "You're upset about something."

I know. I know what I'm upset about. Too much.

I know too much.

I speak without thinking because thinking leads to crying. "I'm still embarrassed I threw up all over Bethany at her party and you had to clean it up."

"Don't you worry about that. That was months ago."

She doesn't believe me. She believes I was embarrassed but not that it made me cry.

"I'm fine," I tell her. I make myself take another drink of lemonade, a normal-sized mouthful. Does she see the glass shaking in my hand? "I'm fine." I force a smile, widening it, making it brighter. "I feel much better. Thank you."

She doesn't believe. Mrs. Zubecki stands up and pats my shoulder before she walks around the table to return to her lattice. She moves the unfinished pie to the serving counter and begins laying out the identical strips of dough. "I'm here for you if you want to talk."

I want to. I can't.

I say, "Okay." And that one tiny word keeps the

door open. I don't know when or if I'll breathe the truth to anyone, but here is a bridge. Here is a start if that day comes. It would be a terrifying, welcome, earth-shattering day.

I closed the book slowly. I wanted to cry, but the narrator's secrets affected me too much. I felt numb. It was too much for anybody to handle, let alone a defenseless teenage girl. I set the book aside and laid my head down on my hands on the comforter. I knew every book couldn't finish with a happy ending, but I longed for the upbeat final pages of *F*CK, F*CK, F*CK*, the glimpse of hopefulness that Chessa walked off with. What would've changed if this narrator had run into Toria the way Chessa did? Would a close friend her own age have helped her see her own worth? Helped her get out of that terrible house of pain and torment?

I was in no mood to start *Hypocrisy*. I had to shake off the eerie effects of *Satan, My Father* first, but I knew where it was when I was ready. It hid in a fraying box in my closet marked OLD SCHOOL BOOKS. It was XZA's third and final novel. When I finished it, there wouldn't be any more to turn to, but that didn't really bother me. I could reread these three as many times as I wanted and hopefully, I would still have Willa as a friend to talk to about them. If anybody I knew could understand the way they made me feel, it would be Willa. The books obviously affected her, or she wouldn't be so obsessed with them. She wouldn't have bought me *F*CK, F*CK, F*CK* and encouraged me to hunt down the other two during our first face-to-face conversation in over a year. Willa must have thought I was worth being in her life, too, or she wouldn't have called. I hoped she was still glad she made that decision.

Chapter 12: Xan

Sensual pop music pervaded the small boutique. The vocalist, a young woman of probably no more than twenty, sang of a sexually charged relationship with more dysfunction than she should be so chipper about. The bass shook the floor under my feet, reverberated in my ears, and hummed through the metal racks of lingerie around us. Stacey thoroughly enjoyed herself, a smile stretched across her thin lips as she bounced her hands in time to the music.

"I love this place," she said. "It's like being at a concert and shopping at the same time."

I tried to imagine it the other way around, shopping in the midst of a gyrating crowd. "I can't remember the last time I was at a concert."

Stacey laughed and reached the first row of round, metal racks. "I can't picture you moshing, Xan."

"The last concert I went to had about thirty people there. I stick to small venues and bar shows mostly."

"That sounds more like you." Stacey lifted a racy, red babydoll off the rack. In case the cut of it wasn't revealing enough, I could see through it as clearly as a window. "What do you think?"

"I thought you wanted something for when Nick and John come down."

"I do. You don't think it can lead to anything after?"

I paused, trying to guess how the evening would go. Michael and I had our suspicions but no concrete opinions.

Stacey hung the babydoll back on the rack and turned to me. "I didn't want to ask this again, especially in front of Michael. I don't want you to think I'm shallow or anything, but what do these guys look like? And don't do that thing my mom always does where she skips that part and starts talking about their personalities. That means they're ugly."

"They're not ugly."

"But they're no Michael Singer."

"But who is?" I interjected before Stacey could say it.

She smiled in appreciation.

"They're not bad," I insisted. "They're good people. You could do a lot worse. Look at who Marcy's dating. If that's not settling, I don't know what is. It's been months since I saw Nick and John, but they're very smart and endearing people."

Stacey wrinkled her cute little nose and started for the next rack. "See, there you go with the personalities. That's what I'm afraid of."

"Smart, ugly men?"

"No, somebody I really like who's not as attractive as me. I hate those looks you get from people, you know? The ones that make them look like they're thinking, 'How did he get her? How did she stoop to his level?' You never have to put up with that. You and Michael are pretty well matched."

"Maybe we should keep Michael in another room so the others won't look so bad."

Stacey looked up. "He should definitely join us. He's a good baseline. If I like anybody as much as I like Michael, I'll definitely need something from this place."

"Maybe you shouldn't rush it."

Stacey turned away. She searched the pastel green and blue babydolls on the next rack, but I knew her tricks. She didn't want my advice if it was going to be practical.

I tried a different approach. "We'll both buy something sexy, how's that? I'm not telling you not to hope for the best case scenario. Pick out whatever you want."

"I will."

"Okay."

Stacey glanced at me. "I thought you *were* picking something out. Are things finally slowing down for Xan and Michael?" Her green eyes sparkled.

"Never. Don't get your hopes up that high. You're not Michael's type. He likes them moody and brooding, apparently."

"Is that what he said, or is that how you see yourself?"

"Stacey, don't patronize me. I know what I'm like."

"That's not true. I don't see you that way." Stacey hung a lacy, baby blue chemise over her arm. "There's no way Michael does, either. He loves you."

I tried not to wince hearing the L word from Stacey. I'd come to terms with Michael's feelings, but I wasn't ready to discuss them with my friends. "I know he does. It doesn't make me perfect. We're supposed to be talking about you."

"Why me?"

"Do you even know what you're looking for in a man these days?"

"Honesty would be nice. And faithfulness." Stacey moved on to the next display. "I miss the excitement of having somebody to look forward to. I want somebody who doesn't see anything but me in a crowded room."

I watched Stacey dig through a bin of underwear marked *Clearance*. "Marcy or your other friends could give you better advice than I could. You know how I feel about relationships."

"But you've been with Michael for ten years."

"As lovers and cohabitators. I don't understand how you can go through such a nasty divorce and want to get into a relationship again."

"We're not all as strong as you, Xan. Maybe I won't get married again, but it'd be nice to have somebody. All those times you're watching TV or you see some cool bumper sticker when you're driving, you get to tell Michael all about it. I don't get to do that anymore." Stacey lifted out a pair of purple boyshorts shot through with metallic magenta thread. She draped them over the butt of her jeans. "How about these?"

"What are they marked down to?"

Stacey checked the tag. She grinned. "Four dollars. I don't care how gaudy they are. I'll take them."

"That's one of the pluses of being single. You can do whatever you want."

Stacey's eyes bulged, and her mouth dropped open. "You're going to talk like that when you have Michael? I'd throw out all my clothes and start over for someone like him. That's not a joke. I'm serious. Michael Singer is the perfect man."

"You would seriously prefer having to bend your life around someone else than doing what you want to do all by yourself?"

"In a good relationship, you wouldn't have to choose. It would all be right there. The lingerie and the sweatpants." Stacey pointed at me, the bold purple underwear hanging from her hand. "That's a good title if you still need one for your book."

I skipped over the topic of my book and stayed on Michael. "Do you think I would let Michael live with me if it was an inconvenience? If we had different schedules? Different diets? Different ideas on what I should wear?"

Stacey dug to the bottom of the clearance bin. "You never learned to compromise, did you? You were an only child. You never had to share. You don't know what it's like when nothing is ever completely yours."

"That's not what it is. I didn't have that much when I was a kid, not that it was uncomfortable. You don't know everything about me."

Stacey threw me an interested glance. She would be waiting a very long time if she thought I was going to explain Uncle Grigori's tragedy to her. She was too much of a hopeless romantic to see it as the cautionary tale I had always used it for. In an instant, I was twelve years old again, looking into his lined, constricted face. His hair had never been such a mess, the overgrown locks crisscrossing each other like the wind had torn through them. He hadn't left his apartment in days. My mother had driven me over, and she lingered in the kitchen across the apartment, tidying while we talked in private.

His voice could barely scrape out of his throat. "I loved her, Xan, and she broke my heart."

I was in seventh grade. I was no stranger to heartache. I saw it on TV all the time, heard it in songs, saw the way my parents hurt each other, watched the tension between my friends' parents. It had never touched me this closely before, and it clawed at my heart. Uncle Grigori's desperate eyes stared off at the window, where my mother had raised the shade a few minutes before.

I wanted to promise him everything. It would be all right. She could come back. He could find another woman, much more beautiful who would love him for the rest of his life. I couldn't say these things because I didn't know if they were true. If I lied to him, it would only cut him deeper. Seated on the bed with him, I scooted towards him and hugged his neck. "I love you, Uncle Grigori. I'm still here." It seemed like the most comforting thing I could say. It had only evoked the smallest of smiles, the minimum of relief.

By the next summer, he was dead. I stood by his open casket the entire wake until my mother pulled me away by my sleeve. "They have to carry him out now," she told me in a loud whisper. I kept my eyes on the sleek black box every moment it was in my sight. My father and the other pallbearers carried it out of the church. I stepped outside too late to see it loaded into the hearse, but I saw it through the window of the car as I passed by. I rode with my mother in the family car, driving behind the van of pallbearers, which I knew was directly behind Uncle Grigori.

At the cemetery, my eyes followed the casket from the hearse to its place beside the open, rectangular grave. It seemed like such a strange shape for a person, so rigid and formulaic. It was unconcerned with Uncle Grigori's shape, which was a little round in the middle. He always dressed so well, in a kind of vintage style with green or brown tweed vests, that most people forgave the body stretching them out. Now he was closed away in the casket, which was lowered after most of the guests had left. I stood stubbornly at the graveside, my mother tugging at my clothes again. "We'll be late to the luncheon. We're family. We're supposed to be there with everyone else."

I waited, expecting the grave to be filled in right away. "I want to see him buried so I'll know this is where he's staying."

My mother took my hand. "He'll be here. Trust me. Grigori wouldn't go anywhere that you didn't know how to find him."

I knew even then there was a hint of bitterness in her reassurance, but I went with her to the car. I left my uncle in the bottom of the squared-off hole, never to see more of him than his tombstone ever again. In the coming days, I thought a lot about the kind of pain that had left Uncle Grigori so despondent. Over the next few years, I heard enough hushed conversation between my parents to know Uncle Grigori had taken his own life. That gave rise to a whole new line of thought. Romantic entanglements were not only full of uncertainty and the threat of personal decline. They threatened one's existence if they went wrong.

That would never happen to me. I would never give anyone that power over me. The easiest way to do that was to stop it at the door. Keep the love out, the tenderness that crawls into the heart and makes it so painful to remove later. It was easy for years until Michael showed up. Once I warmed up to him and never found a way to push him away as I first tried to, that door creaked open. Now he lived in my house, slept every night in my bed, and I watched him eat muffins across the breakfast table.

Stacey snapped her fingers two feet from my face. "Whoa, I triggered a memory or something."

I blinked, caught off guard by the vivid succession of details. Thirty years had done little to erase Uncle Grigori or the pain of his loss from my memory. "Yeah, I was thinking about something else. What were we talking about?"

"It doesn't matter. I didn't mean to upset you."

Stacey had turned to give me her full attention, ignoring the clearance underwear behind her. I didn't want her focusing on me until I could collect myself. "Let's go back to finding you something to wear. You can't meet Michael's friends with holey underwear."

"No, I can't."

Stacey moved farther into the store, never passing a rack without stopping to look at the merchandise or slide some fabric through her fingers. "How are things going with your book?"

I still didn't want to talk about it, but it was better than the alternatives. "I'm still writing, but I have no idea how it's going to end."

"What's it about? Where does it start?"

"The main character, Leifa, decides she doesn't want to get married."

Stacey cringed despite her grin. "Your mom's going to love that one."

"That's part of my freedom. She'll never read it, so I can write whatever I want."

"So what happens to Leifa?"

"She calls the wedding off in the morning. It was scheduled for that evening. Obviously, everything's been bought. All the guests have RSVP'd."

Stacey, having gone through the planning and execution of a

wedding, shook her head. "That's so evil. Do you have any idea what a nightmare that would be?" She paused. "Then what?"

I had her hooked and tried not to show I enjoyed it. "She has to decide what to do with her life. Mostly, it means making new friends who support her new lifestyle. Leifa starts getting involved with men who are nothing like her ex-fiancé. The friends she shared with Barry go a little crazy in their own ways."

"What happens to him?"

"I'm not sure. He's been trying different tricks to win her back, but Leifa's happier without him."

"She likes getting some strange."

"She likes what we were talking about earlier. The freedoms of being single you want to overlook."

Stacey groaned and shuddered. "If wearing granny panties is your idea of freedom, shoot me now."

"It's about a free schedule. Not having to worry about problems between your friends and your significant other. Not worrying about jealousy and hurt feelings and getting drawn into things you don't really want to do."

Stacey flipped through the negligees hanging on the next rack. "Why don't you leave Michael if you miss being single so much?"

I opened my mouth but stopped myself when I realized what I was going to say. I didn't miss being single. But I was single. Michael and I weren't together in that way. Or were we? Is that what I was so cranky about, finding myself in the situation I was so thoroughly against? I gave Stacey the answer I was most comfortable with. "I'm not leaving Michael."

"There's a surprise. But what about your schedule? All these things Michael supposedly impedes on."

"He doesn't. He did for a while, but he changed a lot of his habits so he wouldn't bother me."

"You're the one impeding on him?"

"I guess I am."

"So what's the problem?"

A slightly older woman wandered into my peripheral, flipping through the hangers on the racks. I stepped closer to Stacey to keep from broadcasting my private life into the shopping space around us.

"Why would he put up with that? Why would he stay with me if I'm so demanding?"

"Because he loves you," Stacey said, her emphasis making it sound obvious. Her tidy eyebrows bunched up above her eyes.

"But he's been like this the entire time I've known him, including the night we met. He's always been ready to do whatever I want him to."

Stacey shrugged under her jacket. "He respects you. He adores you. I don't know what he was like back then, but I know him now. I could come over to the house completely naked, and he'd rather look at you in old yoga pants and a dirty T-shirt. He wants to be with you."

"What's so special about me?"

Stacey searched my face. Her eyebrows knit together in total confusion. "Xan, I'm saying this as a friend, but sometimes you scare me. How do you get to your forties without knowing how relationships work?"

I lowered my voice. "I never had one. I always cut them short and kept them shallow. It's the easiest way to get attention without the risks of a relationship."

"By attention, do you mean sex?"

"No." It meant a lot of things, but I realized sex was what I'd been thinking of. "Sort of."

"Why were you trying to be like that? Did you have bad experiences with boys when you were a kid? Like, a teenager, I mean?"

"Why does everybody ask me that?"

"It's the obvious question, I guess." Stacey stopped to hold up a red bra and panty set. "How about this one?"

I stopped to check the cool tone against her features. "Try it on."

Stacey hooked the hanger to her wrist. "How did boys react to you when you were in school?"

"They either loved me or they ignored me. They either thought I was brilliant and mysterious, or they didn't know what to think of me."

"Welcome to the club. Rejection is part of the game."

"I knew that, and I decided I didn't want to play."

"Until Michael."

It wasn't exactly true. I fought Michael tooth and nail every step of the way. But he was still in my house, and I accepted that. I accepted Michael as a part of my life.

Stacey glanced at my empty hands. "Aren't you going to pick anything out? You did make him change his habits. It's the least you could do."

"I didn't make him. He did it on his own." I realized as soon as I said it, Stacey would pounce on it.

She shook her hands at me in frustration. "You don't even know how good you've got it. Listen to Marcy. Her boyfriend won't change for common sense."

"It doesn't matter if I buy anything or not. We're having Michael's parents down from Chicago for the weekend. This wild, sexy evening you're envisioning will be put off anyway."

Stacey made a dismissive exhale through her teeth. "You both work from home. Why do you need a weekend? Pry yourself off the computer for twenty minutes and help yourself to the man buffet."

Stacey picked out a red satin chemise and held it out between us, considering my face above it. "You should try this one. Red looks good on you."

I tried to ignore the customers glancing at us. There was a reason I didn't usually go shopping with Stacey or Marcy. They didn't mind sharing their preferences with overhearing strangers. I preferred my privacy. I took the chemise, not impressed by it but not opposed to trying it on. I needed answers more than I needed lingerie. "What do you suggest I do?"

"About Michael?"

I nodded.

"Are you kidding? If it was anybody else, I'd say marry him as soon as possible. I know you're not a fan of marriage, and I don't blame you. The only thing worse than being single is being divorced. But I don't understand the way you talk about Michael. Like he's a stranger or somebody you rarely see. Don't you trust him after ten years?"

"I do, but trust doesn't mean he won't leave me. It doesn't mean he can't pick up bad habits down the line."

"You're always so logical. You know my ex put me through the ringer. If I'm saying you can trust Michael, that should tell you something."

I picked out a black chemise trimmed in white lace.

Stacey shot me another question. "Don't you want to be with Michael?"

I hesitated.

"Or whatever you want to call it. You're so picky with words."

"Yes, I do."

"Then you don't have a problem. I'm the one with an actual, serious problem here. I'm going to try these on. Do us all a favor and get something for yourself." Stacey snatched the chemise out of my hand and hung it on the nearest rack. "You don't want to look like a mortician."

"It's classic. Black and white."

Stacey ripped a hot pink chemise off a rack and thrust it into my hands. "The expression is a lady in the living room, a whore in the bedroom. Are you trying to reverse it? Please tell me you know what Michael would want to see you in."

Stacey didn't wait for an answer. She strolled away toward the fitting room signs at the back of the boutique. I looked at the lingerie around me. I didn't want to admit I hadn't asked Michael for suggestions. I had met Stacey here to talk about her life and help her feel good before Michael's friends came down. Buying lingerie was one of the furthest things from my mind, and I wasn't in the mood to sift through any of it.

Left alone in the sea of satins and silks, I tried not to let my thoughts stick to our conversation. I moved through the racks, trying to slow down and look through them as carefully as Stacey had. I needed to pick something she wouldn't rip out of my hands.

Chapter 13: Jessie

Professor Styles turned to the white board, black marker in hand. "King Vortigern," he recited, writing the name in large letters across the board. He stepped back to double-check the spelling of it. "Vort-i-gern. Yes. He wants to save his crumbling castle. So he sends out for a fatherless young man whom he can sacrifice according to the counsel he's been given. But what saves Merlin after the king's men drag him there?"

I looked at my notes. They were sparser than I expected. I hadn't written anything for at least ten minutes. I rubbed my eyes and tried to force myself to focus. My pen was still in my hand, and I took my time in writing *King Vortigern* as if the name needed no explanation.

A girl about nineteen or twenty spoke up on the other side of the room. "His story? His personal story? When he tells it?"

"The truth," a slightly older student said, her voice deeper and more assured.

"You're both right," Professor Styles said. "But I don't want to go into themes quite yet. King Vortigern finds out he was wrong about how to fix his situation, and Merlin gives him a completely different story than his advisors did. Who can sum it up for me?" Professor Styles pointed to a raised hand.

"These dragons are fighting or something," a middle-aged woman said breathily, stuck between amused and confused.

I tried not to sigh out loud. The clock above the white board was moving, but I didn't feel like time was passing.

"Exactly," Professor Styles said, noting something about dragons on the board. "What else?"

The thinning patch on the back of Professor Styles' head drew my attention. He spent so much time with his back to the class, it gave us plenty of opportunity to study the ring of golden hair that grew wispier every semester. Sometimes the other students pointed it out while he was turned or drew sketches of it in their notes. I wished Willa was still in school. She was surprisingly good at sneaking notes, and with Professor Styles glued to the board, we could've had an entire conversation by now.

I stared at the open page of my book, hoping to tune out the discussion. I'd be so relieved when class was over. An hour and fifteen minutes didn't sound like much, but it felt like hours had dragged by. Professor Styles continued marking on the board, every dotted *I* sending a soft thump to my ears in the back of the room. By this point, I was siding with the middle-aged woman in her reaction to the dragons. Until we started talking about theme, I wasn't interested in simple questions meant to find out who had done the reading and who hadn't. All I wanted to talk about was modern literature, how important it was, how overlooked the best of it always was. Here we were babbling about red and white dragons and kings and advisors when modern literature was tackling problems and issues all of us could relate to. But I guessed even the modern lit courses would never put an author as edgy as XZA on their reading lists. Too risky. Too controversial.

The bells rang through the speaker system, and I realized I'd made it through class without having to answer a single question. I started packing up.

Professor Styles tried to get all of his words in. "Remember to continue the reading. We'll discuss the sword in the stone and Excalibur next class, so be prepared. Good discussion today."

I picked up my backpack and joined the line filing out the door. Each of us picked up speed as we broke into the hallway and fanned out from our cramped formation.

I hit the stairs and hurried down toward the waiting line of metal doors on the first floor. I pushed one open and burst out into the bright sunlight. My eyes blinked hard, but my feet kept moving. I adjusted to the light, picking up the bursts of color in the flowerbeds around me. They were the same colors every year, both familiar and unoriginal. Other students wandered past me, but I didn't pay much attention to them. I followed the path from the rear of the building toward the center of campus. The nearest bench sat empty as I'd hoped, and I parked myself on it. A few students I knew from other classes waved to me as our eyes met. I waved back and laid my backpack next to me to keep anyone from sitting there.

I opened my backpack and pulled out *Hypocrisy*. For being the newest of XZA's books, it had the most wear of the copies I owned. The corners of the front cover were creased and bent. The bottom corner was splitting the artwork from its plain white backing. The art was less dramatic than the other covers but just as provocative. In the right-hand foreground stood a teenage girl with her hand tentatively resting on her pregnant belly. Behind her, just left of center, loomed a male figure in a black suit. I assumed the girl was the main character, sixteen-year-old Lourdes Falzone. I was pretty sure I was about to find out who the man was, if I'd learned anything about the way XZA wrote. The last images of Merlin and dragons drifted from my mind. I glanced at the people on their way to class or standing around talking. They were too busy to notice me. I flipped the book open and slid my bookmark aside.

Lourdes closed the door to Pastor Ozbeck's office. He gestured to the empty chair across the desk from him. She settled into it, finding it more comfortable than the worn quality of the nubby turquoise fabric had led her to believe. She still didn't know why he'd asked to see her, but she didn't want to seem rude by asking too many questions.

Pastor Ozbeck folded his large hands on the desk in front of him. "I didn't know if you would come to see me. I thought you might not want to take the time."

Lourdes couldn't imagine not responding to someone's simple request, especially the head of her church. "Why wouldn't I come in?"

"You have school. You have friends and homework. I'm sure you have chores to do at home."

"I do." Lourdes didn't consider any of those a reason to brush him off. Other girls might. They had cars and vacation homes and loads of friends. Pastor Ozbeck hadn't been at the church very long, and this might be why he underestimated her character. If he had known her mother and how strict she was on ethics, he would've known Lourdes would be there the first afternoon she was available.

Pastor Ozbeck sat quietly as if he expected an explanation.

Lourdes sat up straighter in the boxy chair. "I do have things I need to do, but you wanted to see me. My mom dropped me off on her way to pick my brother up from school."

"You have a close-knit family, don't you?"

"I suppose I do."

"Does your mother work?"

"No. She stays home with us."

Pastor Ozbeck offered a friendly smile. "That must be nice for you. You probably have a clean home and tasty meals every night."

"We do."

"I remember your mother's cooking from the pot luck. She made the lasagna, didn't she? It was very good."

"Yes. I'll tell her you liked it."

Pastor Ozbeck tilted his head slightly. "You're very mature for your age, aren't you?"

"I don't know. I guess so. My dad just calls it being accountable."

"That's a very good attitude to have. I called you in because I could use a little help around the office and getting to know the church a little better. I could use a young person who's dependable. Would you help me do that?"

Lourdes didn't mind the idea, but she didn't want to step on the toes of the other staff. She had known the secretary for as long as she could remember, a tall, thin woman with glasses who never spoke above a whisper. She was always polite and generous, handing out sugar-free candies to the kids on Sundays. Lourdes didn't want to cause problems doing someone else's work. "The office secretary could help you with that. She's worked here a long time."

Pastor Ozbeck dipped his head in a big, smooth nod. "She could, but she has a lot of work that has to be done. There's a lot of mailing, typing, and deadlines to meet. I thought if I could find a volunteer, some knowledgeable young person from the congregation to help me, I might have an easier time moving into this position."

"Oh, I have no problem helping you. I'd be glad to. I was looking out for the secretary. I didn't want to take over her job."

"That's very kind of you. I assure you I won't let that happen. Are you sure you could find the time?"

"Sure. I could walk over after school and be home in time for dinner. Is that what you were looking for? Someone in the afternoon?"

"That would be perfect. Would two or three times a week be too much?"

"No. I don't think so."

"Did you like your other pastor, Pastor Klein?"

"Yes. He was very friendly. He was very funny, too. Everybody thought so."

"It sounds like I have big shoes to fill."

"You do, but you shouldn't worry. Everybody likes you. My parents think you're a very good replacement."

"Is that what you think?"

"Sure. I think you'll fit right in."

Pastor Ozbeck leaned back. "I certainly hope so."

"You're only the second pastor here I can remember. My parents have been coming here for years. They would know what the other pastors were like before Pastor Klein if you wanted to hear about them."

"Thank you. I'll have to remember that. Do you think you would be able to come by on, let's say, Mondays and Thursdays? Or do you need to ask your mother?"

"I'll ask her when I get home, but I'm sure it's all right."

Pastor Ozbeck smiled, and his small grey eyes turned up at the corners. "Very good. I'll wait anxiously to hear what she says."

"I'll call you as soon as I know."

"I'd appreciate that. You're a very responsible young lady."

"My parents taught me to be on time for everything. My father says if you're on time, you're already five minutes late."

"I'll be sure to have you out on time, then."

"I'm sure Mom wouldn't mind too much if I was late from helping out at the church."

"I'll try not to make you late just the same. I wouldn't want your dinner to get cold. I want to make sure you have time for your homework. I don't want your grades to drop because of me."

Lourdes shook her head. "I wouldn't let them."

Pastor Ozbeck tented his fingers under his chin, and his deep voice rolled out even lower. "Good girl."

I shuddered as I reached the end of the chapter, Pastor Ozbeck's voice surprisingly real as it rumbled in my head. Hard footsteps raced toward me, and I tucked my feet under the bench to keep them out of the way. I was afraid it was Dick, but it was two students I didn't know. They ran past me, dodging the standing students to disappear into the crowd.

I checked my watch. There was enough time left before class to read a little more or grab a snack on the way. As much as I dreaded reading more about Pastor Ozbeck, I had a feeling if I didn't, his leading questions and menacing form would haunt me until I did. I turned to the next chapter. If I read fast, I could get to a more satisfying place and still have enough time to get something from a vending machine.

Chapter 14: Xan

The Singers' SUV hummed into the driveway, accentuated by two signature honks. I heard the blasts from the second floor hallway and smiled. Michael's dad must be driving. I folded the last bath towel, still warm from the dryer, and tucked the short stack of them onto the closet shelf. I jogged down the stairs, joining Michael as he walked out to meet his parents in the lingering sunlight. Mark and Claire lowered their luggage from the back of the SUV, pulling up the handles to roll them along behind them. They both held a bottle of wine in their other hand. They laughed as they leaned in for hugs, swinging the bottles aside.

"How are you?" Claire asked, upbeat and cheery.

Michael's answer came easily despite the hard work he was putting in reading and reviewing student writing. "We're good. Looking forward to some golf."

"And a lot of wine, I hope."

"Of course."

Mark lowered his wine bottle to arm's length like a golf club. "I hope you've been practicing, Mike. I'm ready to retake my title as reigning champ this year."

Michael smirked. "Practice isn't everything."

"No, but it's a start."

Mark's cropped hair was a mix of dark and grey. Unlike Michael, he'd never hidden the silver. It had gradually won out over his natural color in the last few years. Claire, in her casual honesty, had told me years ago she dyed her locks to maintain their original honey-blonde luminosity. It was easy to let them into my house and assign them the biggest guest room we had. It was the more luxurious of the two, the one Marcy and Stacey fought over when they stayed with me before Michael moved in.

Getting along with Mark and Claire had always been effortless for me. I'd met them informally at a party in Michael's apartment. Even that night, they never questioned my presence in his life or made me feel awkward for my reluctance to make a long-lasting commitment to him.

Claire patted my arm. "How are you, Xan?"

"I'm good," I echoed, less convincing than Michael. The unfinished state of my book hounded me, and I was relieved to see his parents. Keeping up with Mark and Claire made it too hard to think about my characters, and they faded from my mind.

I took the wine bottles. "How was the drive?"

"It was all right. The traffic got thinner once we got out of the city."

Claire stayed at my side, and we led the men into the foyer.

Michael reached for his mother's luggage. "Let me take that upstairs for you."

Claire waved him away. "I can manage it, thank you. The room around the corner, right?"

Michael and I nodded.

Mark and Claire disappeared upstairs. I carried the wine into the kitchen and set out glasses in case they wanted to open it right away. Michael lingered in the hall, making slight rustling sounds hanging their jackets in the closet. His parents came down, and they all joined me in the kitchen. Mark went straight to the bottle opener and uncorked some wine. He filled Claire's glass and handed it to her before he filled the rest of them.

Claire took a sip and sighed happily.

"What's new?" Michael asked them, picking up the next filled glass.

"Your father," Claire answered, gesturing to Mark with her glass, "has decided he'd like to try a cruise next summer."

"What's wrong with that?"

"The last time I was on a boat – " Claire chuckled. " – was fifteen years ago. Remember that tiny rowboat of a watercraft, Mark? We were riding in it, and he turned around too fast because he thought he saw a snake in the water, and I lost my balance and fell in. It turned out to be a stick."

Michael didn't miss a beat. "I told you not to get in a boat with this man. Dad and water don't mix."

"I thought I'd give him a chance. You were right."

"Well," Mark said good-naturedly, "there won't be any chance of me flipping you in from a cruise ship."

Claire raised her eyebrows. "That's what you think."

"It was just an idea."

"An idea you talk about every night," Claire muttered into her wine. She winked at me.

Mark filled my glass, but just listening to them talk was enough to relax me.

"What are we making for dinner?" Claire asked, raising her wine glass. "I'm halfway through this glass, and I want to be coherent when I try to help."

I motioned to the recipe tacked to the front of the fridge. "We found a recipe for no-bake shepherd's pie. That way we're not sitting around for half an hour waiting for it to bake."

"That sounds good. There are so many places to find good shepherd's pie around Chicago. If you're interested in different versions of it, the next time you come up, we'll take you on a tour."

"That sounds nice."

Michael looked up with interest from reading the recipe. "Do I know all the places already?"

"Some of them, I'm sure. But there are some new restaurants we really like."

Mark spoke up. "You do mean a *tasting* tour, right, Claire? Otherwise, we're gonna be pretty full after that second restaurant." He patted his stomach and puckered his face. "Oof! That's a lotta lamb."

"Of course I meant tasting," Claire told him. "We can order one dish and all share. They have take-home containers."

Michael glanced at his father. "Believe it or not, there are worse ways to spend a day in Chicago than getting stuffed on shepherd's pie."

Mark laughed and topped off his wine glass. "That sounds ominous, Mike. What were you doing behind our backs when you were younger, or is it better your mom and I don't know?"

Claire swatted playfully at her husband's arm. "Michael's never done anything you haven't. Although, there was that time he had the motorcycle. How were old were you, Michael? Eighteen?"

"Nineteen," Michael corrected.

"Well, you had it for three weeks, and let me tell you, Xan, they were the longest three weeks of my entire life. If I didn't color my hair, I could show you all the greys that came in that year." Claire swept her fingers through her hair. "I was relieved when he sold it back. I'll never forget that kid. Barney Slomak. You could tell he was trouble from a mile away."

"He didn't force me to buy it, Mom," Michael reminded her. "I wanted it for months."

"Yes, but after you sold it back, what did you say to me?"

Michael barely hesitated under his mother's sparkling gaze. "It was too dangerous, and I was done with it."

"So I was right. Still glad it's done and we can stand here in the kitchen with all of our bones intact."

Claire's insinuation made me wonder what Mark's most outlandish adventure was, but I didn't want to pry. Not knowing the truth, my imagination ran the gamut between drunken disasters and good intentions gone wrong.

"Did you know about Michael's motorcycle, Xan?" Claire asked. "Does it surprise you he had one?"

"No," I said, smiling. "He never told me, but it doesn't surprise me."

Michael was seldom what he seemed. He still looked clean cut except for his hair, and it fooled everyone into assuming he was always on his best behavior. I'd heard enough stories to know he wasn't the poster child for good manners we all thought he was at first glance. He'd confessed to seasonal flings and stealing other men's dates. He'd played his share of pranks and slacked off on the job. He had a dozen stories about going to weddings with Nick and John, sometimes as an uninvited additional guest. The bright, easy smile and well-cut clothes disguised the kind of personality many of us secretly hoped he possessed: spontaneous if not slightly debaucherous. Maybe he got that from his father. If so, both men had cleaned up their acts a long time ago.

Michael tasted his wine. "I wasn't thinking of anything too wild, Dad. Before I moved out of the city, I spent several hours one time changing a tire with John." Michael glanced at me. "You know what he's like. The plan changed every minute. I was seriously worried it was going to take the whole night. I finally talked him out of going for help, and we put the donut on. The car was fine to drive after that, but it took us forever to get to that point."

Mark held his arms out in a dramatic display of defeat. "How does that make me look that you can't change a tire, even with help?"

"We were in suits, Dad. We were trying not to ruin several hundred dollars' worth of good clothes. We already went to our meeting, which was good, because the rest of the day was pretty much shot. I had to calm John down and convince him I already knew a good place to buy a replacement tire."

Mark was shaking his head.

I came to Michael's rescue. "That's the way John is. There's nothing sadder than a well-dressed man covered in tire grease."

Michael pointed to me. "That's true. I've seen it. Saddest man I've ever seen in a gas station. Covered in grease."

Claire motioned her nearly emptied glass to the recipe on the refrigerator. "So, before I'm completely wasted, how do we do this? I haven't made shepherd's pie in ages."

Michael took the recipe down and looked it over. "We need somebody on vegetables, somebody on the lamb, and somebody on potatoes."

He handed the paper to me, and I skimmed the ingredients list. "Whoever's left over can be in charge of what gets added to the lamb."

Mark took a more solemn tone. "That sounds responsible. Better leave that to Claire."

Claire shook her head. "Give me the vegetables. I'm too out of practice with everything else that goes into it."

In one coordinated swing, we raised our glasses for a final sip of wine before setting them out of the way. Michael filled a pot with water to boil for the potatoes, and I set Claire up with a cutting board. Claire sliced the carrots and onion with patient accuracy while Mark sighed in playful exasperation as he waited on us, tapping a spoon against his leg. I laughed, adding the chopped vegetables to a pan on the stove to soften in butter. Within minutes, I caught the first luscious smells of the evening, the milky butter a rich compliment to the sharp onion and earthy carrot. Mark kept an eye on the vegetables, waiting for his cue to add the lamb.

"I'm on the lamb, you guys," he chuckled.

Claire groaned. "Are you going to list every lamb joke you can think of?"

Mark continued without acknowledging Claire, speaking in a hoarse whisper. "Don't tell anybody. I have to figure out what I'm going to do on the lamb."

Michael replied over his shoulder. "Keep talking, Dad, and we'll turn you in. I promise you."

I stifled a laugh so I wouldn't encourage Mark's antics. I collected the rest of the ingredients from the cabinets, the fridge, and the freezer.

Claire, done with her duties, popped out of the room long enough for Mark to sneak in another joke. "I'm just so tired from being on the lamb."

Michael rolled his eyes to the ceiling, and I laughed into the back of my hand.

Claire breezed in from the dining room. "I can set the table if you tell me where the linens are."

I tried to match her mood, more casual than the wacky humor Mark brought with him. "Thanks. They're in the dining room cabinet." I opened the drawer in front of me and sorted through the measuring spoons, trying to keep up with the intricate timing of the recipe.

Claire disappeared, and I measured out a tablespoon of flour.

Mark glanced at me. "Michael says you're still working on your book."

My muscles tensed. I didn't want to think or talk about the progress of my book. "I am."

"Good luck with it. We can't wait to read it when it's done."

I focused harder on the recipe to keep my mind from leaping to the unfinished plot on my computer one room away. I had to add the flour next, but the lamb wasn't ready. I could open the can of tomato paste while I waited. "I appreciate that."

"Have you kept up the year-to-year age progression with your narrators?"

"No. I skipped ahead. She's about twenty-four, twenty-five."

"That should be interesting. I'd like to see how you write a story about someone that age."

The lamb browned through, and I scattered the flour over it. "Stir that in." I glanced back over the recipe and noticed Michael standing casually at the other end of the island, waiting on the potatoes to soften. I brushed tickling hairs off my forehead with my wrist. "Do you have everything you need to mash the potatoes?"

"Yes," Michael said, much more relaxed than I was. "I should've taken your job. The potatoes are a hurry-up-and-wait game. You're supposed to be resting your brain."

Mark interjected. "From what?"

"Writing," Michael and I answered in different tones.

Mark gestured to the breakfast table by the windows. "Pull up a chair and relax. I can add the other stuff in. I was just being funny about shirking responsibility."

Michael raised a disbelieving eyebrow at his father. "You, make a complicated dish? You'd rather change a tire with one hand than make something with more than six ingredients in it."

"To some people, that's a style of cooking. I'm trying to be a good guest." Mark reached for the recipe, and I handed it over.

I didn't drag a chair over from the nook, but I joined Michael in standing around by the island.

Claire came into the kitchen, raising a deck of playing cards into view. "Look what I found from the last time we were here."

Mark measured the tomato paste. "You'll have to reteach me, Claire. The only card game I can remember is Solitaire. Who wants to watch me play several hours of that?"

Michael groaned.

Claire opened the box and slid the cards out. "I can teach you Rummy in no time. Should we bake the shepherd's pie and play some cards? Or do you think it would dry out? Do you want to play, Xan?"

"I'll play."

Michael set the temperature for the oven. "I don't think baking it will hurt anything."

Mark added the final ingredients to the pan on the stove, and

Michael carried the steaming pot of potatoes to the sink to drain them.

Claire sidled up to me, shuffling the cards. "How's your book going?"

I tried not to cringe. Every time I left it alone, the book caught up to me. "It's all right. Just a little stalled."

"Oh." Claire crinkled her face up and patted my arm. "Don't worry about it. One little idea, and you'll be off to the races."

"The races!" Mark exclaimed. "That's something we haven't done, watched horse races."

"I thought you were on the lam," Claire said dryly.

I set out a casserole dish while Michael finished mashing the potatoes. Mark spooned the cooked lamb and vegetables into the dish, scraping every last bit off the bottom.

"What have you been up to?" I asked Claire. "Besides planning trips?"

"Is there time for anything else?" Claire glanced sidelong at her husband. Her lips pulled to one side in a light smile, and she nodded at him. "I've been trying to plan a vegetable garden, but this one insists it look like a work of art, too."

"Form and function, honey," Mark spoke up, relishing the idea.

Michael pulled out two spatulas, and the two men began covering the meat mixture with a thick layer of mashed potatoes. Mark's need for speed overshadowed Michael's careful sealing of the dish's outer edge, splattering instead of troweling as he tried to shoulder Michael out of the way. Michael laughed and planted his feet more firmly, maintaining his ground.

"Those two," Claire muttered to me. "They could make a contest out of anything. You should've seen Mark the first time I saw him. He was such a show-off, even then. Strutting around the basketball court like he owned the town."

The oven beeped, and Michael slid the potato-topped dish onto the rack. He set the timer, and Claire shook her head as she brushed globs of mashed potatoes off Mark's shirt. We picked up our wine glasses, and Claire led us into the dining room, refreshingly cooler than the dinner-heated kitchen.

Michael and I rarely used the dining room by ourselves. It was nice when we had company, but otherwise, it seemed too formal to me. Thanks to Claire taking over with napkins and placemats, it actually felt inviting to be in there. Claire sat herself at the head of the table and guided us through the rules of Rummy. She beat us at several rounds before the timer went off. Michael ducked into the kitchen to take the shepherd's pie out of the oven, and we played another round while it cooled.

Michael set his cards down, hunger driving urgency into his voice. "I think dinner's ready."

Mark passed his cards to Claire and stood up before anyone else did. He slapped a hand against his belly. "Let's eat."

Claire looked up at him with a knowing smirk as she reached for my cards. "You're only in a hurry because you're in last place."

Mark smiled at his wife. "But I'll be the first to refill the wine."

Michael passed out bowls, and we huddled around the dish on the island to pile them high. It was the best shepherd's pie I'd had in months, and Mark stayed true to his word over the hours we sat in the dining room. No glass fell below the halfway mark before he hastily refilled it.

Finally, Claire placed her hand over her glass as Mark extended the bottle her way. "Mark, it's late. We should go to bed. It's been a long day."

Mark swished the contents around the inside of the bottle. "There's still half a bottle left in here."

"It'll be here tomorrow, too." Claire's eyes were shining, but she did look tired. Her makeup was gently smudged, and I was sure mine was, too.

Michael went to the kitchen and returned with a stopper. He sealed the bottle tightly and put the wine away before Mark could find a good reason to finish it in the next half hour.

I led Mark and Claire upstairs while Michael locked up the house. "Clean towels are in the bathroom for you."

Claire gave me a hug before she wandered away toward the guest room. "Thank you, Xan. Good night."

"Good night."

I left the bedroom door open for Michael, and we slipped under the covers less than fifteen minutes later.

I knew I'd sleep soundly next to Michael that night, content and relaxed from sharing good wine with even better company. I might not have solved the ending to Leifa's adventures, but for once, I didn't want to think about them. I just wanted to be.

Chapter 15: Jessie

The closer we got to the diner, the more I realized what a horrible idea this was. Every time I stole a glance at Dick, his eyes were intense, piercing the road. His hands squeezed the steering wheel when he wasn't using them to slap the top of it in time with the radio. When I wasn't looking at Dick, he was impossible to ignore. He muttered every word of every song, emphasizing the angry, four-letter ones.

Dick was in no mood to talk to anybody, and we were meeting Willa. How did I think putting Dick and Willa in the same place was a good idea? I closed my eyes for a moment and tried to convince myself it could still work out. It could be fine.

But it wouldn't. I couldn't trick myself that easily. Dick was a handful when we were by ourselves. There was no way he was prepared to be civil, and Willa wasn't the type to hold her tongue, either.

Dick lifted his hand and cranked the rearview mirror around to adjust it. He spat curse words at it, and I shrank down in my seat. I was more afraid of his behavior than Willa's. Willa was straightforward, but Dick was blunt. He was going to blurt out whatever thoughts he had. This could turn into a war, and I would be caught in the middle. Maybe it was my fault, and I deserved it for pushing so hard. I wished Dick hadn't agreed to it, but I kept trying to remind myself it hadn't happened yet. I didn't know how it was going to play out. It was the only way I could make myself walk inside.

Dick turned the truck in a wide, growling circle into the diner parking lot. As usual, it was the tallest vehicle around. I felt like we should be speeding toward a ramp that would shoot us over the parked cars instead of parking among them. The truck swung into an empty space and stopped abruptly, my face swinging toward the dashboard before it bounced up again. I grabbed my purse and climbed down past the monstrous black tire too big to fit inside the wheel well. I'd had enough practice by now to keep my footing and not almost fall.

I was simultaneously relieved and unnerved to see Willa waiting for us outside the diner. I had never understood her uncanny ability to stand around by herself, completely unconcerned about what other people might think of her. She was dressed in the same overalls I'd seen her in two days before. The bright orange shirt under it had holes near the ends of the sleeves where her thumbs poked through, something the rest of my friends had stopped doing in high school. I'd never been embarrassed of Willa before, and feeling it crawl over me now bothered me more than the embarrassment itself.

Dick walked around the back of the truck to where I could see him. "Yeah, that's who I meant. The weird one."

I shot him a warning glare. I hoped he wouldn't say anything like that to her face. "Her name is Willa," I whispered harshly.

I started toward the diner, and Dick reluctantly fell into step with me. Willa gave a casual wave. I almost wished they didn't know each other so I could waste time introducing them. Instead, we converged and said nothing. Willa opened the door, and we filed inside.

A teenage waitress smacking a giant piece of pink gum showed us to a booth in the middle of the dining room. I sat down with Dick sliding in next to me and Willa plopping down across the table from us. We grabbed the laminated, single-sheet menus from behind the wire condiment basket.

We spent several minutes studying a menu that didn't take very long to read. I couldn't be the only one feeling the weight of the silence. I glanced at Willa, who readily looked up to meet my gaze. Faced with her frown, I had to say something.

I tried for neutral ground. "How are you and Frank?" I asked.

"Okay. How's it going?"

"All right."

There was a pause, and I tried to think of something else we could talk about. I didn't want Dick to accuse me of excluding him from the conversation.

Willa beamed and raised her eyebrows. "Where are you at in *Hypocrisy*?"

I tensed whether I wanted to or not. I'd hoped she wouldn't ask me about it, but hadn't I known Willa wouldn't censor herself for

Dick? That was what she wanted to talk about, so that's what she was going to bring up. "I'm not too far in. I haven't been able to read it very much I've had so much to read for class. I'm at the part where Lourdes is volunteering at the church, and she doesn't know why the secretary's hours have been shortened. She never sees the secretary around anymore."

Willa dropped her fist lightly and repeatedly onto the table. "You're so close to the creepiest shit ever. You don't even know."

I stopped myself from cringing at her reaction. "Is that good?"

"It's awesome. *Hypocrisy* picks up where *Satan, My Father* left off."

A black uniform shifted in my peripheral, and I realized the waitress was standing at the edge of the table. She was tall and middle-aged, her bold blonde hair sprayed into a helmet the dry consistency of a bird's nest. We mumbled some drink orders, and the waitress walked briskly away.

Willa picked right back up again. "Which one's your favorite book so far?"

I could feel Dick sitting beside me. His silence was a bad sign, but I felt obligated to Willa to keep the conversation going. "I don't know. It seems kind of unfair to judge them when I haven't finished this one."

"It's an unfair question to begin with. You almost can't even compare them. They're all works of genius. How do you pick which main character you like best? How do you decide who the best villains are? I mean, I think the narrator's dad wins that one hands down, but Pastor Ozbeck is seriously screwed-up in the head."

"He seems pretty creepy," I admitted.

"Oh, yeah. The guy's a real winner. You can see a whole arc through the books." Willa gestured over the table, illustrating her points. "Dad as bad guy. Most characters as bad guys. Then Pastor Ozbeck. It's one person, then it's everybody, then it's one person again. Some of the same themes come back, too, so it's pretty cool. It's almost like a sequel."

"Yeah, I can see that."

"Who didn't want a sequel? I could read her books forever. I don't care how bad things get. I just want to keep reading. You know what I mean?"

Dick exploded next to me before I could answer. "Jesus Christ. Do you do anything but talk?"

Willa narrowed her eyes at him. "I wondered how long you could keep your mouth shut. What was that? Three minutes?"

Dick turned to me, his brown eyes flashing. "You lied to me. You said she didn't read that stuff. I should've known she did. Is that where you got it from?"

Willa set her hands on her hips. "What if it is? What if I gave her a book? So what? It was her birthday. What did you give her other than grief?"

"I gave her my dick."

My face burned like it was on fire. I struggled to find my voice. "Shut up. You did not."

Willa regarded Dick with solemn disdain. "You impotent man-boy."

Dick leaned in front of me to put his menu away. "What does that even mean? I told Jessie you were weird."

"*I'm* weird? I don't drive around in a two-story truck. If it had rust holes in it and was an homage to *F*CK, F*CK, F*CK*, maybe I'd think it was cool."

"Yeah, whatever. I'll let you know when you're qualified to judge what's cool."

Willa held her wrist up and tapped it. "Where'd you get that bracelet you gave her?" Willa jerked her thumb at me. "Did you steal it or just trade some old junk for it in a pawn shop? You seem like the kind of guy that would steal stuff from his own mother and pawn it."

Dick's face scrunched up, and his tone took on a bitter sarcasm. "Like I'd give Jessie some second-hand bullshit. What kind of question is that?"

I repeated the only phrase that ran through my head. "Shut up, Dick."

"Stop telling me to shut up. You said we'd go out with Willa and find out what she's been up to. She's been up to nothing but shit."

Willa folded her arms and regarded him for a long moment. "You're a real piece of work. Would it kill you to take an interest in something Jessie thinks is cool?"

"Maybe I'd be interested if what Jessie thought was cool was actually cool."

Willa shook her head. "How does it smell up there, Dick? With your head that far up your own ass?"

Dick jumped to his feet, the table jumping with him. The salt and pepper shakers rattled violently in the wire basket. Dick pointed to the door. "Why are you in my diner? I want to come back here, you know, and you're messing everything up for me."

"Trust me. I will gladly get out of this dump. Never mind the fact I drove here to spend time with my friend." Willa lowered her eyes from his face to mine. "Are you coming, Jessie, or are you staying with Dick?"

My heart rose into the back of my throat. I wanted to slump under the table and stay there until everything was worked out. I wished Willa hadn't asked me that directly. I could barely look at her.

Dick leaned over and poked me in the side, making me wince. "Don't even think about leaving me here by myself. And tell her she can't talk to me like that."

I shifted on my part of the bench, feeling Willa's eyes weighing on me like dumbbells on my shoulders.

Dick jabbed me again. "Come on. I'm starving."

I cleared the lump out of my throat. I couldn't meet Willa's gaze. "I'm pretty hungry. I should stay and get something to eat."

"And she can't talk to me like that."

Dick wasn't going to let me off the hook. Maybe if I stayed silent, Willa would go away with her feelings only half hurt, and Dick would order, and we would eat, and I could go home, and I'd never have to parrot his words after him again, and the diner would burn down so I'd never have to come here again. But Willa wasn't moving, and I heard my strained voice escape from my throat. "You shouldn't talk to him like that. He's my boyfriend."

Willa said nothing for a long time. I was beginning to wonder what she was going to do. She could walk out without ever talking to me again or grab another table's plate of food to dump over Dick's head. Instead, she pulled a few napkins from the dispenser, its silver cover dotted with greasy fingerprints. She handed them to me. "Here.

It's to mop up the liquid fat off whatever you order and keep it out of your heart." Willa slid out of her seat with the smoothest dignity any of the three of us had at the moment.

I couldn't look at her, but I knew if I didn't reach out to her before she left, I might never see her again. I raised my hand to my head where Dick couldn't see it, forming an ear piece and a microphone out of my thumb and pinkie. *Call me*, I mouthed.

"Oh, I will. You bet I will." Willa gave Dick one last disapproving glare and strode out of the diner.

I buried my face in the fistful of napkins. "Goddamn it," I muttered into the muffling paper sanctuary.

My body rocked as Dick sat down next to me. "Did you see that shit? Was I right?" Dick's eyes blazed as he turned to me. "The first mistake was Willa. The second mistake was bringing her here. And the third mistake was you telling me to shut up. Nobody tells me to shut up, okay? Jesus Christ." Dick craned his neck to search the aisle behind us. "Where's the waitress? What does a man have to do to get a couple of sliders around here?"

I felt awful. As I lowered the napkins, I hoped for two things. I hoped the diner food wouldn't make me throw up where I sat, and I hoped Willa would forgive me. All I could hear in my head was Willa proudly saying "Bam!" to all the people she'd kicked out of her life who didn't deserve to be in it. I could live with keeping Dick and Willa apart as I should've done, but I liked having Willa in my life. I didn't want to lose her friendship because I couldn't stand up for myself. She shouldn't have to suffer because of Dick.

Chapter 16: Xan

Mark offered to drive us to the golf course. The Singers' SUV, built for serious vacations to mountainous states, gave a smooth, plush ride on the bumpy county roads.

"You'll wish you'd practiced, Mike," Mark baited his son in a sing-songy threat.

Michael remained unshaken and confident. "We'll see how well your practice pays off."

"Maybe I'll win," Claire taunted.

Mark laughed loudly, prompting a defensive "Hey!" from Claire even though she laughed, too.

I chuckled, but my mind wandered from their conversation. It fixated on one tiny detail Claire had given me the night before: the way she and Mark had met. It was easy to imagine how Mark's overactive ego put a bounce in his step as he no doubt knew exactly who was watching him. And Claire, sitting on the bleachers with her friends, saw through the macho displays to his sense of humor and decided she wanted to get to know him.

It was a good story, believable and straightforward, the complete opposite of the strange story of my parents meeting. I'd heard it several times since I was a child, and it was such an inexplicable incident, I often tried hard to imagine it.

They said my father was a lonely, independent teenager. This was impossible for me to grasp. As long as I'd known him, he was every bit the traditional, hard-working man. He clocked in on time, stayed late when he had to, and introduced us regularly at company functions. My mother tried to obscure his teenaged hobby in fancy terms, but in short, he was fascinated by toying with other people's locks. Most of us called it breaking and entering.

My father never took anything. I believed him when he said that. He was mostly intrigued by gaining access to private places and having a quick look around. He liked the precision involved with the locks, the feel of a small eyeglass screwdriver or a dentist's tooth cleaning pick in his hands. He would smile at the click of success, and he smiled when he talked about it, which wasn't often.

One afternoon, my father was tinkering with the lock of an apartment on the backside of a building, out of sight of the road and the family who just stepped out of it. He was adjusting the tools in the lock when he heard the slightest gasp off to one side. There stood my mother, not horrified, just surprised to find a stranger there. My mother liked to interject that his clean face and decent clothes convinced her she shouldn't be scared of him. His hair was ruffled by the wind, but it was short and neatly trimmed. Instead of running or screaming for help, my mother approached him with her unique sense of boldness and asked what he was doing. My father, recovering from being discovered, explained he was going in for a few minutes to have a look. The kicker and the high point of the story was my mother's line. She'd always wanted to see the inside of her neighbor's apartment. She had her schoolbooks wrapped in her arms from studying with a friend and offered to serve as lookout.

Their youthful rebelliousness astounded me. It was nothing they ever would have encouraged or condoned in me. But in a way, my parents' chance meeting was almost more romantic than the way Michael and I met. Of course, Michael and I usually told an abridged version – we met at a signing. There was no way to clean up my parents' meeting without obliterating the context, and the one time I'd heard a distant cousin ask about it, my mother quietly and briefly said they met at a party.

Michael laughed next to me in the SUV, and I refocused on the conversation around me.

Claire was shaking her head at Mark. "We've got the whole day ahead of us. Why cause so much trouble now?"

"Dad without trouble?" Michael mused. "Dad without air."

Mark pointed through the windshield. "There's the sign, kids."

The mini golf course was buried between restaurants and shopping centers but stood out with a huge sign at roadside. Mark pulled into the parking lot and parked close to the building, rubbing his palms together in anticipation. We climbed out of the car, and Mark insisted on paying before we'd reached the window. While he joked with the attendant, Michael motioned Claire and I forward with a flexing finger. She blocked Mark's view, and we picked our differently colored golf balls from the silver bucket. We hid them in our hands as Mark tucked his wallet away.

Mark lifted the last remaining ball with a cock-eyed grin. "Who left me with yellow when I was trying to pay?"

Michael smiled broadly.

Mark held his ball up. "Okay, wise guy. As long as you know what color to look for as it knocks yours out of the way to drop a hole-in-one."

Claire looped her hand around Mark's arm. We started up the path to the fork, forced to choose between the green phoenix and white tiger courses.

Mark considered both paths, peering over bushes and short fences to see which one looked more interesting. He made the same choice he always did with fresh enthusiasm. "Let's try the white tiger. It sounds more exciting."

We followed the trail marked with round signs bearing the stark white profile of a tiger. Mark passed out the scorecards and tiny pencils from the attendant. The October wind died down, and the sunshine warmed us much more than expected. We peeled our jackets off before we started the first hole.

Mark sighed dramatically at the inconvenience of holding his jacket.

"We'll pass them," Claire suggested, reaching for the jackets. "It'll be fine. You guys go first."

Michael motioned Mark up to the black dot where a tee should be. Mark set his ball down and spent so long lining up his initial shot, Claire started up a conversation with me.

"I've been thinking of putting a few fall plants in the front now that the summer ones are done. I don't usually change them over, but I think it'd make for some nice pictures."

Halfway through her list of possibilities, Mark gave the ball a decisive swing. Claire's voice faded as she watched the ball bounce off the red brick boundary to squeeze between two concrete barriers. Mark chuckled triumphantly and pointed his club at the ball. "Top that one, Mike."

Michael replaced Mark at the starting point, taking just as much time to figure out his best approach. He tried a more complicated shot, ricocheting off one of the concrete circles to end up about even with Mark's ball.

Mark backed up a few steps as he turned to me. "Xan, you ready?" He probably remembered some of my past plays posing a danger to the safety of the group.

I was never ready for golf except to enjoy chatting with Claire while the men battled it out. I placed my ball with accuracy but paid little attention to what else I was doing. The layout of the green told me nothing. I knew two options from watching Michael and Mark, but my aim wasn't sharp enough to try them. My sloppy technique sent the ball flying past the concrete shapes into the far corner of the green, no closer to the hole than when I'd started.

Claire handed the jackets to me and took her turn, playing as casually as I did. She lined up her shot in seconds and swung the club as soon as she could while still trying. The ball bounced several times between the brick boundary and a concrete circle. It stopped where a solid triangle blocked any clear shot to the hole.

Mark dropped his head into his hand with a slapping sound. "I've told you how to pick a good starting shot, Claire."

Claire shrugged and took the jackets from me. "I can't get the hang of it. It's all right."

Mark took up his solemn stance at his ball and managed to pass it through another close-fitting channel to within inches of the hole. He stepped off the green while Michael followed up. Michael spent half a minute scouting his next move. It paid off as usual, getting the ball close enough to the hole for a stiff wind to blow it in.

They tied for the hole, and the competition ramped up from there. Every time Michael took his turn, Mark lingered a few feet away, his club propped in front of him with his hands folded on top. He'd offer advice like, "Go for the angle shot, Mike. You can make it."

Although humor warmed and shook Mark's voice, Michael would leave his ball to walk over to see beyond the rock pile or miniature water fountain blocking his view. He'd laugh and return to his ball. "It won't fit between there and the wall. What do you want me to do? Pop the ball over it?"

"Why not? If you get enough momentum, you can bank it off the bricks and launch it right over."

"I'll stick with the safe shot, thank you."

Michael would work himself back into the perfect position and take his time gauging how much power to use on the swing.

Claire and I moved our conversation from gardening to home improvement to television shows. Between subjects, I watched Michael and Mark. Michael succeeded in every way that I failed. His patience allowed him to spend adequate time on every shot, ducking his head for a closer look at a straight line or considering a bank shot off the bricks. He saw opportunities I never would've seen, narrow gaps and available angles.

Mark kept trying to chip away at Michael's focus. "It's in a good spot, Mike."

Michael's tone barely registered any preoccupation with his father's conversation. "The trick is not to shoot it past the hole and down the ramp."

"You shouldn't overdo it, then."

"No."

Michael's eyes never left the ball, finally letting the club knock it exactly where he wanted it to go. It careened off the bricks, sailed between the smirking tiger's crouching legs, and sank neatly into the hole, saving Michael the trouble of navigating the slope beyond it.

"Well done, Michael," Claire said. She glanced at Mark with a knowing smile. "You can't distract him, dear."

"I can," Mark insisted, thrilled by the concept. He struck the end of his club on the path. "It can be done."

I watched Michael's parents, too. He wasn't so unlike them that they weren't some indication of the kind of relationship he was after. Through their arrival, several meals, and golfing, I missed little that passed between them. There was so much unsaid shining in their eyes and lurking in the tilt of their lips, but they understood it all. Sometimes I thought they only spoke for everyone else's benefit.

"Where's your sense of adventure?" Mark teased his wife.

"I left it in the Grand Tetons rock climbing with you." Claire winked at me, the same coy, reassuring gesture Michael used from time to time.

"We should go back there and get it. We've never been to Washington state. We can swing by the Tetons on the way."

"The Pacific Northwest in the winter? I'd rather hit California this time of year."

Michael took the coats from me, and I stepped up to take my turn.

"Take your time, Xan," he said. "We've got all afternoon. You don't have to play so fast."

"We're not all as good as you are."

Before I could finish my cursory assessment of how to get my ball somewhat closer to the hole, a hand landed on my elbow. I glanced up to find Michael passing the bulk of the coats to Claire.

"This shot's not that hard." Michael positioned himself behind my right shoulder and pointed out the best path in front of me. "Look. Aim for the curve in the bricks. If you hit it hard enough, it should get right up next to the hole if not in it."

"How hard is that?"

"Here." Michael stepped almost behind me. He reached his left arm around my waist and wrapped both of his hands around mine on the club handle. "Take a couple of practice swings next to the ball."

I took a small step forward, and Michael moved with me. Holding the club a few inches past the ball, I swung it about as hard as I'd been planning to.

"Whoa," Michael laughed. "It's that kind of swing that sends my dad diving behind the bushes."

I laughed at myself and tried a few slower swings.

"That one," Michael said. "Straight and sure, but not too hard."

We moved back into position with Michael's hands guiding mine. I lined up the ball and tried to swing with the same velocity. My self-consciousness and old playing habits gave it a little more energy than I intended. The ball bounced off the curve in the bricks and passed the hole by an inch. It stopped a few feet beyond it beside the barricade.

"Closer," Michael acknowledged. He patted my hands and stepped away.

I reclaimed my place next to Claire, and she walked up to take her turn.

Mark didn't move a muscle. "I'd offer to help Claire, but she doesn't want my advice."

"I take your advice when we're driving. That's more important."

Claire lined up her shot in seconds and swung the club too gently. Her ball stopped between a well-trimmed topiary and a two-foot parrot halfway to the hole.

"What was that?" Mark exclaimed. "Hit it again."

"No, that was my play. Rules are rules, Mark. No favorites."

Mark held up his left hand, his thumb twirling his gold wedding ring in the sunlight. "You've been my favorite for forty-seven years."

Claire laughed good-heartedly, and Mark replaced her on the green. After a lengthy deliberation, he sent his ball straight into the hole, tying Michael for the hole but trailing close behind him for the course.

By the time we finished the white tiger eighteen, Michael was still ahead. Mark groaned but offered Michael a congratulatory handshake. Claire and I had close scores, too, far above the winning one.

Claire sighed as we walked back to the parking lot. "Ah, well. It was Michael's help that pushed you ahead. Next time I'll know to take a few lessons from somebody."

Mark pressed the unlock button on the keyless remote, making the SUV's lights flash. "You beat us at Rummy. Now we're all even."

Claire packed the jackets in the back of the SUV. "But by the end of the weekend, I'll come out ahead."

"How do you figure?"

Claire laid her hand on my arm, her eyes shining above her mischievous smile. "Tomorrow's the day planned for me: wine tasting."

Chapter 17: Jessie

Willa hadn't called. It had only been two days since the blow-up at the diner, but I waited for her phone call more desperately than I'd waited for a call in my life. I checked my phone every hour to make sure I hadn't missed her. When I took a shower or ate at the table with my parents, I hoped that when I got back to my room, I'd find a message from her on my phone, but it didn't happen. She said she'd call, but I wasn't sure she would.

I wasn't proud of myself for telling her what to do, and even though I wanted to be the kind of friend who could call and apologize, I wanted to take Willa at her word. She'd call me.

It wasn't like I didn't have a lot of other things going on. I barely had time to read *Hypocrisy* anymore. My teachers were so busy loading me up with *The Odyssey*, the short stories of Franz Kafka, and numerous interpretations of Harry Potter, they seemed oblivious that I might have something I wanted to read on the side. If I had known about XZA before I signed up for fall classes, I might have taken at least one class that didn't revolve around literature.

It was hard to concentrate on it, though. I kept realizing over and over, as if for the first time, that I'd invited Willa into a sure-fire trap. Hadn't I known it was going to blow up between her and Dick? Hadn't I known I wouldn't be able to hold a decent conversation with her about anything without Dick jumping in?

My fear and guilt got the better of me, and I shoved my homework away to call Willa. It rang a couple of times, my heart pounding as loudly as the ringing on the line. Mid-ring, the call went to voice mail, and my mouth dropped open. She'd rejected my call. I pictured her scrunching her face in disgust when she saw my name on her phone and ending the call before I even got a chance to explain myself.

"Hi, Willa, it's me, Jessie," I babbled, unprepared for the prompt to leave a message. "I guess I just wanted to apologize and, um, see how you were doing. That's, um, that's about it. Call me back. I'd really appreciate it. Thanks."

I hung up feeling stupid. If she wanted to talk, she would've called me already, and she wouldn't have sent me to voice mail. I should've made a joke or something, like it was nice to see her again if only for a couple weeks. Maybe it would've stirred up some sympathy. Now I sounded pathetic.

The phone rang in my hand. The screen said *Willa*. I answered it immediately. "Hello?"

"Hey, kiddo." Willa sounded casual, almost chipper. "Sorry I didn't take your call. I was in the middle of talking to Frank. Whatcha up to?"

Willa's voice sounded better than I wanted to admit. We were still friends. I tried to be as cool as she was about things. "I was doing some homework, but I wish I was reading *Hypocrisy*. You were right. Things are starting to get creepy. Pastor Ozbeck's got some issues."

"I know, right? You almost don't wanna read it, but you gotta know how it ends."

"Yeah." I paused and jumped into what I wanted to talk about. "How are you? After the diner?"

"You mean the Dick debacle? I'm all right. It's gonna take more than that ignorant hillbilly to get under my skin. He didn't take it out on you, did he?"

"No," I lied. Dick had ranted in the diner for an hour, barely comforted by the fact he'd pushed me into siding with him. He ranted in the truck after we left, cut off an old lady with a handicapped license plate, and flipped off somebody else who honked at us. I liked Willa's carefree attitude better than my hurt feelings, and I wished I could forget what happened. "I'm really sorry I stood up for him. I feel terrible about it."

"Ah, whatever. Apology accepted. It's not like it's the worst thing that's ever happened to me."

Somehow, her forgiveness made me feel worse. I didn't agree with my choices, and I didn't want Willa pretending she was okay with them, either. "I think the next time we get together, we shouldn't include Dick, though."

"Good idea. Then we can really talk. You should come by the laundromat some night and talk to me."

I cringed, although I was a little intrigued. I didn't know who I wanted to avoid more, the other employees or the customers. "I don't know. Maybe I will."

"Are you scared?"

"Yeah. A little. Laundromats always seemed kinda dirty and skeezy to me."

"They're not dangerous."

"Wait – dangerous? I didn't know that was an option."

"*Not* dangerous," Willa interjected.

"Are you talking about the people who come in or the people you work with?"

"All of them. Okay, most of them. But there's usually only one lady working with me in the evening, and the customers are doing their own thing. You'd be fine. It'd be entertaining."

"Entertaining how?"

"Sometimes I get hit on. Sometimes it's cool, sometimes it's not."

"When is it ever cool to get hit on in a laundromat?"

"That's what makes it fun. It's like a lottery. Out there in the regular world, there's like one attractive person for every fifty people or so. In there, it's like one in a hundred, but they're really hot."

"Are you thinking of leaving Frank?"

"No. Hell no. All I'm saying is if I'm going to be hit on, let the guy have all his teeth. Is that so much to ask?"

I laughed a little. "What's the lady like who works with you?"

"She's a mess. More like a train wreck, actually. Her hair is never combed or brushed. She has these big, crazy eyes. She always brings a book to read, but it's always something weird that I've never heard of. Or she reads trashy magazines. She dresses the way my grandma would if she was homeless. You gotta stop by. I can't do these people justice."

Only Willa could make me laugh that hard. "Maybe I will. It'd be crazy not to go."

"Cool. You know which laundromat it is, right? Suds on Lincoln Way."

"I'll write it down." I picked up a pen and dug out a notepad my mom had given me with a border of flowers and stars. I scribbled a note. *Suds on Lincoln Way – Willa. Evenings.* "How late are you there?"

"'Til about ten. Don't come too late 'cause I have to close up."

"I won't."

"The owner takes this ridiculously long dinner break about six. That's always a good time."

6, I wrote. "I don't have class on Fridays."

"Perfect. The Friday night freak show. This week's episode will feature the usual 'I don't want to do laundry on a Friday night' special with a light twist of 'How you doing, baby doll?'"

"Is that how they talk to you?"

"Yeah. That's the guys talking to me." Willa lowered her voice. "'How you doing, sweet thing? Why don't you smile for me? That's it. That's right. How long you work here, baby?'" She slipped into her own voice again. "That's always better than the guys who try to badger me to death, the ones who keep asking me out. 'Why won't you go out with me?' 'I have a boyfriend.' 'Oh. Why won't you go out with me?' 'My boyfriend.' Like they don't understand what that means. I'm taken. I have somebody I like. Thank you. Move along. Have a nice day."

"That sounds crazy."

I didn't know what else to say. I'd never understood Willa's ability to attract male attention. When she was a student, we'd gone to a small Christmas party for the English department since we knew most of the professors. Dick had broken up with me the week before because I wanted him to spend more time with me and a little less goofing off with his friends. I wore one of the nicest skirts I had. Very few members of the faculty were dressed better than I was, and the rest of them made me look stylish.

Willa showed up in a khaki jumper with her hair in two low pigtails. We sat on cold metal folding chairs in a corner of the room sipping fruit punch from clear plastic cups. We barely made eye contact with anybody else most of the party, and several guys still found their way over to Willa. They said hi to me, but they were only interested in getting to know her. She had just started dating Frank, so she was polite without flirting. She seemed to take it in stride, but I thought the endless stream of suitors was a sign the world naturally favored Willa. If I knew why and thought there was the smallest chance I could duplicate it, I'd try. As it was, I was stuck in the "I like you," "Don't call me," "I'm here again" cycle with Dick.

Willa spoke up through the phone. "It'll be nice to see you and be able to talk this time."

"Yeah." I felt one apology wasn't enough, even if she did accept it. "I'm sorry about that."

"Don't worry about it. Two comments from my coworker Friday night, and we might be even. I'm excited to hear what kind of batshit stuff she'll come up with to say to you."

"What's your boss like? About the same?"

"A little slimy but not too bad. His hair's kind of greasy, but he gets hit on all the time. It's not as obvious as when it happens to me, but I can tell. I'm asking the customer if she needs assistance, and she's looking past me at him with this little smile on her face. I'm always petrified when I have to go into his office for something I'm gonna open the door and find him half naked with somebody. I could be eighty before that image leaves my head."

"Is he married?"

"No, he's divorced. I always say there are at least two women in this town with discerning taste, me and his ex. We are not interested."

"You can count me in there, too. Greasy's not really my thing."

Willa hesitated, but any bad remarks she wanted to make about Dick she didn't say. "Unfortunately, if you were looking for eye candy at the laundromat, he's the closest thing we have to a man around here. There's this young guy I have to work mornings with sometimes. All he wants to do is play bloody knuckles."

I scrunched up my face. "What's that?"

"Pretty much what it sounds like. You ram your fists at each other and try to dodge the other person's hand. There was a two-week period I had to work with him because the lady who works mornings hurt her ankle and couldn't come in. I'm kind of glad we weren't hanging out then because my hands looked like shit. Frank wanted to kill him. It looked like I had leprosy."

"That's disgusting."

"And painful. His knuckle-ramming skills are about all he's got going for him, so at least he's good at something."

I put my pen down and taped my note to the calendar.

"His brother's an ER nurse. If you want some fucked up stories, he's your guy."

"No, thanks."

"I don't blame you. There's some stuff you don't wanna know about the human body."

"Definitely."

"So I'll look out for you Friday night. You should bring some laundry in case my boss sees you."

"Okay."

"The prices aren't too bad, so at least you're getting a good deal. Of course, you could always complain that the washer shredded your stuff, and I could give you a refund. That would involve my boss, so you'd get an extra good look at his hair."

I covered my eyes and groaned. "No, thanks."

"Yeah. I'd pay money to avoid him, too. I'll see you on Friday."

"Yeah."

I hung up, feeling much better this time as I hit the red button. My textbook gaped open on the desk, and I didn't want to look at it anymore. I left my phone beside it and pulled *Hypocrisy* out from under my pillow. Talking to Willa had given me a huge relief, and I felt I deserved an even longer break from studying. I stretched out on the bed and flipped the book open to my bookmark.

Lourdes poked her head into Pastor Ozbeck's office. "You called me?"

"Yes." He motioned a broad, flat hand at the empty seat across from him. "Sit down."

Lourdes sensed trouble in Pastor Ozbeck's warm but solemn tone. She sat down across the desk from him. "I'm sorry if I asked too many questions about Mrs. Barrett not being here. I'll try not to be so nosy from now on. I'm sure it's none of my business."

"It's not about that."

Pastor Ozbeck's eyes wandered over Lourdes, searching her hair, which she had pulled into tight, secure pigtails that morning. He studied her blouse and the modest but popular knee length of her skirt.

Lourdes smoothed the fabric of it, feeling slightly uncomfortable at the extra attention. "Am I not dressed nice enough? Mom said I shouldn't wear jeans to church, even if I'm helping you out during the week."

"You're dressed fine. I only wondered…" Pastor Ozbeck shifted his focus past Lourdes. "Would you mind closing the door?"

"There's no one else here." Lourdes stood up despite her statement of fact and closed the door as she'd been asked.

"You've mentioned you have a boyfriend."

"Yes." Lourdes sat down in the chair.

"What's his name?"

"Reese."

"Is he in your grade?"

"Yes. We met in school last year."

Pastor Ozbeck stroked his chin, a remarkably weak chin with so little definition, it was hard to tell if it had any bones in it at all. "As your pastor, let me ask you a delicate question. Are you saving yourself for marriage?"

"Absolutely."

"Has he said he'll wait for you?"

"Yes."

"And you're sure you will not waver?"

"Yes, sir. I know what'll happen to me if I don't."

"What is that?"

"I'll go straight to hell. Mom and Dad already told me."

Pastor Ozbeck adjusted his position in his chair. "I need you to do another kind of favor for me."

"What do you need?"

"You've done a good job helping me learn the congregation. You've done everything I asked you to. Now I need you to keep me company in a little more personal way."

"Do you mean at your house?"

"No, here at the church. I get so lonely, you know. I'm not married as Pastor Klein was. I have no children to care for or play with."

"You can get married as a pastor. It's priests that can't."

Pastor Ozbeck nodded, the motions shaky and impatient. "I might, but for now, there's something you can do for me I would appreciate very much."

Lourdes waited, the clock hands on the wall ticking away the hollow seconds.

"I am in need of female companionship."

Lourdes merely blinked at him, not understanding.

"Are you naïve, child? I'm asking you to have sex with me."

Lourdes crossed her legs without thinking. "Pastor Ozbeck, I told you. I'll go to hell if I do that."

Pastor Ozbeck managed a crooked smile. "Would you? I speak for God. He asked me to speak for him. If you did something I told you to do, surely you wouldn't be punished for it."

"Mom told me to guard my virginity with my life."

"Wisely so, but I am not just any man, Lourdes. You know that, don't you? God chose me to work for him, and I have chosen you to help serve me."

Lourdes found herself shaking her head. "I don't think it's right. It's not like sorting pamphlets or telling you about the people pictured in the church directory."

"No, it's not. It's a special request I'm making of you because you're a very special young woman.

You're not like other girls your age, and you know that. You're kind and generous and honest. You care about other people's needs."

"I don't understand why Mom wouldn't have told me there was an exception."

"Not all girls are chosen. She didn't want you to feel disappointed if you weren't."

Lourdes pushed the new logic into her mind, forcing it to fit where its odd shape fought against her. "Mom always does have my best interests at heart."

"Yes, she does." Pastor Ozbeck stood up. "And I know that because you care about your classmates and the other girls in the church, you won't tell anyone about my special request."

Lourdes felt the full weight of her dread in her chest. The thin muscles tightened around her ribs, constricting her like a snake. "No, I wouldn't tell."

"You *won't* tell," Pastor Ozbeck corrected with a subtle change in emphasis.

Lourdes watched him coming toward her. "I won't tell."

Knocks echoed against my bedroom door, and I jumped.

"Dinner in five," Dad said.

"Thanks," I said, trying to catch my breath. I was pretty sure I'd just lost my appetite.

Chapter 18: Xan

I stood in the master bathroom, looking at the pool of purple satin in my hands. Stacey had talked me into it, a thin, flimsy chemise outlined in white lace. I hesitated because I hadn't done anything special for Michael in a long time. I wanted to think we were still spontaneous, but some of that had faded, probably because we were so impulsive in the beginning. Running off to a hotel in a city foreign to both of us would have been a hard pace to maintain.

I wasn't sure exactly what I was afraid of. Michael rarely turned me down for sex, although it did happen when work exhausted him. Even though my body was changing and had changed since the night we met, I wasn't ashamed of it. I'd never tried to hide my imperfections from him. I knew better than that. It never worked for anyone, and I had nothing I needed to hide.

Michael's voice reached me from the bedroom. "I like having my parents down, but they're almost like borrowing kids for the weekend. I hope I have half that much energy when I get to their age."

I called back to him. "Are you that worn out?"

"No. All the wine we drank last night and the night before made me sleep like a baby."

I opened up the chemise and slid the smooth, silky tube down over my head. The thin straps settled onto my shoulders, and I adjusted the length of it to rest over my thighs. It draped well, the hem rising in two gentle points on either hip to show off a few extra inches of skin. Mine was pale as usual, having spent most of the summer indoors working on the computer.

Michael continued to sum up the weekend. "I'd call it a success. Dad was placated by the mini-golf. Mom went home with new bottles of wine to entertain with."

"I'm almost concerned about the amount of wine they can put away." I would've worried if I didn't remember the amount of vodka Uncle Grigori could tolerate. He only drank when he was happy, at parties, during holidays, or any occasion he deemed reason to celebrate. He'd brought a bottle of Popov to the small dinner party my parents hosted when I graduated from elementary school. He brought a flask to the funeral of a cousin who died too early, claiming the world was better without his endless carousing and shady business ideas. My mother had refused the Popov, but she had a small sip with him then, agreeing quietly before she went back to giving her condolences to the family.

Before Michael moved in, I spent Uncle Grigori's birthday alone one year. I drove to the cemetery and poured out a bottle of Eristoff for him, quite an improvement from the Popov, as disgusting as it was cheap. I thought about taking a few sips for myself, but it didn't seem appropriate. I never felt like drinking when I thought about him. Alcohol was for enjoyment, not for drowning one's sorrows. It would've been inexcusable to break his rule over his own grave.

When my mother and I visited him during his depression, she'd found a single bottle of vodka in the cabinets. He usually had an entire selection, half of it opened and enjoyed. This one was unopened, and he expressed no interest in having it opened.

My mother carried it into the bedroom doorway while I sat with Uncle Grigori on the bed. She held it up, interrupting our conversation. "You haven't even cracked the seal. Let's open it up for old times' sake. Those were good times we used to share a drink or two. Come on. I'll have a shot with you."

Being twelve, I studied her strangely, wondering who would drink in the middle of a rainy afternoon and why. All I knew was that Uncle Grigori never drank when he was sad, which was rare, or angry, which was usually the result of creative defensive driving, arguing politics, or having one of his historical articles turned down for publication. I was about to explain this to her when Uncle Grigori answered her.

"I don't want it."

My mother held the bottle up in front of her and read the label. "It's good. It's not the well stuff you used to drink."

I knew now, at forty-three, my mother was trying to cheer him up. She wanted a sign he was okay and he would pull himself out of this. Did she know he was losing his will to go on? I felt his pain, but I thought he'd come out of it. I'd never known him to stay in a bad mood longer than a few days.

"I'll get some shot glasses," my mother pressed on.

"Don't do that, Anna. Leave me alone."

My mother left the doorway. Uncle Grigori and I sat in silence. I couldn't remember what we were talking about when my mother came in. We talked about everything but his feelings and the woman who caused them. I told him about school and the extracurricular activities my mother was forcing me into. They were either school related and about to expose me to a world of mind-numbing pseudo-intellectuals, or they were more feminine than I cared to be as I grew out of my tomboy years: ballet, gymnastics, or sewing lessons, my choice. Gymnastics seemed the obvious decision and lasted a short six weeks.

I began to babble about the recent weather fluctuations. "It's been going back and forth between hot and cold a lot. I wore a t-shirt one day, and I needed my coat on the next. It rains off and on no matter what the temperature's doing."

Uncle Grigori barely looked at me. "I hadn't noticed."

My mother broke into the conversation as she entered the room. "Of course not. How could you? You have the shades down every time we come over."

Uncle Grigori shifted away from her. "I don't want to see the world."

I saw that my mother had carried the bottle of vodka back in along with two shot glasses. She held one out to Uncle Grigori, and I gave her a harder look than before. How dare she? Her disrespect for him cut me to the bone. Uncle Grigori refused to look at her or speak. She finally gave up, opened the bottle on the dresser top, and poured herself a shot. She threw it down her throat in one swift motion, and I wasn't sure I'd ever seen her do that.

My mother held the empty shot glass for a moment, and I wondered if she was going to take another. By the far-off look in her eyes, she considered it but probably remembered she was responsible for driving me home. She set the shot glass on the dresser. "You need to go outside."

"I do leave. I've been to work. I've been to the library."

"I mean you need to be out there among people. Do something fun. Take up a new hobby. You'll meet someone new."

Uncle Grigori looked at her now. It wasn't accusing. It wasn't even a warning stare. It was sadness. He was begging her to understand and stop pressing him.

My mother ignored this. "You need adult company. You need more than a twelve-year-old girl to talk to a few times a week."

Uncle Grigori clenched his face, bringing his features in toward the middle. His voice became gruff, a growl. "I talk to people, Anna."

"Who do you talk to? You've got me, and that's it. I'm the only one in the family you talk to. There's almost nobody left."

This time he warned her. His eyes were so sharp. "Xan might be the last one I talk to."

I felt my name change the air. I was leverage now. *Do as I say, or I'll only talk to your daughter.* It didn't bother me then except for the glare in my mother's eyes, a shade darker than Uncle Grigori's mottled grey. They flashed with resentment for our friendship and his new lifestyle.

"Become a recluse," my mother dared him. "See if I care."

"You don't know what it's like."

If the tension between them hadn't been so thick, I would've interjected to side with him. As it was, all I could do was watch and learn.

My mother scoffed at him. "I don't know what it's like to hurt?"

Uncle Grigori gave a slight pause. He must've known his words would sting, but he proceeded anyway. "What it's like to love before you lose."

My mother's gaze burned holes in him before she turned away to screw the cap back on the bottle. Her stiff jaw ground her words down and shot them through the narrow gap in her lips. "Make sure you finish this, or it'll go bad."

"Vodka doesn't go bad. You can't trick me like that."

"Come, daughter."

Once again, I was confused. It took me years to figure out why she didn't use my name. It was the same reason he made a point of using it repeatedly in the next few minutes.

He had given it to me. She gave me life, but he gave me a name.

Uncle Grigori pulled me into a hug, almost moving me into his lap. "Goodbye, Xan. I'll see you soon. Keep an eye on the weather for me, Xan, and keep doing so well in school. It makes your uncle very proud. I love you, Xan."

"I love you, Uncle Grigori."

I blinked, and the scene vanished. I was barely aware of my reflection in the mirror, something I would've been studying if I hadn't been gripped by such a strong memory. I had said *I love you* so freely, without apprehension or hesitation. It had been possible once. I'd merely forgotten.

Why were these memories coming to me now, months after the anniversary of his death? I thought about him often, but not like this, not in pictures and snippets of dialog.

Michael called out to me, safe and secure in the present world. "Are you falling asleep in there?"

I pushed myself into action, briefly rearranging my hair. "No. I'll be right out." I pulled my toothbrush out of the holder and quickly brushed my teeth. "How about you? Are you asleep yet?"

"Nope. Just reading."

"What are you reading?"

"One of those former-cop, recent-widower-gets-the-killer kind of deals."

"Not my thing," I said as Michael added, "I know they're not your thing."

I rinsed my toothbrush and replaced it in the holder. I started paying more attention to my reflection. I still had my makeup on. The mascara was starting to smudge across my bottom eyelids, and I ran my fingertip under each one to wipe them clean. "Are you enjoying it?"

"It's not bad. The characters are surprisingly fresh. The city's kind of a character in itself. I care what happens. I'm interested in how it turns out."

I liked the way Michael's voice lowered and slowed when he talked about books. He sounded careful and deliberate in his descriptions. He also just sounded sexy. "Are you dedicated to reading more tonight?"

"Not necessarily. Why?"

I stepped back from the mirror, glancing at it to make sure the chemise flattered me as well as I remembered. The loose fabric bunched at the waist, forgiving any weight I'd gained entertaining over the weekend. So much of my legs was showing, my wider-than-average hips looked shapely and inviting. I walked into the bedroom. Michael sat up in bed, a few pillows crammed behind him for support. The thick comforter covered him to the waist, leaving his bare chest and arms exposed. He was wearing his new reading glasses, a pair of narrow black rectangles stretching across his face. The book yawned open in his hand where it rested on his knees, but his focus was entirely on me.

I was a very lucky woman.

"You did get something," Michael murmured. Without looking away, he reached for his bookmark and slid it between the pages before he closed them.

"I did."

"You look amazing."

"So do you."

It was a credit to Michael how good he looked at the end of a long day. His hair curled against the pillows behind him. Even though the excitement of the day had worn him out, his eyes shone. And Stacey was right. No matter what my friends tried, I was the one Michael wanted. He looked at me with the same intensity he had those first six months he drove out one night at a time to see me.

I moved toward him and crawled onto the bed. Michael took his glasses off and set them on the bedside table. He sat up to meet me, but I pushed him down against the pillows in the same way I'd guided him onto his back ten years before. I eased my chest down against his and kissed him with more reservation than he probably expected, cruelly teasing the fire out of him.

The paperback landed on the carpet with a slap. Michael rolled me on my side, lying above me against the mountain of pillows. His eyes flashed as he gained the upper hand. He held me close and moved his lips definitively against mine. Michael's hand swept over the satin of the chemise, running its softness against my awakening skin until I had no choice but to give in and return the hunger. Michael's fingers slid down my thigh and followed its warmth up under the chemise. I pressed my hips forward, the thick comforter between us keeping me from meeting Michael's body. My hand trailed down his side, smooth skin all the way to his hip. My other fingers flexed in his hair, the long, thick waves other women only dreamed of touching.

Michael's persistent hand pushed the skirt of the chemise up toward my waist. I pulled the comforter away from him as much as I could, and he caught on immediately. Michael climbed over the covers, and I met him on my back. His hair dusted my chest as he ducked his head to kiss my breasts through the chemise. It was a different feeling than I was used to, so close but thinly separated. Michael tugged at the neckline, but it barely moved. He covered what skin he could in open kisses, eventually bringing his mouth back up to mine.

I rubbed my shin against his calf, enjoying what skin to skin contact I could find. Michael held me tighter, his hand brushing the inside of my thigh as he guided himself toward me. I kissed him harder and arched my back in pleasure as the tip of him settled into place. I pulled my hips back as he slid in so he could only enter partway, but it still felt good enough to make my body shiver. I relaxed my hips and let Michael fill me deeper. In the slow, smooth repetition of retreating and returning, all I could focus on was Michael. The weight of him around me. The subtle changes in speed and depth. The dozen scents I caught as we moved – the creamy scent of his conditioner, the soap smell in his stubble, the muddled heat of his breath. When I came, I wrapped my legs around Michael's to keep him close to me. Michael's hard breathing reminded me we were in this together, that I gave as good as I got. I came again, trying as usual to count the waves of spasms in my body, but it was too easy to lose the number as they blended together in fading trickles.

Michael slowed his thrusts as he came, and I tried to match his rhythm with mine. He laid his chest against mine and kissed the space behind my ear. He gradually stopped moving until he rested against me. He nudged his slick temple against mine, his chest filling with heavy breaths against my ribs. After a moment, he shifted his weight to lie next to me. He trailed his lips along my jawbone to my neck. It was another few minutes before he could speak. "You should go shopping more often."

I chuckled. I could agree with that. The annoyance of lingerie was its allure, hiding what was often exposed and keeping our bodies from touching as much as we were used to. My mind, free from all of its worries and preoccupations, skipped aimlessly across my shopping trip with Stacey. "Stacey said you were the perfect man while we were out."

Michael's voice purred beside my ear. "What was the context?"

"I don't know."

"Did she say I was the perfect man for you or just perfect in general?"

"In general, as a statement of fact."

Michael kissed my shoulder. "I'll be interested to hear what your friends think of my friends."

I swirled a wave of Michael's hair around my finger, watching the unique way it curled around itself with little prompting. "No offense, but I wouldn't expect to hear the word 'perfect' get tossed around."

"I'd be happy if no arguments erupted and no one got drunk enough to pass out on the lawn."

"Is there a chance of either of those happening?"

Michael leaned back from me and shrugged. "You know Nick and John. They can get pretty opinionated when it comes to what they do. As for the drinking, we're introducing four single strangers to each other. It could get ugly with or without the wine."

I rested my hand on Michael's arm. "Better lie and say we only have one bottle."

"Good idea." Michael sat up, patting my leg as he got off the bed. He walked into the bathroom and ran the faucet.

When the water stopped, I said, "I think it'll go well as long as all desperation is kept to a minimum."

Michael poked his head out of the bathroom, his toothbrush in hand. "Whose desperation?"

"All of them. It's easy to pick on Stacey, but Marcy's obviously looking to jump ship."

"She hasn't broken up with the milkman?" Michael disappeared back into the bathroom.

"Not that I know of. She would've told me if she did." I got up off the bed and peeled off the chemise. I dropped it into the laundry basket.

"Please tell me she's not really going to wait until Nick and John drive down."

"She might. She likes the drama. She likes sharing outrageous stories with people about what she puts herself through."

I joined Michael in the bathroom to get ready for bed. By the time I was ready to climb under the covers, Michael was straightening them out from our impromptu rendezvous. I sat on my half of the mattress and finished arranging the far corner of my covers. Michael picked his book up off the floor and set it on the stack on the bedside table. He got into bed with me and turned off the light.

I settled my head onto my pillow, my mind stuck on the subject of our friends. "I keep thinking Marcy wants me to put half her life into one of my books."

Michael chuckled. He adjusted his covers and position next to me. "Would she get her life in order if you finally did and she saw it for what it was?"

I snorted. "Of course not. She'd want a sequel."

Michael leaned over and kissed me. "I think you're right, and it scares me. Good night, Xan. I love you."

"Good night, Michael."

He rested his head on his pillow, and I felt the L word hanging in the room like a heavy echo. It was put out there to be answered and echoed back. But I couldn't. Michael lay still as his breathing slowed and evened out. Did he feel it too, or had he learned to accept the nagging silence? Had he given up on ever hearing that from me?

Chapter 19: Jessie

I dug through the dirty laundry crammed into my hamper. I wasn't going to parade my underwear through the laundromat, and I was pretty sure I didn't want to trust my parents' good towels to its overused machines. I picked out my worn jeans and sweaters, and threw them into a small black garbage bag. I tucked *Hypocrisy* into my purse in case Willa got too busy to talk to and I got stuck doing laundry without her. There could be other customers. Her boss could call her into his office for something. I was going in prepared.

I lugged the surprisingly heavy bag out of my room. My parents sat on the couch, happily oblivious to Dick's near disasters on its upholstery. A *Seinfeld* rerun played on the television. I recognized the episode, so I knew my parents had seen it a thousand times. I didn't understand why they thought it was funny, but they laughed at every joke and sometimes in between. They often made a game of asking ludicrous questions about the characters as a running gag between them.

"Do you think George is gay?"

"Why didn't Elaine and Kramer ever get together?"

"Do you think Jerry ever got tired of wearing those tight jeans?"

"What ever happened to Mr. Peterman?"

"Do you think George's dad is gay?"

They weren't trading questions now. They were chuckling their way through an Elaine and Jerry conversation. Mom turned first and saw me behind them. "Are you going to meet with Willa?"

"Yeah."

"You can have her over here, you know. You don't have to do your laundry at a laundromat to talk to her."

I walked past the couch and dropped my bag of clothes on the carpet to put on my shoes. "It's okay. She's really busy, and she wants me to meet her crazy coworker, so it's not a big deal."

Dad spoke up with solemn concern straight from an after-school special. "Do you need any quarters?"

I cringed. I had friends in middle school whose parents wouldn't have lent them a nickel to buy food. Here I was in college, and my parents were trying to anticipate my smallest needs. "I've got some."

I wiggled my feet into my shoes and faced my parents directly for the first time since I came in the room.

They'd gone back to chuckling at the TV, but I wished they would focus on me, *really* focus on me. I had no job, and they never encouraged me to get one. I was dating somebody they hated, and they pretended he didn't exist. Spending money to do laundry to talk to a friend was ridiculous, but they didn't push me to find a better way. They just accepted it. If I wanted to live like this for the rest of my life, they'd let me, and it bothered me. I was tired of being treated so passively. It would've been condescending except they didn't show any preference one way or the other.

I picked up my lumpy garbage bag. "I'll see you later."

My parents waved, and I pulled my keys out of my purse. I stepped out into the sunlight, knowing it wouldn't last too much longer. I walked to my car and dropped my clothes in the passenger seat.

The drive to Lincoln Way took less than five minutes. I turned onto it and looked for the sign for Suds. Past the Arby's ten-gallon hat and a huge glazed donut for a local donut shop stood the light-up overflowing wash basin for Suds. I pulled into the small parking lot. A couple of cars sat there, including the same maroon two-door Willa was driving when we met. I grabbed my bag of laundry and headed inside.

Noise assaulted me from every angle. Several machines were running, banging and buzzing as they turned. A talent show played through squeaky speakers on the television in the far left corner of the room, bolted to the wall near the ceiling. A mom and her two kids were pointing to it from molded orange chairs, having a light-hearted argument about who was the better dancer. A young woman stood behind them at a folding station, tapping her foot to the music in her ear buds. Behind the customer service counter to my right, Willa dropped bored fingernails onto the surface one by one. The counter looked like wood, but the laminate was peeling at the edges. Between her and the office door beyond her, her greasy boss and a frizzy-haired coworker were carrying on a barely civil conversation.

The boss's black hair was slicked back so smoothly, I was surprised it had any volume to it at all. By the laws of physics, it should've been plastered to his scalp like an old swimming cap. "You. Be nicer to the customers, or you're gone."

This had to be the coworker Willa had told me about. She was dressed in an unbelievably eclectic outfit, even by Willa's standards. I stepped closer for a better look. The woman was wearing a long-sleeved shirt with thin stripes in a multitude of colors – blue, purple, white, green, black. She wore a brown corduroy vest over it, which wouldn't have been so bad except for the childlike animals embroidered on it – lions, giraffes, an ostrich. "I don't give them lip. They give me lip. All I have are quarters. I don't have the secret to life back here."

Willa, looking tame in a shiny gold blouse, stopped tapping her fingernails on the counter. "Not in front of the customers," she advised them over her shoulder. To me, she said, "Can I help you?"

I walked forward, trying not to laugh and ruin our charade. "Maybe. I have this small load here."

"Okay." When I got close enough, Willa whispered, "Help me. Help me escape." She smiled at me.

The boss offered me a polite but brief "Good evening" and closed himself in his office. Willa's coworker came out from behind the counter, where I could see the lower half of her. She was wearing a long, calf-length skirt with tiny blue flowers on a white cotton background. At the ankles, I could see a few inches of pale blue jeans above her sparkling red glitter ballet flats.

Willa glanced at the office door to make sure her boss was locked away. "Hey, Marlene. What'd you bring to read tonight?"

The woman turned her focus from the customers in the far half of the laundromat. "National Enquirer and a book about frogs, the life cycle of frogs."

Willa raised her palm in a smooth gesture towards Marlene. "What'd I tell you?"

I nodded. Marlene defied all explanations.

"Hey, Marlene. Come meet my friend Jessie."

Marlene waved to me. "Hi, Jessie. I'm Marlene."

I didn't know what to say. I hadn't expected to be formally

introduced. "Hi."

"Do you like animals?"

"Sure."

"I read a lot of books about animals." Marlene, apparently done talking to me, shuffled on toward the customers.

"Liar," Willa accused under her breath. "Last week it was aliens. The week before that, it was true accounts of ghost stories from the Civil War. She changes her interests all the time."

"Do I really have to do my laundry?" I asked.

"Nah. You made it look good, though. I appreciate it."

The office door opened, and the greasy-haired boss emerged with a box of frozen dinner. Willa launched into her spiel. "The laundry carts are back there." She pointed past me. "Most of the machines are open. Please take your laundry out as soon as the machine stops. I can make change for you if you run out of quarters."

The boss ducked into another room marked *Employees Only*.

Willa sighed, her perfect posture slumping. She checked her watch. "There he goes. Two minutes after six. Perfect timing. How are you doing on that book?"

I set my garbage bag of clothes on the counter. "All right. Did you finish it?"

"Almost. It gets so good, Jess. You gotta read faster."

"I'm going as fast as I can. Trust me. I've been blowing off my reading homework to read *Hypocrisy*."

Willa grinned. "How are your grades?"

"They were good. They're dropping now."

"How are your parents taking it?"

"They don't know yet."

"They don't have to know."

My fingers played with the plastic tie holding the bag closed. "I don't know if I want to be in college anymore. I'm barely inching toward a degree. I thought I'd figure out what I want to do by now, but I think all I've figured out is that I don't want to be in school. I don't want to live with my parents. They treat me like I'm a kid, but I can't really blame them. I rely on them more than I should."

"My couch is open if you want to crash with us."

It sounded tempting, but I had to remember that the other half of that "us" was Frank. I didn't want to intrude on whatever they had going on. I shook my head, even though if Willa lived by herself, I'd try it out to see if it could work. It was easy to imagine the freedom I could have staying with Willa. I could read whatever I wanted, stay up late joking about people we used to know, and watch current shows my parents hadn't heard of. I could spread out beyond one room's worth of space and feel like an adult for a change. "I don't want to mess things up for you and Frank. He might not even remember me."

"He does. He mostly remembers Dick because he was such a spaz." Willa leaned toward me over the counter. She lowered her voice. "Seriously, though. What the heck do you see in that guy? Why are you still with him?"

I lifted my shoulders in a long, procrastinating shrug. "He's funny. He gives me stuff. He's somebody to go out and do things with."

"So am I."

"But I get to see him around school all the time, and you left."

Willa took a second to answer, but she didn't sound mad. "I guess I'm just surprised. He broke up with you a couple of times, didn't he? After you guys started dating?"

I didn't want to answer that. "Yeah," I said gruffly.

"I remember him really upsetting you more than once, and I'd hoped you'd moved on. It's a total mystery to me why you're toughing it out."

I fiddled with the tie on the garbage bag, twisting it with lazy irritation. "I haven't told this to anybody, but it's been on and off the whole time."

Willa cocked her head and stared at me.

"When the fighting gets really bad, we break up for a couple of weeks, and then we get back together." I felt stupid saying it, but it also felt like a relief to admit it.

"That's messed up. How does that work?"

The relief faded as quickly as it arrived. Willa knew exactly how it worked. "We don't have that much in common. You know that. We try to compromise, but we always get to a point where we can't stand each other. Then either he breaks up with me or I break up with him."

Willa's eyebrows shot up in excitement, interrupting me. "Really? You break up with him?"

"I broke up with him at the beginning of the summer. We were having the same stupid argument for weeks. I couldn't take it anymore."

"I wish I could've been there to see that." Willa clamped her hand over her mouth and lowered it again. "Look, I'm sorry. I'm trying to be polite, but I don't understand the attraction. Why do you take him back? What can possibly be so great about Dick that I don't see?"

"He makes me laugh. He's as directionless in life as I am. He can be supportive when he wants to be, and he's really cute."

Willa made a watery gagging sound in her throat. "First of all, ew, and when does he support anybody? All I've heard him do is tear us down."

"You haven't spent that much time with him."

"And I don't plan to."

The kids erupted into cheers, taunting their mother. "We *told* you we knew who could dance!" They burst into wavy-armed marches of victorious joy.

Willa tapped her fingers on the counter. "I don't understand why you haven't moved on. It sounds like you had plenty of chances for it."

"Move on and do what? Hang out by myself? All of my friends have already graduated, and there's nobody else to talk to. It's easy for you. Guys notice you all the time. They want to be with you. I'm not even on their radar. It's nice having Dick around sometimes whether you believe me or not."

Willa raised a single eyebrow. "Did you just say 'nice'?"

I pulled my hand away from the tie on the bag. "He's familiar. He's more genuine than my parents are when he encourages me to stay in school. He tells me I'm doing a good job with it, which is more than they tell me."

"How many boyfriends did you have before Dick?"

"One."

"Was it serious?"

"Not really. It was only a couple of months. We barely even made out."

Willa propped her elbow on my bag of clothes. "So you're scared of the dating pool. I get it, and I don't blame you. It sucks out there. But to watch you cling to Dick for dear life is depressing."

"Come on, Willa." I leaned toward her and kept my voice down. "He's the only guy I've ever slept with. It's weird to think about finding somebody else."

Willa's face shrunk up like she'd eaten an entire lemon. "We're reaching whole new heights of 'didn't need to know' here. I get it, and no offense, but he can't be any good." She shook her head. "Forget it. I don't wanna talk about it. You gotta think about your future, Jess. Do you honestly think you can have any kind of enjoyable future with Dick?"

I tried to picture it. Someday we'd be thirty, forty, fifty. I couldn't picture anything but Dick lounging on my parents' sofa, one muscle spasm from spilling dark soda all over the light blue cushions. "I don't know. I didn't think we'd be together this long."

"Does it really count as being together if you're not together?"

I shrugged. "It might as well count. I couldn't find anybody else when we weren't together."

"Did Dick?"

The question sunk its claws into me. "I don't know. I never asked him."

Willa stood up straighter. "I mean, when I look at my future with Frank, it's not perfect, but it's not bad. We're not rich. We work crappy jobs with shitty schedules, but we're okay. I can talk to him. I never have to worry he's going to bite my head off over something stupid. I don't think you know what that's like."

The door opened behind me, and a middle-aged couple carried in two huge bags of clothes.

"Welcome to Suds," Willa called over to them.

They ambled up to a row of machines and started opening their bags.

"I've been in bad relationships before," Willa said. "I think a change would be good for you."

I fought the thought of it, looking around for someone I liked and then waiting for him to notice me back. "Dick's not as bad as you think he is. There's a lot worse guys than Dick. You know that's true. Even at school."

"Yeah, but you should be happy. Dick doesn't make you happy."

"He can. You won't give him a chance."

"I might be wrong, but I don't think I am. He's not my problem – or boyfriend – so maybe I don't have any room to talk. If you need a place to stay or a book to read, I can help you. Otherwise, I don't want to talk about this anymore."

Nothing had ever been off limits with Willa. I wanted to be glad the argument was over, but I was hurt that she was cutting me off. "Okay."

Marlene wandered back into view and behind the counter.

Willa's face perked up with a mischievous look. "Hey, Marlene. Are you dating anybody?"

Marlene paused. "Nope."

Willa turned to her, grinning. "What, did you have to think about it? Did you forget?"

"No. I used to go with this boy who'd take me fishing up at Clear Lake."

"Where's that?"

"Out past the highway."

Willa scraped her nails along the counter. "There's, like, a million highways."

"What do you care? You don't fish."

"How do you know?"

"You never talk about it."

"Would you catch anything?"

"Sure. There's catfish and bass and trout all around here."

"Would you eat what you caught?"

"Sure." Marlene folded her arms in their striped sleeves over her corduroy vest. "He'd clean the fish, and I'd help him. We'd load 'em up in the back of the truck and take 'em over to his mom's house and cook 'em up."

"Did he live with his mom?"

"Nope, but she had the biggest grill out of everybody we knew. Sometimes we'd bake 'em or broil 'em, but grilling 'em tasted the best. We got the whole meal cooked right at the same time."

Willa turned to me. "There you go, Jess. If you're bored and looking for something to do, grill up some catfish."

"Oh, yes," Marlene encouraged us. She moved her hands from side to side to illustrate while she talked. "All you need is a little lemon juice and some fresh black pepper. You can roast some red peppers right alongside it. Throw in a salad and some ice cream, and you've got yourself a meal."

Willa dared another question. "Would you make the ice cream?"

"No, but I can. It's a newer ice cream maker, not the old crank ones, but it still tastes good."

Willa returned to facing me, shaking her head in wonder at Marlene.

I widened my eyes to share her disbelief, but I couldn't care less about Marlene's crazy stories. I'd taken Dick's side again without meaning to, and he wasn't even there to make me do it. I wished Marlene had somewhere else to go so I could explain things better, but she lingered behind the counter next to Willa.

Dick had better be worth the stress I was putting on my friendship. He had to be as funny and supportive as I said he was, or Willa might never talk to me again. It was obvious Willa didn't think he was worth it, but I needed Dick to prove me right.

Chapter 20: Xan

Michael's schedule had never been so full. I looked over the list of his appointments, hours of interviews with students eager to talk to him about their work. I envied him more than I could say. Instead of gradually unveiling each author, all I could do was make arbitrary guesses based on their names and Michael's brief notes. It was hard to tell if a senior named Ted was working on post-modern novels or quirky, real experience-based short stories. Self-professed free spirit Mallory could be writing hopelessly romantic poetry or biting, witty chick lit.

"You're bringing samples home, right?" I asked, even though I'd already asked him.

Michael patted his jacket pockets, making sure he had everything. "I promised you I would."

Michael picked up his folder of fliers he'd had printed so the students could find their reviews after he posted them. He reached for the list in my hand, and I regretfully handed it over.

We'd spent all week discussing what we expected to find in these pieces. We were counting on the usual rough, unrefined poetry and long, unfocused novels-in-progress, but somewhere between three and nine o'clock, he would stumble across a few real gems. I couldn't wait to read them, the polished pieces and the scattered efforts. I was just jealous Michael got to peek at them first.

I kissed him a little longer than I usually did when I saw him off without me. He walked out to the garage, and I heard his car rumble out of the driveway.

I hadn't told Michael about my own plans for the day. I picked up the phone in the entry hall and dialed my mother. It rang a few times, and I hoped I wouldn't miss my window of opportunity.

My mother answered as I was preparing a message to leave on the answering machine. "Hello?" She sounded guarded as usual, expecting either me or a telemarketer.

"Hi, Mom."

Now she sounded wary. "How are you?"

"All right. I wondered if you had some time. I wanted to talk about some family business."

"Okay. Your father's at work. You can come now if you want."

"I'll be right there."

I settled the phone into the base. I realized my mother's easy compliance was based on how vague I had been. I expected the real battle to begin when I arrived and uttered the most loaded name in our family's history. I wanted to talk about Uncle Grigori.

My parents' house sat in a quiet but active neighborhood on the far side of town. The same style of 50's efficiency and lack of creativity lined most of the streets. It would've been depressing if the gentle crumbling wasn't alternated with sharp, modern restoration. As I pulled into my parents' driveway, I noticed the neighboring house had finally shed its dated metal overhangs and put up an attractive waist-high fence.

I knocked on the door, and my mother answered in a sweatshirt and pressed slacks. She didn't look noticeably older than the last time I'd seen her, usually a sign that Dad's heart was in decent shape. Streaks and wily strands of silver decorated her nearly black hair. I walked inside, disappointed but not surprised I didn't find anything new. The couch had been given a fresh sage-green slipcover, but I recognized the old bulky form beneath it.

"Do you want something to drink?" My mother closed the door behind me, a sound that made me feel trapped and uneasy.

"No, thank you."

"I was making some bread."

My mother led me into the kitchen. The smallness of the house reminded me why I'd chosen my own. After growing up with so little space, I appreciated spreading out and being able to breathe. There was no place to run or hide here. The rooms were packed tightly together, every smell easily transferred, every atom touching the rest. My mother pulled a clean tea towel out of the drawer and laid it over the ball of dough resting on the counter. She gestured to the small kitchen table, and I sat down across from her. My mother stood up to fill herself a glass of water at the sink and sat down again.

"Family business," she said. She took a sip of water, prolonging the inevitable. "What did you want to talk about?"

I'd gotten myself in the door. I didn't need to mince words now. "Uncle Grigori."

My mother huffed through her teeth. "I thought you were finally ready to admit what your books have done to this family. I should've known better."

I jumped on the change in subject, eager to defend myself. "What my books have done is give me an outlet. They make me part of the solution and not the problem, no matter what you might think. What I'm writing about is important. You can't see it because you've never read them."

"I don't need those kinds of images floating around in my head."

"Is that why you never told me how Uncle Grigori died?"

My mother hesitated. "I don't like to think about it. He spent the last five or six months of his life holed up in his apartment pining over that girl. Nobody even remembers what her name was anymore."

I hadn't thought of her name in years, but it bubbled to the surface without any effort. "Evalisse."

"Whatever."

"Do you blame her for what happened?"

My mother shrugged. She ignored her water, and I wondered if she would've preferred vodka, the other smooth, clear, odorless liquid. "It doesn't matter. She had the right to break up with him if she wanted. I blame him for closing himself away, for never getting help." She blinked, gazing off into space. "It was a long time ago."

"Thirty years this year. I've been thinking a lot about it. Does it still hurt you?"

She looked at me. "Of course. He was my only brother, my only sibling. He took his own life. What do you want me to say?"

"I want to know how he died."

My mother's fingers fidgeted around the base of her water glass, picking at crumbs or loose threads I couldn't see. "No, you don't. It's awful."

I leaned forward. I wanted to take pity on her, but I was unable to silence the decades of bitterness inside of me. "It was awful finding out about his suicide from conversations I overheard around the house. You weren't honest with me when I was thirteen. I hoped you could be honest with me now. I have a right to know what happened to my own uncle."

"He hung himself, Xan."

I cringed, not sure what I was expecting. I pressed ahead. I'd started this conversation. "Where?"

"In the kitchen. Remember how the ceiling had those long beams?" My mother's voice cracked as she raised her hand to run it back and forth along invisible boards. "He paid his rent early. I remember his landlord saying that."

My heart fumbled. "Who found him?"

"Your father. I was afraid to go in. We hadn't visited Grigori in maybe a week. I hadn't heard from him. We didn't take you with us that day. I took your father instead. I knew what might've happened, what he might've done."

I waited, hoping my mother would continue without my prompting her.

Her eyes were glassy. "I couldn't find our key to his apartment. I hoped we wouldn't need it, but we knocked on the door, and there was no answer. Your father still knew how to pick locks from his younger days. That was how we met, remember. But once he got the door open, I couldn't force myself inside. I had so much dread. I started crying, and I told your father, 'We shouldn't go any further. We should call the police.' Your father said if Grigori was dead, family should find him, not them. He went in, and the furthest I got was just inside the door."

My mother paused to take a drink of water. "It was a tiny apartment. One bedroom. It didn't take long to search. The kitchen was in the back, past the dining room and the bedroom. Your father looked sick when he came back to me. He said, 'Grigori's here. We have to call the police.' He was too shocked to call, so I did it for him. I said, 'My brother's killed himself in his apartment.' The police were there in maybe half an hour. Did you know your uncle killed himself in his best suit? We had to find his second best suit to bury him in."

I recovered enough to ask another question. "How did he have an open casket after all that?"

"The funeral home was very good. They covered his neck up and the whole nine yards. I'm sure he was a mess when they got him."

"And there was no note. I thought I heard you say that once."

My mother shook her head slowly. "What need did we have for one? We knew why he did it. That's why we wanted the open casket. We covered up the whole thing as much as we could, not just for you. We told everybody he had a heart condition. It was better to hear 'That's too bad' because of a heart condition than suicide."

"But we were so close, he and I. I wanted to know what happened to him. I was hurt you never told me."

"If I made the wrong choice, I'm sorry, but you were already so affected by his depression. I didn't want to make things worse for you."

Hearing my mother apologize relieved most of my tension. She meant well. She didn't do it to spite me. I'd never considered that. "I guess I didn't appreciate how much it affected you."

"I was afraid he might do it, but it shocked me. It shocked me for a long time. I still can't believe he actually did it. But I realized you had more hope than I did he would snap out of it. I tried to get him to grow up and go back to the world, but he wouldn't do it. He was so stubborn."

"I remember."

"So that was it. He loved and lost one woman, and we had to go on without him."

"Were you closer before you got married and had me?"

My mother's voice rose, becoming more conversational. "Of course. Having children changes everything. Getting married changed everything. I moved in with your father and had a household to take care of. We couldn't afford to pay someone to take care of the lawn. We had to do it ourselves, not that we have that much yard. After you were born, half my time was spent keeping you out of trees and out of the street."

I thought of the neighbor's recent outdoor updates. "Why didn't you put up a fence?"

My mother almost chuckled. "With what money? I could baby-sit you for free."

"I remembered I wanted to stay at the cemetery and watch Uncle

Grigori go into the ground."

"Of course you did. I wasn't surprised. You wanted to go anywhere he did. If I wanted to take you to the zoo, you had other things to do. If Grigori wanted to go, you couldn't wait to go with him."

I tried, as I often had over the years, to find the best explanation for this. "He understood me. You and I could disagree on anything, but Uncle Grigori thought like me."

My mother took her time to answer. "There were times your father and I would get into bed at night, and I would say, 'She loves Grigori more than she loves me. Our own daughter loves him more than us.' Your father would say it wasn't true."

I sighed. "Mom, I never loved him more. I just got along with him better."

"I saw it reflected in your books, or in what people told me about them. They never asked me if they were based on anything true, but I saw a light in their eyes like a question. They wanted to know why you were so angry, why you would write about such things if they didn't happen to you."

"A lot of people are angry. They just refuse to admit it and talk down about those of us who are open about it."

My mother finished her water. "That's the way Grigori thought, too. If there was any way to stir up the buried truth, he'd find it. That was what he loved about history, all the upsets and allegiances no one else knew. If anybody knew what he was talking about, he'd move on to something else." She tipped the glass to see if there was any water left. "Did you know that woman showed up to the wake?"

I leaned closer. "No."

"Did you ever see her? She had kind of a horse face."

"Yes, I remember."

"But Grigori loved her. He thought she was beautiful. I recognized her immediately."

"How far did she get?"

"Just to the door." My mother carved out a square area of the air with her hands. "In the doorway. As soon as I saw her, I left the casket and the people waiting in line. I couldn't let anyone see her. They'd have a fit."

"What did she want? Did she know he killed himself?"

"No, she was genuinely concerned about what happened. I think she feared the worst. I didn't tell her the truth, but I didn't cover up how broken up he was after she crushed him. I think she wanted to know if she caused his death, but the damage was already done. What was I going to gain – what was she going to gain? – from knowing how badly he took it?"

My mother pushed herself up from the table. "Are you sure you want nothing to drink?"

I waved at her. "I'm fine."

My mother went to the sink. "I didn't let her stay any longer than the few minutes that I spoke with her."

"Do you think she guessed what happened?"

My mother refilled her glass and returned to the table. "I think she wondered but she wasn't sure. She didn't say much. Their relationship was over. But she cared enough to be upset. I imagine she's as haunted by those days as we are."

"What did Uncle Grigori do in the months between the break-up and when he hanged himself? I remember going to visit him a lot. Did he really just sit around in his apartment all that time?"

"He kept teaching, but that was about all he did. It was terribly dark in there."

"Did you know he was going to do it?"

My mother shook her head slightly. "No. I thought he'd get over her and move on. Everything else about his life seemed normal. Library books piled up on tables. Newspapers and magazines coming in. Laundry washed and put away. That's why I pushed him so hard to get over her. She didn't want him – fine. I wanted him to have a good, full life whether she was in it or not. And then he was – " Tears formed a shiny film over her eyes, and her voice shrank to nothing.

My mother had never shown so much vulnerability in front of me, even after he died. Concern pulled me into motion, and I slid from my chair to the one beside her. I laid my hand on her wrist, thin and bony beneath the sleeve. "You're not blaming yourself, are you?"

"I wish I hadn't pushed him. Those are the conversations I replay in my head." My mother swirled her free hand slowly around her ear.

"I try to think about the good times we had. He loved Russian folk music. He'd play it so much when we were kids, it'd drive me crazy. I told him a thousand times to put on something else. He had even gone to the trouble of learning some old Russian dances."

"I forgot about that. It was everything else I remembered." I could see him now that the memories had been loosened. He would dance at any occasion, even if no one else was dancing or the music wasn't appropriate for it. He'd always motion for my mother or me to join him, but she never wanted to embarrass herself. I joined him a few times and tried to learn a few steps, but mostly I just liked watching him.

"Oh, he loved parties," my mother remembered. "The music, the drinking, the dancing. But most of that was before you were old enough to walk around. He'd rather take you roller skating or something than go drinking with any friend he had."

The brighter side of Uncle Grigori's life made me happy and regretful at the same time. I was glad to hear about his better days, but I missed him terribly. Like my mother, I dotted fingertips to my watering eyes. She and I had more in common than I'd ever thought. We'd never spoken this openly about Uncle Grigori, my writing, or anything else. It was something I hadn't realized I'd wanted. I wanted the conversation to keep going, to keep us on the same page as long as I could. "Where did he learn to dance like that?"

My mother's eyes sparkled with pride and knowledge. "You'd be surprised what kinds of dance lessons he paid for. That was how he met her, I think. Doing the cha cha or something."

"He didn't have to take it so hard when she broke up with him. People break up and get together every day."

My mother clutched my hand. Her skin was wrinkled and dry. "You wish he was still here?"

I nodded.

"I do, too."

"How did Dad take it? Finding him like that."

"How do you think he took it? He took it hard. He started having heart palpitations not long after. That's why I tell you to go easy on the fathers in your books. His heart can't take it. We lied that Grigori had heart problems, and your father developed them for real."

This stunned me. "I had no idea Dad's heart problems went back that far. How much did you keep from me?"

My mother patted my hand. "As much as I had to, especially where Grigori was concerned. You've been writing since you were a little girl. Do you think I wanted to see poems about dead people all over the house?"

"My writing was a lot brighter when I was a kid. You could've taken that chance."

"I wanted to keep it that way."

I slipped my hand away gently. "I found out a lot of harsh truths with or without you, Mom."

She seemed to grow exhausted before my eyes, her head drooping as her hand rested lazily beside the water glass. "I know a lot of them, too."

"I'm sorry about Uncle Grigori."

"It's okay."

Thinking about those last conversations between my uncle and my mother, new questions begged to be asked. I wanted to know what Uncle Grigori meant when he said, "What it's like to love before you lose." Had my mother been in love before my father? I'd never heard a whisper of anything like that. Was it something my father didn't even know about? I'd accused my mother of looking out for my father in the name of duty rather than love, but what did Uncle Grigori know that I didn't? Was my father a second choice? Had she lost an opportunity to be with someone, someone she cared a lot about? Maybe she'd never gotten the chance to express her feelings to him before he died or married someone else.

My mother had gone to so much trouble to cover up Uncle Grigori's death, I doubted she would open up to me about her own life so easily. I'd learned enough for one afternoon. I stood up to go. "I'll let you get back to your bread."

My mother stood up, and we met for a hug. "I'll talk to you soon," she said. "Try not to think about these things too much."

I didn't answer. I'd be obsessed with our family's complexities until I died. I thought about making a joke of being buried next to Uncle Grigori when I did but decided against it.

We moved toward the living room and the front door.

"How's Michael?" she asked.

"He's all right. He's interviewing students from the college for the website."

"What do these students write about?"

"I don't know yet."

I stopped at the door, trying to figure out the puzzle that was my mother. She openly admitted she didn't like Michael living with me and didn't want him for a son-in-law, but she always remembered exactly what he did. The fact that his job was computer based never seemed to throw her although she had never owned one. My mother was giving me more new questions than old answers today.

I decided to put her at ease. "Don't worry about Dad. My next book isn't about families."

"That's good."

My mother pulled the door open, and I walked out into a light drizzle. The air was cool for fall, but I didn't have far to walk. I climbed into the car. My mother remained at the screen door, and she waved as I turned on the engine. I waved and backed the car out of the driveway. Some traditions were reassuring, and they never died.

Chapter 21: Jessie

I thought a lot about what Willa said. She thought I was scared to move on and a change could be good for me. Mostly, I replayed her unabridged enthusiasm about me breaking up with Dick. She had looked so proud of me at the thought of me sticking up for myself.

But I'd never been so disappointed in myself. I kept trying to force my brain through my homework, but I couldn't stop trying to figure out what was going on with me. Why couldn't I do what Willa wanted me to do? I'd broken up with Dick before. It seemed like a big deal the first time, but it was just habit now. I couldn't shake the idea that maybe the only reason I'd ever been brave enough to break up with Dick was because I knew we'd get back together. I wasn't the strong, independent person Willa hoped I was. I broke up with him to prove how mad he made me. That was it. As soon as he thought I'd cooled off – right around the time I started missing him – he showed up, and I took him back. I was no more independent now than I was in the days when only Dick broke up with me.

I pushed my chair back from my desk and rubbed my eyes. I needed a break from books and the ideas swarming through my head. Occasional noises reached me from the kitchen, metal clanging and cabinets bumping shut. I hadn't talked to my parents much since they got home, so I got up to check on dinner.

I used to help with cooking when I was younger, and I didn't know when that stopped. The kitchen was too cramped to fit all three of us at the same time, but we could at least take turns.

When I was a teenager, we had a system for it. We each had our own strengths. Dad was good at pasta duty. He'd set the water up to boil and stand in the doorway to the living room, watching TV with a spoon in one hand and an oven mitt on the other. It kept him out of Mom's way, and he always knew exactly when to pull the pasta off the stove to drain it. Mom usually called me in for casseroles and stews. I measured everything exactly the way she taught me, as accurately as I could. It drove Dad crazy to watch me. He wanted dinner done as soon as possible, but Mom was more patient. She just wanted good results. Even Dad had to admit things tasted better when I helped instead of his hasty scooping techniques.

Mom always handled the meat. When I explained this to Dick, he laughed for ten minutes, but it wasn't a dirty joke. Mom could put a mean Cajun rub or a perfect, creamy dill sauce on anything that had once been alive. At the same time, she could layer a vegetable lasagna better than most people's grandmas.

I reached the kitchen and peeked in the doorway. Dad was stirring a boiling pot on the stove, and Mom was pulling a casserole dish out of the oven.

"How much longer?" I asked.

Mom glanced at me and set the dish across two unused stove burners. "A couple of minutes. How's your studying?"

"All right." It didn't sound all right. I sounded depressed. The only reason I was attempting to study instead of reading *Hypocrisy* was my fear of how bad my midterm grades were going to look. I wanted to ask my parents what they thought about me leaving school, but I was too sure they'd freak out. They wanted me to get a degree. They were already being patient, letting me skip summer school and drop my course load down for the semester. The first question they'd ask would be, "What are you going to do instead?" And I had no answer for that. I didn't know where I could look for work or if I should get some sort of certification that would only take a year or two. I didn't want to admit I didn't know what kind of career I wanted.

Dad lifted the wide spoon and pinched a few grains of rice in his fingers. He tasted them with a disapproving tilt of his eyebrows. "Too tough. This is taking forever." He turned the flame up a little higher under the pot. "You've got another ten minutes, Jessie. You can keep studying if you want. We'll call you."

"Okay." I didn't want to study. I wanted to be a part of dinner or read or be out having fun with Willa.

I slunk back to my room and closed the door most of the way. I sat down at my desk and pulled *Hypocrisy* out of my backpack.

But I didn't want to sit. I was always sitting. My body felt restless, and my legs ached for activity. It was the same aimless buzzing that used to make me grab my camera and run outside.

Suddenly, I missed it more than I had in months. It wasn't the best camera in the world, but the photos came out clearly enough to impress people. They were good enough to get into the school literary journal two years in a row.

I still couldn't believe what happened to it, and if I told Willa the truth, she might finally be stunned into open-mouthed silence. I lent it to Dick so he could take pictures of his truck after he put those huge, obnoxious wheels on it. He wouldn't tell me exactly who broke it, but either Dick or Kyle dropped my camera while making a video of the truck backing up, and the other one ran it over. Dick returned it to me a smashed hunk of junk with tiny pieces falling off of it. I'd cried as I tossed it in the trash, and when I broke up with him over it, it was the longest time we ever spent apart. After a couple of weeks, though, I missed him, and I was glad he called me. I forgave him even though it hurt, and all I'd been left with since then was reading, television, and school. Most of my friends had graduated or fallen out of touch with me like Willa did. My only other option was hanging out with Dick.

No wonder I felt like shit.

Not even close to being able to replace my camera, I turned to *Hypocrisy*. I left my lit book open on the desk in front of me for an alibi and immersed myself in somebody else's problems.

13

Lourdes and Reese sat at a respectable distance on the couch, close enough to touch although they didn't dare. The movie was one all their friends had already seen, one Lourdes hoped wouldn't be too racy for her parents. She had heard there were jokes about sex and flashes of underwear. She'd been assured, however, that the heartwarming message at the end would win over the most conservative of parents. Lourdes certainly hoped so.

Reese loosely overlapped Lourdes' hand with his. Ever since she had given in to Reese and had sex with him, she found it ridiculous to sit with half a foot of space between them. Only her parents' disapproval and her guilt over the secrets she had never told him kept her from scooting closer. Reese stroked her fingers with his, and she flashed him a timid smile.

Behind them, the bathroom door slammed open against the wall. Lourdes sucked in a terrified breath, turning her head to stare over the back of the couch. Her mother stormed into view, holding up the one thing Lourdes had never wanted to see again. Perhaps it was the second, a reminder of the thing she really didn't want to see again.

Mrs. Falzone shook the pregnancy test at her daughter. Her voice was a shriek. "What the heck is this?"

Lourdes shrank down, wishing she could disappear under the couch or lower, under the carpet and the floorboards.

Mrs. Falzone hovered over her, waving the white plastic stick in the air. "There are two women in this house, and it isn't mine. I think I'd remember peeing on a stick."

"It's mine," Lourdes sobbed, hoping honesty would lessen any punishment her mother was hatching.

"Well, which is it? Yes or no? Are you pregnant or aren't you?"

Lourdes lowered her stare to Reese, who slid his hand away. His eyes bulged from his head. Lourdes thought she might pass out. She couldn't tell if she was breathing. "I am."

Mrs. Falzone screamed, a cry of shock and disappointment.

Her husband rushed into the room. "What is it? A spider?"

Mrs. Falzone pointed to her daughter. "It's

Lourdes. She's pregnant."

"Pregnant?" Mr. Falzone marched closer to the couch, peering over it at Lourdes. "Good God, why did you do that?"

Lourdes fought to give her voice traction. "I didn't mean to. I'm sorry."

"I suppose Reese is the father."

Lourdes knew better, but she wished she didn't. She nodded to keep the lie from passing her lips.

Mr. Falzone threw his hands up in defeat. "I can't believe you, Lourdes. You're going to have a baby when you're seventeen. I guess you can get married the next year when you're eighteen. Reese is no name for a son-in-law. It's never what I pictured on my little girl's wedding invitations."

Reese glanced up. "I thought I was being careful."

Mr. Falzone wheeled on him with bulging eyes. "Abstinence is being careful."

Reese cringed. "I'm sorry. I didn't know. She didn't tell me. I'll do the right thing, I promise. I'll be here."

"You already did the wrong thing. Now you're trying to do the right thing. It's a little late, Reese."

Mrs. Falzone caught a glimpse of the television and drew her lips back from her teeth. When Lourdes turned to the movie, three teenaged girls were flipping up the backs of their short skirts, flashing their underwear at a trio of boys.

"What is this garbage? Where's the remote control?"

Reese picked it up from the cushion next to him, and Mrs. Falzone snatched it from his hand. She turned off the TV without bothering to stop the DVD.

Mrs. Falzone held onto the remote. "Reese, I'm

sending you home, and I'm giving you three days to fess up to your parents. If I don't hear from your mother by then, I'm calling her myself."

"Yes, ma'am." Reese stood up and brushed nervously at his jeans. He worked at meeting Lourdes' gaze. "I'm sorry I let you down, babe. I don't know how I screwed up, but if I did, I'll help you through it. It'll be ours, and nobody can take it away."

Lourdes wanted to cry, and she bit her lip to chase the tears back. She cared more about Reese in that moment than the first time they'd kissed or the two times they'd had fast sex in his bedroom. Lourdes squeezed his hand quickly in agreement before she stood up and walked him to the door. She kissed his cheek. "I don't know when I'll see you again."

Reese looked past her at her parents. "I don't know. Be cool, okay? It's going to be all right. I won't make any more mistakes with you, I promise."

Reese kissed Lourdes on the cheek and disappeared out the door. She wanted to go with him. She ached to grab his hand and run away. She could leave her parents and her brother behind if it meant leaving Pastor Ozbeck forever.

Lourdes didn't want to turn around. She knew her parents stood there, waiting, expecting an explanation, expecting more from her decisions. Her eyes wandered over the back of the white door. She found she couldn't glance at the handle because when it filled her vision, she could barely keep her hands from shooting out and twisting it. Her throat tensed, ready with the only words she wanted to say: "Reese, please wait for me."

Chapter 22: Xan

The new chapter heading and all of its white space stared back at me. I leaned back in my desk chair, admitting temporary defeat. I didn't know what came next. Leifa stood at a crossroads, and so did I. Whatever path I chose for her would deliver the final message of the book, which still didn't have a title I could propose to Sheryl. She'd have a good laugh over *Bitches and Assholes*, but the book had changed enough that the working title was more ironic than accurate. Starting with Barry's disbelieving tirade when Leifa called off the wedding, several characters labeled her a bitch for leaving him in the eleventh hour, but her former best friend was the only woman who deserved that moniker. The number of assholes was diminishing, too. Barry had grown up a lot since that morning, surprising the other characters – and me – with moments of real insight and understanding. The friend who betrayed him by pursuing Leifa was showing a soft, relatable side I hadn't anticipated. Leifa had a handful of options, but I couldn't decide which one worked best.

A few light knocks sounded on the doorframe. Melody called to me. "Do you need anything?"

"I need a break." I shrank the program so I didn't have to look at the empty page anymore. I stood up and met Melody at the door. "Where's Michael? I had an idea I wanted to run past both of you."

"In the nook."

Melody led me down the hall. Her long hair swung in a loose ponytail in front of me. Her practical style had rarely wavered in the time she'd worked for me, but everything else about her had changed dramatically. She wasn't the skinny, shy twenty-something I'd hired twelve years ago. Melody walked taller, her shoulders set with assurance. She had slowly traded her cutesy t-shirts for looser fits in seasonal colors. Henry and motherhood had been good to her. I liked to think my influence helped, too. Today, she was more confident than I was.

Michael sat across the kitchen, reading in the sunlight pouring through the windows.

"Xan's taking a break," Melody announced.

Michael read a few seconds more and closed the book. He laid it on the table. "How'd you talk her into that?"

"I didn't. She has something she wants to tell us." Melody walked over and stood next to him.

Michael watched me, his expression expectant but calm.

I folded my arms, not sold on what I wanted to suggest. "I'm thinking of doing a small book tour in December before the holidays. I don't know how much longer this book will take, and it'd be good to do something proactive about my career to take my mind off it."

"I think it's a great idea," Michael said.

Melody's smile took up half her face. "That's exciting. Do you have anything booked?"

"Not yet. I know there are bookstores within a few hours' drive where I haven't signed. I'm not sure how open they'll be to hosting an author who hasn't published anything for several years."

Michael retained his reassuring grin. "It'll be a reunion tour. Seriously, you're still a published author. Your books are still relevant. I guarantee you can still draw a crowd, and that's what bookstores need. They'd be ridiculous to turn you down based on the publication dates of your books."

"Does anybody remember me?"

"Are you kidding? You're hard to forget. Maybe it's time to take a tour and see if you can hook some new readers."

"I should've known you two would be in favor of it. You always support me."

Melody laid a hand on her chest. "Xan, your readers love you. The second I post online that you're doing a book tour, they'll spread the word. Trust me. They're waiting for this new book, and while you're working on it, a tour is the perfect opportunity to keep in touch with them."

"Okay."

Michael tapped my arm to get my attention. "They want to know you haven't forgotten them. You don't have to tell them you don't have an ending for this book. Just tell them you're working on something."

"What if I never finish it?"

"If you don't give them any details, they'll assume whatever comes out next is what you've been working on. Have you talked to Sheryl?"

"No."

"Maybe she'll have advice for you."

"Maybe."

Melody's voice called my attention back to her. "Let me pose it as a question online. 'If you live within five hundred miles of XZA, is there a store in your town you'd want her to come to?' If we can get people involved, it'll make it that much bigger."

"You can ask them if you want, but no promises. I just thought it'd be nice to get out there again."

"It will be. The response will be better than you think." Melody couldn't stop smiling. "I can't wait to post this."

"Go ahead. There's no point in me getting on the computer until tonight. I have nothing to type."

Melody patted my shoulder and breezed past me out of the kitchen.

I stepped closer to Michael. "Do you really think it's a good idea? It's been several years since I've signed anything."

"Why not? There are a lot of people who haven't heard of you. It never hurts to get your face out there. Your writing, your name."

I looked out the window into the backyard. The trees shed more and more foliage every day. They were half barren now, some trees still bushy with burnt orange and faded green. The honey locust tree was stripped to the bone, a few brown withered leaves hanging on the end of each naked branch. Fallen leaves littered the lawn.

Michael tossed out another idea. "We could do a ten-year anniversary interview for the site."

I shook my head although I appreciated the offer. "Too suspicious. You can interview me when my next book comes out."

"At least let me post about the book tour when you have the details worked out."

"Okay."

Michael leaned toward me. "Stop worrying about your book."

"You say that a lot."

"You worry about it a lot. I never saw you like this over

Hypocrisy."

"I was in a groove back then. My main characters were close in age. They had big, in-your-face problems. Leifa's completely different. She's like a grown-up version of Chessa or Lourdes. She's messed up but not as badly."

"Maybe you should mess her up a little more." Michael took my hand, the contact reassuring me that he was on my side.

I held his fingers lightly. "I just want to find the right ending. I can do whatever I want to it once I can see the whole scope of it."

Melody strolled into the kitchen. "The idea's out there. I'll check it before I leave to see if you get a response. Flora will be thrilled."

I turned a doubtful but appreciative expression on Melody. "She's three."

"She likes your books. The colors, at least." Melody's face lit up, and she clasped her hands together in front of her chest. "Her art camp is having an exhibition next month if you want to go. She'd be so happy to see you."

"All right."

"The theme is 'fancy fall' to make the kids feel like real, important artists."

"What's Flora making?"

"She's not sure. They've been working with leaves and all sorts of different mediums. They made clay figures last week. Flora made this sort of snowman with a monkey head that was pretty cute."

A cell phone rang somewhere, and it took a moment for me to recognize the ring tone as Michael's. He got up from the table and walked across the kitchen to the counter. "It's Nick." He put the phone to his ear. "Hello?"

I whispered to Melody. "We've been trying to set something up with our friends for weeks."

Melody nodded.

"Good. That works for us. Seven." Michael paused, listening. He shifted the phone away from his mouth. "Xan, how would you describe Marcy and Stacey? Nick thinks you'll be biased, but I think you'll be fair."

I considered my two oldest friends. "How many words do I get?"

"Two. One for each."

"Stacey I would describe as foxy. Marcy... intense."

Michael spoke into the phone again. "Did you hear that, Nick? Foxy and intense." He laughed. "I don't know, and I don't know if Xan wants to know." Michael directed another question to me. "Does Marcy's intensity translate to the bedroom?"

"I can only imagine."

Michael reported back to Nick. "Probably."

I posed the same question to Michael. "Can you sum your friends up in two words? I want Melody to know the kind of evening we've gotten ourselves into."

Michael covered the microphone on his cell. "Particular and scattered."

Melody laughed, making a dissipating gesture with her hands. "I don't envy you."

"Come on, Melody," Michael teased, lowering his hand from the microphone. "You don't want to join us? You're very balanced. We could use you."

"I'm sure you could, but my balance is needed at home to keep the dogs from killing the cats and my husband from killing the dogs. And the cats from attacking any leg that walks past them. There's a whole cycle I keep in check."

"Where does Flora fit in?" I asked.

"She chases the dogs and the cats, whichever she sees first."

Michael grimaced through his smile. "What a circus."

Melody shrugged and laid her hand over her swollen abdomen. "I have a feeling this one's going to fit right in."

I glanced at her belly, not nearly as round yet as she'd gotten with Flora. "Hopefully as a spectator, not a participant."

Melody laughed. "I hope so, but I doubt it."

Michael brightened his smile and returned to his phone call. "Yeah. Seven on the twenty-eighth."

Melody patted my arm. "Good luck. You'll do fine."

I raised my eyebrows. "I'll be fine because I'm not one of the desperate singles."

"They'll be fine, too."

I set my hands on my hips and turned to Michael. "Tell Nick this is a one-time deal. I'm not running a dating service."

Michael pulled the phone away from his jaw. "He lives in Chicago. He doesn't need to come down here to find women." Michael laughed. "He says maybe he does."

I remembered what my friends used to say about Michael driving down to meet me. "Marcy started calling the drive here from Chicago the 'sex drive' years ago."

Michael winked at me. "Maybe it's time somebody made that drive other than me."

"Maybe it is." I pictured my shopping excursion with Stacey. "At least one of my friends is ready for that."

Chapter 23: Jessie

I finished my quiz with a long-winded answer and glanced over the rest of my work. There was no way I'd get full credit, but my efforts had to count for something. I was grateful I'd pushed myself to catch up on class reading. At least I recognized the character names in every question.

Half the room was still writing, and I let my mind wander ahead to the end of class. I wanted to read *Hypocrisy* the second it was over. I just needed to find the best place to do it. The library would've been my first choice if the weather was warmer – quiet and hidden, but way too hot as the building adjusted to the fluctuating temperatures of fall. The break rooms scattered through campus would put infinite snacks within reach, but they were hit or miss – silent and empty or loud and obnoxious. I would've settled for my car if I didn't have to run the heat on low the whole time I sat there. I was leaning toward the library when Dr. Casey's voice rose over the shuffling of papers.

"Pass them to the front, please," she instructed.

I held my quiz out to the girl in front of me who barely turned before she snatched it.

Dr. Casey checked her watch. "That took a little longer than I wanted, but that's fine." She collected the pages from the student at the head of each row. "Are there any questions about the reading, what we just finished or what we're starting on?"

No one spoke or raised a hand.

"First one hundred pages for next time," Dr. Casey reminded us. "Don't blow off these tests and quizzes, guys. They could really help your grade later if you goof on the final. It's cumulative, which means it's going to cover everything. Don't wait until the last weekend to try and read everything, okay?"

The bells rang, and the class stopped paying attention as they dropped their stuff into their backpacks and headed for the door. I packed up my bag, grabbed my coat, and walked out behind them, sharing a small smile with Dr. Casey. It'd been a year since I was in a class with her, but I appreciated the chance to learn from her again.

I reached the doorway, and as soon as I saw Dick, my chest tightened. My half-made plans were over before I got twenty feet from my seat. He stood across the hall, his body slumped against the wall, crushing the contents of his backpack.

He straightened as I walked through the doorway. "I'm starving. Let's get something to eat."

I scrambled for any excuse to creep off to the library, but Dick's insistence wasn't giving me much time. "Why are you always so hungry?" I asked, irritation sharpening my voice.

Dick squinted at me. "I'm just hungry. Jesus. Are you coming or not?"

"Yeah, fine," I mumbled. I shrugged out of my backpack to put my coat on.

Dick started down the hall without me, and I caught up with one sleeve on.

"What class was that?" he groaned. "It sounded boring as shit."

My jaws clenched together. I'd told him about this class every week, and the semester was halfway over. "Absent Parents in Modern Literature."

"What kind of stupid class is that? Who made that one up?"

I ground my teeth against each other. It was easily my favorite class of the semester, and I'd told him that, too. "I don't know. Probably Dr. Casey. It's not as boring as it sounds, and there's a ton of material for it. It's a really common theme in children's books. Roald Dahl – "

Dick let out a crackling laugh, and I cut myself short. A blonde girl came toward us, either a few years younger than us or just so pretty that she looked eighteen. Dick aimed his index fingers at her like twin pistols and made little firing sounds with his lips. She grinned back at him, her blue eyes sparkling. Her tight-fitting sweater put a wide white stripe across her breasts between two solid blocks of pink. She walked past us, and I was relieved she didn't stop to talk.

"Who's that?" I asked, trying to sound casual. I sounded suspicious and angry.

"I don't know her name. I just know who she is."

"Is she in a class with you?"

"I don't know. I'm not in class that much."

"You should be. You're paying for it."

Dick made a scratchy, amused sound in his throat. "I'm not paying for it now. It's called student loans. Who cares if I learn anything if I get the degree?" Dick glanced at me. "You know what I'm talking about. All your classes are blow-offs."

My eyebrows flew up in disbelief. "Because they're literature? None of them are easy."

"Why aren't you taking blow-offs, then? Don't you know what to ask when you sign up for classes? You have to ask things like, 'Does the teacher have an attendance policy?'"

"I guess I don't ask that."

"Well, you should. You shouldn't spend more time in class than you have to. That's the smart way to get through this. You're always talking about how smart you are."

We reached the stairwell and started moving down to the first floor. A gorgeous brunette in cat eye shaped eyeliner gave Dick a wave of her fingers. He shot an index finger pistol right back at her. The legs of her skintight jeans were stuffed into fur-topped boots that looked more expensive than half my closet combined. I wondered how she could strut around campus in those heels. I could hear them striking the floor even over the buzz of conversation.

Dick's gaze lingered on her, and Willa's question reared in my thoughts. Had Dick dated other girls when we weren't together? I was beginning to wonder if he dated other girls while we *were* together. I didn't sound edgy this time, just defeated. "Do you know her name, either?"

Dick scrunched his face up, trying to remember. "Katie? Candice. Courtney. Something like that."

"How long have you known her?"

Dick shrugged. "I don't know. Why are you asking me so many questions?"

I wanted to ask him why he was being so defensive. "You asked me about my class, and then you interrupted me to wave to people. I thought I'd ask about them. I never saw you wave to them before."

"What were you talking about?"

"Roald Dahl."

"Who the hell is that?"

Maybe Willa had another point. Dick didn't read that much. "Never mind."

I pushed the door open to a stiff blast of wind. I could almost see Willa shaking her head. *He doesn't even open doors for you*, she'd say. *Literally or figuratively.* The wind was bitingly cold. It hadn't warmed up at all while I sat in class. The tops of my ears stung in preparation to go numb. Dick and I followed the sidewalk toward the back of the campus and the new parking lot.

The building started blocking most of the wind, and my hair stopped whipping into my mouth. I remembered my failed plans to run to the library, and I suddenly wanted a few minutes to myself if I couldn't grab quality reading time. "I forgot my book," I blurted out.

"What?"

"My book. I have to go back for it."

"Get it tomorrow."

"It won't be there tomorrow. It'll be there now." I turned to head back. "Just wait for me, okay? I'll be right there."

I hurried away. I heard Dick offer a "Fine. Whatever, Jessie" before I turned the corner and ducked inside the building.

For a moment, I stopped in the corner to catch my breath and try not to wince as my ears warmed up. I made my way up the stairs at a normal pace in case Dick peeked in. I didn't want him to see me standing around in the entryway.

I looked to see which hallway had the least traffic in it and wandered past a half-dozen meandering people. One guy started to raise his hand, and I thought maybe he recognized me from class. Instead of waving, he pointed at my feet.

"You got some paper stuck to your shoe or something," he said.

"Thanks," I muttered, glad I hadn't waved back. Clinging to the bottom of my shoe was a bright white piece of paper folded sloppily in half.

I leaned against the wall and pulled the paper off, leaving a disgusting wad of lime-green gum behind. The flier, once used to advertise a math club meeting, was already ripped, so I used it to pick the rest of the gum off my shoe. I balled it up and took it to the garbage can.

The floor was littered with papers, some face up, some face down. I could picture somebody running down the hallway with his arms out, knocking everything off the bulletin boards with some goofy grin on his face. I threw the gum paper away, and another flier on the floor caught my attention.

It had a drawing of a bracelet on it. It was simple and the proportions were bad, but it looked like the one Dick had given me.

I picked it up, my stomach lurching as I reached for it. *LOST BRACELET*, it said in big black letters. *Gold chain with daisies on the connecting part. Please call!! Reward!!!*

All I could do was stare at the picture. Did Dick steal the bracelet, or did he find it? He certainly hadn't bought it as he'd tried to assert at the diner. Either way, I'd been wearing it to school a couple days a week. Somebody could've accused me of stealing it or at least of not turning it in. Some present Dick had given me. So thoughtful of him to act like he was doing me a favor while setting me up to look like a thief.

I pictured Dick out on the sidewalk where I'd left him. It was probably time to head back. I let the sheet of paper glide to the floor and walked out of the building. I kept my shoulders shrugged up to protect my ears and squinted through the wind for Dick's truck. I could see him sitting in it as I got closer, his head thrashing while his fingers drummed wildly on the steering wheel.

I climbed up into the passenger seat, the door slamming shut in a frozen gust.

Dick flicked the volume down on the stereo. "Take it easy. This is my baby." He patted the steering wheel affectionately.

"Sorry," I growled through gritted teeth. I was too cold and too angry to accuse him of giving me some other girl's bracelet. It could wait for another time.

"It's Thursday," Dick said, his hands accompanying the low-playing music with another riff on the steering wheel. "The waffle stack's on special today."

"At the diner?" I could taste the grease in my mouth already. It was usually followed by the tight throat of dehydration and an uneasy churning in my stomach.

"Yeah. Where did you think we were gonna go?"

I didn't want to argue. I just wanted to be home, pretending to do my homework while I read XZA. Willa was already done with *Hypocrisy*. I still had a few chapters left to go.

"What's the matter?" Dick pressed me. "You're not hungry?"

"The diner's fine. I'll just get some tea or something."

Dick snorted. "Tea? What are you, my grandma?" Dick studied me, his head cocked to one side. "You've been hanging out with Willa."

"What?"

"That's the kind of thing she'd do, drink tea like some blue-haired old lady."

"I always drink tea when I want something other than water."

"I've never seen you get tea. Get a soda."

I pulled my backpack off in the confines of my seat and dropped it at my feet. "I get tea all the time. I can't have caffeine. You know that."

"Since when?"

I looked out the window so I wouldn't give him a dirty look and start a fight. I knew the answer faster than I wanted to. "The very first time we went out. You asked if I wanted a soda. I said no. The caffeine hurts my stomach."

"Not every soda has caffeine in it, Jessie."

"I know that. I told you that. It's easier to cut it all out."

"I guess I can't remember back that far."

My irritation crept deeper, making me feel tired and wired at the same time. "We went to the movies."

Dick stretched his face into a long expression of indifference. He still couldn't remember.

"We saw *Borat*."

Dick laughed, slamming his hand against the steering wheel. He clutched his stomach. "God, that was hilarious. I forgot you were with me."

Why had I come outside? The first time, the second time? Why had I gotten in this truck? "It was your suggestion."

Dick pulled his phone out of his pocket. "I gotta send some jokes from it to Kyle."

Dick typed quickly with his thumbs. I stared out the window, exhaling with boredom. A quick stop by the diner, then Dick would drive me back to the school where I'd jump in my car and drive home. I made a new plan, one I wouldn't let anybody break. I'd say hi to my parents, lock myself in my room, and not come out until the reruns of *Frasier*.

Dick's hysterical chuckles interrupted my daydreaming. He tucked his phone in his pocket. "Let's see what Kyle says to that. I put my phone on vibrate." He elbowed my arm a few times to make sure I got his meaning.

I wasn't as brave as Willa wanted me to be. I was starting to think I wanted to know the answer to her question, a question I'd buried a long time ago. But the other girls Dick knew intimidated me, and I didn't want to feel that sinking feeling in my stomach when he answered me. I already lived with a general version of it every day. I made a new list of questions for Dick, ones I didn't want to hear any of his attempts to answer. How long had we been together? When was the last time we broke up, and for how long? I knew all the dates and details. Did he?

He wouldn't even bother to guess. None of that information stuck in his head. A movie about a make-believe foreigner stayed in his brain forever, but the fact that I was there with him and paid for my own ticket was lost to him.

Dick jerked unexpectedly and pulled out his phone. "There's the feeling I was waiting for. Been a while since I had a good hummer." He read the screen and laughed, leaning his head back and showing his teeth. "Kyle, you sick bastard."

He slid his phone away, and I was glad he never read his texts to me. I didn't want to know. I just wanted to get the next hour or two over with so I could go home. I'd never thought of my good memory as a bad thing. Maybe I'd be happier if all I could remember were the funny lines from movies and forgot all the things Dick didn't do for me. Or the things he did that I wished he didn't. He was lucky I wasn't wearing the bracelet now. I would've torn it off and thrown it at him. I could've walked away and never looked back.

Chapter 24: Xan

I popped the cork loose from the wine bottle and poured myself the first glass of the evening. I set everything else aside to take a few small sips before the guests arrived. Michael's footsteps sounded in the entrance hall, coming closer to the kitchen. He walked in and caught me self-medicating.

A slow grin slid across Michael's face. "What are you doing?"

"Preparing."

"That's the only bottle we're opening, so don't prepare too much. What are you worried about? Do you think they're going to pair off and sneak up to the guest rooms?"

"I hope not, but it's possible. You didn't see what Stacey bought." I set my wine glass on the counter beside the five empty ones I'd pulled down from the cabinet. "I'll tell you exactly what I'm afraid of. Nick is going to start talking about movies, and the second he realizes neither one of my friends knows the first thing about them, he's going to wonder why he's here. John is going to go on and on about music until my friends have no idea what he's talking about."

"True, but Stacey and Marcy are going to show up looking like they're the entertainment at a Victoria's Secret fashion show. I think they're expecting more than Nick and John."

I pictured Michael's friends as I'd seen them over the years. They weren't flashy guys, usually tooling around in t-shirts and corduroy pants. "I don't know what they're expecting, but I think my friends are being more honest about why they're coming here. I think Nick and John want it to work out, too. They just won't admit it."

Michael poured himself half a glass of wine. "They both sound pretty skeptical to me."

"They don't think I can have interesting friends?"

"They're skeptical of everything."

Michael took a sip of wine and kissed me. We both tasted like wine, and the evening hadn't started yet. I wanted to call it off and stand there quietly kissing Michael in the kitchen, but the idea was interrupted by the insistent chiming of the door bell.

Michael pursed his lips, rueful that our moment was past but mischievous about the evening ahead. "Let's see who it is."

I followed him to the door, and Michael pulled it open. Marcy and Stacey stood on the porch bundled in their coats.

"Did you drive together?" Michael asked.

Marcy raised her eyebrows. "No. We agreed to get here at the same time. I followed her the whole way out of town."

Michael stepped aside and motioned for them to come in, extending his hand toward the center of the house. "Fish, meet barrel."

Marcy came in first and unwound the scarf from around her neck. "Who says we're the fish?" She took off her coat, revealing the lowest cut V-neck I'd seen her wear. It hugged her well, leading the eye down to her dark-wash jeans and black heeled boots.

Michael closed the door, and Stacey shrugged out of her coat. Her button-up blouse was modestly but noticeably see-through. The balconette bra I'd tried to warn Michael about was making its appearance in cream-colored satin with black vertical stripes and a bow between the cups. Stacey's skinny jeans showed off her long, thin legs. Sparkling gold sling-backs decorated her feet.

I took their coats since Michael was holding his wine glass and hung them in the closet.

"You're drinking already?" Marcy asked him.

Michael raised his glass. "It's one of the benefits of being the host."

"You look delectable as usual, Michael."

"Thank you."

Michael was wearing another of the sweaters his parents had given him, a black one striped with narrow bands of tan. Anybody else would have begged Bill Cosby comparisons, but on Michael, it almost looked chic.

Stacey turned her big green eyes on me. "How do we look?"

"You look fine."

"You look nice, Xan."

I glanced down. I'd almost forgotten what I was wearing. I was also in black, a pullover tunic with cuffed three-quarter sleeves. Unlike my friends, I'd ignored jeans and heels to opt for leggings and ballet flats.

Marcy spoke up again. "Are we the first ones here?"

"Yeah." Michael interrupted himself to sip more wine. "Nick and John were driving down together. They should be here in a couple of minutes." He gazed through the wide doorway to the living room to check the clock on the far wall. "You got here early."

Marcy propped one hand on her hip, pressing her breasts forward. "Are you trying to suggest we're eager?"

Michael chuckled into his wine glass as he went for another sip. "I know you are. It's no mystery."

The doorbell chimed, vibrating the air.

Marcy tucked her fingers under one shoulder of her shirt and then the other, pulling her bra straps up and raising her breasts with them. "Lift 'em high, ladies," she muttered.

Stacey addressed her with a toss of her smooth blonde hair. "How did your STD testing come out?"

Marcy's eyebrows settled low. "Clean, thank you."

Michael pulled the door open. Nick and John stepped in, each rubbing his hands together for warmth. John offered Michael a handshake. Nick gladly stepped around him to escape the cold and give me a hug.

"Good to see you, Xan," he said.

"You, too."

I could hear John complaining to Michael. "Did you hear their new album? I waited six years for that thing."

Michael shook his head.

Nick glanced around the foyer. "The house looks nice."

I looked it over with him. "Thanks, and thanks for coming. We've got wine, and snacks are already out."

Michael gestured John off the entry rug and shut the door against the cold. "These are Xan's friends, Marcy and Stacey. This is Nick and John that work with me."

They started shaking hands, and I slipped into the kitchen to grab the wine. Michael followed me, claiming he needed a refill.

I held as many wine glasses between my fingers as I could. I glanced behind me at the foyer and spoke in a hush. "That's horrible leaving them all out there alone when they just met."

"Horrible for who?" Michael flashed his mischievous smile. He picked up the bottle of wine and the last empty glass. "Are you more afraid they won't like each other or they will?"

"It's not polite to throw people together who live so far apart. What happens if they do like each other, any of them?"

"If we can make it work, they can, too."

Michael leaned over and set a brief kiss on my lips before he led me out to the foyer. Nick and John were hanging their coats in the closet. Nick was dressed in a well-fitting dark blue button-down. His closely cropped, tight dark curls gave him a younger appearance I thought Stacey might like. His mixed heritage gave him an envious golden honey complexion complimented by striking burnt sienna eyes. John was wearing a lightweight suit coat and dress pants turned casual if not ironic by a white Joan of Arc t-shirt featuring a stick figure robot shielding himself from a host of pale blue raindrops with an umbrella. He was, in many ways, Nick's opposite. His short, brown-blonde hair fell straight, and his blue eyes shone a few shades brighter than Marcy's.

John offered me a short stack of CD's in slim cases. "I brought you some new music to write to."

"Thank you." I never asked for them, but I always looked forward to him bringing me more.

Nick took the empty glasses from my hands, and I shuffled through the CD's, not recognizing a single band. I set them on the hall table to go through later in more detail and followed the three men into the living room. Marcy and Stacey had already staked out their seats. Marcy took up the recliner, and Stacey sat on the far end of the couch. Nick and John filled in the two cushions between them, leaving the love seat for Michael and me with a clear view of whatever was about to unfold.

John snatched up the bowl of snack mix and cradled it while feeding small handfuls to himself. Nick filled the empty wine glasses one at a time. Marcy and Stacey reached their hands out, making it easier for Nick to pass them.

Marcy thanked him and cleared her throat. "So, what's this website about that you all work for?"

I knew she'd heard a little about it from Michael, but it was a good question to start with.

Nick swirled his wine gently around the inside of his glass. "Underrated Media dot com centers around the three kinds of media we work in: movies, music, and books. We're still trying to expand that to magazines and possibly video games, but mostly TV."

"What counts as underrated?"

"Anything that's good that hasn't gotten the press or reviews it deserves."

"Who decides that? Who decides what's good?"

Nick turned a pointed finger to himself, John, and Michael. "Us."

"And nobody questions you?"

"Sometimes the readers do, but our bosses mostly agree with us if that's what you mean. Sometimes they second-guess us, but we mostly know what we're doing by now."

Marcy narrowed her eyes. Her voice dragged with envy. "You're so lucky. College politics can be a nightmare. What happens to all the media that's not underrated?"

"We get to enjoy it without breaking it down into a review on the site."

Stacey turned to me, her eyes wide with surprise. "Michael interviewed you, Xan. You're not underrated, are you?"

Michael and Marcy groaned on my behalf.

I tried not to burst Stacey's naivety bubble. "Have you read my reviews?" I asked, trying not to sound grumpy.

Michael patted my leg. "Let's not go there tonight, Stacey."

John spoke up, rescuing me. "I've been trying to institute a new section on the site called Overrated where we highlight a few trends that have gotten more than their fair share of good publicity."

Nick shook his head in decisive swings. "They won't go for it. We're known for spreading the word on everything that gets overlooked and providing honest reviews with a touch of humor. What you're talking about is a section where we pick things apart. I don't think our readers will go for that."

"What about new readers?"

Nick shrugged.

"We pick things apart all the time," John insisted.

"In our off time. It wouldn't look professional. It won't hook new readers. And it'll take time away from the things we actually want to review."

John looked for back-up. "How do you weigh in, Michael?"

Michael didn't take long to think it over. "Once a month I'm fine with, but in the process of saying these things have already gotten too much attention, we'd be giving them extra attention."

John tilted his head from side to side. "I guess you're right."

Marcy jumped back into the conversation. "What kinds of things have you reviewed? Music or movies."

Nick spoke up first. "We've reviewed pretty much everything from pop culture to indie faves to stuff nobody else knows about. I like to throw a foreign film in there every once in a while to keep it interesting. But what I really like to do are movies about music. Those are some of the best, but most reviewers don't know enough about music – or know someone who does – to give a proper review. Everybody loves *Spinal Tap* and *Walk The Line*, and they're great, but I still stand by *Pirate Radio*."

John threw him an irritated glance. "It got good reviews."

Nick raised his index finger. "Decent reviews. Not high enough. Therefore, it's underrated and fair game for the site." He reached over and grabbed a handful of snack mix.

John turned to Marcy a few feet from him in the recliner. "This is what happens when we're left to decide what's underrated or not."

Marcy smiled at him.

Nick chewed and swallowed. "That's why I write movie reviews, and you do music. The site would be dead by now if we did them the other way around."

Marcy chuckled and leaned toward them. "I always picture Xan's mom as Anjelica Huston. I met her once, but the way Xan talks about her, I always think of her as this brooding, imposing figure."

I laughed. Nick and John looked to me for an explanation. They'd never met my mother. "Try Cloris Leachman, only shorter."

Stacey spoke up pensively. "*Pirate Radio*. Was Russell Brand in that?"

Nick's posture stiffened. "No. Completely different kind of humor."

Stacey shrugged. "I'm still trying to figure out who he is. I mostly just watch movies that have Leonardo DiCaprio in them."

I nudged Michael, whispering, "Here we go."

The conversation broke down completely. Marcy sidetracked John with a question about his Joan of Arc t-shirt, which led to a long and rambling description of the Chicago independent music scene. I knew how insightful he was, but I wondered if Marcy did. Her scrunched eyebrows, lightly bunched to stay polite, told me she didn't. Nick, who could talk for hours about movies and genre conventions, steered his conversation with Stacey as far from movies as he could. They talked about the horses she rode as a child, the places Nick lived growing up, and what they liked best about their current vehicles.

Michael and I talked intermittently, whenever a random thought popped into our heads. He'd squeeze my leg and say, "Mom called. She's still excited about their weekend here. She's making her way through the wine she bought at the vineyards." Minutes later, I'd turn to him with my own thought. "We should find a different golf course for next year."

This made Michael's eyes sparkle. "I can get in extra practice."

The rest of the time, we listened.

Marcy seemed to be doing well while John skipped through the decades and across continents to compare musical styles. She eventually laughed, overwhelmed, and changed the subject. "How did you and Michael become good friends if you're into music and he's into books?"

John glanced at Michael. "It's not all we have to talk about. We always had fun at meetings, so that's how it started. He's a great guy to work with, so it was easy to hang out afterward."

Marcy wrinkled her nose in protest. "Michael Singer's not a man. He's an institution."

I wanted to drop my forehead into my hands and not watch anymore. John had to be thinking the same thing I was. If Marcy was so enamored of Michael, why were John and Nick even here?

Stacey distracted me with cries of, "Me, too. Me, too," and I gladly switched over to her conversation with Nick.

He was leading her into a movies discussion one baby step at a time. "Ninety-nine percent of movies in any genre are going to follow the same rules and basic plot points."

Stacey rolled her eyes up as she thought about it. "No, they don't."

"They do," Nick insisted patiently. "They really do."

Marcy interrupted any hope I was nourishing for the evening. She tapped her fingernails against her empty glass. "Is there more wine?"

I stayed firm in the face of her sourness. "No. That's all we had. It was a special bottle from Michael's parents. I hope you didn't drink it too fast."

Marcy gave me a puckered expression of defiance and disbelief. She knew we had more wine, and she knew why I was keeping it from her. If I knew her at all, she was already debating her revenge.

John lured her back into conversation. "There are a lot of completely different songs that have similar or identical pieces of music."

Marcy leaned over to set her wine glass on the coffee table. "That's not illegal?"

"Not necessarily. I'm sure most of it happens by accident, and the bands aren't even aware of it. The frontman for How I Became the Bomb is often confused for the frontman of Hot Hot Heat, and they're not even from the same country. You have to listen to a lot of music very closely to start hearing these tiny little connections."

Marcy barely sounded interested. "I guess I don't listen to that much music. I haven't bought a new CD in a couple of years."

"I always keep Xan stocked with music I think she'd like. She might be able to lend you something, or I could find some recommendations for you if your tastes are different."

Stacey leaned past Nick to jump into John and Marcy's conversation. "I wouldn't worry about it. Marcy's stuck in the nineties."

Marcy scowled at her. "That's the late nineties to you."

I wasn't surprised when less than a half hour passed before Nick looked at his watch. "It's getting late, and we still have to drive back."

Stacey, for all of her simplicity about movies and life, seemed to pick up on Nick's intentions to flee. She supported him with a casual sigh. "It is a long drive. We all worked today. I'm a little worn out, too."

Marcy grabbed the opportunity to make a jab at Stacey. "Worn out from touching strangers all day."

Nick stood up and set his glass on the coffee table. "I respect anybody who does a job I wouldn't do."

Stacey stuck the tip of her tongue out at Marcy, who turned her head and pretended not to notice.

We all stood up in our own time and found a place to leave our glass. John took one last handful of snack mix, and I realized the bowl of chocolate-covered peanuts hadn't even been touched. The snack mix was almost gone. We moseyed toward the front door while dry, expected phrases popped up between the singles.

"It was good to meet you," Nick said to no one in particular.

"Yes, you, too," Marcy assured him, Stacey nodding beside her.

I opened the closet and pulled out the men's coats. Nick and John slid into them and fastened them up. They shifted their focus to Michael and me.

"Thanks for the hospitality," John said.

Michael shook his hand. "Thanks for coming down."

"We miss you up there. You don't know how many times I'm at a bar show and I think, 'Was that lyric based on something?' And you're not there to answer me."

"Email me."

"I would if my notes were legible. You know how dark some of these shows get."

They said goodbye to me, made a few last parting pleasantries to my friends, and disappeared into the dark, cold breeze. Michael switched on the porch light and shut the door.

Marcy's clouded blue eyes regarded me coolly. "It wasn't a complete waste of time. Parts of it were entertaining."

Stacey patted my shoulder. "Good try, Xan. They were very nice."

"Polite, at least," Marcy added.

Stacey looked at her. "Did you break up with the milkman yet?"

"No, so I have something to go home to if I want."

I defended myself. "Don't blame this on me. This is something the two of you cooked up with Michael. I didn't think it was going to end in fireworks and foot rubs."

Stacey folded her arms. "Why didn't you say that from the beginning?"

"Would you have listened to me?"

Marcy answered for her with a resounding, "No." She gestured to Stacey's revealing outfit with the smooth, flat-handed motions of *The Price is Right* models. "May I present exhibit A?"

Stacey pulled her coat out of the closet and put it on. "I still had a nice time."

Michael sounded relieved. "I can tell Nick you won't be calling?"

"Sorry. He's not my type."

Marcy reached for her coat. "Your type already has their clothes off."

I tried to pry past Marcy's defenses. "What did you think of John, Marcy?"

"Oh, he's weird." Marcy buttoned up her coat and bundled her neck up in her scarf. "He went on and on about songs and bands I've never heard of. Maybe it's a good thing you were hiding the wine. I might be dizzy by now."

Michael lingered by the door. "So that's it. Those are the only friends of mine you get to meet."

"That's fine. I'll go back to the milkman and pining for you." Marcy left a small, tasteful kiss on Michael's cheek. "Let me know when you make some new friends in the area. I can track them down myself."

Marcy waved and let herself out.

Stacey pulled her hood up over her head. "Good night, Xan. Good night, Michael." She left an endearing kiss on my cheek and then Michael's. She followed Marcy out the door.

For the first time in several hours, I could breathe. I took a long, deep breath and let it out as a sigh. Michael locked the door for the night.

"It was an adventure," he agreed.

"Maybe I should've let them have more wine."

Michael shook his head. "You made the right decision. I wasn't expecting fireworks, either. I just wanted to give them what they wanted and let it be done."

I walked over to Michael and let him wrap his arms around me. "I think we're safe from double dating."

He laughed and kissed my forehead. "Thank goodness for that."

I glanced through the rectangular doorway into the living room. Six empty wine glasses and the tall dark bottle decorated the space like a staged play. I wandered in and started collecting the bowls of snacks. "John could eat anything we put in front of him. I'm surprised he left the peanuts behind."

Michael walked in and picked up the glasses. "He couldn't get to the peanuts without asking for them or getting closer to Stacey. The mix was an easy target."

"What's wrong with Stacey?" I stacked the bowls and grabbed the empty bottle.

"The appropriate question is, what's wrong with John?"

I smiled and moved to the doorway. "It could be worse," I reminded him. "Stacey's underwear could be peeking out from under the couch."

Michael groaned. "How do we know it's not?"

I stepped into the foyer. "You can look if you want, but I think I've seen enough of her underwear for one night."

Chapter 25: Jessie

Willa had never been able to keep a secret from me before. She called me out of the blue and refused to tell me what was going on. She could barely stop giggling. "Come down to the laundromat. I have something to tell you, and I want to tell you in person."

She reminded me of a crack kid detective pretending to hold some super-secret knowledge that was going to knock my socks off. When I got there, it could be anything. Maybe Marlene had knitted her a sweater so they'd look like twins or Frank had given her a really expensive piece of jewelry. Maybe they'd gotten engaged. I didn't know how I felt about that. I'd be excited for her, but it reminded me how far I was from getting engaged to Dick or anybody else.

It was frustrating to wait until six o' clock to leave for the laundromat. I sat through dinner with my parents, which was mostly uneventful because I didn't bring up anything that would move them to notice me. As usual, they carried on their own conversation, throwing me an occasional question or two. I smoothed over my disappointing mid-term grades by blaming the slump on a few hard tests armed with tricky questions.

"Almost everyone's grades are down," I said, but I didn't know anything about it. I promised to do better, and my parents merely nodded. I spent the last half hour before I left the house writing an essay on the surrogate parents in *The Book Thief*.

At five to six, I rushed out of the house and drove the short distance to Suds. I parked by the door and almost ran inside, the dark was so cold. My face was stinging as I walked up to the counter, blowing warm air on my frozen hands.

Willa was beaming, her secret twinkling in her eyes. "You'll never guess what's happening."

"Probably not," I admitted. Her excitement felt more contagious as I warmed up and stopped worrying about frostbite to my tingling nose and ears. "What's going on?"

Willa rolled her eyes in a big, dramatic circle. "Come on, you have to guess."

"You're getting engaged."

Willa snorted and laid her hands out on the counter. Her fingers were bare. "Fat chance. Do you see a ring on these fingers? I'll give you a clue. It has to do with a certain author we both know and love."

"XZA." Now I was getting excited.

Willa could barely stand still. "She's doing a book tour."

"When?"

"Next month."

"New book?"

Willa shook her head. "It's kind of a reminder tour while she finishes what she's working on."

"But she's working on a new book?"

"Yeah."

"Is she coming close to here?"

Willa grinned knowingly, teasing me for not already guessing all the right answers. "She'll be an hour away. December tenth. I'm taking all my books and making her sign them."

"An hour away," I repeated. I leaned against the counter. "That's so close."

"I'm saving up for gas money. All I need is directions."

"Frank's letting you go?"

"Of course. Do you think he'd risk life and limb to stop me?" The corners of Willa's upturned lips fell as she searched my face. "Don't tell me Dick won't let you go for some reason because that is some serious bullshit."

I tried not to act like it could cause a fight between Dick and me. "It's not a big deal for me to blow him off to do something with you."

"Yeah, right," Willa muttered.

I offered the simplest explanation I could. "He's not a fan of XZA, so he doesn't understand why we like her books so much."

"No, I know exactly what it is. She's smart and mouthy and thinks for herself, and that's everything he doesn't want you to be."

Willa was probably right, but I couldn't let her know that. "That's not true. He wants me to get a degree. He tells me that all the time."

Willa pursed her lips doubtfully. "I'm driving up there to that bookstore, and I want you to go with me. There's no reason you can't."

"I know."

"Meeting XZA is worth any argument you have with Dick about this. You could go and not tell him. Did you think about that?"

It wasn't a bad idea, but Dick was going to find out sooner or later. I wouldn't be able to hide my good mood after the signing. I'd rather try my luck at introducing our plans head-on. "There's nothing for him to disagree with," I said, determined to go no matter what Dick said. "I'll split the cost of gas with you. I won't have to buy copies of her books because I already have them. That's one expense taken care of."

"Exactly. So tell him you're driving up with me. It doesn't have to be a long trip. It's one afternoon, a couple of hours. And who knows? Maybe we'll say something that ends up in one of her books someday."

A grin lit my face. "That would be cool."

"Unspeakably cool."

"I'm in. I'll tell Dick I'm going, and that'll be it."

Willa eyed me, her eyebrows skeptically askance. "You're not going to back out on me, are you?"

"No. I'm not backing out."

"I'll go by myself if I have to. Hell, nothing is going to stand between me and shaking that woman's hand. But it'll be significantly cooler if you're there."

"I know."

"Exponentially cooler for you if you're there and not stuck hanging around with Dick."

"I'll be there," I promised.

Willa brought her fist down on the counter to emphasize her words. "The *tenth*. Go straight *home* and *write* it on the *calendar*. In *ink*. I'm not *joking*. If I have to go without you, Dick is a dead man."

I raised my hands in surrender. "Do you honestly think Dick can talk me out of this?"

Willa shrugged. "I don't know. I hope not. He's got this weird hold on you that you don't seem too aware of."

Anger and guilt flared in my chest. I'd sat in Dick's truck and let him babble at me knowing my bracelet belonged to someone else. "What hold?" I asked, trying to ignore it. "We'll see how strong it is on the tenth when I go with you to meet XZA."

Marlene walked out of the *Employees Only* door. She wore a loose blue blouse decorated in a fishing lure pattern tucked into neon green jeans. I didn't even know they made jeans that color. The legs were tucked into the ugliest quilted snow boots I'd ever seen. Marlene almost didn't notice me as she walked past the counter.

Willa called out to her. "Hey, Marlene. Jessie's here."

Marlene smiled and waved to me. She kept moving and started checking the row of machines. Some of them were running, two were stopped but full, and the rest of them sat silent and empty.

Willa turned to me. "Do you know what questions you want to ask her?"

"Questions?"

"Yeah, in case we get a few seconds to talk to her. What are you gonna say?"

"I don't know."

"Which book are you going to tell her is your favorite?"

I considered the question as carefully as I had the others. "I don't know."

"Well, you've got a month to think about it. She probably won't remember us, but I want to say something really cool in case she remembers me."

Willa's chances of being remembered were much higher than mine. "Nobody ever forgets you."

"I bet she'd remember you if you went dressed like the cover of *F*CK, F*CK, F*CK*." Willa pantomimed something standing on top of her head. "Get a mohawk wig and some red plaid pants. You'd have to wear a shirt, obviously, but I think everybody would remember that. Her fans would totally applaud you."

It sounded like way more attention than I was looking for. "You do it. You have the attitude for it."

"I wouldn't look that different than I normally do except for the hair." Willa gestured to her outfit, a short-sleeved blouse with white flowers on a yellow background layered over a long-sleeved waffle-knit shirt. Her black pants looked professional until I noticed they were tightly laced up over the side of each hip.

"How does your boss want you to dress?" I asked.

"We just have to look better than the customers." Willa lowered her voice. "I mean, come on, it's a laundromat. Who are we trying to kid here? I draw the line after khaki pants."

That reminded me of another problem. "I wonder what kind of job I'll end up with."

"What's your major?"

"English. Because my advisor made me declare something."

"I know what I declared. See ya!" Willa gave a feisty salute above her beaming smile.

I couldn't blame her, but I didn't want to face the job market without something to show for my efforts since high school. My parents never had much advice for me about it. They usually suggested I stay in school without mentioning why. It bothered me they wouldn't come right out and say it wasn't me, it was the number of jobs available, but now that Willa mentioned it, I didn't want to talk about it. It made my school decision completely arbitrary. It was just something to fill the time. "Is that all the news you had? XZA is coming close enough for us to meet her?"

"That's enough news for anybody. But yeah, that's all I had."

Willa's greasy-haired boss opened his office door and stuck his head out. His eyes darted to Willa then settled on me. "Good evening. Willa, when you have a minute, I'd like to see you in my office."

Willa gave an amiable reply over her shoulder. "Okay."

The boss closed his door.

Willa jerked her thumb toward it. "See what I mean? He sounds creepy as hell, but it'll be something simple like calling a customer about something they lost or asking me what I think about another employee."

"Does he ask you stuff like that?"

"He values my opinion for some reason." The smooth confidence in Willa's voice told me she knew exactly why he wanted her advice. It was the same reason we all gravitated toward her. She was objective and didn't judge. Except when it came to Dick, and I couldn't blame her for that.

"That sounds like job security," I said.

Willa stuck her tongue out. "I don't wanna be stuck here for the rest of my life."

I shrugged. "You're doing more with your life than I am. Good luck whatever happens in there. It doesn't sound good."

"I know Carl. He's all grease and no bite." Willa waved her hand over her head. "Lotta grease, though."

"Yeah, don't get too close to it." I took a step back from the counter. "I'll call you in a couple of days, and we'll keep making plans for next month."

"Let me know what Dick says about it."

My mind filled with dread. "I will."

I walked to the door, making sure my coat was fastened all the way to my chin. Willa called Marlene to the counter to watch the register. I offered Willa one final wave and pushed the door open. The skin on my face shrank against the prickling cold.

Dick was going to be pissed.

Chapter 26: Xan

The Fancy Fall Art Exhibition was better done than I'd expected. Michael and I checked our coats for free in the first hallway of the civic center and followed the signs to a large room buzzing with people. Plain fabric in bold colors draped over every table, showing off sculptures ranging from animals to more elusive, dramatic shapes.

Michael gestured to a grooved white vase rising from a wide base to a narrower opening. The textured clay made it look like a volcano made out of mashed potatoes. Michael spoke in a low voice beside my ear. "Devil's Tower."

I smiled but didn't let myself laugh. The chance of the artist understanding the reference was too small.

Two-dimensional art, water colors, finger paintings, and crayon drawings hung on the walls. A few larger, more detailed pictures stood on easels in the middle of the room. The simple and dexterous, elementary and advanced mingled together, giving a much better effect than that of moving from the toddlers to the preteens. Seeing the observers, parents, and friends dressed in pressed slacks and long skirts must have given the young artists the intended thrill. Very few children lingered near their artwork except to point it out, saying, "This one's mine, Mom," or "Daddy, it's a giraffe."

The formal clothing and slow pace of the crowd lent an air of reassuring pageantry. The guests hadn't taken their time getting ready to rush through ill-presented artwork. The children hadn't spent several weeks getting ready to have their artwork barely looked at before it was relegated to the refrigerator or packed away in a box as a keepsake. Everyone got what they wanted, and I always appreciated a supportive atmosphere towards creativity.

Michael and I deviated from the obvious path many others took around the room. We floated back and forth between the tables and the pictures on easels. A slip of white paper mounted on black cardboard accompanied all of the artwork, naming the artist but not listing their age. It kept the guests from comparing the pieces in those terms. The only comparisons I heard were about color, subject matter, and style. Toddlers giggled as they chased each other through the crowd. The older children congratulated each other and introduced their parents with assumed maturity.

Michael bent his head down by my ear. "What if this dark, moody watercolor was done by a three-year-old and the post-modern almost-giraffe was done by a twelve-year-old?"

I raised my eyebrows as I considered the two pictures. "Then art camp had a child genius and someone else who really didn't want to be there."

Michael brushed his hand against mine but didn't take hold of it. I'd told him years ago how I felt about public displays of affection, but I wondered what would happen if we pushed that boundary. I avoided contact in front of strangers out of independence more than modesty, but who was I kidding? Michael drove us here from the house we shared. We'd drive back to it and sleep in the same bed when the art exhibition was over. If I was so worried about my independence, the linking of our hands in public was the least of my problems. Numerous couples of all ages strolled around us with fingers linked or one arm around each other. I thought about slipping my hand into Michael's, but I wasn't sure how he'd react. Would he throw me a quizzical glance, or would he mysteriously take it in stride?

Michael pointed out a detailed drawing of a teenaged girl running through thick woods. While the artist's style was still developing, it was a talented picture for the age group. The subject's clothes were slightly torn, but the determined angle of her eyebrows showed no signs of her stopping. "I like this," Michael said. "It could be one of your covers."

"Chessa, maybe. Is there a picture of a disenchanted bride-to-be nearby?"

"Maybe."

Michael and I kept making our way around the room. We passed most of the artwork before I spotted Melody with Flora and Henry. They stood in a tight grouping by one of the tables. Flora recognized me with a widening of her eyes and ran right over. She grabbed my hand. "This one's mine," she proclaimed and led me to her parents.

True to Flora's name, Melody had dressed her daughter in a bright pink floral dress. I barely had time to wave to Melody and Henry. Flora stuck her hand out and presented us with a small grey sculpture. "It's a cat."

"I see that," I said. The ears were loosely shaped, pointed but short and close to the head. The whiskers were scratched into the cheeks. It stood sturdily on four straight legs with rounded paws, and the long tail protruded out from the rear end at a high angle. "It's very good."

"Good job, Flora," Michael chimed in.

Melody set her hands on her hips. "She's been very excited to show it off to you."

I looked down at Flora, who played absent-mindedly with the skirt of her dress. "Why did you make a cat?" I asked.

"Because they're soft and cuddly. It's not a mean cat. It's not a scary cat. It's just standing there. It probably wants something to eat or a place to sleep." Flora placed her palms together and rested her head on them like a pillow.

"It probably does."

Michael added his own questions. "Were you hungry when you made it?"

"Yeah," Flora said right away without thinking.

"Were you tired?"

"No. I'm never tired at art camp. We're just making art. If we were playing basketball, it might make me a little tired."

Melody surveyed the room. "It's a pretty good turn-out." She waved to someone she recognized. "I think if Flora does it again next year, I'm going to suggest hors d'oeuvres, except I worry somebody would drop food on the art."

"That would make new art," Michael pointed out.

"Smelly art," Melody agreed, "after a couple of hours."

"Good point."

We talked for a few minutes more before saying goodbye. I lowered myself to my haunches to give Flora a hug. Feeling her tiny arms around me reminded me of the way Uncle Grigori must have felt when I hugged him. I gave Flora an extra squeeze of affection.

"I'll see you Monday," Melody promised me.

Flora looked up at her mother. "Can I go, too?"

Melody smoothed Flora's feathery blonde hair. "No, sweetie. I'm going there to work, not to play."

"You could work. Xan and I could play together."

I smiled. "I have to work, too, Flora."

"Why?" she pouted.

"That's how I make money."

"You don't need money. You just need hugs."

Melody laughed. "We'll go over there to play sometime, okay?"

Flora folded her arms decisively. Michael and I complimented her cat statuette until she felt better and made our way out of the room. He pulled our coat check numbers out of his pocket and traded them for the coats. We shrugged into them and walked out through the cold night to the car.

We'd been inside the civic center long enough to let the car cool past comfortable. Michael adjusted the heat setting and the vents. He turned the music down a little, one of the CD's John had brought for me. It struck me that even in Michael's car, he would give me control of the CD player. He must've done it countless times, and I had to have noticed it. I just didn't read anything into it until now. I hadn't been willing to let it sway my feelings for him one way or the other.

Michael drove us out of the parking lot onto the street. The sun had set early, leaving the streetlamps to light patches of each neighborhood.

Michael glanced at me. "What do you think? Will Flora want to be an artist?"

I thought about the times I'd spent with Flora. She was spontaneous but ultimately practical. "She'll want to be an artist until she realizes there's no money in it."

"She doesn't care about money yet."

"Maybe she never will. She'll do what we all do and work some barely related day job while we spend our evenings chasing art."

"I'm just saying an artist is more likely for her than a lumberjack. She might want to be a teacher or something helpful like that."

I recalled our brief conversation with Flora and her parents. "Did she really bring up basketball?"

"Yes, she did."

"Where did she get that from?"

"Henry, I guess."

I studied Michael's shifting profile in the various lights of the city. "How are your interviews going?"

"They're good. I almost feel bad, like I'm promising them something I can't deliver. They're so eager to talk to me and tell me about their writing. I'm sorry I can't do more for them than post short reviews online."

"That's more than a lot of people can do for them."

"That's true."

It wasn't hard to picture myself in the students' shoes. "I would've jumped at that kind of opportunity when I was in school. When you're young and unpublished, all you want is somebody to read your work and see its potential."

Michael turned onto the road that led us out of town. "I'm sorry I didn't meet you until you were older and published."

"That's okay. I needed a few years of growing up before that interview."

Michael made a sound between a scoff and a chuckle. "Really? Offering an interview with the intentions of sleeping with the interviewer is an act of wisdom and maturity?"

My lips widened into a smile. "If I'd met you in my twenties, I would've skipped the interview and propositioned you first."

Michael laughed. "It would've done wonders for my self-esteem, but nothing for my career."

"I haven't done very much for your career anyway."

"Not in a huge way, but the website was only a few years old back then. That interview was no small deal. I was treated like a hero even if the rest of the guys had no idea who you were. They weren't getting interviews like that."

"That's funny. I told my friends I slept with my interviewer, and they treated me like a hero, too."

Michael laid his hand on my knee. "It was more important to me on a personal level that you were willing to sit down with me. The interview made me look legitimate as a reviewer, but personally, I was honored. There was no reason for you to give me your time. You had no clue who I was."

I leaned my head back against the seat to take the weight of my head off my overworked neck. "Don't be silly. I flirted with you. I offered you the interview. And when you walked away, at least half a dozen of us were checking out the view. Come to think of it, wherever you go, there's still a group of us checking out your butt."

"The reason my friends don't do that with you is because they're intimidated by you. They've read your books. They're afraid of getting their asses kicked for being creeps."

Crossing through one final intersection, we left the city lights behind. Darkness and shadow overtook the car.

I squinted to see Michael in the sparse remaining light. "I'm not that scary, am I?"

"Not really, but who wants to risk it?"

"I didn't intimidate you, did I?"

"No, but I realize there's a difference between what authors write and who they are. You're not a vigilante. You're not Toria. It's just a matter of finding out how big of a gap there is between an author and their work."

I turned my head to look at the trees passing the window as still, black shapes. "You weren't too worried, obviously. You didn't take that much prodding to get into bed with me."

Michael paused. "Would you have let me say no?"

"Yes, but you were worth taking the time to convince."

"It was you who got out of bed and wouldn't get back in."

I gave no answer. I wanted to see how much Michael remembered and what his take on that night was now.

"That's okay," Michael obliged. "You got back in eventually. It just wasn't the same night or the same bed."

"Why did you call me the next morning? I couldn't possibly have charmed you enough to invite that. You must've been expecting a tirade."

Michael shrugged, shifting the shoulders of his coat. "I thought you might stand your ground, but I didn't think you'd be cruel. What was it you said? Something about being worth taking the time to convince. That's how I felt. It was worth risking you hanging up on me to try to see you again."

"Really?"

"Yes. Really."

"You have a thicker skin than I give you credit for."

Michael threw a glance at me. "Everybody does that. It's the smile. I look like I'm ruled by shallow happiness, but there's so much depth here they don't see." Michael gave a melodramatic sigh. "It's probably because they're too busy staring at my ass."

I smiled at his joke, but I was serious. I'd been so preoccupied with thickening my own skin and checking for cracks in my armor, I'd never noticed how strong and sturdy Michael was. It comforted me, even though I didn't know what that meant for us in the future, even the near future.

Michael drove us home. The evening was young, not even nine o' clock. We trudged up the stairs to the bedroom and the bed Michael had mentioned as the second one we'd occupied together. Except for a few trips to Michael's apartment in Chicago, my bed had been where most of our escapades had taken place. Before he moved in, it was a matter of convenience. He was willing to make the drive, and to spite him for being so hard to resist, I made him drive down when he wanted to see me.

Michael said nothing about this. He didn't seem to notice the bed as I did, as a symbol of my giving in and everything I'd made him work so hard for. He started undressing. He unbuttoned his shirt and traded it for a plain white tee out of the dresser drawer. I kicked my shoes off and slid my skirt down, but taking off my clothes was only a front to keep watching Michael out of the corner of my eye. He traded his sleek black pants for a pair of familiar, gently faded blue pajama pants, and I realized that I loved him. I recognized the swell of affection for what it was, strong enough to get my attention but reassuring in its sincerity. I almost opened my mouth to tell him or at least tell him something in that vein. I wanted to tell him how much he meant to me, his jokes and his observations on art and the way he dealt with Melody and Flora. I wanted to thank him for putting up with my friends, buffering the harsh criticisms of my mother, and introducing me to the hope-inducing role models of his parents.

But I couldn't say a word. I stood there with my black silk shirt in my hand like I didn't know whether to hang it up or drop it in the hamper.

Michael forgave this, too, my momentary lapse in action. He spoke unexpectedly, the gears of his mind turning as mine did. "Those are the kinds of memories that stick with you, evenings like the art exhibition. Anything special like that when you're a kid makes you feel amazing."

All I could do was nod. Michael moved toward the door. I couldn't let him leave the room without saying something. "I'm sorry Jack died."

Michael tilted his head, caught off guard by my dated reference.

My fingers kneaded the collar of my shirt. "I know he was important to you, and you would've liked to move down here with him because of the big yard and everything. It would've been so much more room for him than your apartment."

"It would've. He would've liked it here, but I wasn't sure how you felt about having a dog in the house."

"I would've gotten over it." At least, I hoped so, and I was glad I could say so in hindsight.

"Thanks, Xan." Michael walked out the door into the hall.

I watched him go. I was never more aware of how inept I was at expressing my feelings. Maybe I didn't deserve Michael. Maybe I should throw him to the hungry wolves that were Marcy and Stacey. I deserved to see him out in public buying fresh, hot muffins for another woman, smiling when she said what I couldn't: "Michael, I love you."

The affection that filled my chest turned into something else as it shifted. Determination. Michael wanted to be with me, and if I loved him, I would fight for this. I'd fought him every step of the way as we always said. He worked his way into my bed after that first night, then into my schedule, then into my house. I'd fought ever loving him or needing him, but we were a couple. It made me shiver to think the C word, but we were. We'd attended a children's art exhibition as a couple. We made food, tasted wine, and played mini-golf with his parents as two couples. And I wouldn't have it any other way. I needed to fight for Michael before he decided to move on. That was still possible no matter how he felt about me tonight.

But I had no clue where I could start.

Chapter 27: Jessie

My stomach churned when Dick suggested the diner for dinner. I refused to go, but now I wished I'd given in. We'd compromised on grabbing fast food chili dogs, but I couldn't even eat mine for fear Dick was going to squirt something onto my parents' couch. I stared at him from the recliner, holding my chili dog over a plate on a tray table. Dick refused to eat over anything. He relaxed on the couch, the chili dog poised above his chest, his shirt catching the crumbs falling off the bun.

Dick never swallowed before at least beginning if not also finishing his sentences. He tried to say something, but it only sounded like muffled, grunting syllables. He swallowed half his mouthful and tried again. "There's still a month left before break. This semester's taking forever."

I took a small bite, hoping Dick would see I was chewing and not make me answer. I hadn't come close to telling him the plans Willa and I had made.

Dick tore off another chunk of chili dog with his teeth. "I hink…" He swallowed part of the visible dog and bun. "I think we should get outta here for winter break. Go someplace warm. Fuck this snow. You know what I mean?"

I shrugged. "Sure." I'd never gone anywhere to escape the winter weather. I didn't like it, but I dealt with it. I'd always considered it something to survive, something that brought us all together as we complained about it, but never something I had to run away from.

"We need a beach somewhere like Miami. A lot of old people, but a lot of action."

Dick finished his chili dog and brushed his fingers off on his shirt. The longer he didn't speak, the more I knew he was waiting for me to back him up.

I set the remaining half of my chili dog on my plate. "It sounds great. I'd love to get out of here for a week or so."

Dick's bushy eyebrows lowered in suspicion. "But what? What'd you do? Are you planning something behind my back?"

"No." I didn't want to say her name. "It's just that Willa…"

Dick threw his hands up in the air. "I knew it. What'd she talk you into this time? How stupid is it?"

"It's not stupid. It's something I really wanna do."

Dick leaned over and picked his soda can up off the coffee table. He didn't take his squinted eyes off me.

I made myself say it. "We're driving to this bookstore on one of the Saturdays to go to an XZA book signing."

Dick stared at me. Then his eyebrows shot up his forehead, and he laughed. He laughed in spurts, calming himself down only to find humor in it all over again. His whole body shook, and I thought he was going to spill his pop. "A book signing? With that XZ whatever? And you're going with Willa? I don't know who's dumber, you, her, or that writer."

My chest tightened. "We're not dumb."

"What do you wanna go to that for? Who came up with that brilliant idea?"

I tried to keep my voice even while my body vibrated with rage. "Willa saw online that XZA is doing a small book tour in the area, and we decided to go."

"But why? I don't get it."

"Because she's different, and we want to meet her. We want to tell her how much we like her books and maybe ask her some questions."

Dick laughed, spitting a burst of soda all over his shirt and pants. He set the can on the coffee table. "You two girls think some writer chick wants to hear your thoughts on her book? That's ridiculous. That's the best joke I've heard in a long time, Jessie."

My fingers flexed toward fists. I stuck an image of Willa firmly in my mind the way she shook her head at me in the laundromat, daring me to stand up to Dick. "It's not a joke. We're driving over and meeting XZA on the tenth of December. That's right before finals, so it won't even be over break. It doesn't mess up any plans you want to make with me."

Dick chuckled and wiped at the wet spots on his shirt and jeans. "You wanna waste the weekend before finals on this chick? Are you worried about your grades or not?"

"Yeah, I am, but it's my only chance to meet her. I can't pass it up."

"So you're willing to let everybody down so you can say hi and bye to somebody who's not even gonna remember you?"

I stiffened, pulling my arms in toward my sides. "It's not going to let anybody down. I'll do fine on the finals. It's a few hours on one day."

Dick slowed his speech and emphasized his words. "Who the *fuck* wants to hear what you two *girls* have to say about their books?"

The intense conviction in Dick's eyes shut out the image of Willa in my head. I couldn't say anything. He'd found my secret fear and voiced it.

Dick took another sip of soda. "She's written, like, two books, right?"

"Three," I breathed.

"Yeah, so why does she need your opinion? She's written, like, hundreds of words. Why does any one word you say matter to her?"

I didn't feel like eating anymore. The second half of my chili dog might as well have been a packing peanut. "I still want to go talk to her."

"Okay. Whatever. Don't complain to me when she looks at you like you're retarded."

"I'm not retarded."

Dick turned his head toward the kitchen. "Doesn't your mom have any cookies or cupcakes or anything?"

I stared at my chili dog. "There might be some chocolate in the pantry."

Dick got up and wandered into the kitchen. I wanted to grab my phone and call Willa. She'd assure me in a second that XZA would want both of us there. I couldn't imagine XZA turning us away or giving us dirty looks for asking questions. Why would her books empower us so she could put us down?

Dick came back with a Mars bar, tearing the wrapper apart. "I don't even know which of my classes have finals."

It took me a second to pick up on the new topic. "You should probably find out."

"I don't know what I did with my syllabus." Dick crashed down on the couch.

I remembered where I'd seen it last, and I considered keeping my mouth shut. I decided I'd help him out. "I think it's crumpled up in the bottom of your backpack."

"Probably."

There was no gratitude. I wasn't surprised. Just disappointed. In me. For trying.

Dick peeled the wrapper off the candy bar and tried to throw it to the coffee table. It missed and fell out of my view. He left it where it landed. "So we're doing a beach somewhere for winter break?" he asked.

"Yeah," I said, barely paying attention.

"I bet I could get somebody to sell me some pot, and I could resell it for some extra money."

"Yeah."

"How are you going to help pay for it?"

"Student loans, I guess. The same way I pay for everything."

Condescension twisted Dick's voice. "You're not worried about having to pay it back?"

"It's the only money I've got."

"You better stay in school, then. You don't want it to come due."

I knew that. It was half the reason I stayed in college along with my parents' approval.

Dick took a huge bite of the candy bar and chewed it with noisy slurping sounds. "I don't want mine to come due."

"Is that why you're still in school?"

Dick shrugged. "I don't know what else to do." He chuckled. "The T and A ain't bad, either."

I grabbed my plate and carried the remains of my chili dog into the kitchen.

Dick called after me, suddenly serious. "Hey, are you gonna eat that? I'll eat it."

I stomped my foot on the pedal to the garbage can lid, exposing a mess of old potato salad Mom had cleaned out of the back of the fridge. She'd gagged when she opened the container. It was a stinking, gelatinous mess wriggling atop slimy spinach and tin can wrappers. I dumped the chili dog off my plate into the thick of it. If I was too chicken to confront him about the bracelet, it was the next best thing. "It's too late. I already threw it away."

Dick accepted this with a groan. "That sucks."

I rinsed my plate off, taking my time in the kitchen. A Saturday with Willa could be good. Dick would never suggest coming along, so our plans were safe. All I had to do was wait until a few days before the tenth to remind him I'd be out of town. Then I wouldn't have to listen to him whine, and I could go meet XZA in peace.

Chapter 28: Xan

I sat on the living room carpet with a dozen of my novel's scene cards laid out in front of me and the rest of the deck in my hand. Melody had written them out for me while I lingered over my coffee, dreading this part of the process. I was hoping visualizing my novel this way would help me see the full story of it, but it was often easier set up than understood. Michael was out conducting more interviews with local writers, some of them students and some of them referred friends, family, and graduates. This left me free to ponder my novel without his continuous coaching to take it easy.

Melody came in with a fresh mug of coffee for me. She set it on a coaster on the coffee table.

I stared at the cards. The answer had to be somewhere in those words. I barely glanced up at Melody as she hovered over me. "I think there's another folder for this book in the back of the filing cabinet. It has my original ideas in it. Could you grab it for me?"

Melody's stocking feet made a light, quick exit to the foyer. I laid out a few more cards, forming a gently rising line as the action built toward the climax I had yet to write.

Melody returned with a plain beige file folder. "Is this it?"

I took it from her. The tab read *Leifa?* in my handwriting. I opened it to pages of handwritten notes on various sizes and shapes of paper. "I think so." There was an early, partial character list and a list of major plot points on a white fast food napkin. "Yes. Thank you."

Melody sat down on the floor across from me past the growing row of cards. She folded her legs under her. "I wish I could help you more."

"Michael's right. I'll get it eventually."

"You could work on one of your other projects. It might help clear your head."

"I'm afraid of stuffing too many stories and characters in there at the same time. The market's changed, anyway. It'll be tough to find a home for this book, but not so tough that it's not worth it." I laid out a few more cards, finding the ebb and flow of the story. I shifted the conversation away from my book. "I was thinking about getting my parents a computer for Christmas. They've never had one, and that way, they could check on my writing and Michael's work whenever they feel like it."

"That's a great idea."

"It's strange, though. My mother's never been shy about disapproving of Michael, but she likes him enough to ask about him and what he does. I've never understood it."

"My parents weren't wild about all of my boyfriends, either, if you remember."

I laughed. Melody's most rebellious boyfriend was only half as compulsive as Michael, as far as I knew. He raised red flags because he wore black leather jackets and boots instead of polo shirts and sandals. Unbeknownst to Melody, her disagreements with her parents had spawned several book ideas. I'd never seriously pursued them, so I never mentioned it. "I knew you'd be fine. I wish they would've trusted you more."

Melody shrugged. "I don't blame them. If you go back and look at how different they all were, it's a wonder my parents didn't send me to a psychiatrist."

I marveled at Melody's leniency. "You have a patience I've never had. I'm surprised our parents didn't try to switch us at birth. You would've been polite to my mother, and I would've explained my every move to your parents."

"There's a bit of an age difference there," Melody reminded me lightly.

"They'd notice. They just wouldn't care."

Melody loosened her focus, gazing off past the furniture. "Sometimes I think about being fifteen, eighteen again, just starting out dating. I thought I knew so much more than I did." She shook her head and looked at me. "Here I am, married, second baby on the way. Is this the same lifetime or what? Where do all the years go, huh?"

I'd been thinking a lot about years. Ten years with Michael. Thirty since I'd seen Uncle Grigori. I laid my index cards on the floor and looked Melody in the eye. "I've never told Michael I love him."

Melody scrunched her eyebrows together. "What?"

"I've never told Michael I love him." It sounded incredible, even to me.

"What are you talking about?"

"You've been with Henry almost as long as I've been with Michael."

"Yeah." Melody still sounded perplexed. "About eight years."

"And you've told him you love him."

"Of course. Every chance I get."

My hands bounced in the air, fueled by frustration. "That's what I'm saying. I never had that urge until a couple of days ago after Flora's art exhibition."

"What happened that changed your mind?"

"Nothing." I almost laughed. "It was the smallest thing in the world. He was putting on his pajamas. It was the most perfect thing I've ever seen."

Melody leaned toward me. "That's good, right? You're getting more comfortable with your relationship."

"Ten years in? Michael says it to me, and I say nothing. What am I, deaf? He knows I hear him."

"Do you know why?"

It was the same reason I'd given Michael ten years ago. It sounded logical then. It sounded inadequate and implausible now. "My uncle killed himself."

"Oh, my God." Melody scooted closer to me, used to crawling on hands, knees, and shins after Flora. She moved much more carefully with her pregnant belly. "You never told me that."

My voice cracked when I spoke, and I didn't bother to stop it. "He fell in love with this woman named Evalisse, and she broke his heart. He stopped caring about everything else, and he hanged himself in the kitchen of his apartment."

Melody wrapped her arm around my shoulders. In all the years she'd been my assistant, she had never needed to comfort me. "Does Michael know?"

"He knows about it for the most part. My mother never told me how he died until recently. I just knew what I'd picked up from my parents when they didn't know I was listening."

"I'm sure Michael understands. You obviously saw a relationship end in a pretty painful way."

"That's not even half the reason I'm upset." I didn't have to reach for the hard truths. They bubbled up like lava shooting from a volcano. "There's the complicated relationship I have with my mother. I don't even call her Mom most of the time. And I blamed her. I blamed her for her own brother's death for thirty years."

Melody's voice remained sturdy and consoling. "You were young. His death really hurt you."

I shook my head. "I blamed her from the start, right when she told me. I had no decency, no respect for the fact that her brother died."

I'd been home in my room, reading a book I'd since forgotten the title of. I used to worry about losing that detail and would wrack my brain for twenty minutes at a time trying to remember which book it was. Who was the author? What was on the cover? In the end, everything else remained except that one ultimately unimportant piece.

When my mother called my name, I knew something was wrong. She never called for me. She waited for me to crawl out of my bedroom, my hovel, my hole, to greet her in my own time. I stayed where I was. I didn't want to see her if she had bad news.

By the time I forced myself up and reached the door, she was on the other side. She knocked slowly. "Xan? There's something I need to tell you."

"I don't want to hear it," I said, but she opened the door.

Her face was stricken, drawn in places and puckered in others. I backed away from her, frantic tears irritating my eyes. She reached for my hand, but I jerked it away.

"Sit down, Xan," she told me.

"No." I didn't want her suggestions or her revelations.

She took a shaky breath and lowered her voice even further. "Uncle Grigori passed away."

"No!" I was already hysterical, my knees loosening beneath me.

My mother reached out to hold me up, but I slapped her arms. I slapped at her until she stopped coming towards me and backed out of the room. She pulled the door closed, and I fell to the floor.

I never apologized for this. On the contrary, when my dinner appeared on the other side of the door a few hours later, I took it as a sign of her apology for ruining my life with her words. As I ate, I longed for Uncle Grigori and blamed my mother with a blazing hatred for pushing him so hard in the previous weeks. He wanted to be left alone or on some days to talk to me. He had never wanted my mother to barge in and order him around.

I'd never considered her burden of relating this news to me. I'd never stopped thinking about my own loss long enough to look at that day from her point of view. She lost her only brother to the depression of his apartment months before he died, and after finding him dead there, all I could do was offer her more pain.

No wonder she thought I loved Uncle Grigori more than I cared about her. I had the irrepressible urge to call my mother and apologize thirty years too late.

Melody stroked my hair rhythmically, and I decided I owed her an explanation. "I never got to say goodbye to my uncle. When I found out he'd left me most of his money, I felt this crushing guilt. It stirred up new problems between my mother and me. I heard her tell my dad they could've used it to renovate the kitchen, but it was stuck in CD's and investments for me, waiting for me to grow up."

Melody said nothing.

I went on, the same thoughts I'd been holding onto for thirty years. "He was a teacher, so his salary wasn't great, but he lived very simply. There were rumors he'd been saving up for a house or an engagement ring for Evalisse. He had a decent-sized nest egg when he went."

Melody rubbed my back and cleared her throat. "Maybe you should look at it another way. It's horrible that he passed away, but maybe something good came out of it."

I covered my face with my hands. "How do you think I was able to afford the down payment on this house? I love this house, and I'd never live anywhere else. But I wouldn't have it if Uncle Grigori hadn't died. Every year I don't get enough editing work or publish a book, I fall back on that money. Part of your salary came from my inheritance."

Melody tried again to soothe me. "It's no wonder you've been reluctant to commit to anyone. Xan, that's a lot for anyone to take in, let alone a teenage girl."

"I can't stop thinking about his final months. He was horribly depressed. My mother couldn't get him to do a damn thing, but he waited so long to end it. I can't help but wonder if he was growing that inheritance for me. Was he keeping himself alive to help take care of me? It cuts me too deeply to think about." With no note from Uncle Grigori, I'd never be able to answer that question.

Melody set her head on my shoulder. She was good at nurturing. I'd always known that. Her sensitivity and trustworthiness had made me hire her and keep her on no matter what my financial situation.

I grieved into my hands.

Melody admitted what she was thinking. "I've never seen you cry."

I hadn't meant to break down in front of her, and I tried to dry myself up. "I shouldn't have stuck Michael in the middle of this mess between my need for people and my issues with the ones I already know."

Melody reached for the box of Kleenex on the end table and handed me a tissue. "I'm sure he'd understand if you explained it to him."

"That's not the point." I dotted the Kleenex at my wet eyes and nose. "At least with my mother, I had a reason to believe she hurt me, no matter how twisted it was. But Michael never did. He was kind and generous and did whatever I asked him to. Except for not saying he loves me. That he wouldn't do."

Melody shook my arm in encouragement. "So you got lucky. You should embrace it. Not everybody has it so good."

"Melody, you don't understand. I don't deserve this. I've done nothing but push Michael away ever since he hinted he might want something more in life than a fleeting one-night stand. I came home from that interview determined to never speak to him again, but you know how the next morning went. He's charming, and he's sexy. I gave in that one time. Then I gave in again. And it just went on like that for years. I put him through much more than I would've put up with from anyone."

"He loves you. That's all. It's not complicated."

"It's not simple, either, but I feel like if he's still here, I have a chance to make this work. I don't think I'd be the same if Michael left. I always thought I'd move on like *that* if it happened." I snapped my fingers. "But I know now it would hurt me for a long time. I never wanted to give someone that kind of power over me, but I trust Michael."

"You shouldn't feel bad about caring for somebody. If you love him, it's because you can't help it. You've made it your whole life without getting hurt, but you have to ask yourself, is Michael worth the risk of getting hurt?"

I searched for a dry patch of Kleenex and touched up my face. "I think he is. I can't let him go without telling him how much I care. I really do love him."

"He'll be happy to hear that. I know he will."

I squeezed Melody's hand. "Thank you for making me take that call ten years ago. I resented it, and I was short with you, but having Michael in my life has been a good thing."

"Sure. How could I resist? He's such a smooth talker, if he was closer to my age, I might've gone out with him."

I smiled to think of the way Marcy and Stacey hounded Michael. "My friends have picked up where you left off."

Melody softened her voice. "You should rest and look at all of this later."

I abandoned the stack of index cards in my hand and the line of them spread across the floor. Melody guided me to the couch. I sat down, and she handed me my coffee.

"What if I'm too late?" I asked. "Expressing my feelings to Michael."

"It's not possible," Melody assured me. "'Too late' would mean he'd moved out by now."

I cringed at the image of Michael leaving. I'd gotten used to sharing my house. What would I do with a three-bedroom house and a nice yard by myself? I bought it to spread out in after years of small houses and cramped apartments. My friends and I weren't young and restless anymore. Marcy's and Stacey's lives had changed too much for sleepovers. Stacey worked more hours, and Marcy had her strange relationship with the milkman to keep her busy. Without

Michael, the house would feel empty.

"What if he leaves me?" I asked.

Melody perched on the couch arm next to me. "He won't."

"We don't know that."

"Michael does. All you have to do is talk to him. I'm sure he'll answer you as honestly as he can. Then you'll know what he's thinking, and you won't have to keep guessing."

I knew Michael was the only one with the answer, but the thought of it being the wrong one petrified me.

Chapter 29: Jessie

I finished wiping dust off the stereo and looked at the clock. Willa was supposed to be here in five minutes. The rest of the room looked better than it had all semester, not exactly tidy but straightened. I didn't have enough time to get started on something for school, but it was all the time I needed to read a few pages of *Hypocrisy*. I threw the dirty paper towel away and grabbed the book out of my backpack. I tossed myself across the bed, bouncing a few times with the mattress, and opened the book. I hadn't been able to read it for days.

Lourdes stood outside the high school. The light rain pelted her face, but she made no effort to shield herself. She looked out for her mother's car. After several minutes, Lourdes checked her watch. Her mother was running late. Lourdes stepped closer to the curb where her mother could see her more easily than against the immediate backdrop of the building.

Lourdes felt her hair soak up the rain and begin to fall limp against the top of her head. She looked at her watch again. Her mother had never run this late. She wondered about her brother, if he was also standing in the rain in front of his school. Maybe there was a problem with him that had demanded her mother's attention and was keeping her from picking up Lourdes.

Lourdes might never know the problem was not a matter of personal safety or a simple slip in paying attention to the time.

Mrs. Falzone reclined in a motel bed across town, her legs wrapped desperately around those of Mr. Hayes. There was no tenderness in their motions, just a hurried coupling of moving parts. She remembered how little she knew about him, and their anxious friction did little to teach her. They were merely filling a space, and she was terrified her life would feel empty again within a couple of hours.

When Lourdes' mother pulled up in front of the high school with her brother in the back seat, Lourdes climbed in beside him. She was glad his face and jacket were dry. She wiped her face with her jacket sleeve, the fleece feeling more soggy than useful.

Mrs. Falzone said simply, tersely, "I lost track of the time."

Lourdes piped up right away. "That's okay, Mom. I didn't wait long."

By the time Mrs. Falzone pulled the car into the garage, a tear slipped down the curve of her cheek. She wiped it away, but Lourdes saw it. She didn't know what had caused it exactly, but she was sure it had to do with her pregnancy.

The doorbell rang, and I was forced to put the book down mid-paragraph. I slid it under my pillow and hurried out to the living room. My parents sat on the couch in their usual spots, Dad closest to the kitchen and Mom on his left. They made no move toward the door.

"I'll get it," I said anyway.

Mom glanced at me. "Thanks, Jessie."

She meant well, so I ignored the fact that her casual gratitude made her sound condescending. I pulled the door open. Willa stood on the porch in an old fur coat I hadn't seen before. The reddish-brown color of it was either the coolest or the ugliest thing I'd ever seen. I let her inside and closed the door against the wind.

Willa kicked her boots off and left them on the rubber mat with the family boots. "Hi, Mrs. Taylor, Mr. Taylor."

Dad offered a subdued, "Hi, Willa."

Mom waved and smiled. "It's good to see you again, Willa. I didn't know if we would."

Willa unzipped her coat. "It's pretty hard to get rid of me.

What're you watching?"

"*Seinfeld*," my parents chimed in together.

"I'm surprised I didn't recognize the voices. My parents are stuck on *Cheers*. Can you believe it?"

"*Cheers* was good," Mom agreed. "So was *Taxi*. I didn't know you knew all those old shows."

"Sure. Life with my parents filled me in on everything that happened before I was born. I'm lucky I saw anything in color." Willa turned to me. "What're you up to?"

"Studying." I lowered my eyelid in a slow wink.

Willa grinned. "Gotcha. Why don't you show me what you're working on, and I'll see if I can help you with it?"

I led Willa past my parents to my bedroom. I couldn't remember the last time we'd hung out there together. It must've been at least two years ago, not long after she stopped going to school.

Willa looked around longer than I expected her to. "It looks the same."

I couldn't believe it. I looked everywhere she had, eager to find a difference, but she was right. The walls were the same bold purple they'd been since I was nine. I'd moved some of the furniture at one point or another but had moved it all back. It looked exactly the same as the last time Willa hung out here.

Willa leaned over to study the black and white photo of my clean room. "This is new, I think."

I gave a slight exhale, more embarrassed than relieved.

"Did you take this picture?" Willa asked.

"Yeah."

"It's good. I like it. Do you still run around taking pictures?"

I shrugged, uneasy about what happened to my camera. I wanted to lie, but I was afraid she'd see right through it. I settled on an evasive half-truth. "Sometimes. It's been a while, though."

"That's too bad. You had a good eye for it." Willa moved on to the bookcase and touched my knickknacks. She picked up a plastic snow globe Mom had bought me on a family vacation and turned it over in her hands to shake up the glitter inside it. "Where's your special homework?"

I walked over to the bed and pulled out *Hypocrisy*.

Willa set the glitter globe back on the shelf and held her hand out. "Let me see. What part are you on?"

I gave her the book without having to open it. "Lourdes' mom just cheated on her husband."

Willa opened it up to my bookmark and laid on the sarcasm with a rise of her eyebrows. "Really romantic, isn't it?"

"I hope she gets caught."

"She won't, at least not by the time the book ends."

"That's too bad." I sat down on the edge of the bed.

"I wanted her to get caught, too. I wanted to see the whole family fall apart the way it actually is instead of getting to put up a front." She closed the book and held it up. "Have you told Dick we're getting these autographed yet?"

"Yes."

"And?"

"He threw a shit fit, but I'm going."

"Good for you. I can't wait to meet her." Willa opened the back cover and showed me the author photo above the short bio. "That's who we're looking for."

I'd looked at the back-of-the-book photos of XZA before. She was pretty in a shrewd way. Her hair was as dark as her skin was pale. She had dark dramatic eyes, narrow cheek bones, and a small arched mouth. I wished I looked more like her, but I didn't say it.

Willa smiled at the picture with approval. "It's gonna be great. I'm so glad you're going with me." She inhaled sharply with another idea. "You should bring your camera, and we can get our picture taken with her. Then we'll always have evidence of our little adventure."

"What if it's not so awesome?"

Willa's eyes opened wide as her head tilted to one side. "What are you talking about? It's going to determine the rest of our lives."

"What if we don't really get to talk to her?"

"Then we email her later or leave her a Facebook message and say, 'Hey, great to meet you. You're awesome.' And then she responds with, 'Hey, great to meet you, too.' It's fine. It's not the only chance we'll ever have to talk to her. It's just the best chance we've gotten to see her face to face."

I looked down at my socks. "I'm trying not to get my hopes up too much."

"Why? What did Dick say to you?"

"Nothing I wasn't already thinking, and that's the truth. I don't think it's going to be as great as you think it is."

"We'll see then, won't we? I'm not saying she's going to make us her new best friends. We're not going out to dinner after. We're meeting our favorite role model. It's going to be awesome no matter what she says."

I didn't argue. I didn't want to fight about something that hadn't happened yet.

"Trust me." Willa set the book down on the comforter, also something I'd had for too long. "I was right about the books, wasn't I?"

"Yes."

"And I was right about Dick not liking our plans."

I reluctantly admitted to that. "Yes."

"So what are you worried about? Is Dick ever right about anything?"

"Sometimes."

"Sometimes?" Willa made a clicking sound with her tongue. "What's that old saying my grandpa always used? A broken watch is right twice a day."

"He's right about me staying in school. I don't have the money to start paying my loans back."

"You get some time before you have to do that. He's not wrong, but he doesn't know everything. If you hate school so much, leave. You can always go back."

"That's true."

"Glad to hear I'm smarter than Dick." Willa glanced at the clock on the bedside table. "What do you wanna do? We should go do something."

"We should." I pulled at the fibers of Willa's coat. I couldn't tell if it was real fur or not. "Where did you get this thing?"

"Oh, you like it?" Willa adjusted the fit of it on her shoulders. "I found it at the thrift store. You don't have to be rich to shop. You just have to dig through other people's old junk to find what you want. You wanna go?"

I shrugged. "Why not?"

"Cool." Willa zipped up her coat. "Shake the change outta the couch, and let's get rolling. We want to get to the good stuff before it closes."

"How much junk do we have to dig through to get to the good stuff?"

"A hundred pieces to one. Most of it's left over from the eighties, but if you're really lucky, some rich, spoiled housewife just made a huge donation."

Chapter 30: Xan

Finding Uncle Grigori's grave was a numbers game I'd invented when I was sixteen so I could find it without relying on my mother. I still used it even though I'd seen her find his plot much more quickly than I could. She found it instinctively, while I always seemed to forget exactly where it was. Maybe I always hoped I'd never find it, a sign that he was alive and it didn't exist.

He'd given me Zenobia as my middle name. As I pulled into the cemetery, I reminded myself that Queen Zenobia reigned during the third century. I guided my car along the path, passing the statue marking the third section of graves and parking as far to the right as I could.

I picked up the bottle of Russian Standard from the passenger seat. I'd brought it to honor Uncle Grigori, but the ceremony of it would benefit me more than it would affect him. I climbed out of the car, the newly lowered temperature stinging my face. I was glad I could park this close but sorry I couldn't park closer.

Unlike my visits in the summer, I wasted no time crossing the path to the correct section of graves. Fifteen cities in the US were named Alexandria as I was. I hung the bottle discretely at my side and walked down the row to the fifteenth column of headstones. They were all low, about knee-height, no impressive monuments blocking my view for at least fifty yards. I'd never liked the openness of cemeteries. In some sense, I wanted to hide when I visited. I appreciated the easy access to the public, but knowing a total stranger – or worse, someone I knew – could interrupt my private business set me on edge. I wrapped my scarf tighter around my neck, grateful as I was every winter for the soft alpaca wool from Stacey.

I waded into the section of graves, searching the headstones row after row until I found Uncle Grigori's. It was a simple pale grey, a color I'd never seen except in headstones and winter skies. Its relative plainness only underscored its serious purpose. In the row behind it, several double headstones loomed in a line, marking those who had died as married and widowed. They made it easier to notice Uncle Grigori's was a single plot, the reason he had gone in the ground to begin with.

I lingered a few feet away near where his feet might be, keeping a distance I didn't usually hesitate to cross. Reading his name, birthday, and estimated date of death etched into the stone always sobered me. He hadn't even made it to fifty. I hadn't yet, either, but I planned to.

Brave birds sang to each other in other parts of the cemetery, breaking the fragile silence. I didn't look for them even though I probably could've spotted them among the bare branches. I focused on Uncle Grigori's headstone as if it were him, as if he could answer me.

The cold hung light and airy around me, but my motions felt sluggish. I crouched down on my haunches, almost eye to eye with his name. "There are a lot of things I wished I'd said while you were alive," I said, the sound of my voice alone between the plots. It came out low and convincing, encouraging me to go on despite my uneasiness. I'd never spoken out loud here unless I came with my mother.

"Why didn't you tell me you intended to do this?" I asked. I sat down on the hard ground with the bottle of vodka in my lap, obscuring it with my arms. "You shared everything with me. When I was six, you told me about articles you'd written that my mother couldn't understand. But you understood me, and you knew I was interested in anything you wanted to tell me."

Uncle Grigori was more than those two dates memorialized on his headstone. There was a whole life lived between them, filled with triumphs and joys before his heartbreak. I'd usually seen him happy, which made his life-altering decision all the harder to understand. "You must've known your death would change me, change my life. I would've done anything to keep you with me. You left me alone with Mom, who's never known how to talk to me, and Dad, who I didn't know how to talk to. Do you know how much I would've given to keep you with me?"

My voice peaked, and I threw glances over the headstones to make sure no one had approached me. I wanted to say more, to shake the headstone that taunted me, reminding me where Uncle Grigori was. I hated that this was the closest I could get to him.

But I didn't need his answer for this. Of course he'd known. And the one way for him to go through with what he wanted to do was to keep me from knowing. He must've felt guilt, horrible, crushing guilt as he went through with it. If he'd told me what he was planning, the look in my eyes would've trapped Uncle Grigori in an even harder choice: dying to end his heartache or living to spare me mine.

"How did I not know you were going to do it?" I wondered, thinking over those last conversations in his apartment. "My mother knew. She saw the signs. But I was young, and I was so excited to spend time with you, I didn't pay attention to what you wanted or what you needed. If I had, though, I couldn't have replaced Evalisse for you, so I would've been left in the same spot. All I could do was give you my sympathy and a hug."

I pictured his small, dimly lit apartment, which had never been bright even on sunny days. If it wasn't for his money, I'd probably live in a similar place. One bedroom, small closets, beige carpeting. The only thing my house had in common with the other places I'd lived was the beige carpeting, just softer and longer-lasting.

My mother hadn't painted a very pretty picture of Uncle Grigori's death, and I cringed at the story she'd told me. "Why did you hang yourself?" I recalled touring the apartment with my parents, how much they cooed over its unique characteristics despite the cramped amount of space. "I remember when you first moved into that apartment, how much everyone admired those beams in the kitchen. They don't see them as such beautiful architectural details now, do they?" I paused, caught between wanting to imagine Uncle Grigori's final moments and hoping to spare myself the gruesome details. Had he dragged in a chair from the dining table or used the little stool he kept in the coat closet? I hadn't thought to ask my mother how much she knew. Where did he get the rope from? Why wear his best suit?

That last detail told me more than any note could've. The uncle I loved wasn't completely gone. The conscientious man who took pride in his appearance and always put his best face forward still clung to some hope of better days.

"I guess there's no good way to go, but what made you choose something that was used as capital punishment for years? Maybe you thought you deserved it for what you were doing or for whatever reasons made Evalisse leave you. Maybe it doesn't matter and it's none of my business."

I wished Uncle Grigori was here. I wanted to know what it would've been like to be friends with him adult to adult. "It's so hard to be mad at you. We were the only two people on the planet who understood each other. Not knowing why you left or why that was the best choice you could come up with would've killed me if I'd thought about it with any real depth."

No wonder I'd put it off for so long. Loving Uncle Grigori meant accepting his decisions, and no part of me had wanted to face that possibility. I turned the bottle of vodka slowly in my lap, my fingers on the cap. "I accept that you're gone. I don't accept that you did it to yourself." My eyes fell on his last name, my mother's maiden name. Thinking of her broadened my focus, pulling me out of my selfish grief. It wasn't *my* tragedy. Losing Uncle Grigori was a *family* travesty. "I'm not the only one who's changed. Mom was more angry and upset after you died than she was before. Dad's heart gets weaker and weaker since he found you. I hope he was an acceptable member of the family to be left with that task."

There was no answer. Not even the birds came closer or gave a response. There was nothing to pull me out of my reverie, and I drifted in it. "Mom got so jealous after you left me the money, but I think that was just to keep her from fixating on what you did. She had no trouble being furious with you the way I did. I would've rather had you than the money. I didn't care that she was mad. She's always been mad at me, but I've always hated the feeling that I benefited from your death. I see now you didn't mean it that way, but I wish you would've asked me about it before you did something that would impact the rest of my life."

My eyes traced the dates emblazoned in the headstone. I could still remember gazing at them when they were fresh. It'd seemed strange to shift into the next decade and then the next millennium. It seemed so far away. "I wonder what you would've been like now. You'd be halfway through your seventies. A stubborn, cantankerous old man, probably. I imagine you would've gotten over Evalisse at some point. I guess you didn't think you would. The rest of the family kind of resents her, but I don't think anyone pores over her very much these days except for me."

I raised my knees, planting my feet on the ground and wrapping my arms around my legs. I could still call up the voices and vague faces of men I'd known before Michael. Some I'd snubbed, and others had snubbed me, igniting indignant anger much more than sad regret. That was the way I'd wanted it. "No one has hurt me the way Evalisse hurt you. I worked hard at that. It was easier than you'd think, but I had such a strong example to learn from. It kept me honest and never let me sway."

I shifted my fingers inside my gloves, smooth burgundy leather on the outside and soft, warm cashmere lining the inside. Michael had bought them for me several winters ago, but I took such deliberate care of them, they almost looked new. "That brings me to why I'm here, the man who gave me these gloves. He loves me, Uncle Grigori. That terrified me for a long time. I wish you could've met him, but I didn't meet him for twenty years after you died."

I tried to picture the two men together, shaking hands and swapping stories. Uncle Grigori would've regaled him with tales on giving lectures and traveling to St. Petersburg before I was born. It was a city I'd loved to hear him describe – not so much cold as wet. In return, Michael would've unveiled entire collections of stories revolving around bar-hopping and various Chicago attractions. They would've made plans they may or may not have kept – world travels and book exchanges and drinking. It would've warmed my heart to watch them, at once understanding and disbelieving. The antics they could've cooked up together were unimaginable. They would've dragged me into their conversation eventually, putting an arm around me or finding a new story that started with, "Remember the time, Xan...?"

But that could never happen. My mind turned to sadder memories, the tense afternoons I spent in his apartment, and I felt twelve again. I was sitting in the bedroom that grew stuffier and stuffier every time my mother brought me to visit. I sat on the edge of the bed with him, facing him, touching on subjects that mattered and didn't matter. I kept talking because when I didn't, it was easier to hear my mother inspecting the rest of the apartment. The kitchen cabinets thumped as she shut each one. The bathroom shower curtain sang along the metal rod and grated back again.

"I saw a bird today," I'd say. "A cardinal."

Uncle Grigori would nod but not say anything.

"Robins are everywhere."

"They always are."

Finally, my mother would come into the bedroom. She would only talk about his condition, mental, physical, and living. She wasted no time on small talk. Her hand rested on the dresser, her arm above it straight and rigid. "This isn't a life, Grigori. Do you want to come live with us for a while?"

"No," he answered before I could get my hopes up.

"Do you want me to come stay with you for a few weeks?"

"No."

"I don't know what to do for you, Grigori."

"Then do nothing. Please, do nothing. There's nothing you can do for me."

My mother paused. "Come on, Xan. Let's not bother him anymore today."

I didn't want to leave, but my mother's expression was insistent and Uncle Grigori made no argument. His shoulders slumped even though he had the self-consciousness to dress in a nicely made, thick cable-knit sweater. I leaned over to hug him as I always did. "Goodbye, Uncle Grigori. We'll be back soon."

He closed his arms around my back. "Goodbye, Xan. I love you."

"I love you, Uncle Grigori."

I blinked, and the image faded. It wasn't a scene from a random visit. It was the last day I'd ever had with him, the last time I'd ever seen him alive. *I love you* were the last words I'd ever spoken to him. We held his wake and funeral two weeks later.

For thirty years, I'd avoided love thinking – knowing – that the person you love the most can disappear when you don't expect it. Keeping myself at a distance from everyone I met, I never understood why Uncle Grigori would give up so much over losing Evalisse. Loving Michael showed me a fragment of what Uncle Grigori felt even though I still hated the way his story ended. He never told me what he planned to do. He never mentioned suicide or money. He never looked me in the face and said, "I have to do this. Forgive me. Know that I love you, Xan." He'd simply said, "Goodbye. I love you," like it was an ordinary day. And I left his apartment like it was an ordinary day.

A car drove by on the path fifty feet away, passing my parked car. I wiped a tear off my cheek with my glove. I lifted the bottle of Russian Standard and unscrewed the cap. The dates on the headstone caught my eye, his birthday in the summer and his death only weeks before my birthday in the spring. "I always wondered why I celebrated your birthday and ignored every anniversary of your death." I pocketed the cap. "Now I know."

My thirteenth birthday party reared up in my memories. It was as painful and inescapable as Uncle Grigori's funeral. I hadn't wanted the party at all, but my mother threw one anyway. All the rest of the family was there except for him. I didn't invite my friends, but my mother got a few to come and chatter in the midst of my family.

I sat in the middle of the chaos, no smile on my face and no thrill in my heart. The presents piled up on the table meant nothing. The whispers I'd heard over the past few weeks replayed in my head, the unbelievable reason Uncle Grigori wasn't there to celebrate with me. My mother's voice echoed those two most condemning of words: *to himself, to himself, to himself.*

My heart split open with loneliness and longing as I thought of it. A girl adrift, surrounded by laughter and presents and cake. Reaching my teenage years without my best friend to guide me and give me hope was the hardest day of my life.

I pulled my glove off and wiped the swathes of tears off my cheeks. I burrowed my hand into the glove's warmth once again. Uncle Grigori's headstone sparkled through the salt water clinging to my lashes. I gave myself a minute to calm down, to let the broken edges of my heart heal as they pieced back together. "I don't want to cry about things I can't change. I wanted to remember the happy times. I just wouldn't let myself. This is goodbye to regret and assumptions and trying to hide. This is to us and the lives we led when we were together. You taught me so many things that were more important than learning not to get close to somebody. We could enjoy anything together. You supported anything I wanted to do. We stood by each other while my mother wondered what to do with the two of us."

I held the bottle out over the grave a few inches in front of his name and poured the vodka out slowly. "This is for you and drinking during happy times. I don't want to focus on the end anymore. I want to think about the happy times we had and enjoy the good that I have now."

I poured out most of the bottle and took the last mouthful for myself. I swallowed its subtle taste and held the empty bottle low in my lap. "I was so terrified that changing my mind about Michael and love would make me a hypocrite. Being critical of love was something I was known for, but I don't think it makes me a liar. I needed to grow up and look at things for what they are. What was true for me then doesn't have to be true for me now. I think you'd understand that."

I wished for a sign that Uncle Grigori heard me, but I didn't need one. The strength of my realizations was enough. "I love you, Uncle Grigori. I love Michael, too. It's strange to admit, but it's the truth."

I pulled the cap out of my pocket and screwed it back on the bottle. I wanted to leave the bottle with him, but I didn't want his grave to look like it had been littered by disrespectful drunks. My mother would be upset to see it there if she stopped by, and I'd have to explain why I put it there. She would never understand it. Thirty years after her brother's death, she would still be shaking her head at my kinship with him.

A breeze picked up and tried to pry its way under my scarf. I pushed myself up, warm enough in my coat but ready to move on. Uncle Grigori's name looked strong but sad in the stone. "Thank you for naming me what you did," I said. "No one ever got the joke until Michael. My mother wanted to change it, but I wouldn't let her. I always enjoyed it. It was something different, something that set me apart. It was something you gave me, deliberately, and I wasn't going to let anyone take that away."

I sifted through the other good memories I had of Uncle Grigori. We'd watched the animals at the zoo and fed the geese swimming in ponds around the city. He gave me a book for almost every occasion, no matter how much my mother insisted I didn't have room for any more. He offered me sips of vodka when I was five or six, always behind my mother's back. There were so many wonderful memories, in brief flashes and long vignettes, but I wished I had more of them. "I'm sorry I didn't spend more time with you when you were alive." The wind mercifully moved to my back, pushing me forward but curling over my shoulders like gentle fingers to hold me in place. "I love you, Uncle Grigori."

I hung the bottle at my side and walked away to my car. I hid the bottle under the passenger seat before I drove out of the cemetery. The other car was parked by the exit, and I could see an older woman standing at the far end of a row.

The still quiet of the cemetery stayed with me, or maybe it was the full weight of changing long-held opinions that calmed my mind. Falling for Michael had taken me ten years. Rather, realizing it and coming to peace with it had taken this long, much longer than it should've. And whatever his reaction was, I had to trust him to give me a response I could live with. I couldn't imagine what the right time to tell him would be, but I knew I had to do it soon. I didn't want to go another ten years until I did what needed to be done.

I didn't want to live or die with regrets.

Chapter 31: Jessie

Willa wasn't kidding when she said she didn't want to talk about Dick. Like my parents, she avoided the subject as if he never existed. She stopped bringing him up, and I could barely bring myself to mention his name. When I did and even when I didn't, I sensed her disappointment in me, and I felt bad about staying with him. It was a bunch of little things I couldn't tell if I was imagining or not. Willa forced a smile when she greeted me, or her eyes dimmed while laughing at a joke, and I remembered what she hoped I would do. Her voice played in my head when we weren't together. Every time I hung out with Dick, the arguments we had over him echoed in snippets like a skipping CD. I tried to tune it out, sometimes so focused on this, I didn't do much talking with Dick.

But Dick wasn't talking much, either. I worried he was doing the same thing, keeping too many thoughts to himself. There was a lot he wasn't explaining. He said hi on a regular basis to girls at school and even the diner when we went there. He winked at the woman tearing the stubs off our movie tickets at the theater. I couldn't go on with this much longer. I had to ask, but I knew I wasn't going to like his answer. I could already hear what Willa was going to say when I repeated it to her. It was going to be bad, and Willa was going to raise her eyebrows a little and say, "Why am I not surprised?"

I tried not to ask Dick, but the question itched under my skin until I wanted to blurt it out at the top of my lungs. *Did you date other girls when we weren't together!?*

Instead, I kept my calm, hoping I'd get a better response out of Dick that way. It was a rare night we sat at his house instead of going out. His mom and step-dad were gone, trying to salvage their relationship with a date night consisting of dinner and a movie. Judging by the roll of his step-dad's eyes when his mom explained this, it wasn't going to help.

Dick and I sat squished together on the couch. He flipped through the channels impatiently, moving on to the next one the second a commercial started. The constant changes in images and cut-off sound clips made me feel ungrounded and uneasy.

"It's coming right back on," I said.

"Commercials are stupid. I wanna watch a real show." Dick smashed his thumb down on the remote in such an erratic rhythm, he had to hit it twice sometimes to make the channel roll over.

I could barely stand it. "Can I ask you a question?"

"I don't know. Is it a stupid question?"

I ignored him. "During the times we were broken up, did you date other girls?"

Dick made a scraping sound in his throat that passed for lazy laughter. "Did Willa tell you to ask me that?"

"No."

"Of course I did."

"What do you mean 'of course'?"

"We were broken up, right? You're not the only woman on the planet."

I shifted away by an inch or two. I'd expected the answer but not the attitude. "I know that. I thought you might've mentioned it on your own."

Dick sounded agitated. "Why would I do that? So you can compare yourself to them? I know how you are. You compare yourself to everybody."

I snapped back at him. "You're right. I compare myself to the girls you say hi to because I wonder if you've been with them or girls like them."

Dick widened the gap between us, his tone falling flat. "You've got a serious problem, Jessie. Do you realize you're jealous of people you've never even seen?"

"Yes, I do. But how can I feel good about what we have or what you think of me if you never tell me anything? Why don't you tell me who else you've dated?"

"Why? So you can tell Willa what a terrible boyfriend I am?"

I couldn't find an answer to that even though it seemed like it should be easy. I was too worked up to think clearly. "This isn't about her. Are you dating other people right now?"

Dick chuckled. "Are you shitting me? You're not just jealous. You're paranoid."

"Who wouldn't be? You're more excited to see people I don't even know than you are to see me."

Dick shrugged. "I see you all the time. How excited do you want me to get?"

I stared at him. "Do you even care about me? I told Willa that you do. I stood up for you."

"Of course I do." Dick leaned over and put his arm around me. He left a wet, sloppy kiss on my cheek. "Why do you think I keep coming back for more?"

"I don't know."

"If Willa can't help you figure it out, stop telling her everything about me. She's not that good of a friend. She went months without talking to you."

I didn't let Dick sidetrack me. I could've kept in touch with Willa if I'd wanted to. "How many girls do you think you dated when we weren't together?"

"I don't know. I don't remember that stuff."

"Was it a little or a lot?"

"I don't know. If somebody was interested in me, I went for it."

"What does that mean?"

Dick's smirk twisted his face. "You understand how dating works, right? If somebody likes you, you go out with them."

I pulled a few inches away. "That's not what I'm upset about. How far did you go?"

"With who?"

I jumped off the couch to my feet and leaned over him. "How far did you go, Dick?"

"What are you yelling about? God, you act like I cheated on you." Dick was still hunched over the cushion where I'd been sitting. He pushed himself up straighter.

Dick had slept with somebody. His indignation was all I needed to hear, or at least, all I wanted to hear, to know that.

"What?" he asked. He patted the couch cushion next to him. "Come on. Are we watching TV or not?"

In a small way, Dick was right. I was hurt he'd spent time with someone else and rounded the bases, but I didn't believe he'd cheated on me. Maybe I was hurt he'd found someone else and I hadn't. Marlene had probably dated more guys than I had. Maybe Dick's other experiences were private and I shouldn't ask him to tell me about them.

After a long half a minute, I sat down next to Dick. He wrapped his arm around my shoulders and pulled me up against him.

In his other hand, he picked up the remote. "You act like you weren't free to do the same thing."

"I was," I agreed.

"Did you?" Dick sounded much less interested than I was in his past.

I wished I didn't have such a pathetic answer. "No. I hung out with Willa and my other friends from class."

I'd also watched rerun marathons with my parents. Comedy shows had saved me from a deeper depression during more than one break-up. I'd alternated between studying too much and not studying at all. My weight had fluctuated terribly, making me feel even worse. Dick always looked the same with his trim, sculpted chest and arms and the slight beer belly around his waist. After not seeing him for a few weeks, he'd call or show up with a hug. We'd get back together, and I wouldn't ask him a thing about what he'd been up to.

He usually hung his head for a minute and tried to look sorry, but Dick had shown up with a big smile to apologize this summer. I'd assumed it meant he was happy about the possibility of getting back together. It was actually more enticing than his sad-and-guilty routine. Now all I could assume was that he'd been happy to see me because he knew he was pulling one over on me. He knew there was no way I wouldn't take him back. He'd swept me right back into our relationship, and I was too happy to see him to question it. Or was the word I was looking for 'desperate'?

How stupid was I to let him back in my life? That's what Willa wanted to know, but I was starting to wonder it, too. Dick held me against his side, but he wasn't looking at me. He wasn't even thinking about me. He was already sucked back into the television, trying to find a new show to stop on. I wasn't so easily distracted. When faced with Dick's hostility, I'd backed down from getting answers, but now that he was quiet, I wanted them even worse than before. I didn't need to see the other women. I just needed to know what I was getting myself into. Was it going to be more years of this, or would Dick eventually grow up? I knew Willa's answer, but I needed the objective truth to come from him.

Chapter 32: Xan

The buzzer sounded in the laundry room on the other side of the living room wall. I finished the paragraph I was reading, an old favorite I'd chosen to take my mind off writing my own book. I slipped the bookmark between the pages and left the book on the coffee table. Melody had the day off, or she would've beaten me to the laundry. I walked through the foyer and turned into the back hall. I passed my office and went into the laundry room. Half the load was Michael's button-down shirts from conducting interviews. I wanted to hang them up before they wrinkled, otherwise I would've let them sit until I'd read several more chapters.

The first time I toured the house with the realtor, I'd thought its sole shortcoming was putting the laundry room in the back corner of the first floor. I still felt that way. Every week when I carried laundry, I thought about converting a spare bathroom upstairs into a laundry room. I could at least have hook-ups installed in a closet and tuck the washer and dryer in there. On the other hand, it kept me active, so I couldn't complain.

I emptied the dryer into a plastic basket and lugged it across the first floor to the stairs. I carried it up, careful not to scrape the lip against the wall. I found Michael in the bedroom. He reclined on the bed, entranced by a book in his hands.

Beside him, the sunset colored the sky outside the window. I hadn't noticed the snow falling as I'd passed the windows downstairs. It wasn't the first snow of the year, but I wasn't used to it yet. It felt like a sentence, promising we'd be lucky to have any jacket-weather days until halfway through spring. I set the laundry basket down and lowered the shade across the window.

Michael turned the page quickly, more engrossed in this book than most of the ones he'd read lately. He'd started it that morning and was over halfway through it. When he spoke to me, his words were mumbled and preoccupied. "I'm going to keep reading for a while, all right?"

"Okay."

"What time is it?" Michael glanced at the alarm clock. He exhaled through parted lips and rubbed his hand against his face. "How long have I been reading?"

"Hours."

Michael flipped through the pages of the book as if he hadn't realized how far he'd read. "What's for supper?"

"Leftovers."

"I want to finish this chapter, then I'll help you, and we can eat."

"All right."

I slid the basket closer to the closet and started hanging Michael's shirts up. I glanced at him from time to time as I reached for a new shirt. His head hung down over the book, his eyebrows knit together in concentration over whatever danger or drama the characters were involved in. The curtain of his hair was tucked behind his ear, or I wouldn't have been able to see his face at all. These were the moments I liked, the quiet ones without pressure or pretense. There was no one else around to compare ourselves or our relationship to, just Michael and me.

"Michael," I said.

"Mmm?" His eyes loosened their intense grip on the page, and I knew he was listening.

"I love you."

Michael took a few seconds to reply. He sounded as laidback and detached as ever. "I know."

Indignation flared up inside me, and I whipped his shirt down into the laundry basket. I exploded at him. "You know? What do you mean you know? It's taken me ten years to realize I love you and tell you how I feel, and you act like it's no big deal?"

A grin spread across Michael's face. I took a deep breath to calm my temper. He knew he was messing with my head.

Michael reached his hand out, and I moved closer to take it. He kissed my knuckles and lifted his shining eyes to my face. "I know. Thank you. Don't think it doesn't affect me to hear you say it because it does. I didn't know if you ever would."

"Then why did you stay with me? You could've found someone who appreciated you more than I did."

Michael closed his book over his fingers like a makeshift

bookmark. "I know how you feel about me."

"Really? I wouldn't let myself know how I felt about you."

Michael pressed back against the pillows. "Look at the facts. You wouldn't have kept seeing me if you didn't like me. You wouldn't have let me move in with you if you didn't trust me."

I joked with him to test his theory. "Maybe I just really like sleeping with you."

"Maybe, but you would've made me drive down from Chicago every week for the last ten years if that's all it was. We did that for a while."

"And I'm sorry." I squeezed Michael's hand, grateful I still had it to hold onto.

Michael squeezed back. "It's all right. I wouldn't have done it if I minded."

"I mean for everything. I've been nothing but difficult. We laugh about it, and it's part of our history, but it couldn't have been easy for you. You didn't do anything to deserve that."

Michael slipped his real bookmark between the pages and laid the book aside. "That's why you didn't want a relationship, remember? You didn't want to put up with someone else's habits and idiosyncrasies."

"I didn't, but I didn't mean to push all of mine on you. It wasn't fair. I didn't realize how much I was changing you."

"Again, I wouldn't have let you if I didn't think you were worth it."

"I have no idea how I gave you that impression."

Michael considered my face with a slightly sharpened focus. "You have the most interesting combination of an open, honest book and someone who completely closes everybody out. When I met you, I wanted to know what made you tick. You didn't have to answer all my questions, but you did. I knew you were telling me things I'd never read in other interviews."

"I wanted to be honest with you since you were being genuine with me." I slipped into joking again. "My books never got me so close to getting laid before, so I had to do something."

Michael laughed.

"I'm serious, though. All I've been thinking about for months is how this whole thing got started, with the interview and my uncle dying thirty years ago." I sat down on the edge of the bed next to Michael's legs. "There was a lot of stuff I didn't know and a lot I never thought about as I got older. I didn't realize how much I needed to grow up."

Michael cradled my cheek in his hand. "Listen, I didn't know if we'd last months or years or a couple of hours. I wanted the chance to know you, and I was willing to do whatever it took. I didn't care if I looked desperate. You'd push me away if you didn't want me."

"You never looked desperate, Michael. You sounded like a stalker."

"I couldn't have been that bad. Melody put me through to you."

"Don't underestimate the impression you make on young women." I thought of all the times Marcy and Stacey had devoured Michael with wide-eyed hunger. "Or middle-aged women, for that matter."

Michael tucked my hair back from my face. "You didn't need to grow up, Xan. If anything, you needed to grow down or grow out. You needed to believe something good was possible for you even if something horrible happened to your uncle."

I put my hand over Michael's, feeling more finely tuned to its warmth and smoothness. "I'm sorry I didn't let you talk me into celebrating our anniversary. I cheated you out of celebrating something special."

"It's nothing I can't live without. I'm sorry I scared you with the L word our first night together. I lost my ability to communicate clearly for half a second, and it sparked ten years of debate."

I laughed at myself. "I overreacted. It's made a good story. I was afraid to celebrate our anniversary. It's taken me a long time to process all these things."

"I know, and I would've helped you if I could."

"You have helped me. If it wasn't for my guilt for the way I treated you, I might never have reevaluated what happened with Uncle Grigori. I don't know how I would've gotten through the last ten years without you. You know how many projects I started and gave up on that might never get published. You know what a struggle I've had with my mother. It was easier to move on because you believed in me."

"Melody believes in you, too."

"Are you trying to write yourself off?" I looked Michael over, this incredible man with earnest but mischievous eyes. He was still his own brand of mystery in polo shirts and long hair. "Melody's invaluable, yes, but she goes home. She's only here part of the time. She can't stay up with me all night, spooning and talking over the finer parts of my novels."

"What's the point of living with a writer if you never talk about writing? It's something that kept me pursuing you. The critic and the writer together. How perfect is that?"

So perfect, it'd scared me senseless until days ago. "You're sure you wouldn't want a relationship more like your parents have?"

Michael smiled. "What do you mean? Where I drive you crazy, and you pretend not to notice?"

I laughed and pressed my lips to Michael's hand. "They're not that bad. I thought you might've wanted more camaraderie, more back-and-forth like they have."

Michael pulled his hand away from my face and held my hands between his. "It takes too much energy to be a comedy team. I like what we have. It works for us."

"I love you, and I'm sorry it's taken me ten years to say it."

Michael cupped my face in his hands. "I love you, too. Thank you for sharing it with me."

I leaned forward and kissed Michael gently. I let him draw me into his part of the world, familiar lips and comforting touch. I breathed in the scent of his skin and reveled in the tingle of energy between us. It wasn't for several minutes that I realized we'd neglected our responsibilities, the book to review and the laundry to put away. Michael didn't seem any more worried about it than I was. He lowered me onto the bed beneath him, still more focused on each other than the book that lay unforgiving beneath us. My legs trailed over Michael's, but we didn't adjust anything. We just were.

Michael moved his mouth to my neck, and I stole the opportunity to kiss his earlobe. He pulled the book out from under me. "Is this what I was doing?" He tossed it aside and returned his arm around me.

"Yes. We were doing laundry and reading."

"I'll finish the laundry. Then we should eat."

"You need to finish your book."

"You need to finish yours."

I'd barely thought about *Bitches and Assholes* for days. "I've given up on it for now. I'm taking a week to recharge my batteries. I was probably working so hard on it to keep me from thinking about all of this other stuff. Now I've taken three months off work, and I still have to finish the book."

Michael regarded me solemnly. "Don't let that bother you. You've made brilliant progress with everything else. Just don't let it be one of those books nobody gets to read. I was looking forward to this one."

"So is Melody and Stacey and Marcy and me. I mostly care about the ending. I know the rest of it."

"From what I hear, it might be something your mom would read."

"Could be, but there won't be recipes included. That's what she likes now."

"Slip a few recipe cards in it and call it a birthday present." Michael kissed my forehead. "I'm starving. That's what a good book will do to you, steal your afternoon from you."

"At least you get to read for a living and not struggle with writing."

Michael laughed. "Try telling that to Nick and John. They say it's easier for me to forget bad writing than it is for them to get bad songs and movies out of their heads."

"I'd like to set them straight on that. I'm constantly haunted by the bad phrasing of my fellow authors. Do you remember that group book signing where that woman started an impromptu reading? 'Eyes like tumbled emeralds' has stuck in my brain for years."

"I remember that. I wish I'd forgotten." Michael sat up and patted my leg. "As for me getting to read instead of write, nobody builds statues to critics. I should be ashamed the best I can do is critique other people's creativity."

"Nonsense. It's feedback that makes us better. Feedback we can use, anyway." I pushed myself up.

Michael's features softened. "I'd really like to interview you again when this book comes out."

"That could be three years from now."

"That's okay. I'll wait." Michael slid to the edge of the bed and stood up. He picked up the shirt I'd thrown down and found a hanger for it.

"You're a patient man," I said.

Michael hung the shirt on his side of the closet. "I'm not patient. I'm just hoping after we do the interview, I can get you to sleep with me."

I laughed. "That old trick."

Michael hummed thoughtfully. "That sounds like something your friends would call each other."

I stood up and gave Michael a kiss before he could reach down into the basket again. "What should I call you? You're not really my boyfriend, but you're closer than a lover."

"How about partner?"

I wrinkled my nose and folded my arms even though it fit. Perfectly. "I always hated it when people used that term. I never knew what they meant by it."

"Probably the same thing I do. We weather the world together. We stand by each other and put up with each other. It's the label for people who don't want to use labels."

"Is that how you've thought of us? As partners?"

"Not really. I just figured I was lucky enough to be in your life. I didn't see the need to call it anything."

"But why me and not someone else?"

Michael fished out the last shirt in the basket. "I spend most of my professional life explaining why I like things. Do I have to critique you, too?"

"You liked me from the night we met. You owe me an explanation."

"I had a head start on you. I'd been reading your novels since they came out. I read most of the interviews you gave. I knew a lot more about you than you did about me."

"Did you know I was going to be stubborn?"

Michael reached for a hanger. "I didn't think that much about it. I figured I'd meet you and get my book signed and that would be it.

When you offered me the interview, that's all I expected you'd give me."

I grinned. "You didn't read my interviews very closely. I was a man-eater back then."

"I didn't think it would extend to me. I didn't expect to say 'love' any more than you wanted to hear it." Michael hung the shirt in the closet and turned to me. "I thought there were a lot of times you didn't want to hear me say it."

"I was an idiot."

"You were in pain, Xan. People do a lot of crazy things when they're in pain."

I unfolded my arms and gave Michael a hug.

His arms encircled my back, steady and solid. "Did you find out what you needed to about your uncle?"

"I could never know enough about Uncle Grigori, but I found out enough to know I should move on. He killed himself and hurt the family. I shouldn't let Evalisse's breaking up with him hurt you, too."

Michael lifted my chin and kissed me. "We should make something special for dinner. The leftovers will last until tomorrow."

"What do you want to make?"

"Anything. An old favorite or something new. It doesn't matter to me."

"The cookbooks are downstairs."

"Waiting for us."

I studied Michael's face. This business of being in love changed things. He seemed handsomer. His eyes glowed, less apprehensive than they used to be. I felt a bit lighter myself. "I do love you, you know."

"I know."

"Did you hope I'd say it one day?"

"Hope, yes. Expect, no. I know better than to put any expectations or limitations on you."

I tightened the loop of my arms around his neck, bringing him closer. "And that's why I love you."

Chapter 33: Jessie

Willa had been done reading *Hypocrisy* for ages. It was taking me forever to get through the last few chapters. My homework got more and more involved as the semester went on. I could blow off the stories and short essays assigned at the beginning of the semester without hurting my grades. It was all novels and ten- to twenty-page literary criticisms now. I was writing my own papers for the end of the semester, researching in the computer lab and checking out library books I could use as sources.

Hypocrisy, which I wanted to hold against my chest as much as I wanted to read it, traveled everywhere with me, unread. Seeing it in my backpack at school or feeling it jab my ribs through the thin fabric of my thrift store purse gnawed at me. Willa was physically biting her lip to keep from spilling the ending. Her face scrunched up whenever I admitted I hadn't gotten much further, and her arms writhed with the discomfort of keeping quiet.

I hunched over my desk, struggling through dry, winding sentences deconstructing *Beowulf. Hypocrisy* sat in my backpack on the bed behind me. I was so close to the end, but I had to finish this paper.

I glanced at my backpack. It was just a bag, but it taunted me. My fingers twitched to rip the zipper open and devour the rest of *Hypocrisy*. I couldn't take it anymore. I left my homework on the desk and grabbed *Hypocrisy* out of the bag. I hurried down the hall and locked myself in the bathroom. Stripping my clothes off, I drew myself a bathtub full of water somewhere between warm and scalding hot. Being careful not to drop the book in the water, I lowered myself in and opened it up. I laid the bookmark on the edge of the tub and settled in to finish the only book I'd ever gone through this much trouble to read. It made absorbing the story that much more intense.

Pastor Ozbeck's unruly eyebrows rose in surprise. Lourdes continued into his office.

"What are you doing here?" he asked. "How did you get here?"

"I walked." Lourdes lowered herself into the chair across the desk from him. For her age, walking a few miles was nothing, but as her belly grew, her swollen feet and ankles couldn't stand the activity.

"Close the door."

Lourdes shook her head, too weary to obey. Her ankles throbbed. "I can't."

Pastor Ozbeck stood up from his chair and walked around the desk to the door. He closed it quietly even though Lourdes expected him to slam it. "I suppose you came here to talk."

"Why wouldn't I?"

"It's private business. You should close the door when you want to talk about something private."

"You mean embarrassing." Lourdes watched him return to his chair, slightly doddering and uncoordinated for being middle-aged. His belly protruded farther than hers did, and it turned her stomach. "Embarrassing for you."

"For me?" Pastor Ozbeck did not sound convinced. "It could only be embarrassing for me if you told someone."

"I might," Lourdes admitted, trying to keep her calm as much as he was. It wasn't hard in her tired state to fake some understated confidence.

"If you did, it would embarrass you, not me. I would tell them my side of the story, in which a confused, hormonal teenaged girl mistook my friendliness for romantic invitation. You took advantage of me."

Lourdes' jaw dropped. "You couldn't tell them that. They'd never believe I overpowered you. How could I force myself on you? You weigh so much more than me. You're much stronger."

"You charmed and confused me, of course. I'd say I was too embarrassed to admit my mistake before. Who could blame me for wanting to comfort you if your less mature peers left you lonely and you sought wiser companionship?"

Lourdes laid her hand on her belly. She would never let this liar near her baby if she could help it. "They wouldn't believe you."

Pastor Ozbeck grinned at her, his upturned mouth a combination of condescension and pity. "Wouldn't they? People are capable of believing the strangest things."

"Like how you got me to believe in you. I did think you were friendly. I thought you were wise and you wanted to teach me things. You taught me how to lie and how to hide things. You taught me to hate myself and let Reese take the blame for what you did."

"Reese?" Pastor Ozbeck echoed with disinterest. "Is that your boyfriend?"

"Yes. I told you his name. He's the one who's going to be the baby's father, not you."

Pastor Ozbeck shrugged one monstrous shoulder. "How do I know the baby is mine?"

Lourdes lunged toward him. In her usual health, she could have thrown herself across the desk and hit him. She felt confined to the chair by her condition, afraid she would collapse if she jumped to her aching feet. "Can you count, Pastor Ozbeck? I am way too far along for the baby to be anyone else's. Unless the doctor doesn't know what he's talking about, it's yours. I wish it was Reese's, but it's not, not in reality."

Pastor Ozbeck folded his hands together on the desk. "What good do you think it would do to tell the truth?"

"We're supposed to tell the truth. You said so yourself in your sermons."

"Should we tell it always? Do you want to be known for the rest of your life as the woman who manipulated and seduced her pastor? Do you really want to test Reese's feelings for you? He would leave you. You know that."

Lourdes shook her head vehemently. "No. He would believe me. He's seen a picture of you. He knows I would never go to you instead of him for anything."

"But you did. I asked you to come to the church and talk to me, and you did."

Lourdes' jaw clenched until it hurt. "You asked me to."

"You were so willing, so eager to help. You were so innocent."

"And no matter what I do, what story we tell, I'll spend the rest of my life being known as the teenage mother. People already give me dirty looks. I can't wait until I look older."

"You will look older. As soon as you have your baby, the lack of sleep will begin to age you terribly."

Lourdes hung her head. She didn't want to look haggard, just a few years older so people would think she was twenty.

Pastor Ozbeck's voice rumbled again. "You shouldn't be so worried about what people think about you. You have the perfect alibi."

Lourdes gripped the chair arms, her knuckles straining white. She narrowed her eyes at Pastor Ozbeck. "Reese isn't an alibi. He's my boyfriend."

Pastor Ozbeck continued unaffected. "The way the story runs now, your baby is the product of two teenagers making the same passionate mistake other teenagers have made for far too long. The version you want to tell holds an abuse of power, and people seldom react kindly to that kind of accusation."

Lourdes loosened her hold as she realized what he was saying. "You're worth more to them than I am. They'll throw me away."

Pastor Ozbeck did not verbally agree, but he did not discount her revelation. "I think it's best for you if you keep this our little secret."

"I want to forget any of it ever happened."

He leaned forward. "One of the best ways to do that is to keep other people from knowing that it happened."

"I hate you, and I don't want to be your assistant anymore."

Pastor Ozbeck leaned back and pursed his lips for a moment. "I know the congregation well enough now that you don't have to spend your afternoons here with me."

Lourdes stared at him. "You're letting me go? You can't. I quit. I already said it."

"No, I let you go. If you press the issue, I'll say it was because of your unwanted advances. If you agree to it now, I'll simply say I wanted you to have more time for friends and school."

Lourdes wondered how he would know what she said. She was already trying to think of a reason to tell her parents she had decided to quit volunteering at the church.

Pastor Ozbeck supplied the answer. "Your parents come here every Sunday. Imagine how interesting it would be if we gave them different reasons for you leaving the position."

Lourdes supported her weight on the chair arms as she stood up. "I hope we'll be leaving the church. I can go somewhere else with my friends. I can go with Reese. You might never see me again. I don't want to see you."

"You were so polite when you first came here. 'Yes, Pastor Ozbeck.' 'No, Pastor Ozbeck.' 'I don't want to go to hell, Pastor Ozbeck.'"

"Oh, I've seen hell. That place doesn't scare me now."

Pastor Ozbeck's eyes bulged at her. "If you think you've been through the worst that can happen to you, hell will be worse."

"I hope that's true for you." Lourdes turned away and started for the door. She thought Pastor Ozbeck might have one last comment or suggestion for her, but he didn't speak. She let herself out into the hallway and left the office door open behind her. She walked out of the church and crossed the parking lot to the gas station at the end of the block. Lourdes pulled a few quarters out of her coin purse for the payphone and called to have her mother pick her up. Her mother agreed in a tired voice, and Lourdes sat down on a wooden bench to wait for her.

I closed the book, almost as sad and aimless as Lourdes felt. I tried to be happy for her standing up to Pastor Ozbeck, but her situation was too overwhelming to be called bittersweet. His influence seemed like it would affect her life no matter where she went or what she did. I tried to shake off the heavy gloom, looking ahead to where the characters went from there. It would make a good question for XZA. What would happen to Lourdes? Would she and Reese stay together and raise the baby? Would anyone ever find out who the father really was? Would she ever tell? Or would Lourdes live every day of her life with that terrible secret? Her mom would come pick her up and never question the story that Lourdes decided to stop volunteering. And Lourdes would always feel trapped between bringing an unfair judgment down on herself and loyalty to the truth.

I dropped the book on the rug outside the tub. I was glad Lourdes was better able to stand up for herself by the end than the nameless narrator of *Satan, My Father*. I thought of a great joke about the two titles and tried to hold onto it while I drained the bathwater. I toweled off, put my clothes back on, and snuck the book back to my room. My cell phone sat on the desk, and I snatched it up. I dialed Willa from my contacts list.

She answered with her usual high spirits. "Hey, you. What's up?"

"I finished the book."

"Great. How'd you like it?"

"It was good. I wanted to tell you XZA could've named this one 'Satan, My Pastor.'"

Willa chuckled. "That's a good one. What should we call *F*CK, F*CK, F*CK*? 'Satan, My Mohawk'?"

I thought back to the book I'd read several months before. "'*Satan, My Father*: Redux.' Chessa's dad was the bad guy, too."

"He was hardly in it, though. Her mom was the obnoxious one. She couldn't stop crying and trying to control everything."

"Yeah, I don't blame Chessa. I would've been making myself throw up for some sense of control, too." I turned and noticed my mom standing in the doorway. She was watching me with a quizzical tension between her blonde eyebrows. "It's Willa," I explained.

Mom smiled, the tension smoothing instantly. "Tell her I said hi. Dinner will be ready in about twenty minutes."

"Okay. Thanks."

Mom walked away down the hall.

Willa giggled in my ear. "Busted."

"Totally busted. Somehow your name explains everything."

"It's probably the same reason my mom accepts your name as the reason I've seemed more focused."

"I haven't noticed you focusing."

"Me neither. I never focus. Everybody knows that."

I ducked down on my haunches and slid the book under the bed. "I think we should ask XZA what happens to her characters after the books end."

"Great idea. I would love to know. I wonder if she knows."

"I bet she knows everything."

"Maybe that's why she works on them so long."

I wanted to keep talking to Willa, but it picked at me that my parents were making dinner for me again. If I went out there now while they were still cooking, I could set the table before they could stop me.

Willa spoke up. "You know what'd be awesome? If you took a picture of XZA, and she used it in the back of her book."

I blew air into the phone line. It would never happen, but it was a pretty awesome thought. "I don't actually have my camera anymore," I heard myself admit.

"That's okay," Willa whispered. "That's what student loans are for."

"You don't think that's a bad idea? It's supposed to be for books and stuff."

"No, especially if you went to school for it and turned it into a career."

The suggestion hit me hard and sunk in deep. Why hadn't I thought of this before? Plates clinked in the kitchen, reminding me my parents were pushing themselves to make dinner. "I'm sorry. I should go set the table or something."

"Okay. Less than three weeks until the big day. Keep those questions coming."

"I will." I hung up and left my phone on the desk. I could think of a dozen questions I wanted answered about *Hypocrisy*, and I wasn't going to stop dwelling on them until I'd picked the best ones. My parents were about to have a very silent helper in the dining room.

Chapter 34: Xan

From the hallway, I heard Michael typing diligently on his laptop. He sat at the desk in the small spare bedroom with his back to the door. The book he'd finished reading rested beside his computer, and the Underrated Media site showed on what I could see of the screen. The floor creaked under my weight before I could leave him uninterrupted.

Michael stopped typing and turned to look at me over his shoulder. "Did you want something?"

I lingered in the doorway, wishing I hadn't come close enough to disturb him. "Marcy called. She's stopping by in a few minutes."

"All right."

"I'll tell her you're working so she doesn't try to impose on you."

Michael gave the barest hint of a grin. "She'll try it either way. Her fascination with me supersedes her respect for me."

"That's probably true."

Michael returned to his work and typed a few more words. "What's she stopping by for?"

"I don't know, really. She wants to talk, I guess."

"Do you think she dumped the milkman?"

"I hope so. As much as he disgusts her, she's held onto that one for a long time. He must be good."

Michael turned towards me again, relaxing against the back of his chair. "She could've used some pointers from the old you on how to let go."

"She could use some pointers from the new me. I gave her my old pointers. They obviously didn't catch on."

The doorbell chimed below me.

Michael flicked his eyebrows up. "Good luck."

"Thank you." I pulled the bedroom door shut for him, latching it quietly.

I took my time moving down the stairs, trying to guess why Marcy was dropping in. When I opened the door, Marcy's expression was blank but pensive, making her mood hard to read. I let her in and shut the door behind her.

"How are you?" Marcy asked as if we hadn't been through this on the phone.

"I'm fine."

"How's Michael?"

"He's busy working, but he's good."

Marcy peeled her thin leather gloves off and stood holding them. "The heat feels so good in here." Her eyes wandered the foyer even though nothing had changed and she'd been to my house a thousand times.

I folded my arms. I'd never seen her stall. She always came right out with whatever was floating or flying through her head. "Marcy, was there something you wanted to talk to me about?"

"I wanted to ask you, uh..." Marcy moved on from the artwork in the foyer to the furniture in the living room through the wide doorway. "I remembered somebody saying Michael's friend brings you music."

"Yes, he does."

"I wondered if any of it was any good."

"Yeah, it is. I don't love all of it, but some of it's really good."

"I wanted to know if I could borrow some of it."

"Of course." I knew there was more, but I didn't let on. "What kind of music were you looking for?"

"Whatever. I'm not that picky. I just need something for the drive to work and back."

"I think most of what he brought me is here in the living room." I led Marcy onto the carpet and over to the CD rack. I sifted through a stack of jewel cases filled with CD's John had burned for me. He'd noted the artists and album titles with a green, thin-tipped Sharpie.

Marcy stared at them. "That's all from him?"

"Yeah. It's added up to quite a collection." I handed Marcy a few CD's in varying styles. "You and Stacey show your appreciation for Michael with sexual innuendo. His friends bring me offerings of music and movies."

Marcy read over the writing on the CD's, adopting a dry humor. "Xan, you're so naive. We don't use innuendo with Michael. We mean everything we say."

I pulled a few more CD's off the rack and echoed her tone. "If you ever do try to steal Michael from me, you'd better cover your ass before my boot gets to it."

"Ooh," Marcy cooed with a shudder. "I finally hit a nerve after all these years."

The door popped open upstairs, and Michael started down the steps. "Marcy, how are you?"

Marcy watched him descend into the foyer. "Too sober. You look divine, Michael."

"Thank you."

"Xan said you were working."

"I was."

"On what?"

"A review for the site."

"I'm sorry I barged in."

Michael batted his hand at the air, unconcerned with Marcy's intrusion. "I was intrigued why you might've stopped by. Is it private?"

Marcy smiled at him, tickled and goading. "You know there's nothing about me I wouldn't share with you, Michael. Was it a local author review you were working on? Xan said you've been busy with students at the college."

"This one wasn't, but they have kept me pretty busy. Luckily, only about two or three of the students have novels or trilogies for me to look at. It's a lot easier to get through the poetry and the short stories."

"I didn't know you reviewed poetry."

"Not as a rule."

"You've never reviewed my work. I have a new poem I've been working on called *Death of a Vibrator*. True story."

Michael warned her lightly with his eyes. "We all know where my interview with Xan went. I'm not opening that door for you." Michael pointed to the CD's in Marcy's hands. "Did you come here for music?"

Marcy hesitated. "Yes. Partly. Don't change the subject. Xan said some of the student work she read was pretty good."

"The reviews I wrote are up on the site. I couldn't include full poems or stories along with them, but I used some of the pieces I liked the best. You can go online and read them."

"I'll have to check it out."

I handed two more CD's to Marcy and put the rest of the stack away. "We wanted to know if you broke up with the milkman yet."

"Yes, I did."

"How'd he take it?"

"Sour," Marcy deadpanned. She laughed. "Really, I don't care how he took it. He's out of my apartment, and I haven't seen him. I haven't smelled him or his milk for days, and it feels good." She flipped through the CD's again.

I couldn't stand her charade. "Marcy."

She raised her startled blue eyes to my face. "What?"

"What did you come here to say? You don't know how to be subtle. What's the preamble for?"

"God, I wish I could smoke in here." Marcy crammed her gloves into her coat pocket. "Look, here's the deal. I know I thought John was really weird when I met him at the party. It was sort of like a swinger's party without the swing. But I keep thinking about him, and I think I kinda like him."

I blinked at Marcy. I had no idea how to process that.

Michael was stunned and silent, too, before he gave a breathy laugh.

"I know, right?" Marcy said. "But I think I was overwhelmed by all the information he gave me at the time. He really knows music. And any guy who knows music that well has to have some good rhythms of his own, you know what I mean?"

Michael raised his hands to stop her there. "I don't need to know anything like that about my friends. I don't mind having a little mystery in my life."

"Is that why you won't sleep with me? I have more mystery than that, Michael." Marcy grinned at him and tossed her hair back over her shoulder. "I was thinking you could tell me what John said about me."

"He said, I quote, 'We're never seeing either of those women again.' And Nick agreed."

"What did he say about me, though? That's a general statement of what we all thought that night."

"He didn't have much to say. I'm not even sure he realizes how much he dominated the conversation he had with you."

Marcy dug around in her purse and pulled out her pack of cigarettes. "I'm having one of these as soon as I get out the door. Michael, will you tell John if he wants to talk my ears off about music some more, he can give me a call? If he's shy, pass his number on to me, and I'll do the rest."

"I'm sure you would."

Marcy turned to me. "It's embarrassing, Xan. It really is. You think some guy's a total nut job, and then you can't stop thinking about him."

Michael winked at me.

My friends had apparently forgotten that Michael was once little more than a nut job to me. "Speaking of nut jobs, Marcy, have you met my partner, Michael?"

Marcy's eyebrows shot up under her bangs. "Partner Michael? I've met lover Michael. Did you upgrade him to partner?"

I noticed I didn't cringe when she said it. I liked the sound of it after all. "I did."

"Congratulations. Right past love machine to partner. It's very romantic." Marcy studied our faces back and forth, her expression growing suspicious. "What's going on with you two? You look like you just left one of those relationship retreats or something. You look happy."

"I'm partnered with a living legend," I said. "Why shouldn't I be happy?"

"You're never happy. Years ago, when I decided his initials stood for Much Salivation, you told me he needed too much attention." Marcy glanced at Michael. "You tamed the best known cynic of our time."

"Go home," I warned her, "before I find the milkman's number and tell him you want to reconcile."

Marcy moved toward the front door. "You'll tell John I'm interested, won't you, Michael?"

"Yes," he assured her, ever dutiful.

We trailed Marcy to the door. She tried to juggle everything in her hands and find her keys in her purse. "I'm calling Stacey the second I'm done with my cigarette and telling her your engagement might happen this century."

Michael spoke up. "Don't push it, Mars."

"Please. It's taken you ten years to make it to partner. This isn't a law firm. I know I give you two a lot of grief, but partner isn't good enough. You have the greatest relationship ever made. You're a force of nature. You have nowhere to go but up."

"We've been doing just fine moving slowly forward."

"Maybe so, but the thought of Xan wearing white in front of fifty or a hundred people is hysterical. I'll talk to you later. I have too much to do."

Marcy turned and let herself out.

I didn't linger on the E word: engagement. Marcy couldn't force Michael or me into anything we weren't ready for. I couldn't help feeling sorry for John. He had no idea what was coming his way. "The humane thing might be never to mention this to John."

Michael smiled, that uncanny mix of agreement and mischief. "But I will."

"Be careful. She's already got marriage on the brain."

"I'll leave that out and see what happens."

"I thought you liked John."

"I do. The joke is on Marcy. John drives all of his dates crazy. If you thought he was scattered and talkative here, wait until she gets him one on one. His social anxiety will kick in, and he won't stop talking. The horror stories are incredible."

"From John or the victims?"

"The victims. Nick refers to all of John's girlfriends as 'survivors.' The stories from both sides are mind-boggling."

"More proof of why dating is futile."

Michael put his arms around me and kissed me. "I'm proud of you."

"For telling her I made you partner?"

"For not telling her about your uncle and letting her sensationalize something that's very personal for you."

It wasn't hard to hide my private life from Marcy, but I appreciated Michael's support. "I'm used to keeping my innermost thoughts away from Marcy. Stacey I can trust, but never Marcy."

"Then why are you friends?"

"It's safer than having her for an enemy," I said, only partly joking. "I don't have to trust her implicitly. Who else would I talk to, anyway? You know I've always believed in having friends. They keep life exciting. If you're waiting around for the perfect friend, you might wait forever."

"That's good advice."

My lips twisted in a disapproving frown. "Don't tell anybody I gave you good advice. The second they hear that, they'll want to talk to me. I don't have time for advice. I have a book to finish."

"I won't say anything," Michael promised me.

The gentle rumble of his voice turned my lips into a smile. "Do you want to make bets on how far this thing goes with John and Marcy?"

Michael grinned at me. "My first instinct, too far, but it'll be very interesting to watch."

Chapter 35: Jessie

I left my academic advisor's office, resettling the weight of my backpack over my shoulders. Mrs. Conover had told me everything I needed to know, and the final decisions were up to me. I slipped through the light traffic in the halls and left the building. Not many students lingered outside today, the snowy paths covered in hasty boot prints. I headed for the student center as quickly as I could without sliding and stomped hard on the welcome mats as I walked in. I snaked my way through the halls to the cafeteria and scouted out the best place to sit. There wasn't much of a line at the cases and counters. Most of the tables sat empty. I dropped into a chair in the back corner of the cafeteria, away from the doors and the dwindling lunch line. I opened my backpack, smiling at the stack of papers Mrs. Conover had printed off for me. I pulled out a notebook and a newspaper Willa had given me for the short article encouraging readers to come meet XZA a few towns over.

The paper had a more recent picture of XZA than the *Hypocrisy* book jacket. Her hair was still dark, her face pretty, just a few years older. I opened my notebook to the list of questions Willa had put me in charge of. We'd brainstormed for an hour at Suds the other night while my laundry swirled and rotated in the machines. It was a pretty comprehensive list, and the only question left was what should we actually ask her? Did we want to know what inspired her stories or what came after they ended? If it was up to Willa, we'd ask her everything, but I didn't think it was appropriate. It was a book signing, not an interview.

I felt a hard jerk on my ponytail and reached automatically for my hurting head. Before I could guess who it was – and I only needed one guess – Dick's voice boomed above me. "Whatcha doing?"

"Homework." I folded the notebook closed before he could read the questions and call me a liar. "What are you doing?"

"Cutting class." Dick pulled out the chair in the corner and flopped into it. He slouched against the molded plastic and ran his hand over his hair. "What do I need to learn economics for? Money comes in. Money goes out. Somebody's keeping track of it, and it's not gonna be me."

I made sure my notebook covered the article on XZA. "I think there's more to it than that."

"I wouldn't know. I'm never there."

"You're gonna flunk your finals."

Dick shrugged. "Who cares? I'll try again next year if I feel like it."

I fit the notebook and newspaper into my backpack. "You're willing to throw the whole class away? I thought you thought school was important."

Dick cocked an eyebrow like he hadn't heard me right. "What?"

"You're always telling me to do well and graduate with a degree I can do something with."

"Yeah, so you can take care of me."

I stopped fiddling with my backpack and stared at him. "You were joking?"

"Hell, no, baby, I'm serious. I want you to graduate and take care of me so I don't have to keep doing this shit. You're smart. It's easy for you."

"Well, I might not be here much longer."

Dick took a turn to look surprised. "What?"

"I just met with Mrs. Conover – "

Dick's mouth opened, and I quickly guessed his question. "My advisor," I explained, my voice even but my jaw clenching. "I want to go to an art school so I can get a degree in photography. I haven't decided if I want to finish with an associate's degree here or try to transfer some credits."

"What the fuck, Jessie, you're leaving me?"

"I'm leaving the school, maybe not for another semester."

"To take pictures?"

"It's what I want to do. It's what I always wanted. Nobody supported it before."

"Who told you to do it?"

"Willa," I said with a satisfied smirk.

Dick's eyes bulged, and his lips twisted wordlessly before he could respond. "Willa. Of course. That's how you know it's a stupid idea. I can't believe I said you were smart."

I leaned across the table. "You're the one who broke my camera and never offered to pay for it. I don't think you get to choose what I do with my life."

Dick huffed and slumped even lower in his chair. "Whatever. Like you really care about school. You're the one going up to see what's-her-name instead of studying for finals."

"Her name is XZA. I'm studying as much as I can before I go. I'll do fine. I remember better when I don't stress myself out studying too much."

"That's bullshit. Willa left without a degree, and now you're letting her pull you down with her." Dick scraped at his teeth with his fingernail.

There was no point in explaining what a photography degree could do for me, but I didn't want to back down. I stole a play out of Dick's book and said exactly what I was thinking. "Like I'm gonna go really far with you and that obnoxious truck of yours."

Dick sat up a little. "What are you talking about? You're the one with no sense of style." He snorted. "Look at your car. And that goes for Willa, too. Jesus Christ. She walks around like she got dressed in the dark with the help of a blind man."

My fist pounded down on the table harder than I anticipated. The blade of my hand throbbed, especially in the tender joints of my pinkie, but I didn't care. Words were already pouring out of my mouth. "Shut up, Dick. You have no room to talk. None of your clothes fit you. Your friends are hideous losers. You don't know anything about Willa or me, but you certainly pretend to. You don't know anything about school or what you're doing. Don't criticize me just because you have nothing else to say. Don't be such a dick, Dick."

My heartbeat thundered in my ears. Trying to catch my breath, everything seemed clearer than it ever had. For the first time, I noticed how scruffy Dick's hair was getting, way past the point of skater cute. He was either too cheap or too lazy to get it cut. I was surprised he hadn't asked me to do it for him. He probably thought I'd screw it up. Even if I did a good job, he wouldn't say so.

Dick was still quiet. He stared at me between long blinks.

He'd never shut up before, and I took the opportunity to say something more. "You have the perfect name. You always did." I realized something even better. "That's exactly something XZA would've written. You know what, Dick? I'm going to that book signing with Willa, and I'm meeting XZA, and it's going to be awesome."

Dick's eyes shrank to their normal rat size. "I tell you not to do one thing, and you freak out on me."

"You always tell me what to do. You think you're so fuckin' amazing, but you're not. It's like Toria said to that dumbass who bothered them in *F*CK, F*CK, F*CK*. You're not extraordinary. You're just an extra dose of ordinary." I zipped my backpack closed in one smooth swipe.

Dick's shoulders hunched as he leaned against the back of his chair. "Whatever. It's not the first time you've broken up with me. You'll be back. You always are."

"Not this time."

"What about Florida? You think Willa's gonna take you on vacation?"

"I only said I'd go to make you happy and make you shut up. I don't care where I spend the winter. Do you think I want to be stuck somewhere with you?"

Dick pulled his shoulders back. He raised his arm to one side and bent his fist up so his bicep pushed against the sleeve of his coat. "You're gonna miss this. I know you will. I better not see your number on my phone when I'm tan in January."

"You won't. If I even think about it, Willa will be there to remind me to stay away from you. No wonder you hate her. She was onto your bullshit years ago." I grabbed my backpack and stood up.

Dick watched me sling my backpack onto my shoulders with sleepy eyes. "I still don't believe you."

I rested my forearms on the back of the chair in front of me. "You know what? I put up with you because I didn't think I could get anybody else. But at least the odds of that person being better than you are pretty close to a hundred percent."

Dick laughed at me with an annoying edge of sarcasm. "You're so full of it, Jessie."

"You're full of it," I fired back. "I know you gave me somebody else's bracelet. I saw the fliers. Did you steal it, or did you just not turn it in?"

Dick sat up straighter, his bushy eyebrows narrowing in offense. "I didn't steal anything."

"Did you know who it belonged to? Did you see her drop it and sit there waiting for her to walk away so you could grab it?"

Dick slipped down again. "Why should I spend money on you? You might not like what I got for you anyway. Then I'm out the cash."

"You know what I don't like, Dick? Liars. Thieves. You." I pulled my cell phone out of my pocket and pushed the button for my contacts list. "You think I'm full of it? I'll delete your number right now."

Dick folded his arms tightly across his chest. "So what? I bet you memorized it."

"Nobody remembers phone numbers anymore. I relied on my phone to call you." I found Dick's name and accepted the option to delete it. His name disappeared, and I could breathe. I showed him the screen. "Look. Dentist. Doctor. No Dick."

"I'll call you," Dick offered with a twinkle in his eyes.

"No, you won't. You'll be so busy chasing all the other women you know whose names you can't remember, you won't remember to call and harass me."

Dick looked away out the windows, where the slanted blinds tried to block the bright, clear sunlight bouncing off the snow. "Whatever."

"At least I'm leaving this school with information I can use. Whether you stay here a thousand years or drop out like Willa did, you're leaving just as simple as you came in. I might never have to see you again."

Dick adjusted his folded arms. "Have a nice life, then."

"Yeah, I will." I walked away from the table and out of the cafeteria. I passed through the brown and yellow hallway, laughing at the crass coincidence of colors. It felt good to enjoy myself without Dick there to question me.

I did not intend to miss Dick. I might get lonely sometimes, I might do something or see something I wanted to tell him about, but there was nothing to miss about Dick but bad jokes, greasy food, and a nauseating kissing style. The next time Dick waved at another girl, I wouldn't be jealous. I'd feel sorry for her. My parents would try to keep from cheering at the news, but only Willa would truly understand what I'd done.

I pushed the metal door open and trudged out into the blanket of snow that had covered the walkway since I'd gone in. The previously shoveled snow surrounded the concrete patio like a low, scalloped fence. I shoved my bare hands deep into my pockets. Once I got to my car, I'd call Willa and let her know I had good news. She could wait to find out what it was from me in person.

After I made her guess.

Chapter 36: Xan

The turnout wasn't my worst. I sat at the table in the small but buzzing bookstore, satisfied with the line of women in front of me. It varied from one to a dozen people at a time, but everybody seemed in a pretty good mood. They shared where they'd driven from, how long they'd been reading my books, and occasionally how much I inspired their own writing. Some of them had never heard of me, and I was glad Michael and Melody had encouraged me to do this. They were right, as usual, and it felt good to get back out there, away from my novel in progress.

Michael had ridden with me. He lingered somewhere out of sight, browsing books or talking with customers. This bookstore wasn't big enough to have its own café, but several women were talking about coffee shops in the area. I wished I could see Michael so I could send him a meaningful, sentimental smile.

My readers seemed to get older as the line moved forward. These were women who'd discovered my books in their thirties and still harkened back to them now. They shared stories of good and bad marriages and raising strong daughters. I never took their honesty for granted. It always reminded me why I wrote what I did. A middle-aged mother of three stepped aside, and I was almost surprised to find a young twenty-something with dark blonde hair at the head of the line. She held a worn copy of each of my books in her hands. Any story she had to tell would probably – hopefully – be lighter but no less important.

I reached for the books, intrigued by their ragged condition. "How long have you been reading these?"

"A couple of months." She seemed reluctant to hand me the books. "If you can't sign all of them, I understand. You can just do F*CK, F*CK, F*CK. That's my favorite. It was the first one I read."

The young woman behind her peeked over her shoulder. "I gave it to her for her birthday."

I smiled as I took all three books. "Of course I'll sign them all. Did you drive far?"

"About an hour."

"Who should I make these out to?"

"Jessie. With an IE."

"Two esses?"

She nodded.

I rarely took chances with names. I opened *Satan, My Father* and poised my pen over the title page. "What can you tell me about yourself that I can make a joke of here?"

Jessie thought for a few seconds. "I've been in school forever. College."

"What are you studying?"

"Literature for now. I have finals in two days."

"And you came out here instead of studying?"

Jessie offered a shy smile. "Yeah. I thought this was more important."

I leaned forward and shared a secret with her. "I have the same priorities. I blew off a lot of things for books, too."

Jessie relaxed and widened her smile.

I set my pen on her copy of *Satan, My Father* and wrote *For Jessie – who puts books first – good luck on your finals.* I signed my name and handed her the book.

Jessie's friend tapped her on the shoulder. "Tell her what you did the other week. What you said."

Jessie said nothing, her mouth shifting uncomfortably.

I opened *F*CK, F*CK, F*CK* and signed it. *To Jessie. Happy birthday always.* And lastly, I left a note in *Hypocrisy. For Jessie, who drove an hour to see me. Thank you. I believe in you, too.* I passed the books to her.

Jessie's face was still lightly scrunched with humility. "Thank you so much."

I felt sorry for her. "You're welcome. Thanks for coming out."

Her friend's index finger poked her arm. "Seriously. Tell her the story."

I set my pen down and folded my hands in front of me. "Tell me. I always have time for a story."

Jessie glanced at the line behind her. "I don't want to hold everything up."

Her friend rolled her eyes and stepped up to her side. "She was dating this jerk named Dick, and she finally called him out on his shit. She told him he was being a dick. Then she quoted your book at him. I wish I would've been there."

I was laughing too hard to speak, and I wasn't the only one. The next few women in line were barely keeping it together, some covering their mouths with shaking hands.

My eyes wanted to water. "You what?" I asked, working hard to speak clearly.

Jessie took a deep breath and answered me more openly than she had before. "I told him he was being a dick, and I realized that was the perfect name for him. I told him he was an extra dose of ordinary like Toria said to that guy at the park, and I left him sitting by himself in the corner of the cafeteria."

"He was a huge dick," her friend chimed in. "Not that he had one in his pants, I'm guessing."

A few of the women chuckled again. I wished Marcy was there. She could spin this kind of humor into jokes for days.

I realized that Jessie's friend was also carrying three worn copies of my books, the spines partially obscured by the way she held them against her hip. I reached for them, and she handed them over right away. The women behind them were still laughing. "Who should I sign these to?"

"Willa. Two L's."

Unlike Jessie, who was wearing a plain but well-made sweater under her open coat, Willa was dressed casually, younger than her age. A striped shirt showed under her baggy overalls. Behind them, the laughing women were passing Jessie's story on to the rest of the line.

"And you were going to keep that to yourself," I teased Jessie to reassure her. "I think you made everybody's day." I turned to Willa, my mouth still open with a smile. "What can you tell me about yourself?"

Willa set her hands on her hips. "I work at a laundromat called Suds. I'm dating this really cool guy named Frank, and we live together. It's such an old man's name, though."

I nodded. "My assistant's husband is named Henry. I always thought that was strange. Melody and Henry."

Willa hooked her thumbs in her slanted overall pockets. "I bet the wedding invitations looked weird."

"They kind of did, but they picked the right design. They looked classy."

"I'm sure they were."

I opened up *Hypocrisy*, sitting on top of the others.

Willa leaned over me. "I've read the first two twice. I just got that one a few months ago. I read it at the same time Jessie did."

"You could've had a book club."

"I wish. It's hard to find people who read good books where we're from."

I wrote, *To Willa, founder of the two-woman book club.* "Which book is your favorite?" I asked. I set *Hypocrisy* aside and opened the next one.

"*Hypocrisy*, I think. I like Toria's character because she's unpredictable, but I like the creepy ending of *Hypocrisy*. I love it when Lourdes tells Pastor Ozbeck to go screw himself."

For Willa, Toria's uncelebrated cousin.

"But I like *Satan, My Father*, too," Willa ran on. "Hey, we were wondering. What happens to Lourdes and Reese and all of them after *Hypocrisy* ends? Do you know?"

I opened the last book to the title page. *For Willa, who asks all the right questions.* I looked up at her. "I always imagined that eventually, somebody would realize the baby looked nothing like Reese. I think Reese would confront her, and Lourdes would finally come clean. It would be really hard for them to get over, but it would ultimately bring them closer. I don't think Reese would leave her. He already has such maturity in the book."

"So she keeps the baby?"

"Yes, for various reasons, I think she would."

"I think so, too. I think she'd be okay no matter what happened to her. She learned to adapt to anything they threw at her."

I agreed completely. "I think you're right."

I caught Michael out of the corner of my eye. He was being as unobtrusive as possible, hanging far back out of the way. He was browsing a section of books I couldn't read the subject of on the end of the aisle, but as he exchanged each book for a new one, he glanced at me. Michael offered me a brief smile, more pride and encouragement than flirtation.

I'd learned to adapt, too. I had found someone I could trust, someone willing to go the distance with me. Admitting my admiration for Michael was new territory. Everything else remained the same. We lived together. We explored life together. But in some ways, we were back where we started. I was signing books and contemplating the innate chemistry between us.

In that moment, I realized why I had no ending for my book. I'd fought it the way I'd fought Michael. We'd come back to the beginning, and so must Leifa. After all of her post-wedding cancellation adventures, she would go back to her ex-fiancé, but with one condition: that they start over. No talk of a wedding. No engagement diamond. They would date from scratch, with a clean slate, and see how it turned out if they tried harder the second time. It was the perfect ending, but I never would've seen it or agreed to it if I hadn't fixed things with Michael.

Willa glanced over her shoulder at Michael, who'd turned away to read the back cover of a trade paperback. The curls and waves of his hair hid his face, and his loose sweater and jeans hid the body that might've snagged Willa's interest. Jessie stood watching me.

I picked up Willa's books and handed them to her. "I'm glad my books have made such an impression on you. It was nice to meet you both. I appreciate your support. Good luck on your finals."

Jessie clutched her books against her side. "Thanks."

Willa grinned with confidence. "Thanks for writing such awesome books. You're working on one now, aren't you?"

I couldn't lie. "Yes."

"Good luck. We'll be first in line for it."

Jessie nudged Willa with her arm but made one final remark to me. "It was really great to meet you."

"You, too."

Jessie and Willa walked away.

Willa's voice trailed back to me. "You should've brought your camera. What's the point in having it if you're not going to take any pictures?"

A thirty-something took her place in front of me, and I reached for the book in her hand. It was a brand new, unadulterated copy of *Hypocrisy*.

"I never heard of you before," she said. "It looks interesting."

My gaze met Michael's, and I waved him toward me. "Excuse me one second." Michael bent his head next to mine, and I asked him, "Can you write something down for me?"

"Sure."

"It's just 'L goes back. Clean slate.'"

Michael must've sensed it had something to do with my book. His eyes darkened solemnly as he parroted my words. "L goes back. Clean slate."

"Yes. Thank you."

Michael walked off to make sure my idea didn't get forgotten, and I turned back to the customer in front of me.

I opened her book to the title page, the freshness of the paper wafting up at me. "Who should I write this to?"

"Nora."

"Is that you?"

"Yes."

I wrote *For Nora, at the beginning of her journey. Thanks for coming.* I signed my name in an illegible flourish and handed her the book.

The next time I saw Michael, several signatures later, he lingered two aisles away. He gave me a thumb's up and patted his pocket. He had either written it down or uttered it into his recorder.

I had a hard time sitting still for the rest of the signing. I enjoyed meeting more readers, but mostly what I thought about wasn't the nameless narrator, dynamic Chessa, or the adaptive Lourdes. Leifa had a purpose now, a direction, and so did the rest of my work in progress. It might not have a new title, but if I could find an ending, I could find something else to call it. Cheryl would be pleased to know the project was finally moving forward. I might have something to show her after a few months of editing.

My mother was getting one of her wishes whether I'd planned it that way or not. I was putting two characters together without false pretenses or a huge distance between them. But would my readers forgive me? I hoped they would. There would still be plenty of life-saving friendships and complicated entanglements to make this book fit into my repertoire.

The signing wrapped up with a few last-minute signatures, and I spent another fifteen minutes talking to the woman who had coordinated it with me. She was lively and pleasant, but every time I noticed Michael browsing across the store, I remembered the message he carried with him. I wondered if I could steal an hour, or even half that, when I got home to get the idea rolling. I shook hands with her, and she went to take care of other business.

I wandered between the shelves to stand with Michael in front of the clearance-priced books. He was looking over a hardcover with a dark and gloomy picture of a key on the dust jacket.

"None of mine are over here, are they?" I asked dryly.

"No." Michael replaced the depressing-looking book on the shelf. "There's a good variety here, though. Mystery, sci-fi, nonfiction."

"Poor little things." The books sat there like abandoned dogs, cats, and children waiting for adoption.

Michael turned to me. "Is everything set?"

"Yes." I pulled my keys out of my purse. "Were there any books you wanted?"

"No, I have plenty of leads waiting for me plus the interviews to finish."

Like Jessie, Michael had put off his own obligations to support me. "Thanks for being here today."

"Of course." Michael patted my arm. "You ready?"

I nodded.

"Let's go home."

Home, the H word if there ever was one. Some people said you couldn't go home again. I could, and I wanted to. Michael would be there. Loving him and even losing him wouldn't be the worst things that could happen to me. Living with him and not loving him until he was gone was unimaginable.

About the Author

Cassandra Leuthold's hilarious fantasy adventure, *The Corundum Conundrum*, won recognition as a New Apple Book Awards official selection. Writing hooked her at age seven, and she never really stopped.

She loves playing with ideas most people think of as opposites: the magical and the everyday, the modern and the vintage, the darkest nights and brightest lights. Even while delving into fictional worlds, she remains a tea aficionado, DIY crafter, and unapologetic music junkie.

Cassandra stretches out in front of the TV with her writer husband and their cats. She wields a Bachelor's in Liberal Studies and a Master's in English.

Find freebies and more book fun at her website, cassandraleuthold.com.